Maverick Men

Maverick Men
The True Story Behind the Videos

Cole Maverick and Hunter

inGroup Press

Chicago, IL

CHAPTER ONE

narrated by Hunter

I think it was that Rhonda Byrne book on the nightstand. *The Secret*. Or that lonely guest bedroom with a single, and two windows wide open to steal a cool breeze from the harbor. As soon as I saw that book I wondered why the hell they'd put something like that in a guest bedroom. I would never do shit like that. It's bad enough when you're not staying in your own place; when you're staying in the beach house of a friend of a friend, who you've never met before. Someone who you don't know how to behave around, or at least not yet. I'd forgotten his name twice already since we got there. But then again, I was always bad with names. Faces, on the other hand, I'm particularly good with.

They stuck me in a bleak room, something that belonged in an old Cape Cod bed and breakfast that was just waiting to be torn down. The furniture wasn't real. I mean—it was *real*, but not something anyone would actually choose to put in their home. It seemed like a room staged for old TV shows. There wasn't any character in the small bed, the dark wooden nightstand with its long, thin legs, and that wooden chair with a egg-white cushion that was too rough to sit on. And *The Secret*, tossed on the nightstand as if someone had been sleeping in that room every night, turning those pages every day. Like someone was expecting to come back and read it again. If it was me I'd at least fill that space with some David Sedaris, or maybe a solid western like my grandpa used to read. Maybe a Louis L'Amour. What kind of host strives to depress their own house guests with a self-help book?

Maybe it wasn't even the book though. I should add that there was a party going on in the apartment that night. Usually I'm a little more social—or at least try to be—but I didn't have any effort that night. We'd gotten to Provincetown around 2 PM on a Friday. I came with one of my co-workers, Chris, and his Irish boyfriend who I'd never met before that day.

Let's face it: 2 PM is way too early to arrive in a vacation spot if you're not feeling the vacation.

I should also add that this Provincetown trip was spontaneous. It went something like this: I was the manager at a high-end restaurant in

Boston, that wore the fuck out of me every single week, and kept me from going anywhere. For two months one of my friends, a server, begged me to go to Provincetown with him for one weekend, a short trip. He had this friend there: Danny, or Donny. Maybe Derek. Maybe it's just Don. I couldn't remember.

This Don (we'll call him Don) had a sweet setup: a 3-bedroom apartment in Provincetown, and a short walk from the beach. Don was also single. And looking. Why the fuck I'd want to meet a single guy who lives in Provincetown was beyond me, and I knew that Chris only wanted an excuse to not spend money on a hotel. I was the solution.

And so at 2 PM on a Friday we arrived at Provincetown, at a 3-bedroom condo owned by this guy Don. He was the kind of guy who had to tell us about five times that he lived in a 3-bedroom in Provincetown, *after* we'd toured the apartment. I think he even ran off the square footage at one point. I knew that the party Don was throwing for us was gonna be flooded with just about every douche bag in the Cape. And believe it or not, the gay Doucheoisie isn't all that different from the straight one. The outfits are Ed Hardy or Ivy-league college sweaters, the conversation is work and money, and everyone is drinking cosmos as if they're about to go out of style.

So that explains why at midnight I was still in the guest room. I wasn't alone—don't get me wrong, if I wanted to do my own thing in Provincetown there are about thirty different options aside from sitting in the world's most depressing guest room. Some people had wandered in; mostly the smokers who wanted a discreet place to light up. I remember a green hookah with three hoses that one of Don's friends lit. I remember a guy in his forties wearing skin-tight black jeans, who sat on the bed with his legs folded, a pensive expression on his face. Something sad just beneath his eyes; maybe the slow way his lips twitched.

"Hunter! Hunter, are you having fun?" Chris had wandered into the guest room at some point, while I was sitting on the bed, in-between puffs from the green-glass hookah, slowly flipping through Rhonda Byrne's book on life and the law of attraction. Chris was drunk at that point, and it was easy to tell. I was used to seeing two versions of Chris every night. There was the work version; trim and proper and perfectly put-together, soft-spoken, big smile, black clothing expertly selected to fit his thin physique. This version could easily pass off as an executive assistant in a big Boston law firm, or as the junior manager of some Copley hotel.

Unfortunately, there was that post-work version, when he'd roll his sleeves up, slouch at the bar, and with each drink you'd see more and more hand waving. It was like Liberace was hiding in his pants and all he needed to do was loosen up his belt with a couple drinks. Sober Chris was cute—not my type, but cute. Drunk Chris was a bit much for me.

"Yeah," I replied. I don't know why I replied to that question. The awful *are you having fun?* line. No one wants to get asked that at a party, especially not by a friend. Did I *look* that miserable? "I'm just hanging out," I added. I don't know why, but I felt like I needed to add something to convince him. As if it would make him suddenly believe me and then return to the party.

"Come on," he playfully called from the doorway, waving at me with one hand. His voice had gone up at least a few scales since pre-party. I wondered if his boyfriend was into that. "Don's really into you, but he thinks you don't like him."

I guess Don wasn't as dumb as I thought. Still, close to it.

"I'll be in—gimme a few minutes. I've been talking to Glenn." I pointed to the guy in tight black jeans who was still lingering on the bed, sitting in bad posture with his body leaned in towards the hookah. He didn't look at me and I had no idea if *Glenn* was actually his name. I wondered if he'd come alone or if there were some people out in the party who knew where he was.

While I was looking over to see if *Glenn* had heard me, I missed whatever Chris had drunkenly mumbled at the entrance. He'd drawn the suspicious attention of two stoners who were sitting Indian-style in the corner of the guest room, and I noticed them stand up to move elsewhere.

"Where's your guy?"

"I don't know," a solemness overtook Chris, as if I'd just told him some really awful news. In fact, his expression changed so quickly that I wondered if the boyfriend had bailed Provincetown. Chris had this sad look, like something you'd see on a cartoon character, or an old stage actress. "I don't think I'm into him anymore," he whined, and pulled his body closer to one side of the doorway as the two stoners exited the guest bedroom, leaving me alone with Chris and the quiet guy in the tight black jeans.

3

"Why don't you go back to the party and we'll talk about this later when you sober up." I really wasn't in the mood to try and reason with a drunk. Chris was acting like an idiot, and the fact that I was his boss at work made things all the more complicated. I could see his eyes widening and contracting as he shifted his balance in an effort to remain erect. *Erect.* What awful word choice with drunk Chris in the room. If anything, I think my penis had shriveled up and retreated into my body.

"Well come out soon," he muttered, but he wasn't looking at me. Something caught his attention in the hallway and he spun around quickly, and within a couple of seconds he'd disappeared from the doorway. A regular David Blaine.

I sighed in relief and laid back down on the bed, briefly resting my head upon the floral-patterned mattress. It really was a hideous mattress. I don't even think they make mattresses like that anymore.

"I can't believe you're still here."

Even though I was sitting so close to *tight pants*, I'd completely forgotten about him. Or maybe it's just that he seemed so mellow and robotic that I didn't actually expect him to open his mouth. It caught me off-guard; especially the warm sound of his voice. Like that older elementary school teacher who all the kids are in love with, who speaks quietly and wisely and wears the same v-neck sweater Monday through Friday. He sounded like a gay Mr. Rogers, clad in tight jeans and a gaudy t-shirt with an Italian designer's name stamped on the front.

I've always been into older guys, but my style is more geared towards a Robert DeNiro in Deer Hunter. And how can you blame me? When he was running naked through the dark streets of that Pennsylvania mining town; that was sheer porn. Who wouldn't want to go hunting with him, and then fuck later, right up there in the Appalachians, on a cold night when it's too windy to make a campfire, and the only way to stay warm is to hold on to each other inside a lone sleeping bag, listening to the sounds of the surrounding forests as we fuck, deep into the first minutes of sunrise.

It wasn't Tight Pants' fault that I didn't notice him. *Glenn.* He just wasn't the type of older guy that I'd notice.

"Oh, I'm sleeping here tonight."

"Doesn't mean you have to *be* here," he said, and pointed one of the hookah hoses at me, waving it like a small wand. He spoke eloquently.

4

"Alright. Well what's your excuse?"

I diverted the attention to him. I wasn't in the mood to be grilled. The fact is, I was in one of those grumpy moods that comes out of nowhere. Maybe *somewhere*, but I was content thinking that it had come out of nowhere. And I felt much better keeping to myself.

I think that he could tell I wasn't in the mood to talk. Maybe because I wasn't looking at him. Because my eyes kept flickering between him, the hookah, those pale yellow walls, and the Rhonda Byrne book, flipped open to a random page that I'd already read before. I'd read it before—or part of it. I just couldn't bring myself to finish *The Secret*, maybe because I knew that the thing I wanted most—or the person I wanted most—wasn't going to return to my life. And as much as I'd thought about him and hoped that he'd come back to me, and pictured the two of us together again, Ms. Byrne's law of attraction didn't seem to be working.

"I'm not in the mood," is all he replied. He was matter of fact. I waited for more of an explanation, but didn't get one. His legs were folded in a position that made me uncomfortable just thinking about it. Or maybe it was just the tightness of those jeans.

"Do you know—."

"No. Two friends brought me."

"Where are they?"

He smiled at me. I didn't know where this was going. He seemed warm enough; non-threatening, despite being much older. I felt safe with him, for some reason. I guess because these types didn't go after guys like me. He looked like the kind of queen who'd be running a Studio 54, divvying out his love between blonde teenager dancers and affected twinks.

"I don't know. I don't feel lonely or anything—," he paused, and rested his chin on one fist in a pensive expression. "They're trying to cheer me up."

"Bad week at work?"

"I wish. No, I think if I'd had a bad week at work, I'd be out there drinking right now."

"Yeah, I guess so. You going to be all right?"

He smiled. I guess he appreciated the concern.

"Um—I don't know yet. A couple weeks ago I lost my life partner."

5

I closed the book and looked up into his eyes. He wanted to talk, and until then, his interaction was the first genuine thing I'd encountered since I arrived in Provincetown.

"How long were you two together for?" I didn't know what else to ask. Not that the length of time really mattered—I mean, there are five-year relationships that are stronger than twenty year relationships. I didn't want to say *I'm sorry*. It would've sounded too cliché, especially when you don't know the person. He had opened up to me, a complete stranger, and I meant to let him know that I respected that. And I *did* feel for him. I could tell by the look in his eyes that he was in love. It was more than sadness—more like the reflection that comes with the realization you've lost something important that you can never get back.

"Twelve years," he replied. He was watching the doorway that led into the hallway. He had a better view than I did of whatever was going on down there, although I don't think he was paying attention to the party. "But we'd been friends before that, for quite a long time. We danced together. Same New York ballet company." He smiled again, but this time he was looking at me. "I was always in love with him though. It was—I don't know how to describe it—. *Amazing* when we finally connected. And I treasured every day. We had so much fun—."

He kept fading off, letting the ends of words slip until they either became new ones or subtly turned into silence. Then, he slowly picked up his head and looked at me through those sad, solid eyes.

"Have you ever felt anything like that?"

"No," I lied. I wasn't ready to get into that. To talk about *Cole*.

"Oh—," his eyes lit up at my answer, like he wished he could reach out and instantly share his own sensations of love with me, so that I could see what it was like, and maybe empathize with him. "It's the most wonderful thing in the whole world," he added. "And it's—it just comes from being yourself, and finding someone who loves you for being yourself. And you can't find it from looking. I learned that—years ago. You know, you can't go searching for it. It's always when you least expect it. Maybe when you're not hoping for anything—."

"What was it like when you guys were together?"

"We could do anything we wanted. Not every day will be perfect, you know, but if you treasure the person you're with, then the little arguments and problems don't matter so much. I really hope you feel something like this, someday. It can be scary—. When you love someone so much, it's hard to—," he bit his lower lip and lowered his head to the floor. I stayed quiet, tense; so much that I felt trapped in my position on the bed. Every sentence was bringing back a flood of memories.

"It's hard to know that you might lose them," he finally finished, after a smile that came out of nowhere. "You'll be tempted to be jealous, possessive, greedy of his time, and repressive of his needs. *Don't.* It's all about honesty. Be honest and it will work out. And if you don't mind me asking again—what are you still doing at this party?"

* *

Three minutes later I was on the street. It might have been quicker than that, even. I wanted to get as far away from the party as possible. It was far too late for the ferry, and I was stuck in Provincetown, thinking about the one person who shouldn't have been on my mind. Cole.

It had been four whole years since I last saw him. Four years since I'd been held the right way, touched the right way. Fucked the right way. Four years of hearing my friends tell me that they were sick of hearing his name, so much that it became uncomfortable to even mention him to anyone. Four years of feeling like I grew up too fast. Four years of struggling through every date and relationship I'd wind up in because I couldn't find anyone like him.

It's not an easy thing, for anyone who's been there. Once you've felt that kind of love, that devotion, that—raw, animalistic passion—with someone, I'm not sure you can find it again. Maybe, if you really look. But I wasn't looking too hard.

I'd compare every guy I met to Cole. It was impossible not to. No one wants to settle; and he'd set the standard. The worst standard possible, since he ultimately broke my heart when he left. But that was our relationship, clandestine and imperfect. Flawed from the beginning. And yet with all the flaws, I still savored every memory I had with him.

There's a disadvantage to not having a firm grasp on the world when you meet someone like Cole. He was a charismatic guy; someone who could talk to anyone—who could relate to anyone. It's that Bill Clinton style. I read once in a magazine that it's a unique thing to meet Bill, because of how important he makes people feel. Like the only person in the room. That's how Cole made people feel. I'd search for

7

that quality in other guys; for that unique charisma, or that ability to always know how to make me laugh. But no one seemed to do it like Cole.

We met at a party back when I was in college and had a girlfriend. Yes, an actual girlfriend. I'd recently moved to Boston for college. This was a huge leap for me, coming from the rural Midwest, where Salt Lake City was the closest I had to an urban experience. I hadn't experienced the East Coast yet. New York City, Boston, Philadelphia, Miami, Atlanta, DC—I knew that I wanted to go to school somewhere along that line. To get as far away as possible, and maybe play around with all these sexual feelings I'd had since childhood.

Going to school in Boston didn't stop me from dating girls, but it did open my eyes to an entire new world of sex. Gay men were no longer the caricatures and stereotypes I'd seen out west. My whole world-view became essentially fucked. "You mean it's not just Catholic priests and heavy truck drivers?" I'd find myself wondering, each time some football or baseball player eyed me up in the gym, or each time I'd walk past Club Café to get a glimpse of what I was missing.

I didn't know what my type was. I didn't even know whether I was a top or a bottom, but I figured at some point the day would come when I'd find out. And even though I wasn't doing anything to speed up the loss of my gay virginity, I was at least open to it. Nervous as hell, but open-minded.

And that day did come, the night I met Cole. At that party—I don't even remember who the host was, but I can pinpoint the building. I can trace my anxious walk home that night—in the dark, cold Boston winter, my cock and balls still wet underneath my jeans as I hurried to get back to my apartment and shower.

And I remember the view—that was the conversation piece. This party was in a penthouse apartment; a beautiful, traditional residence in one of Boston's nicer buildings. Some friend of Cole's—a friend of one of my friend's—had a ridiculous penthouse in a Boston high-rise. And there was a room—I guess you'd call it a study, or just an over-sized office—where an entire wall was one solid window that peered down upon the city. I'd never seen Boston from that view before. And I remember being stunned. The view was high enough that you could see the entire downtown from a clear angle, not like the sloppy view from an airplane flying above the city. This was special.

8

While my friends were scattered throughout the kitchen—along with the rest of the small and intimate gathering—I was in the study, watching my city; absorbing the slow pace of the South End, and the darkness of the Charles under a moon-lit sky. I was so fascinated that I didn't even notice Cole approach, until a hand touched me on the shoulder, and a finger brushed the side of my neck. Instantly there was this sensation, buzzing behind my ears, nervously creeping down my forearms, down to my hands, which restlessly moved in and out of my jean pockets.

Cole stood there next to me, one arm on me—casually, like a straight guy might do to his buddy at the bar—although Cole held his position. And he smiled without showing his teeth, and lifted his head up just an inch. Enough that he drew my attention, so that the view of the South End was overlapped by the charm in his green eyes.

Before I could say anything—or even react to his arm on my shoulder—he turned away from me, and gazed out the same window I'd just momentarily forgotten about.

"What a view, right?" he remarked. I couldn't figure him out. And I couldn't quite figure myself out at that moment. I felt wrapped in anxiety, like it was methodically tightening around my neck—around my upper body. I shifted one leg as my cock hardened uncomfortably in my boxers, rubbing into my tight jeans. I hoped he wouldn't notice. I felt embarrassed that I'd gotten hard so quickly.

Was he hitting on me? I'd totally lost track of time, and my head was spinning with anxiety and discomfort, woven together with such erotic temptation that I felt like at any minute I could rip his pants open and shove my face in his crotch. I knew he had to be gay—what straight guy would put their arm around someone like that, for so long? And then again, maybe it hadn't been long at all. I could've gotten so worked up that my body was just working faster, moving so quick that five seconds seemed to be five minutes.

At some point he took his arm off my shoulder. I couldn't feel that soft touch anymore, but I could still smell him; that amazing, masculine scent, free from any cologne or deodorant, that put me over the edge. I wasn't sure if he was done touching me or not, but just as I wondered if I should touch him back, I felt his large, masculine hands slide down my back, caressing my body through the t-shirt I'd worn to the party. I took one long breath as I felt his fingers ease onto my skin.

9

He lifted up my shirt and kept his hand right above my ass, digging his fingers into me with just enough force to turn my body towards him.

And then he kissed me. I don't remember where I was looking, but it wasn't his eyes or his face anymore. Maybe it was the window, or the glossy hardwood floors. I just felt him come into me, hastily. He pushed his whole body into mine, and I shook against the glass wall. The force of his lips drove me backwards, but as his one hand dipped into the back of my jeans, his other wrapped around my head and pulled me closer. I'd never had another man's tongue in my mouth before. Making out with girls was totally different. As the guy, you're the one in control, and it's your tongue that does the directing. When I kissed Cole, he was in control and it was his tongue taking the lead. I was overwhelmed and fascinated at the same time. Giving up control to someone else was entirely new to me. My whole body felt like it was going up in flames.

Both of my palms were on the glass, sweaty, and I felt like we were laying down, hovering above the city of Boston at twenty-some stories. As if at any moment we could break through the glass and fall backwards, head-first down into the South End. He was pushing me hard enough. Each thrust of his crotch into mine would send us up against the wall.

Every time I'd look towards the door—to see if anyone from the party was about to wander into something I didn't want them to see— he'd pull my head back into his. I couldn't close my eyes while he kissed me. I wanted to see him. I wanted to see those pretty green eyes above dark facial scruff; above a man's lips. And the careful way his tongue moved about my mouth, filling it the way a girl's was never able to.

He was pulling my jeans down—I don't even remember if he unzipped me or not—but I dropped down to my knees before he could take off my pants. He was already unzipped; and so I dug my hands into his gray cotton boxers until I felt him; huge and solid, pressed up against large balls and sweaty thighs. I'd never had a cock in my mouth before, but I'd fantasized about this moment. I didn't know what to do, but I pulled his boxers down so that his dick swung in the air, bouncing against my cheek.

He pushed his crotch into my face so that I was up against the wall, with not an inch of air separating me from the glass. I gently held his big, heavy balls with one hand and pulled him into my wet mouth. I couldn't hear anything at that moment except the sounds of my own

10

moaning and breathing as he pushed himself in and out of my mouth, never taking the head out from around my lips. I squeezed his balls with one hand and felt him balloon in my mouth. Harder and harder, pulling my lips apart as I moved back and forth. I'd never wanted someone so badly, and I didn't want this to end.

He was moaning, and his knees were bending into my shoulders so that my whole body was wedged against the glass. I could feel the sweat dripping from my forehead, down onto his dick where the salty taste poured into my mouth, coupled with the musky smell of his crotch. As his knees dug further and further into me I could feel him on the verge of an explosion. The excitement was too much for me, and as I jerked my cock with my free hand, I could feel that I was close to shooting. I let my dick fall out of my hand, as my cum burst onto the wooden floor, dripping onto my jeans.

And then he came. Wildly; with one whole hand wrapped around the back of my head, forcing his thick cock into my throat, he exploded inside me. I felt the warmth on my tongue; smelled his climax as I kept my lips gently wrapped around him. He leaned his sweaty forehead against the glass wall and passionately placed both of his masculine hands overtop my ears, motioning to pull me up from his crotch. I pushed against the glass wall with my back, sliding upwards towards his head. As I got closer, with the scent of his cum still on my lips, he stuck his tongue into my mouth and kissed me, the way lovers kiss.

That night my entire world changed. Cole and I would see each other again, off and on, and always for sex. It wasn't just for sex, but it wasn't a relationship either. And it wasn't dating. It was the passionate play of two people who weren't ready or willing to be in a relationship. I was in love with him, but I still had a girlfriend who I couldn't shake off. I still had midwestern traits—fears and taboos—that I couldn't get rid of.

The very last time we met, he told me that he was moving to Miami. That he wouldn't be back; or at least if he came back, we couldn't see each other. And that was Cole. When I was with him, I felt like the most important person in the world. Like the *only* person in the world. And when it was over, it was *over*. It's a sad thing, that transition. Even with its complications, I didn't think Cole and I would ever end. And when I had to face the reality of our complex lives (and maybe when he did, too), everything suddenly seemed so finite. Even the things I was sure of, didn't seem all that reassuring.

Some years passed. I graduated from college, got a serious job. I stopped dating girls. I *tried* to date guys. I no longer felt nervous if I walked by Club Café. In fact, I could stop in for a drink. I knew what I liked in a guy, and what I wanted, and how I wanted to talk to them, touch them, be with them. And yet even in all of that growth, there were still little things that I longed for. Simple boyfriend scenarios, like what it would be like to just live with the person that I was in love with. To watch TV with them, shower with them in the morning, make dinner together, and come home to them after work. Or to be the one in the apartment when my partner got home from work. Deciding things to do, other than just sex. That was my only experience—where all of my growth had come from: sexual relationship. I would've killed for a real boyfriend experience with Cole. I guess back then it's not what I really wanted or was looking for, but I quickly learned that this missing component was what I needed to find.

And that's why I sat in the guest room at the Provincetown party, I guess. Because it would be easy to find sex out amongst all the drunk guys in the living room and kitchen, but I wasn't looking for just sex anymore. I needed to find something substantial. And I had to stop looking for the next *Cole*.

I could tell that the bars were closing in Provincetown, because as I found myself approaching Spiritus Pizza after my long walk from Don's apartment, I could see the massive crowds forming. I knew that if anything was going to cheer me up, it would be Spiritus. Not the pizza, but the people. If you've never been to Provincetown, then you're missing out on a circus that takes place every summer night after the bars close. Gay guys from all over Provincetown converge on this pizza shop in the late hours of the night. You can find any type there: from the hottest muscle men to the most outrageous drag queens, to stick-thin scene kids, and even your leather contingent.

This night was no different. Men were piled up, in hundreds. I found myself in-between a group of bears—most of them clad in leather, some dressed in hoodies designed for much younger men—and a couple young twinks who were getting bothered by an older guy with leathery skin and thinning blonde hair. He looked like a porn studio kingpin, complete with gold chains and bracelets, and a gaudy wristwatch that hung loose on one wrist. I couldn't hear the conversation over all the noise that engulfed the area, but I guessed he was asking them to be in a video. Neither of them looked like they wanted anything to do with this guy, and I didn't blame them.

On another night I might have intervened, but I wasn't really trying to make new friends, and twinks have never been my type. I mean, one of these guys had glitter under his eyes. That's where I draw the line.

My cell phone was in my back pocket, although I hadn't checked it along my walk. I had no idea how long the party back at the apartment was going to last for. Even though it was kind of far, I half-expected to see Chris show up at Spiritus. That would be an interesting conversation. Especially if he showed up as drunk as he was when I left the condo.

I walked slowly through the crowds, unsure how long I was going to hang around for. I didn't want to go back to the condo, at least not yet. I thought about meeting someone and just crashing at their place—I mean it wouldn't be hard, with all the guys scattered outside Spiritus Pizza, to find someone who was my type. But I also didn't want to use someone for a bed, especially if they were expecting me to stick around the next morning.

I was open to it. All I had to do was find out the ferry schedule, get my stuff back at the condo, and I could easily crash at some guy's place for a few hours, then wake up and head back to Boston. I definitely wasn't going to last the whole weekend in this mood.

Or maybe that was it: that it was just a mood. And it was up to me to figure out some way to kick it. I was beginning to regret not having a couple drinks back at the party.

"Whoa," I heard someone right near me say. I was walking like a zombie through the dense crowd, my mind focused more on all the shit running through my head than on the people around me. At some point, a few paces past the group of bears and the two twinks and an old couple in Hawaiian shirts, I'd begun to block out the faces and the conversations. It was like my eyes were closed while trying to navigate the crowd.

I kept moving until I heard another sound behind me. A *whoa* or *hey* or something like that—there was so much noise around me that I couldn't tell what I was hearing. I needed to find a place to sit, maybe. I didn't want to go off and stand by myself, because that could look too lonely. I just wanted somewhere to sit, so that maybe I could watch the crowd without being inside it.

A hand landed on my shoulder and I was pushed with a few fingers. It wasn't a friendly touch; more like a quick jab by someone who wanted to get my attention. I thought about ignoring it and going about my walk, but there was some small curiosity to see who it was.

"Apologize when you fuckin' bump into someone, man," a muscle queen in a tank top said as soon as I turned my head. He was older than I was—maybe mid-30s—with huge biceps, and pecs that popped out around the straps of his shirt. *Army colors*, of course. His face was shiny and his eyes were bugged out. He had just got off the dance floor and was clearly still tweaking on *something*.

I don't know what was in me at that very moment. Maybe the way this guy voiced his complaint. Maybe it was just him, and the whole steroid circuit party look. You know, this was the type of guy who gets his eyebrows waxed and has no hair on his balls, but spends two hours per day in the gym, drinks protein shakes, and therefore thinks he's a nightclub God. It would've been easy to apologize and walk away, but I didn't really feel like it.

"Hey, chill out," I said, and I stood my ground. I was surprised that a circle hadn't already formed around us. But then again, two butch guys exchanging loaded words with each other doesn't seem as interesting when you're in a crowd with drunken drag queens performing Madonna songs on the back of automobiles.

"What'd you say?"

How did this sect of gay people even make it out to Provincetown? I guess that's the curse of gay vacation spots. Any place with circuit parties and big name DJs runs the risk of being infiltrated by these tank top-wearing Ken dolls. And this was just one among many; strung out on some party-boy drug. Probably T or G. There were some guys behind him, but I couldn't tell if they were friends or just onlookers.

"You have a hearing problem? I said chill the fuck out. We're in Provincetown."

By the time the words had left my mouth, this asshole was fuming, and I couldn't tell if the new redness in his cheeks was from sunburn or rage. Maybe a little of both. I'd been around these types before though, so I knew what to expect. These muscle queens—bent out on crystal meth—were all the same. Lots of talk, lots of flexing— eventually he'd try to push me. They always push before throwing the first punch. I don't know why they do that. I guess it's just a way to flex their arms out and show off a little, and hope they've scared away whoever had bothered them in the first place.

It wasn't going to be that easy with me. I was ready for the push; ready to rotate to the right, just a couple inches, and nail him in the jaw with my fist. And even if he didn't go down, he'd be too stunned to react. The only downside was that I'd screw up my chances of being able to stick around Spiritus and meet someone for the night. It was *almost* enough to make me want to avoid the fight. *Almost.*

"You have three seconds to walk away," the muscle queen told me. His arms were wrapped in front of him—he must've thought he was Hulk Hogan. In fact I was waiting for the moment when he'd rip his tank top off and throw it to the ground, all while making primal roars meant to frighten me. But *three seconds*? This guy was full of shit. If he was half as bad as he was pretending to be, then he wouldn't have given me three seconds.

"Count it out, man," I told him. I think he was shocked to see someone smaller than him talk back. I could tell in that red face, in those dark, glossy eyes.

Just as I eased my left foot back in preparation for his charge, I felt two arms wrap around me. They grabbed me under my armpits and aggressively pulled me backwards. For a second I thought it might have been one of his friends, coming up from behind to give the muscle queen an advantage, but the latter had this puzzled look on his face as if he had no idea what was happening.

"Take it easy," someone shouted in my ear, but it blended into all the voices around us. Some people were looking, but most were in their own groups, their own conversations.

"What the fuck—," I swung my elbows to try and break free from whoever was dragging me through the crowd. I think I hit him a couple times in the shoulders, but his grip was firm and unwavering. It could have been that guy Don—maybe he showed up with Chris at some point, and they saw me in the crowd. I didn't think it could be a total stranger. It definitely wasn't a cop.

As soon as the muscle queen was out of sight, I felt the two arms unclasp around me, and a firm torso pushed against my back to straighten out my balance.

"What the fuck—," I said as I stood up and quickly looked back to where we had come from, to see if the muscle queen was following. He wasn't anywhere to be seen. What a shame. I really wanted to kick that guy's ass.

15

"Hunter," I heard behind me, maybe two or three times. I hadn't looked back to see who had grabbed me, and so I finally turned my head. I expected to see Don. That's who I was preparing to see, at least.

"You've gotta be kidding me," I said under my breath. I closed my eyes—tightly—just for a couple seconds, and then reopened them to make sure I hadn't gone crazy.

"Hunter," I heard my name again. Why the fuck did it have to be him? Of all the people who could've been in that crowd on that given night. It had to be real. I hadn't been drinking. I smoked a little bit, but that was back at the condo.

Suddenly Spiritus Pizza became the last place on Earth where I wanted to be, and so I turned around and began to move as quickly as possible through the crowd of people. Some were still giving me awkward looks—the ones who had witnessed the confrontation with the muscle queen. Others I pushed passed, trying to get as far away as possible.

I kept hearing my name. I heard once that it's easier for people to hear names than any other words. Even in the chaotic noise of the crowd, I could still hear *Hunter*, shouted loudly in my direction. He was following me, and I had to move more quickly.

"Why are you running from me?" I heard him shout as soon as I broke through the crowd and leaped into a sprint. I didn't want to turn around and look at him, because then I might get stuck standing there, listening to his apologies or hoping that something more was going to come out of our conversation. And I knew that wasn't going to happen. He was on vacation—that was the only solution—he must've been up to Provincetown on vacation. Maybe because at that time it was hurricane season in Miami. Maybe he was visiting family in Boston. I just didn't want him to fuck up the rest of my weekend. I needed to get back to the condo, get my shit, and be on a ferry in the morning.

"Hunter!" he called out to me. "Wait! Why are you running?"

I'd lost track of the route back to Don's condo, and at this point I was just trying to get away from him. To lose him somewhere, where I could hide out and wait until my mind wasn't overwhelmed with all those fucking memories. I hadn't looked back, but the voice sounded closer. He couldn't chase me forever.

I saw a dark parking lot up ahead, just around the next turn. It was full of cars—mostly coupes and compacts, but also a number of

SUVs. This would be the perfect place to lose him. I still hadn't looked back, but I could hear him behind me. His footsteps. Each time he'd call my name. As soon as I neared the corner I split right and ran as fast as I could towards the lot. Again I heard him yell towards me. He was close—I couldn't tell how close—but close enough. Too close.

As soon as I entered the parking lot—full to the brim, with not a single spot open for an incoming vehicle—I realized that this might not have been the best choice. He was too close for me to easily duck under some car, and all the vehicles in my way were just going to slow me down. Without looking back I made a quick right in front of a black SUV, spun around it, and then dropped to the ground. I slid half of my body underneath the car, my palms on the dirty concrete as I tried to listen for him over the sound of my heart beating. I hoped that he'd keep running—slow down enough to look under some of the cars so that I could roll out from under the SUV and sprint off. He'd *have* to give up the chase at that point. My only other worry was that he wouldn't wait for me the next morning at the ferry.

The parking lot was dead silent, and it was clear that he was trying to be just as quiet as I was. I no longer heard my name called out. I couldn't hear his footsteps. I tried to contain my own breathing, but I'd been running so fast that my lungs were finally catching up with me. He was going to find me.

I had to prepare myself—I was going to have to face Cole, after all these years apart. And it wasn't going to be light. There was no chance of that. I mean—he chased me through Provincetown into a parking lot, and I knew that the silence that had enveloped me wasn't an announcement that Cole had given up. He was looking for me. And so I waited, half of my body under the SUV, listening for the sound of footsteps in the windy night. Anything that would give away his presence.

As I was about to inch further under the SUV, he came down on me, covering me like a blanket, his arms wrapped lovingly around me as if to say that everything was okay—that I had no reason to hide. This just made me furious.

As I felt the weight of his chest on my upper back, I pushed upwards, painfully digging my knees into the concrete and twisting my shoulders so that he flipped right off of me. I saw Cole's face as he landed on the concrete; I watched the surprise and sadness in those deep green eyes.

I jumped to my feet, but as soon as I gathered my balance I felt a large hand grab my right ankle. Then two hands—and I let my body drop against the black SUV before he got a chance to yank me back down. I thought Cole would seize the chance to stand up, but instead he charged just above my waist, shoving my body into the SUV and planting his head on the side of my body. As soon as I realized what he was going to do I dug my fists into his shoulders, but it was too late. He picked me right off of my feet and dropped me on my back, coming down overtop of me.

I landed softer than expected—or maybe my head was just so overwhelmed I couldn't feel the pain of the impact. Cole had my legs up over my head and his arms around my shoulders. I was trapped. As his face touched down near mine, our cheeks touching for the first time in years, I smelled that same musk that had aroused me so much back at his friend's condo in Boston. The same musk that would grow more intense when he pushed my body against the glass wall and stuffed his cock in my mouth.

Cole's lips were on my neck; his white scruff brushing up against my cheek, his shoulders pushing into mine. I tried to roll my body back and push my ass upwards so that I could spin away from him, but he just let more of his weight tower down on me. I could feel his hard dick in his pants, brushing up against my jeans. And even worse: I could feel my own hard-on. And I hated it; that he could disappear for so long and a part of me would still want this. That's the fucked up thing about sex and desire. And *my* desire was split in half. Part of me wanted to beat the shit out of him, and the other part wanted him to rip my jeans off.

"Hunter, what are you doing?" he asked in his thick Boston accent, his body hunched over mine and his arms still holding my legs over my head. We'd fucked in that position so many times before.

I didn't respond. In fact, I didn't look at him either. My knees were aligned with my ears at that point, so I wasn't about to start a conversation. I could've punched him in the jaw at that point. Or square in the eye. I wanted to, although he didn't deserve to get punched. At least not in the face. And so instead I just reached one arm up around his neck and pulled his face into my chest. With all my force I rolled to the

18

side, pushing Cole off of me. His body hit the cement and he rolled into the tire of the black SUV with a loud thud.

As I made the dumb mistake of hesitating for a few seconds to make sure that Cole wasn't hurt, he recovered. Before I could even get onto my knees, Cole grabbed my thighs from behind and pulled me into his crotch, his fingers wrapped around the outline of my erection. I swung an elbow and nailed him in the shoulder, but instead of getting off of me he pushed me with two hands, so hard that the upper half of my body flung back down. I could feel the cement dig into my palms. Both hands were black, and my clothing was covered in dirt.

As I struggled to lift my head off the cement, Cole yanked my jeans and boxers down to just above my knees. I could hear his zipper coming undone. I quickly tensed my ass and jerked it upwards, just as his naked crotch was coming down on top of me. He groaned softly and fell on top of me, and I guessed I had probably tapped his groin.

I still couldn't get up from underneath him. My jeans were around my knees and my shoes were still on, and Cole was on top of me, his hard dick rubbing in-between my cheeks, a space soaked from the heat of wrestling. I could feel his lips on the back of my neck, his stubble on my skin. He kissed me in a way that made my legs twitch, my whole body light up.

There was a roughness to the way he held me, which balanced the softness of his tongue as it caressed my neck, reaching up to my earlobe, unloading pleasure into me. The head of his long cock was at my asshole now, in-between my firm cheeks, and he slowly fucked that small space, letting himself glide back and forth, his thick head never fully penetrating me. He was seeing if I wanted it. If I wanted the whole thing. And the truth is, I so badly did.

The sweat from Cole's forehead rolled onto my cheeks as he passionately kissed my neck, all the way down onto my shoulders where he yanked the collar of my shirt so that his wet lips could soak my bare skin. My face was down against the cement, my ass up against his crotch. I began to not give a fuck whether he deserved this or not. Nor did I give a fuck that we were in a parking lot. And so I did what he wanted: as his head dipped down along my neck, I turned my face so that our lips met. As soon as I did this, Cole grabbed me under my right arm and flipped me onto my back, maneuvering himself in-between my legs, underneath the jeans still tied around my knees. He pushed the jeans down to my ankles so that my legs were spread out in a V from his crotch. His sweaty dick was up against my ass, and he grabbed my head and pulled me into him. And for the first time in years we kissed, although it felt like only yesterday when we'd last kissed each other. Sweat ran down both our lips, dragging with it some of the dirt on my face, but neither of us gave a shit.

"Fuck me," I said to him as he thrust up against me. I didn't have a condom on me, and neither did he, but I looked deep into his eyes for that reassurance that after all these years, he could still enter me bareback. And with his muscular arms wrapped tightly around me he returned the look of reassurance I needed.

Cole stuck his tongue into my mouth, and I could feel his dick slowly pushing into me, our heavy sweat allowing for a lube-like entrance. As soon as his thick head was in I felt an instant rush, those old sensations that weren't so much about size as they were about they way he was loving me—even then—covered in dirt and grime, my cheeks and hands darker than night. His dick became the most important thing in the world to me, and I dug my heels into the ground as I pushed my ass onto him, groaning with each inch. This was where he belonged: back inside me, forcing apart my tight cheeks with so much sensation that the entire lower half of my body felt moved to some higher place. And it wasn't the size of his cock or the weight of his body—rather it was the way he looked at me each time he pulled his tongue out of my mouth. I could see right into him. I could feel the way his firm hands dug into my back, rubbing up along my shoulders; digging gently into the sides of my neck. Cole fucked me with an intense masculinity that he paired with the gentleness of a lover. He kissed me ferociously, but his tongue was always soft inside my mouth.

As I slid back and forth on Cole's cock so that my ass cheeks bounced off his legs, he pulled me upwards. With two arms wrapped around my back he lifted me up so that I was riding his cock. My head was just inches above his, and my arms were wrapped around him. I pushed off his shoulders and slid up and down him, breathing deeply as I felt him reach the deepest places of pleasure in my body.

I kissed Cole's forehead, softly, as I moved up and down his chest. The first cold splashes of wind tossed against my back as he slid my shirt over my head to reveal a wet torso, soaked in sweat. Cole stuck his head into my armpit as he lifted me up and down on his erect cock,

20

his fingers squeezing my bare ass, guiding my movements with methodical pull. He was the sole source of heat in that chilly parking lot, where quick, chilling winds stormed in-between the cars, brushing my skin so that tiny goose bumps popped up all over my arms and legs.

I dropped backwards and so did he, so that our bodies formed a perfect ninety degrees—natural and fluid, like the human body's ode to geometry. With my fingers gripping the cold cement behind me, I pushed my ass further and further onto Cole, watching his face as he thrust into me. Watching as his eyes closed each time the head of his cock hit that special spot. His mouth was open; lips dried from the wind. I could feel the coarseness in his hands as they held my ass tightly.

And although it seemed like we were creating the loudest act in Provincetown, our volume was limited to the soft groans—those deep breaths—that blended so naturally into the wind. Somehow I forgot that we were in a public parking lot, but I didn't care if anyone overheard. I was blocking out all noise except that which we were creating together.

Cole's eyes opened as his thrusts got quicker, and we shared an entire conversation in the next few seconds of silence. *This was different.* I saw the change in his face. I felt it below—that hardness, moments before eruption. He pushed harder, throwing the entire weight of his body into me, and I threw my body back into his—over and over, until the sheer thrust of his dick hit my prostate with such intensity that my whole body lit up.

As my dick flopped against my stomach I could feel my climax building from deep inside me. My belly was covered in pre-cum, and a small bead of cum sat on the head of my cock, evidence of our intense fucking. Cole's whole face transformed, and became red in the dimly-lit sky—covered by SUVs and compact cars. We could hear people in the parking lot at this point; and they were loud enough that I couldn't ignore them. I didn't know how many were there, but a crowd had formed. Maybe it had been there the whole time. I kept hearing, "fuck 'em, man," and "take that hole," coming from around the cars. Instead of slowing down or worrying about exposure, Cole just came at me harder.

And just as my whole body shook with explosion—shooting cum into the air, all over my chest, all over dirt-stained thighs—I drove my ass into Cole's cock. He groaned loudly—a celebration of an orgasm— and pulled his dick out of my ass just as he shot streams of cum all over my cock and chest, giving me everything that I wanted. That I'd wanted for years. He'd chased me down for this—to tell me that he loved me and to prove it to me. I'd fucked other guys before, but no one felt like this after I'd cum. There was no one I'd hang onto—staying on top of them, holding them—like they had the only place in the world where I needed to be. As if I'd found that last, sacred battlefront of man, where possessions are on the wayside, and all we have left are our naked bodies, our love, our desire, and our search to find that best feeling on Earth. Unobstructed, like the tip of an old mountain, where we can create something that seems so large compared to the smallness in our view of the world below.

And Cole fell on top of me, his semi-erect dick on top of mine. And for the first time all night, I smiled.

CHAPTER TWO

narrated by Cole Maverick

"Paul! What's going on? On my way to the Cape." I was thrilled to see my friend's name pop up on my cell phone. Especially on such a long drive. I don't mind long drives; never have, really. And you know, it surprises people, because for me it's not about escaping or listening to music or clearing my head. I like to ride out my cell phone's battery talking to friends. Two hours, three hours—doesn't matter. Of everything in my life, *people* are most important to me. And sometimes a long, empty road is the perfect place to connect with them.

"Ah, nothing. Lazy night. On the sofa—thinking I'm gonna order some food. Cole, I was looking at my uh—drawer with the takeout menus. Not a single damn healthy menu in there."

"Not even like a Thai place?"

"Hell no. Thai. Are you kidding me? I can't even find Thailand on a map, let alone want to try their food. I need to slim down, Cole."

"Don't these places have salads? You know that every pizza shop in Boston has some kind of a Caesar."

Paul had been trying to lose weight ever since a nasty breakup. Six months later and he was still feeling the aftermath. It was convenient that I moved back to Boston when I did, because I knew that just being in the city would help him get over his problems. He was a great guy, but didn't like to play the dating game. Something about the slowness and uncertainty of the hunt. He'd go on a date with a guy and look at his cell phone three times an hour for the next couple days, waiting for it to ring. I used to think that sort of thing was obsessive until I met Hunter. Then I knew exactly what it felt like.

"So I'm gonna call a pizza place and ask them to deliver a fucking salad to my house? What a waste of a trip," Paul replied, raising his voice. "It's like going into a sex shop just to get condoms. I can go to fuckin'—CVS—if I want that."

"I don't think CVS makes salads."

"Well, they should," he spat into the phone. "So wait—you with Hunter?"

"Nah, not this weekend. I keep trying to get him to come with me."

"I thought for sure that after that Provincetown story you'd be inseparable."

That's what I'd thought too. Provincetown was a hot rush of emotions and raw physical love that I hadn't felt since I left Hunter years ago to move to Miami. We spent the rest of the weekend together, holding each other, with all the pent-up passion that we'd stored inside ourselves for so long. On our first day together we didn't even get out of bed. All I wanted to do—all day long—was look him in the eyes and tell him how much I loved him. How much I'd missed him. How I'd thought about him almost every waking second. And just how incredibly beautiful he looked, smelled, tasted—every single inch of him. And that weekend I explored every inch of him, as if I was doing it for the first time.

When we got back from Provincetown, something changed between us. Maybe *changed* isn't the right word. I had come back from Miami on a mission, like a Richard Gere—salt and pepper hair and all—in any one of his movies, sweeping in to take the one I love and live happily ever after. I hoped that Hunter would want the same thing. That we'd reunite, and he'd realize that I'm the guy he wants to spend the rest of his life with. We'd get a place together, see the world, and build a relationship that would be beautiful, incredible, and rare.

Unfortunately, my years away had left Hunter with some pessimism. Even after our hot weekend in Provincetown, he wasn't fully ready to trust that I was back to stay. No matter how much I told him. I knew he loved me, and I knew he wanted to be with me, but Hunter wanted to move much slower than I had hoped or expected.

"I'm trying to get him to go on a trip with me," I told Paul. "That'll seal the deal. You know? Just a beautiful trip—I told him anywhere in the world. Right now it's—well it's infrequent, and even when we get together he doesn't sleep over, because he works these crazy long shifts and needs to be clocked in early."

"He just needs to know that it's real," Paul softly replied. He cared a lot about me, and for my happiness. I knew he was on my side, and really wanted to see Hunter and I get together.

"I know. I'm showing him every chance I get!"

"You're a good guy. It'll happen. Hey, what about—."

"Ah, hold on!" I told Paul as soon as I heard my phone beep to announce an incoming call. With one hand on the wheel, I quickly glanced at my cell phone, and my whole face lit up when I saw Hunter's name. "Hey Paul, Hunter is trying to get through."

"Oh, oh, I'll hang up."

"No wait—can you stay on for a second?"

"What if it's a long call?"

"He's at work, it won't be. He said he was working tonight."

"Okay, okay," Paul mumbled. "I'll be here!"

I clicked a green button my cell phone, and could instantly hear the parade of noise that was typical of Hunter's restaurant.

"Hunter!"

"Hey—sorry, it's noisy."

"No problem. Can you hear me okay?" I asked him.

"Perfect. Hey—I'd love to see you tonight. It's been a really long day. Did you go to the Cape?"

"No way!" The words left my mouth before I had time to think about an answer. I was practically at the Cape when Paul called, but I knew that if I told Hunter I wasn't in town, I'd miss my chance of seeing him that night. A small lie would have to suffice.

"You think you could pick me up from work tonight?"

"I'm there. Are you uh—you're not finished right now, are you?"

"Nah, not yet, I'll be here for a couple more hours at least," Hunter told me, and I sighed in relief. "I'll text you when I'm close to done."

"Do you want to do anything tonight? Maybe stay over?"

"I don't know—I'm scheduled tomorrow," he replied in disappointment. "I want to."

"Well how about this—Paul—you know Paul? He's throwing a big party tonight. Let's go—have some drinks, have a good time, and my place is nearby We'll crash there, and I'll get you out of bed in the morning."

"I just need a change of clothes—."

"Done. We'll hit up your apartment first, before the party," I told him.

"All the way to Cambridge?"

"I'll get your clothes. Just text me what you need—tell your roommate I'm coming, and I'll have them in the car when I pick you up tonight."

I waited, holding my breath as I kept my foot steady on the pedal. The last thing I wanted was for him to change his mind over some minor inconvenience.

"Okay," Hunter finally said after some silence. "That sounds great."

"See you in a couple hours!"

"See you soon."

As soon as Hunter hung up, I eagerly clicked back over to Paul's phone call. He was still on the line—breathing heavily into the phone. I imagined him in his living room with food menus spread out on his coffee table, looking in frustration at the options.

"Hey, Paul, I'm back—we're throwing a party tonight."

"A what?" came his startled reply.

"You want to do me a really huge favor?"

"No. Maybe—what is it?"

"What else have you got to do tonight?" I asked him. Then came the silence.

"I was about to order from a Greek place. They're healthy, right?"

"You know how many calories are in a fucking gyro? Paul—come on, it's a Friday night. I want Hunter to meet more of my friends—you know—every time we get together it's late and it's his place or mine. I want him to feel like we're a couple."

"Aren't you in the Cape?" he asked with some shock.

"Turning around."

"You're driving all the way back? Are you crazy?"

"Yes."

"That's fair," Paul said after some laughter. "Alright, so—well shit, forget about the gyro, I'll start calling people."

"Nothing too big, man, no pressure. I'll make some phone calls. We have about—two hours, maybe three tops."

"I'm on it. This is exciting! Beats my night in. So much for eating healthy tonight."

"I'll pick up some celery on the way," I joked.

"Very funny."

"Hey, keep me updated. Let's make this good. I owe you."

"If I meet someone new tonight—hint, hint—then you don't." I could tell that Paul wasn't kidding.

"I'll make some phone calls!"

"See you soon, man."

*   *

If the AC hadn't been blasting on full, I'd have been dripping in sweat. Hunter probably would've loved that. But he and I had a party to attend, and luckily in my rush I was able to stop by my apartment to grab a fresh pair of jeans and a t-shirt.

Hunter and I didn't have many points of contention, but one was his post-work look. He hated it, understandably, because he had to get dressed up and manage a restaurant for shifts of ten to twelve hours—sometimes longer—and leave feeling dirty, sweaty, and smelling like a combination of the night's specials. For me, post-work and post-gym have always been two of the hottest times to have sex.

"Hey," Hunter smiled as he opened my car door and hopped into the passenger's seat. There was no awkwardness, no hesitation; we felt just like a couple. It was like I'd picked him up from work every day for the past ten years, and each time we couldn't wait to see each other. He had this huge smile on his face as he leaned across the car and put his lips on mine, using the muscles in his neck to lovingly push into me. I was ready to pull into a side street and fuck him right there.

"Long day?" I asked as I reached one hand behind him, rubbing two fingers along the inside of his belt. I could feel his damp skin, wet with little beads of sweat that had been collecting all day long. I couldn't wait to stick my face down there and slide my tongue along his cheeks.

"Yeah, I need a drink. Did you pick up—."

"In the backseat."

"I wanna shower."

"No way!" I protested. "You smell perfect. Sweaty, masculine—maybe a little bit of venison and—coriander? Was that on the menu tonight?"

Hunter playfully punched me in the arm, and we both laughed. He never had a problem laughing at himself. One of his great qualities.

"You sure I don't need a shower?" he asked me.

"Do you think you need a quick shower?"

27

"Well—do we have time? I just want to wash the restaurant off of me."

"We can make time," I said. "My place isn't too far from Paul's."

He thought about it for a second and then shook his head *no*. The fingers of my right hand were still wedged down the back of his pants, held tightly in place by his belt, where they rubbed the top of this ass and absorbed his musky smell.

"No, let's just go."

"You want to change now?"

"I'll change in the car when we get there," he replied.

"Deal," I said, and I kissed him one more time before sliding my hand out of the back of his pants. "Here we go." I put the car into drive, put both hands on the steering wheel, and pulled back onto the street.

I hid my nervousness about the party. Hunter didn't seem to be nervous at all, which I thought was great, since in about fifteen minutes he'd be meeting most of my close friends. I was proud to introduce Hunter to them, and knew they'd love him. I wasn't nervous about my friends meeting Hunter. It was more a nervousness about the circumstances. I wanted Hunter to feel like we were a couple; to see what it would be like to have a night out with my friends. I just hoped that it wouldn't be overwhelming or strange for him. I knew he wanted to be with me, but none of the signs had pointed to the kind of relationship I was looking for. Hopefully that would change.

"You sure I don't need a shower?"

"Are you kidding? I've been hard since you got in the car," I told him. I was surprised he hadn't noticed already. Between the thinness of my jeans and my boxers, my erection was pointing right up at the rear-view mirror. Any bigger and I could've used it for a third arm on the steering wheel.

I took a quick look at Hunter, and was reminded why I fell in love with him in the first place. His whole face had lit up after my comment, like I'd turned some switch that had revved up his sex drive. I could feel it pouring off of him—all the sexual energy that he'd repressed during his long shift. And as soon as my eyes went back to the road, Hunter was hunched over me, leaning under my right arm and undoing the zipper on my jeans.

As soon as Hunter wrapped his hand around the base of my hard dick and pulled it out of my pants, I felt a cold rush of air from the AC sweep down into my crotch. I breathed in deeply as his moist lips wrapped around the head, protecting it from the frosty air. I kept my eyes on the road and slowly thrust my crotch upwards so that my dick could slide further into his mouth. Hunter made small groans as he struggled to put all of me in his mouth.

Luckily it was pretty late, so there wasn't much traffic on Boston's city streets. I switched to one hand on the wheel and rested my other on top of Hunter's head full of short brown hairs. My whole body shook as Hunter's mouth maneuvered up and down on my cock, carefully moving his tongue around my head as his lips sucked on the shaft. He lifted his mouth—one of his hands still on the base, his fingers wrapping around my balls—and I felt another rush of the cold air on my wet dick. Hunter blew on it, softly, enough to dry the wetness, and I could feel myself ready to explode. He squeezed my shaft with one hand and dove back down, taking my entire cock in his mouth.

"Hunter," I patted him on the head to get his attention, but he didn't respond. He just kept working his mouth up and down my wet dick as it got harder and harder, sucking more passionately each time as he raised his lips from the base of my shaft to my head. My car was about ten feet from a red light, and an old, beaten up, white tow truck was stopped and waiting in the lane next to us. It looked like it could be something straight out of a horror movie, with some dangerous loner behind the wheel, who'd cruised the streets of Boston each night looking for his next unsuspecting victim.

"Hunter."

He wasn't paying attention, and each time I said his name he sucked harder—dove deeper—so that his lips wet the sweaty pubes that sprung up around the base of my dick. He squeezed my balls, and sent my upper back digging into the driver's seat. My ass was practically hovering over the seat as I thrust my crotch up and down, fucking his mouth with lots of intensity.

Five feet away. I thought about stopping the car short of the light. Fuck it. Hunter and I had fucked in public before. I eased onto the gas, and pulled my car to a stop parallel to the white tow truck.

"Oh God," I said as my foot slammed down into the brake. My other leg dug into the car floor. I turned my head to the left—I couldn't help myself. The streets were empty, and if whoever was in that tow truck happened to look over into my car and didn't like what they saw, I could always step on the gas and ride out of there. I didn't know what to expect when I glanced up into the truck, but there's definitely no way I could've anticipated what happened next.

Two tough-looking motherfuckers were staring down at me. One guy was Latino, and the other was white. One in the driver's seat, the other in the passenger's seat, and both with their heads turned, peering down into my car. We were only inches away. They could see my sweaty face, red forehead, and Hunter's head bobbing up and down as he worked my shaft. And just as I expected one of them to hop out of the car and beat our asses, the hottest thing happened. It was the driver first, and then the hot Latino passenger; both turned to each other, and then looked back into my car with a pair of grins. They ripped their jeans open, lifted their asses off of their seats just enough to get a better look into my car, and out came hard dicks. They nodded their heads and smiled as they watched Hunter suck me off.

As Hunter sucked hard on the head of my dick, I watched as the two hot guys in the truck next to us stroked their cocks, their mouths wide open and their eyes pinned on us. I could see the light change green, but none of us gave a fuck.

"I'm coming," I told Hunter in-between groans, and threw my head into the seat as he sped up, working my shaft and sucking on my head until my warm load exploded in his mouth. I put my hand on the back of his head and shoved him down hard on my cock, gagging him and shooting the rest of my cum down his willing throat. Hunter lifted his wet lips from my dick, and just as he got the first glimpse of what was going on in the car next to us, the two guys in the tow truck were still stroking and smiling. One of them motioned for us to roll down the window. The tough-looking white guy nodded his head from the driver's seat and shouted, "it's a beautiful thing and fucking hot! If you guys ever need a tow[1], or wanna grab some beers, give us a call."

He gave his business card to the passenger, who tossed it through my open window.

"Thanks man," I said, just before stepping on the gas pedal.

1

http://olbmedia.site.metrixstream.com/site/MaverickMen/?page=videos&contentId=14

"What the fuck," Hunter said with a big smile on his face, just before licking the final drops of cum off his lips. "Who were those guys?" he asked, turning back to look at the tow truck. "You should've invited them back. I could've finished them off too," he remarked, and smiled coyly at me. I patted him on his sweat-soaked head.

"Who loves you?" I whispered, and gave him a quick kiss, taking my eyes off the road for just a brief second.

*   *

"Used to be an old cigar factory," I told Hunter as we walked down the hallway of Paul's apartment building. He had changed in the car into a dress shirt and pair of jeans, and looked fantastic. You couldn't even tell he'd just worked an eleven-hour shift. Nor could you tell that he'd just given me the best road head of my life.

"Really? Looks big."

"Yeah—all lofts. I'd love to get a place here, but it's always full."

"I still need to figure out what I'm gonna do about my place," he said, and let out a long sigh.

"Your lease is up soon, right?"

"One month. I have thirty days to find a new place."

"You think you'll stay in Cambridge?" I asked him. My lease wasn't up for another three months, and I'd invited him to move in with me, but didn't want to push it in our conversations. I knew he wanted to take things slow.

"I don't know—maybe. I'd like to try living in Boston. I don't know where, though. I mean—I work here, so it makes more sense to live here, right?"

"Not only do you work here, but it's closer to me," I said, and caught the quick smile on his face. I hoped I was one of the reasons he was thinking about moving downtown.

"Yeah, I know."

As we approached Paul's door, I took Hunter's hand in mine, and leaned in to give him a kiss. He'd been chewing gum since we left the car, so to my disappointment I couldn't taste the cum that he'd swallowed not more than twenty minutes earlier. But we did kiss, the way that two people kiss when they're in love, and as soon as I pulled

31

my head away from his, I whispered in his ear: "I love you, Hunter. I know my friends will too."

Hunter smiled at me, and as I looked into his eyes, I knocked twice on the door with my free hand. It wasn't even a few seconds before the door opened and Paul's head poked out to greet us.

"Finally!" he exclaimed. I watched Paul's eyes as he looked at Hunter, up and down, with a stunned expression on his face. I was proud of my man.

"Paul, this is Hunter," I said, stepping aside as my friend opened the front door.

"Oh, I thought it was the fucking milk man. Who the hell else would it be? Hunter, nice to finally meet you," he said, extending a hand.

"You too," Hunter replied. "I've heard a lot."

"Nothing yet. Tonight you'll get the *true* versions of whatever bullshit stories Cole has told you. Not his *watered down* takes."

"Are you kidding me?" I replied. "My versions are watered down?"

"Come on in, let's meet everyone," Paul said, waving us into his apartment.

I watched Hunter's eyes as he passed through the doorway into Paul's loft apartment. And while everyone's attention had suddenly turned to Hunter, I could tell that he was soaking in the loft: its exposed brick walls, enormous ceiling, open floor plan, and rugged, natural feel. This was an artist's studio; a place of tranquility for the self-employed, where one could feel totally at peace with their home. This wasn't the kind of place you'd want to escape from for fifty to sixty hours per week.

"Wow——," was all Hunter said as his eyes wandered around the first story.

"I know I look good tonight," Paul replied, "but *wow*? I've never gotten a *wow* from you, Cole."

"I think he's talking about your place," I said with a sly grin on my face.

"Of course. I think I need to get an ugly apartment, that way I'll stand out more," he joked. "Let me give you the tour—these people can wait."

As Paul hustled Hunter through the small crowd of people, mostly friends of mine, an idea popped into my head. Actually, an idea and a revelation each popped into my head. For one, I knew at that very moment as I watched the beaming expression upon Hunter's face—the way his eyes shifted back and forth, absorbing each and every small detail of the loft—that I would do anything for this man. Not only that I would do anything for him, but I was *planning* on doing anything and everything for him. And that was my revelation.

The idea? I had exactly one month to beat the clock and convince Hunter to move in with me. About thirty days to prove to him that I was the guy he should spend the rest of his life with. These lofts would be a starting point. Of course, it was easier to smuggle arms across continents than to get a lease in Paul's building, but I knew that I needed to try. I needed to create a home for us.

CHAPTER THREE

narrated by Hunter

"How did you even get a hold of a biochemical suit?" I asked Chris, as he showed up in the basement of our restaurant looking like something out of the Twilight Zone.

"It's cool, right? I got it in orange. It was either orange or white."

"You look like you should be removing asbestos," I told him. "All we're doing is painting the walls. You could've asked me to borrow some clothes."

"But this thing's so cool! It's got *Halloween* written all over it. Not to mention, I'd be swimming in your clothing," he added. "Where's my helmet?"

"The outfit comes with a helmet?"

"Hell yes! Check it."

"I can't believe you bought a suit like that and didn't bring one for me," I replied, shaking my head in disappointment. Meanwhile, I'd shown up in gray sweatpants and a plain white t-shirt. It was a Monday morning, and since our restaurant was closed on Mondays, I'd decided to use the day off to paint the finished basement. The basement was used mostly as a staff space, and for when employees went on break. It consisted of one large room for meetings, a smaller one with plastic tables for lunch breaks, and two unisex bathrooms. The downstairs hadn't been maintained very well over the restaurant's many years in business, and cream-colored paint (that used to be white) was chipping on the walls.

Since Cole was busy all day, and since I'd wanted to paint the basement for a long time, I enlisted Chris' help and arrived at 10 AM on a Monday morning to begin work.

"Uh—do you think I'm that bad of a friend?" Chris replied as he did a one-eighty on the stairwell and stomped back up the stairs. "Hold on!" he shouted.

"Oh no, don't tell me—."

Within seconds Chris had returned with a white pile of Tyvek in one hand, and his orange hood in another.

"We're going to be sweating our asses off in those things," I replied in-between laughter.

"Great. You'll be nice and sweaty for when you see Cole later," he said, his lips stretched out in a wide grin. He handed me the white biochemical suit, complete with white booties and a hood. "You said he's into that, right?"

"Yeah, we love it. Makes the both of us go wild. But he's busy today—I don't think I'll see him before tonight, maybe."

Before I had time to react, Chris flung his hood sideways and wacked me in the side of the head with the visor portion. It didn't really hurt, but the shock was enough to make my eyes widen.

"What was that for?"

"Are you crazy?" he asked me, just before affixing the hood over his head, to complete his outfit. "You've been all about this man for years—for so long all I heard was *Cole this, Cole that*, or that *this guy isn't Cole*. And now he's back and wants something serious, and you're still living in Cambridge."

"I just have to be careful—you know? I got hurt before. I know he's a great guy—I love him. I really do."

"The circumstances are different," Chris insisted. "Right? When you were together pre-great depression—."

"Is that what you're calling the time when he was in Miami? The great depression?"

"Yes."

"I wasn't that bad—," I said unconvincingly. "Was I?"

"Ah—yeah. So pre-great depression, you two weren't trying to be serious. It was just fucking."

"More than fucking—."

"But—but, but, but, he wasn't asking you to move in." Chris made a valid point. "How many weeks are left on your lease?"

"Ah—let's avoid that conversation," I said, and sighed in frustration. "Two weeks. I still haven't found a place. I mean—my roommate found a place, and wants me to move in with him, but—."

"But what?"

"I kind of want to live with Cole. I don't know. I don't know what I want—is that fair to say?"

"You *do* want to live with Cole, or you *don't*?" Chris asked. I always thought he'd make a good cop. Maybe not the kind that arrest people, but at least the kind that interrogate. Especially with a biochemical suit and what was beginning to sound like a muffled, Darth Vader voice.

"I do I'm just a little scared. I'm allowed to be!" I added in my own defense.

"Do you have any doubt in your heart that it will work out?"

"Chris, it's really hard to have a serious conversation with you while you're in an asbestos suit."

"Answer the question," he commanded, pointing a gloved finger at my chest.

"I have no doubt on my end," I answered, honestly. "I wouldn't leave Cole."

"You need to show this man some trust. He's throwing himself at you! Look—call him now, and tell him you really want to see him today. Even if he's working. The moment he can come over, I'll split. As long as you still pay me for the whole day."

"Wha—?"

"You owe me. That white suit you're holding wasn't free. Actually it was—it was two-for-one."

"I could've just given you a change of clothes."

"I didn't want any paint to fuck up my spray tan," Chris admitted with a hint of embarrassment. "Now go call him, and let's get started. I'm sweating already. I'm probably gonna lose ten pounds in this suit today. It's like a walking fuckin' sauna."

As soon as I finished laughing I dropped the white Tyvek suit on the ground and reached in my back pocket for my cell phone.

CHAPTER THREE continued...

narrated by Cole Maverick

The old lady at the front door gave me this funny look after I explained myself. She was wearing pajamas, which I guess is okay at noon on a Monday if you're a senior and don't work. She didn't have any shame about being in her PJs either. She just stared at me with eyes wide and lips pursed, and her little nose scrunching up at random.

"Do I look like I'm going to move out of my apartment anytime soon?" she said squarely, and shook her head like a school teacher addressing a student who had asked a dumb question.

"You never know! It's a hot real estate market right now—don't you think?"

"You know what I think? I think you're damn crazy for knocking on the door of an eighty-year old woman and asking if she's planning on leaving her lease anytime soon."

"Well she said no! But you're the sixty-year old, right?" I asked, trying to charm her, but got no smile whatsoever.

"Stop trying to shit me."

"Hey look, I know you've probably been here since it *was* a cigar factory, but I'm really trying to get an apartment in this building, so if you know anyone—."

"Know anyone? I don't know anyone in this damn place!" she exclaimed, producing an even higher pitch than earlier. "Last time I got a Jello mold was twenty years ago. Now these young people move in—don't even care to knock on my door and introduce themselves."

"If I get an apartment here, I'll bring you a Jello mold," I promised her.

"Yeah, well you're so full of shit you could use an enema."

"Already took one today," I replied. "So you don't know of *anyone* who might be moving?"

"You're really gonna bring me a Jello mold?"

"Jello, coffee—some booze, if you're into that? I don't know what you're into—."

"You come by with a strawberry arbor mist and you can forget the damn Jello," she told me.

"It's a deal."

The old woman gently shook her head full of short, white hair, and then leaned forward to peek down the hallway. A wave of perfume leapt out at me just as her tiny head shifted to the left and the right, checking for passersby. And just as I was about ready to choke on her powdery perfume, she pulled her body back into the doorway, and poked her chin a few inches forward.

"Listen—I was walking Botanica this morning and saw a moving truck around the side of the building. Big one."

"Do you know what unit?" I asked in excitement. A newfound energy poured through my body, all the way down into my toes, and I could barely wait for her to answer me. I wanted to sprint off to find the truck.

"No clue. But if you catch it in time, you might find out."

"Thank you *so* much," I said, speaking from my heart. The old lady smiled at me, for the first time in the whole conversation. And just as I began to jog down the hallway, I heard her call after me.

"Hey—why are you in such a rush to find a place here?" she yelled; her head poked outside her doorway.

"All for the man I love!" I called back. I could see her shaking that little head of white hair, just before I took off in a sprint.

*   *

A red, leather love seat was the first thing I saw, sitting on the ground in front of a truck that was about ninety-nine percent full. My blue dress shirt was wet in the armpits and lower back from running all over the property to find the truck. I was surprised I hadn't been exiled from the property already, given that for the past two weeks I'd shown up nearly every day to drop letters under doors—and sometimes knock on them—inquiring about moving into the lofts. Paul had helped, but neither of us had gotten any kind of response. The answers were always the same. *We're not moving. Maybe in a year or two.* I hadn't even found someone who was relatively close to moving out.

There weren't any people outside with the truck, which surprised me. In the city you'd think people would be more conscious about leaving their shit around! Apparently the movers had gone back for *something.* Just from a glance into the massive truck, I could tell that they weren't going to have an easy time fitting the sofa.

At that point the sun was out in full force, and I was tired and getting sweatier by the minute, so I dropped down on the sofa, resting my back on the leather cushions and extending my arms to cover the full length of the piece of furniture. Just as I let out a huge breath, I noticed a 40-something blonde come parading out of the building, flanked by four teenage boys in white tank tops. She had about six inches on all of them, and they struggled to keep up with her as she marched down the walkway in a pair of hot pink heels.

"Comfortable?" she asked as soon as she reached the truck. The woman came to a full stop just a foot away from the love seat, and placed both manicured hands on her hips. The four boys anxiously moved about—one even walking in a circle—as if they were terrified of standing still.

"Actually yes, it's very comfortable," I replied, patting the cushions with both hands. "Where'd you get this?"

"It's an import."

"Ikea?"

I must have said a curse word. The woman cringed and adjusted her white sunglasses.

"What are you doing on my sofa?" she asked in a tone that suggested she couldn't wait to get rid of me.

"I want to move into whatever loft you're moving out of," I firmly replied, maintaining my game face.

"Have you even seen my apartment?"

"No. It doesn't matter. I want to live in it. I've wanted to live in these lofts for a long time, and as of two weeks ago, I've been waking up every morning and going to bed every single night, dreaming and imagining myself—and my partner—living here. Whether you're moving out of a studio or a three-bedroom, I want it."

"It's a two-bedroom," she replied, her hands still planted on her lips.

"Perfect! Is it available?"

"Well—I was very strict about not letting anyone *see* the apartment while I was still living there. I don't like people in my private space," she said, and I believed her! "How about this—it would be silly for you to not get a proper tour of the unit. I'll go show it to you, and then you can decide if you want to walk over to the management office and rent it. Hm?"

"Let's do it," I enthusiastically replied, and hopped off of the couch.

"Boys! Load the sofa!" she yelled, which—at about ten inches away from her—sent a blood-curdling shock through my ears.

"I don't think it's gonna fit," one of them timidly remarked.

"Make it fit!" she screamed with the ferocity of an Israeli commando. "This way," she continued, addressing me in a milder tone. She then turned on one heel before strutting back towards the doorway.

CHAPTER THREE continued...

narrated by Hunter

"Nothing yet. I left a voicemail earlier—you think I should text also?"

"Huh?" Chris replied in a weary tone. The biochemical suit didn't last very long. He was sweating so much after the first thirty minutes that he stripped down to his underwear. "It's so goddamn hot down here."

"Text or no text?"

"No text," he said. "What'd you say in the voicemail?"

"Just told him that I'm here, painting, and that I'd love to see him. He's usually quick to write back. Hell, I thought he'd be here already," I joked.

"Oh dear lord, please let Cole show up so I can go home. Please," he pleaded as he moved his brush up and down. "I have a newfound respect for the Karate Kid."

"Haven't you like—painted a room in your place before?"

"Hell no, are you crazy?" he responded, turning to me with wild eyes. "And my apartment is never 120 degrees. This basement is ridiculous."

"You're right, for a basement it does get painfully hot down here," I replied. "So no text?"

"Ugh—just move in with him already!" Chris spat, as he returned to painting the wall. "Look at you—you're in love. Can't go two hours without hearing from him."

"That's not true. Well—."

"My balls are so sweaty right now."

"Well, at least your spray tan hasn't come off," I told him. "Oh no—wait—it looks like it's peeling just above your ass."

"For real?" he replied in shock, throwing his head over his shoulder to get a good look.

"Just messing with you! But stay in that position—it's pretty funny."

"Kiss my ass," he said, and after a loud grunt he dropped his paint brush and stretched both arms over his head. "Can we just like—throw the buckets of paint on the wall?"

"No."

"I'm sure it'll dry—."

"No."

"Cole better hurry his ass up," Chris said, shaking his head as he gazed at the basement walls.

CHAPTER THREE continued...

narrated by Cole Maverick

"My name is Tatianna, by the way," she told me, just before she opened the door to her recently vacated apartment.

"Cole," I told her. And as soon as the door opened, I couldn't figure out why she had ever decided to move. Her apartment was beautiful! The layout was different from Paul's, but the quality was spot on. Towering walls of brick, all in different shades of red. A stainless steel kitchen with lots of counter space for cooking. Great living room space for hosting, and all covered by a thick, hardwood floor. And the way that the early afternoon sun poured into the apartment through large windows! It was really a breathtaking sight. This was the home I wanted for Hunter and I.

"Technically they're not supposed to be letting anyone see the apartment until tomorrow, Cole, but I'm willing to go to the management office with you and change that," Tatianna slyly said to me. She lifted her white sunglasses overtop her flowing blonde hair, and smacked her pink lips together.

"I'm ready to sign a lease today. It means a lot that you'd do this for me," I told her. She grinned, and then adjusted her floral dress so that slightly more cleavage seemed to show than it did when we entered the apartment. I didn't like where this was going.

"There's a condition," she said, and I braced myself.

"What's that?"

Tatianna ran a pink fingernail along my blue tie, sending a quick sensation down my chest.

"My only regret," she told me, "in all my time in this loft, was that I didn't get—*pleasured*—enough."

"I don't know, I got a lot of pleasure from my few minutes on that Ikea sofa—."

"It's not Ikea," she snapped back. "Cole, I want to know just how *dirty* you can get?" she continued, just as her finger reached the top of my belt. I had been with women before, but it was much more of a teenage thing. And as far as sticking my tongue in dark, organic places, let's just say that I had a lot more experience rimming than I did carpet munching. I probably could've handled a nineteen-year-old bimbo with minimal bedroom experience, but Tatianna was a straight-up cougar. This woman clearly knew what she wanted and how she liked it.

"Well I never piss in the sink, if that's what you're asking." My sympathy for the four teenage boys out at the truck was getting stronger by the minute.

"Very funny," she replied without breaking a smile. I guess it wasn't that funny after all.

Tatianna put her hands on the thin straps that kept her dress on her shoulders, and yanked them to the side. Instantly the turquoise, floral dress fell down to her pink heels, exposing a white bra and a complete absence of panties. That's right. Where matching panties should've been, an immaculately-waxed crotch stared down at my Italian lace-ups.

"I want you to lick my pussy like it's an ice cream sundae."

"What if I'm lactose intolerant?" I joked, glancing wide-eyed at her lower half. "You know, you're in great shape for—."

"For what?" she snapped back.

"For—nothing—you're just in really great shape."

"The sooner you shut up and get licking, the sooner you'll have a new lease," Tatianna told me, and took a step to the left with one leg, creating an upside-down *V* between her crotch and feet. I scrunched my lips together and blinked a few times. There was no way out of this one. And to be honest, it could've been much worse.

CHAPTER THREE continued...

narrated by Hunter

"I've lost about five pounds already," Chris whined. His red undies were soaked, and I could see the sweat dripping from his body. I wasn't in much better condition. I'd long since abandoned the sweatpants and t-shirt, and was down to white boxer briefs and sneakers.

"Yeah, I think your sweat is gonna flood the basement."

"Good. Then we won't have to paint it," he replied.

"It's good for you! Look—I see some little triceps growing."

Chris frowned at me, and then turned back to the wall. We'd made a lot of progress in the few hours we'd been there, and were working on the first coat of the break room.

"Really? You think I'm getting muscles?" he quietly asked, attempting not to seem too excited by my remark. Chris had been wanting to make the transition from *twink* to *muscle bottom* for the past year, but his genetics simply weren't working in his favor.

"Yeah, I think you should paint more often."

"Hm," he grunted, and I noticed him discreetly flexing his left arm as he painted with the right.

Just as I was about to return to painting, I heard my cell phone ring in the conference room. I had left it on top of my sweatpants and t-shirt, and—hoping it was Cole—I dropped my paintbrush and hurried to answer the call.

"Oh God, please let that be Cole!" Chris shouted.

"It is," I said as I looked at my cell phone, and a smile erupted on my face. "Hey!"

"I am at the door of your restaurant, and ready to paint."

"Seriously?"

"Seriously."

"I thought you'd be at work!" I said, and glanced down at my sweatpants. *Fuck it.* Cole certainly wouldn't care if I answered the door in boxer briefs, and I didn't think anyone on the street would see me. So I hurried towards the stairs to let Cole into the restaurant.

"Is he here?" Chris shouted after me, but I was already halfway up the steps.

"Afternoon off," Cole told me over the phone. "You have a change of clothes?"

"You won't need them."

"I thought you were bringing me here for painting!"

My smile tightened as soon as I saw Cole's outline in the doorway. As I jogged across the restaurant I peeked out the windows for passersby, but luckily the street wasn't too busy.

"Hey!" I said cheerfully as I opened the front door of the restaurant and waved for Cole to come in. His eyes widened and he tucked his chin into his chest as he stared at my sweaty, near-naked body.

"I'm speechless."

"It's really hot down there! I was baking."

"Is this what I've been missing?" he asked. "Damn—I would've rushed here even quicker if I'd known."

"Come in, come in—I don't want anyone to see me," I nervously whispered, glancing over his shoulders for anyone who might be walking down the street.

"Hey!" Cole shouted, placing his palms over his mouth as he turned to face the street. "There's a naked guy in this restaurant! Check it out!"

My eyes widened and jaw dropped as soon as the words left Cole's mouth. On the other side of the street I saw two middle-aged women sneak a peek, although I don't know how much they actually saw given that Cole was blocking the doorway.

"Are you crazy?" I asked him, still keeping my voice low.

"Am I crazy? Am I naked and loitering around a high-end French restaurant? What happened to *sanitary* conditions?"

"It's too hot downstairs to wear clothing."

"Sounds like my kind of place," he replied as he stepped forward and pulled the front door shut. Cole put two fingers a couple inches below my belly button, where my white briefs hid my sweaty pubes. I watched his green eyes as he slid his fingers into my briefs, dipping into wet, thick hair, right down until he touched the base of my cock. His fingers were warm, and all he had to do was touch me once down there for an erection to burst outwards. My damp, white briefs outlined the form of my cock, which dug downwards, pointing to Cole's shoes. Nervously I glanced around the restaurant, watching the few open windows.

48

"Let's go downstairs," I whispered in his ear, and then wrapped my lips around it. My lips were just slightly wet, and after I pulled away from his ear I breathed deeply onto his neck. Cole had a hard-on in his dress pants, and I briefly forgot that Chris was downstairs—and even that we were holding each other on the street-level floor of a Boston restaurant—as I thought about all the things I wanted to do to Cole.

"Are you actually gonna make me paint?"

"Yes," I replied, and laughed as I took a few steps back. "What do you think I invited you over for?"

Cole smiled; I knew he loved when I teased him. If Chris wasn't downstairs I would've taken my briefs off right there and walked down to the basement, bare-ass, beckoning for Cole to come fuck me. I don't even think we would've made it to the basement. I probably would've ripped his pants off on the stairwell. But a small part of me was glad that Chris was downstairs painting. I'd never hooked up at work before, and even though I knew there was only a 1% chance my boss would show up to survey the painting, the pure risk of getting caught and losing my job was enough to repress my sexual need. I was already about two weeks away from not knowing where I'd be living, and joining the unemployment force definitely wasn't going to help me get a new apartment.

"We have company!" I shouted to Chris as soon as I returned to the basement. He had been in the middle of painting—well—in the middle of *pretending* to be painting, and he flashed me a look of surprise.

"Are you sure you don't want me to stay and help?" he asked, before I even had the chance to imply that he could or should leave. He looked at me with a pouty expression.

"Yes, I do, actually."

"Fuck that," he abrasively replied, and hurried down from a small step-ladder with paint brush in hand.

"Whoa, what've I been missing?" Cole asked as he came off the last step leading down to the basement. He peeked into the break room, where Chris—clad in red undies—was dipping his paintbrush in a bucket of cold water. "Damn, it's like a furnace down here."

"Hey Cole," Chris groaned, glancing up from the bucket. "Finally! I thought I'd be here all day—painting this goddamn basement."

"I think you got more paint on yourself than on the wall," Cole said, and with a grin he lifted his chin and motioned towards the break room wall. Chris' lips drooped down, and he quickly inspected his skinny arms for paint marks.

"I've been good about keeping it off me!" Chris said in his own defense.

"It looks great. It does. When Hunter *finally* agrees to move in with me you can come paint our house."

"If it was me, I'd have my bags in your apartment already," Chris said, and after a forced cough he glanced at me with widened eyes. "Two weeks left on the lease, Hunter?"

"Okay, okay, I'll see you tomorrow at work, Chris," I said, not wanting to get into that conversation. Chris picked up his biochemical suit along with a t-shirt and pair of shorts—both drenched in sweat—and waved as he headed for the stairwell.

"He's cute," Cole remarked as Chris hurried up the stairs.

"Yeah, he's a good guy," I said. "A little effeminate for me. But you're into that."

"I'm *flexible*," Cole said. He smiled as he walked towards me. "I have a soft spot for twinks. But you—you're just stunning. I mean look at you. Masculine—sexy—smart—."

He wrapped his big palms around my triceps and squeezed, gathering a firm grip on my muscles. Keeping his tight grip, he slid his hands down my arms, feeling the solid definition. I could see his green eyes making a line down my torso, moving slowly from my chest down to my briefs, where my cock was hard once again from his touch.

I heard the door of the restaurant shut, indicating Chris had left. Or that the owner had come in, and Chris hadn't left yet. I knew it was a ridiculous thing to worry about, but the fear was still present. I couldn't help it. This was my job, and I was in the basement of my workplace.

"You okay?" Cole asked me. I could see the worry in his face. I must've looked distracted, even with my raging hard-on. Cole's eyes were so calm at that moment, and just as I was about to suggest that we wait and not do anything in the basement, I placed my right hand on his zipper.

"If we get caught, are you willing to support me?"

"Hey, we can wait if you—."

"Fuck that."

I un-zipped Cole's pants before he even had time to finish his sentence, and was down on my knees, my toes pressing into the hardwood floor. I didn't even wait for him to take off his belt before I dug my hand into his pants and pulled out his fat cock. Gripping the base with one hand, I rubbed the head of his dick on my cheeks, smacking my face with it and soaking in the hot smell of musk that poured out of his dress pants. I loved when Cole was dressed up for work, in a nice shirt and tie, with a good pair of shoes. I was beginning to wonder what would happen if we lived together, and if I'd ever let him leave the house in the morning dressed like that.

Cole's black leather belt hit the hardwood floor just as I took his thick cock into my mouth. He groaned loudly, as if he'd been waiting for this all day. I stuck both my hands on his thighs, massaging my thumbs and fingers into his muscles as I did vertical push-ups on his legs, each time dipping my lips further and further down his cock. Each time absorbing that musky scent; tasting its salty, thick flavor. I felt one of Cole's hands on the back of my head, drilling my mouth into his crotch.

Cole's tie was in my face, and so with his dick still planted in my mouth, I grabbed a hold of the neck tie and playfully pulled down on it. Cole played along with me and stepped forward as I dipped backwards, trying to keep his dick in my mouth as I tried to lay flat on my back. Once my head hit the hardwood floor, Cole's knees were above my shoulders and his crotch was in my face. I lifted my head, begging with my body language for more of his cock, and he responded by fucking my face as if I was lying ass-up on the floor. He took my mouth as if it was an ass, pounding his thick, wet cock deep into my throat. I could barely breath as he pounded away with full force, and so I snuck chances to exhale each time the head of his cock reached my lips.

"I wanna fuck you so bad," he told me, and pulled his crotch away from my face, leaving my lips battered in sweat, saliva, and precum. Cole grabbed my briefs and tore them off of me, pulling them from my legs as I struggled to get back onto my knees. I spit in my hand and rubbed it on my hole in anticipation.

Just when I thought Cole was going to come down on top of me, he grabbed me under my armpits and pulled me to my feet. My muscles were bulging, and my sweaty body was covered in dirt from the hardwood floor. I wrapped my arms around Cole, my triceps resting on his shoulders, and he hoisted me in the air with his hands under my legs. And he held my naked body—him still in his sexy dress pants and button-down, his tie tickling the base of my hard cock. And with my body up in the air, my weight rested on his chest, I felt him walk forward towards the wall.

My shoulders were the first to hit the wall, followed by my upper back. Cole cradled my legs, which were flung up under his armpits, and I felt the head of his cock rub up against my wet hole.

"Oh fuck—," I groaned as I felt Cole's thick cock dip into me. He thrust his crotch upwards, letting my body slowly slide down the wall so that his dick could climb deeper into my ass. I dug my shoulders into the wall, forming a perfect V between my body and Cole's; one solid, continuous line of sweat and muscle held up by the force of his arms. I was still in the air, and we were connected at Cole's crotch. I could feel his strong fingers cradle my muscular ass, his fingernails scratching along the hair and soft skin.

"Oh fuck—," I repeated, "the paint."

"Huh?" Cole said as he pounded into me. His eyes were focused on my hard cock, which flung back and forth each time he shoved his dick into me; each time banging my back into the freshly painted wall.

"The paint—the paint."

I caught those green eyes race upwards, looking over my shoulder with a flash of surprise. Sweat dripped down his forehead from his short, salt and pepper hair, and he brought his hot fucking to a halt as he stared into my eyes. His dick was shoved completely in my ass, massaging my prostate and bringing me to the edge of cumming without even touching myself. I felt ready to burst.

"Fuck it, we can re-paint it later," Cole finally said, smiling boyishly.

And as quickly as he came to that conclusion, I felt him thrust again, deep into me. My shoulders hit the wall and I arched my back, pushing myself into his crotch. I threw my arms up over my head and pressed my palms into the wall for support, and as soon as I did so Cole stuck his head in my armpit, his nose brushing up against that wet, hairy space under my left arm. His fucking got harder and more intense as he smelled my musk, soaking up the sweat under my arm so that his face and collar were drenched.

As the pressure intensified I could feel myself about to cum. I kept my arms wrapped alongside my head as he pounded me and allowed the pleasure and submission to overtake me. And just as Cole's breathing got so loud that I couldn't have even heard the restaurant door close if someone had slammed it shut, I felt myself explode all over my chest. And I felt Cole explode too—and heard it—as he let out a loud grunt just as his cock came to full stop, deep within me. With little thrusts he fucked me, his newly-sensitive dick stirring an intense pleasure within him.

Just after Cole pulled out of me, he slowly let my legs descend to the floor. And that's when I glanced behind me, to the space on the wall where Cole had planted my back, lifting me up and down as he'd drilled his load into me. Where once an immaculately painted wall had been left to dry, a huge blotch of wet and missing paint outlined the shape of a body. Surrounded by paint, I saw the wet and bare imprint of my head, my thick shoulders, my back, and even my buttcheeks.

Cole was laughing when I turned around.

"You need a shower."

With half of my body soaked in a layer of fresh paint, all I could do was grin.

*   *

"You know what that's gonna look like if my boss shows up?" I said. I wasn't really asking Cole—more of a worrying question to myself.

"Quick shower and then we'll be back before you know it," he reassured me, smiling in the driver's seat of his car. We were able to use plastic bags from the kitchen to protect his seats from our paint-covered bodies, but that still didn't save me the embarrassment of walking down Newbury Street looking like I'd gotten in a fight at Home Depot. "I promise, we'll be real quick. Then we can cover that up, and I'll help you paint until the sun comes up."

"I don't want to paint until the sun comes up," I said, and smiled as I leaned back in the passenger's seat. "Aren't we going to your place?"

"Yeah—yeah," Cole said, his smile fading as—to my surprise— he pulled into a parking spot in a lot for the factory lofts where his friend Paul lived. We'd just been to those lofts a couple weeks earlier for a party, and Paul's apartment had left a great impression on me. It was one of those dream apartments that I would have loved to live in, but it just wasn't economically feasible for me at the time.

"I don't want to be walking around covered in paint—."

"No, it'll be real quick. Paul's not even home. I just have to drop something off at his place. Come with me. We can shower in there."

"You sure it's cool? Paul won't mind?"

"He's working late," Cole told me, and patted me on the leg just before he opened the driver's door to get out. "If you want, then we can just run this into his apartment, and then we'll head to my place. I'd love your company though."

"Just walking into his apartment?"

"I don't care if I'm walking ten feet, I'd rather have you with me than sitting in the car," Cole said, standing just outside the car with the door wide open. He always knew exactly what to say. There was also something about the *way* he'd say things. It never felt like cheesy one-liners. All I had to do was look into those deep green eyes when he talked to me and I'd see all the love pouring out of him.

"I'm coming," I said, and slid out of the passenger's side of the car.

As we walked into the loft building a brief anxiety came over me. My head was ringing with the words *two weeks*, and being surrounded by dream apartments placed me in a peculiar emotional spot. I felt anxious about having to find a new lease and move, and even more anxious about where I'd end up. I'd been thinking about moving closer to Cole—definitely out of Cambridge—but the future was growing so uncertain. And I didn't want to move in with him and impose on his space. Even though I knew he'd want that, it was *his* apartment. And I wanted a space that would be mine too.

We climbed the stairs to the second floor of the building and reached Paul's hallway. The hallway was pretty modest. You'd never be able to tell that such beautifully restored lofts and apartments were behind all those plain, white doors.

"Isn't that Paul's apartment?" I asked as Cole and I passed a familiar-looking door. I could've been wrong, but something about its location and apartment number resurrected a memory from two weeks earlier. I remembered Paul's big, jovial expression when he opened the door to greet us.

"You must be losing it. It's down this way," Cole replied, and waved his hand to point further down the hall.

I took another quick look at the door and kept walking. Cole led me to the very end of the hallway, and stopped at the last door, which faced the long corridor leading to the other side of the apartment building. As he reached into his pocket for the keys, I glanced around the hallway. It didn't look familiar. I was almost positive that we weren't at the right apartment, and the first thing that crossed my mind was that Cole was trying to open the wrong door. But as soon as he placed the key in the lock and twisted, the door opened. He smiled at me—probably the biggest grin I'd gotten from him in weeks—and he held out his hand so that his palm disappeared into the open doorway.

"Oh my God," was the first thing I said as I walked past Cole, stepping into an empty apartment. This wasn't Paul's. It was a different layout, with the same long walls of exposed brick, massive windows, and gleaming hardwood floors. The kitchen put my small cooking space in Cambridge to shame. "What's going on?" I asked, and suddenly my smile was just as huge as Cole's. He shut the front door behind him and walked up to me at a casual pace, a confident smirk gleaming between his cheeks.

"This is home, if you'll accept it. Hunter, I'm madly in love with you. You know I'd do *anything* for you," he said. Cole wrapped his arms around my triceps, squeezing my arms like he had done earlier that day in the restaurant. "I took a big leap of faith this morning and I signed a lease. I want to live here with you. When I left Boston years ago, I made the biggest mistake of my life. You're the guy I want to wake up next to every morning. I don't want to do different apartments anymore. Be with me."

I looked away for a moment, and took in the apartment. I pictured myself living there—pictured *us* living there. Cooking in the renovated kitchen, watching TV in the living room, fucking upstairs in the loft. Well, we'd probably be fucking in just about every room.

"When do we move in?"

I could've sworn I saw some tears in Cole's eyes at that moment. He squeezed my arms again and then dropped his hands down along my forearms until they wrapped inside my palms.

"Tomorrow?"

"But—what about your place—."

"I only have three months left. I'm ready to move in here. *This* is home now," he added. "You think you can put up with me every day?"

"Can I put up with you every day? I think so," I replied, and laughed after a feeble attempt to maintain a serious expression.

"All I want in return is coffee in bed, and a kiss—no matter what—every single morning. You do that, and I'll give you the best life and the most love that anyone could ever give you."

"I can't fucking wait to make you coffee every morning," I said to him. Cole leaned in to kiss me, and at that moment I felt like the happiest guy in the world.

CHAPTER FOUR

narrated by Cole Maverick

It was the best alarm ever conceived by man. No loud ringing or obnoxious tone, or unfortunate snooze button. Just Hunter's moist lips on my body. It was a Saturday morning—late morning—when I felt a warm, wet sensation glide across my balls. My legs were spread open just enough for Hunter to crawl up in-between them, and he buried his face deep down in my crotch. He slowly rubbed his face side to side, reaching between my legs, brushing his scruffy face against my balls and inner thighs, all the while taking deep, slow breaths, absorbing my scent. My morning wood seemed to get even harder than it already was, stretching out in the direction of my belly button.

I kept my eyes closed as Hunter's lips moved in-between my legs, down alongside my dick, where he playfully licked at the sensitive areas around my pubes. Pre-cum dripped from my dick; I could feel the sweet and sticky little puddles of warmth collect on my skin. There was this magical smell in the air, typical of our mornings together. The fresh coffee at bedside mixed with our natural, morning musk to create a scent that was so goddamn sexy I could get a hard-on just from digging my nose into one of our pillows. *That's* chemistry.

At that moment, just when I expected Hunter to take my hard dick in his mouth, savoring the pre-cum with his wet tongue, he lifted his head from my crotch and said those awful six words.

"I have to go to work."

I finally opened my eyes. With them closed I'd imagined Hunter totally naked, stroking his cock with one hand as he kept the other on the bed for support. I saw his muscles flexed and greasy from that late night sweat that sometimes leaves an oily residue on his body. In my mind I saw his messy hair, the hot stubble spread out across his chin and cheeks, and those eyes, gleaming with a boyish fervor, ready to wake up his man in the most pleasurable way possible.

Wrong. That last part, maybe, but unfortunately the rest wasn't the case. Hunter was dressed for work. Well-groomed, with his hair done and his face clean-shaven, dressed up in a shirt and tie, Hunter was ready to leave the apartment.

"What time is it?"

"Ten," Hunter replied.

"It's Saturday."

"I know—and I work in fine dining. It sucks," he said. "Six days a week—off on fucking Mondays, of all days."

"It does suck," I said as I rubbed my eyes. Since I was working as a real estate agent, my schedule was a bit more flexible, and it didn't have the rigid structure of Hunter's job. Sometimes an entire weekend would be occupied with open houses, new clients, and market research. The good thing about our busy schedules was that it pushed me out the door to make money for our household. Paying for my old apartment plus the loft—with Hunter's help of course—had been a tough feat for three months, and I was still feeling the burn in my pocket.

"You think we'll ever reach a point when we can have normal weekends?" he asked me, staring at me with those boyish eyes. God, I would've loved to just spend a whole Saturday and Sunday holding him, making love to him, giving him whatever he wanted and desired.

"We'll get there," I told him. "It's just a couple of jobs. I mean—the income has been real good."

"Yeah, but who cares about the money if we barely see each other?"

Hunter had a point, and it left an awful taste in my mouth. I was madly in love with this guy, and had convinced him to take that big step and move in with me, but I guess I never realized just how frustrating our conflicting work schedules would be. When we were living apart and I was courting him, I knew that he worked a lot, but for some reason I overlooked that detail in all of my move-in fantasies. As if we'd just move in together and have all the time in the world. What a surprise. I was still getting my coffee in bed every morning, but what I really wanted was to have Hunter in bed with me, and not rushing out the door for work.

"I'll figure this out," I said. Thinking back, I don't know why I said *I* instead of *we*. Maybe I felt an extra sense of responsibility since I was the one who had asked Hunter to live with me, and since I'd made so many promises to him. I wanted to do everything I could for this man. There seemed to be no limit to my love for him. Hunter had enough stress at work, and I didn't want him to be stressed at home thinking about career change and all of that bullshit. This was going to be my undertaking.

"Do you have any showings today?" he asked me as he hopped off of the bed.

"Today actually isn't too busy. Perfect opportunity for a massive job search."

"Ah, you have a good job. My job is the problem."

"No, you have a great job," I told him, "but you just have awful hours."

"No joke," he replied, and clenched his lips together. "Jobs like mine aren't designed for people in love." After he said it a smile poured onto his face, and he laughed before heading for the stairs leading down to the living room. Even though it made him laugh, the words were painfully true.

"You want to do something tonight when you get off?" I called downstairs. As I slowly slid out of bed, I grabbed the coffee off the nightstand and took my first sip of the day.

"Yeah!" Hunter shouted from the living room. "Hold on, I'll be right back up to say goodbye. But keep an eye on your phone tonight. We'll definitely go out after I'm done work. At least for a drink or something—maybe catch up with some friends."

"My phone will be glued to my body," I promised him.

*   *

I didn't usually like to jack off without Hunter—I mean what's the point of jacking off alone when you have a hot boyfriend? But on some days—usually around lunchtime—when Hunter had a long shift and I was home on the computer doing work stuff or fucking around on websites, the urge would spring upon me. Sometimes I'd fight it, but on that particular Saturday I just gave in. Maybe it was the way Hunter had woken me up that morning, licking my balls in all the right spots. I so badly wanted him to suck my cock! I was ready to pop.

And so there I was, back at the apartment in the early afternoon in-between showings, sitting at the glass computer table. I'd be able to cum again later with Hunter; I had no doubts about that. I could probably do it five times a day with him.

Just as I was pulling up one of my usual porn sites, my cell phone rang. I'd left it on the computer desk, right behind the keyboard, so that there was no way I'd miss the damn thing if it beeped, rang, or made whatever noise was in its portfolio of sounds.

Paul. As I glanced over the keyboard at the phone, I thought about just letting it go to voicemail. My dick was out and hard, and my computer screen was quickly loading images and videos of hot guys with sweet hairy asses and big cocks.

"Hey," I warmly spoke into the phone, grabbing it after a few rings. The beautiful men on my computer screen would have to wait.

"Cole! You online?"

"As a matter of fact I am."

"I'm gonna give you a website," Paul excitedly told me. He seemed extra-spunky, and my first thought was that he'd met someone. Good for him.

"Okay—what website is he on?"

"Who?"

"Whoever has you leaping out of your seat," I replied. "Is that what you're calling to tell me?"

"I wish—no, not that. XTube.com," he said, slowly enunciating the name of the website. "Like YouTube but with an *x*."

"What are you showing me—," I said as I typed the address into the web browser.

"The reinvention of porn," Paul replied, delivering the line as if he was confidently reading the title of a thesis at a conference of 10,000 people. "*Anyone* has access to the industry, all tied together in a network of user-uploaded videos and pictures. This is the fucking goldmine of porn. Forget the studios. This shit is the real deal. No subscriptions—nothing—I just log on, look at videos that people have uploaded of themselves, and after a fantastic jack-off I've still got money in my pocket that would've bought a gold chain for some sleazebag working out of a basement in Queens."

"This is all free?" I asked, shocked, as I scrolled through pages of videos.

"Some is, some isn't. I sent you an e-mail—go check your e-mail."

My e-mail was already up, minimized in the bottom of my screen. I clicked once on it and the page sprung to life, revealing a couple spam messages plus one from Paul with a long Internet hyperlink.

"What's this?"

"Click it, click it. You'll see," he replied.

I clicked on the link and instantly a new page started to load. I saw the XTube background, the indication that the video was loading, and then the image: a circumcised penis—probably average length and build—wet with lube as a hand worked up and down the shaft. The guy's dick was popping out of a pair of pants that looked oddly familiar.

"Behold," Paul said loudly, "my intro to porn."

"Oh—Jesus!" I bombarded the *X* button on the browser, closing it as quickly as I'd opened it. "What are you showing me this for?"

"Is this not the coolest shit ever? I did it with my webcam. Takes a minute. *Two* minutes. One to take the video, and another to upload it to their website. Look at the comments!"

"I already closed it out," I told him. "You brought me into a danger zone."

"Chill out, Cole. Look—there are two comments already. Almost one-hundred people have viewed the video!"

"When did you post it?"

"Last night," he replied. I was shocked. One-hundred people had already seen it in less than 24 hours? Talk about exposure. "You're a good-looking guy, Cole, you should take a video. You know how many boys would love to see you jack off on cam?"

"I feel like that's something that uh—I don't know—eighteen-year-olds do. Like something I'd have done in high school."

"The technology wasn't even close to existing back then."

"Fuck off," I jokingly replied. "So all I do is turn my webcam on and record a video?"

"Easiest thing I've ever done in my life."

"I'll think about it," I told him.

"I'm serious! You should," he said. Whenever he was excited about something he'd get very emotionally wrapped up in it. "I'll be really disappointed if you don't. So will the Boston gay community. Fuck Boston—the *world* is on XTube. Hey, you should show Hunter this site. Actually—oh my God—do you remember those hot little videos you showed me of you and Hunter from back in the day? The ones you took with that little, piece of shit camera? Do you still have those? You should post them!"

"Whoa, whoa," I immediately cut him off. "If you ever tell Hunter that I showed you those pictures and videos, I'll beat your ass."

"Don't threaten me with a good time," Paul snapped back, and we both laughed. "But seriously, Cole, that would be amazing. That was some hot stuff."

"I don't think Hunter is ready to have his face and naked body shown all over the Internet," I replied. As much as I thought about it, and as much as Hunter liked exhibitionism, I just couldn't see him going that extra step further and including thousands of unknown people in our sex life.

"Pity," Paul said. "I think you guys would be a big hit. *You*—at the very least—should post something."

"I don't know if I want everyone in the world to see me jacking off."

"Cole—really—when have you given a shit about stuff like that?"

He made a good point.

"Listen, I've gotta run," Paul said, lowering his tone. "I'll chat with you soon. What are you doing tonight?"

"Depends on when Hunter gets out of work. I'll call you for sure."

"Sounds great, man. XTube. Don't forget it."

The phone clicked, and I placed it back in its spot behind the keyboard. My eyes wandered up my computer, from my e-mail to the little circle at the top of the monitor. There was a built-in webcam on my desktop that I'd used only to chat with people online. Never to record videos.

My eyes drifted back to the webcam. Would I be able to deal with the consequences of putting a jack-off video of myself online? I didn't even know what the consequences would be, if any at all. But I was bored, and still horny from earlier, and was going to cum anyway. It didn't seem like that big of a deal.

A few clicks later, the porn was back on my screen, and a green light to the right of my webcam indicated that I was about to be videotaped.

*　　*

"I can't wait to fucking lay down," Hunter said as soon as we reached the entrance to our apartment. Work had kept him late—later than usual on a Saturday—and with his Sunday shift rapidly approaching he understandably wasn't in the mood to go out. And that was fine. There was something a lot more important waiting on the computer.

"Before you lay down, you need to see something," I told him as I quickly unlocked the front door for him. I knew he could tell that something was up. After I picked him up from work we sped home, and I practically flew up the stairs of the apartment building.

"What is it?" he asked, smiling as much as he could after such a long, stressful day at work.

"Something pretty fucking awesome. Hey—go up to the computer desk, sit down, relax, and I'll give you a nice back rub."

"Did you book a vacation or something?"

"No!" I replied, rushing into the kitchen to grab a couple beers as Hunter headed for the stairs leading up to the loft bedroom. "Even better!"

"Better than a vacation? Did you win the megabucks or something?" he casually asked, as if he'd respond with a simple *oh ok* if I'd just won a few million.

"Nothing to do with money."

"Are you showing me porn?"

I kept my mouth shut as I popped the caps off our beers. I'd left the webpage on the computer screen for Hunter to see, and I waited in anticipation for the second he'd sit down in the chair and click on the mouse. I didn't know exactly how he'd react. It was something I'd never even really thought about doing until Paul had called me on the phone and showed me that website. And after that, it seemed much more comfortable. I took a video of myself jacking off and watched it, and it wasn't even a few seconds before I was figuring out how to upload it on XTube.

"Did you get on the computer yet?" I called upstairs as I carefully maneuvered the ladder to the loft bedroom with a cold beer in each hand.

"Taking my clothes off first!" he called back. "I couldn't wait to get out of this fucking suit. I'll look at it now—gimme a minute."

I wobbled up the ladder, trying not to spill ours beers. My excitement was mounting up inside me. As I reached the top I caught a glimpse of Hunter, butt naked, taking a seat at the computer. My excitement level exploded. I could feel my heart pounding as I got closer to him, waiting for his hand to fall over the mouse.

"What's this?" he asked, but it sounded like he was asking himself the question. I put both beers on the computer desk and then placed my hands on Hunter's shoulders. And there it was, smack in the center of the web browser and enclosed in a large square: a picture of me, naked, sitting on that same computer chair, hard-on in hand. An eastward-pointing arrow sat in the middle of the image, just waiting to be clicked on.

"Click it," I told him, digging my fingers into Hunter's back. I knew exactly where all his spots were, and as I worked my fingers along his shoulders I could hear him breath in relaxation.

He clicked on the arrow and the video came to life. Unlike Paul's video, my face was in this one. The video quality sucked and the film itself was short, but for a webcam it wasn't all that bad. I mean, this wasn't studio-made. It was just a guy with a webcam, jacking off and waving his dick on-camera. And yet there was something exciting about it. Something that intrigued me to do more. I felt like I wanted to take twenty more videos, not with the crappy webcam anymore but with a real camera. All night I'd been going back and forth, checking my video every ten minutes while waiting for the pick-up call from Hunter. My mind was spinning all night with ideas about camera angles, positions, and what it would be like to do this with my lover.

Even more exciting were all the hot comments that people left under the video. I've never been good at being able to tell when a guy is into me, so I was completely flattered by all the boys and men who wrote in to profess their love for what I'd created. Everyone wanted to see more. More of my dick, more face, and just more videos.

"Is this on a website?" were the first words out of Hunter's mouth. His eyes were glued to the screen.

"XTube.com. Have you ever heard of it?"

"No—what is it?"

"Think YouTube but with porn. People take videos of themselves and upload them for other people to see."

"So—this video of you jacking off is now on the web for anyone who wants to see it?" Hunter didn't sound as enthusiastic as I'd hoped he'd be. "Are you cool with that?"

"It's like—a rite of passage, putting your dick online."

"It's not just your dick, Cole. You're jacking off on camera, and your face is in the video."

"How many times have we hooked up in public?" I asked him, and Hunter immediately turned around and frowned at me.

"That's different."

"It's not that different. It's just voyeurism. This is like—*techno*-voyeurism. Forty people have already seen the video, and I just posted it today!"

"So what if like—your parents saw this?"

"I don't think my parents are gonna be looking at gay porn," I told him. I worked my hands from his shoulders down to his arms, rubbing my thumbs along his triceps. "I think it's hot to be online. That mystery of wondering who's watching—if anyone will really like my video. That's not just an anonymous cock being jerked off, it's *me. I'm* in the video."

"I know, Cole. It's hot, I'm not saying it isn't," he said, turning back to face the video, which had finished its short run and was replaced by ads for other videos. "It's just a little strange for me. Maybe *strange* isn't the right word. *Different.* It's *different.* Like what if I had a video on there, and someone at work saw it, and they told my boss that I was doing porn? There goes my job."

"I understand. Or maybe you'll become the hottest porn star on the Internet and won't need that job anymore," I joked, and Hunter frowned again.

"Do you plan on doing more videos?" he asked me after some short silence.

"You want to do some with me?"

"I don't know—."

"XTube is like a—worldwide site. Who knows where these forty people are from. Probably Russia, South Korea, Germany—who the fuck knows? I know for sure that they're not all in Boston. Come on, Hunter, I think it'll be fun."

"I think our sex life is pretty hot as it is, without putting it online."

"My relationship with you is the best thing in my life, Hunter. The best thing I've ever found. How cool would it be to share this love we have for each other with the world? I'm not talking about that studio bullshit with dolled-up, pretty boy actors. It's fucking hot man-love. Ours will be the real deal!"

"Just let me think about it," Hunter said, followed by a deep sigh. He put his hand back on the mouse and clicked refresh on the page. Up came my face and my cock in a dark yellow background, like the opening to some 80s porno. A porno without decent cameras. "The video's hot, but why didn't you just use your camera? Show off your cock better, you know?"

"Next time I will," I replied. I'd been thinking about this stuff all night.

"In the meantime—," Hunter paused and turned to look up at me. My hands had made it back up to his shoulders and I was moving my thumbs along the base of his neck. "I've missed you all day."

Hunter wrapped one arm around me and pulled me to his side. I kept my hands on him, massaging his neck as he rested a palm on my crotch. He playfully squeezed my cock. I'd already had a hard-on from watching him see the video, and I could feel my cock writhing in my jeans.

"Wanna finish what you started earlier?" I asked him, and Hunter looked up at me. That boyish smile—excited to please his man.

And as he un-zipped my jeans and pulled them down from my waist, one of my hands wandered from the back of his neck to the mouse. With his total concentration on my throbbing cock—his juicy mouth ready to wet down my cock and suck a hot load out of me—I clicked on the webcam icon on the computer. A little green light came on, probably too small for Hunter to notice as he took my huge cock in his mouth. I groaned with pleasure—I'd been waiting for this all day. And although Hunter had no idea, we were about to do it on camera.

CHAPTER FIVE

narrated by Hunter

"Did you post that shit online?" I nervously asked. I don't know why my heart was beating so fast while Cole replayed the video he took from the night before, but I couldn't get into the on-camera sex. I mean, the content was really hot. The video quality was awful, but you could see me giving Cole a passionate blowjob, working my lips from his belly button down to his balls, and digging my face into his crotch until he came all over me. Seeing something like this should've made me rock hard, yet I was flaccid as I thought about the consequences of the video being shown online. Could I handle the world seeing my face as I sucked my boyfriend's cock?

"I haven't put it online yet. Wanted to see what you think."

Cole was in his underwear, hovering over me with a cup of coffee. I was already dressed for work, and unfortunately had to leave for work in a few minutes. Just another Sunday. Most couples get to enjoy Sundays together.

"I don't want to put it online yet," I quickly told him. The words flew out of my mouth. "I'm not—I don't know, I'm just not cool with this yet."

"Let's try again tonight. It's hot—Hunter. Look, the video was choppy—total crap quality, but the content is out of this world. I'll use my camera tonight. We'll do something homemade, fun—make it an exciting Sunday night."

"I don't know. I really have to think about this. Why didn't you tell me you were recording us last night?"

"I've taken naked pictures and videos of you before," he said, which was true. He'd taken a bunch. "You never complained then."

"That's because I knew they weren't going to be uploaded to a website where millions of people could see them for free."

"Then we'll charge five dollars for it, there's an option for that—what do you want me to say?" he joked, and then took another sip of his coffee. A flip had been switched since yesterday, and he seemed totally obsessed with the video thing. I hadn't seen him so excited about anything in a long time, and I wasn't so sure that he even slept Saturday night. When my alarm went off and I opened my eyes to get my Sunday started, Cole was planted at the computer desk across from the bed, busily searching through XTube.

"I just really need time to think this over, Cole. It's a big decision."

"What's so big about it? We're making love for the world."

"Why are you so into this?" I asked him. It truly was puzzling. Out of nowhere he suddenly wanted to show off our sex life online. I'd always found a little voyeurism in public to be a turn-on, but this was a huge step further. This was far removed from a little crowd of onlookers in a Provincetown parking lot. We were suddenly talking about *the world*.

"Because I love you, and I'm proud of you. And it excites me to think that people are into us, and wanna see us fuck. And why not? We're good-looking, masculine guys. You practically live at the gym. I work out every day—."

"*Every day*? Bullshit," I called, and then laughed as Cole stumbled to defend himself.

"Okay, *almost* every day. But come on—I'm not ashamed to show off my body. Are you? And besides, you know how much I love to take pictures and make videos."

"I just need more time to think about this. It seems like a ton of stress—worrying about who will see our videos. I have enough stress at work. I love you, but just give me a little more time."

"Maybe this'll be a stress relief."

"Somehow I doubt it," I replied as I stood up from the computer table to face him. "Look—I don't want to fight about it. I love you—so much. I need to get to work. Can we talk about it later?"

"I'll have the camera ready just in case."

"Yeah, sure," I said, and took a deep breath. "If this is really important to you, then I'll think about it. Just—go easy, because I've never done anything like this and never would've thought about doing anything like this. It's like—getting a tattoo, you know? It's permanent. You put a sex tape online and it'll be there forever."

"I think we've got something that's more than just sex," Cole said. His voice was so warm and loving that it was hard for me to argue with him about the videos. I really wanted to do anything I could for this man, but I was still bothered by how the whole video thing leaped upon me. When I woke up on Saturday I never even knew that XTube.com existed, and all the sudden on Sunday I was on my way towards being one of their contributors.

"I'll think about it. Okay?" I kissed Cole on the lips, and tightly wrapped my arms around him. "Anything that's this important to you, I'll really think about."

*   *

And I did think about it. From the moment I left our apartment the idea of an online sex video between Cole and I was implanted in my mind. I thought about the pros, the cons, and just about every hypothetical imaginable. What would happen if a co-worker saw the video and told my boss? What would happen if my parents found out? What would become of the friendships Cole and I have made over so many years if our friends saw the video? Honestly, I didn't think any of our friends would really care. It was one of Cole's friends who directed him to the website in the first place. But I just needed to go over every worst-case scenario in order to be more comfortable with doing it.

More than just sex. Cole's words were on rewind in my head, all day long. I knew he was right. It was more than just sex—more than just porn with paid actors. This wasn't a studio. I'm sure if Cole and I wanted to make a sex video for money we could find some studio willing to bankroll us. This was totally different. We were putting our love-making online for free, for anyone with an internet connection to jack off to.

When I knocked on the door to our apartment I still didn't have the answer. I needed to look into Cole's eyes and see that he really wanted it.

"Hey," Cole said, his green eyes wide open as he stared at me from the doorway. "Why didn't you call? I would've picked you up, baby."

"I couldn't focus on work. I've been thinking about last night and this morning all day. I don't know why I've been making such a big deal about this video. It's just—well it's—."

"Come inside," he said, and put an arm around me as I walked through the doorway. "Don't you have your key?"

"Didn't bring it. I figured you were going to pick me up after work. I didn't expect to be back this early," I calmly said. I immediately went to the living room and sat down on our big, chocolate brown leather sofa that faced the TV. It was always nice to be back home after work. I loved our loft, and it was such a comfortable place to be in. We had done a great job of turning it into *home*.

"Are you hungry, baby? Can I get you something to eat? To drink?"

"No, just come here," I replied, and patted on the sofa cushion next to me. He was slow to come over, but he took a seat at my side, and put a single comforting hand on my leg.

"If you don't want to do a video, we don't have to."

"I do. I want to give a try. You really want this?"

"I think it would be hot! It's not the—most important thing *ever*. I just think it would be hot and beautiful for us to share what we have— with people online."

I trusted Cole more than anyone in the world. Back when I had a girlfriend and thought I might just be a straight guy with some gay leanings, Cole showed me that I could be both masculine and gay. Sexually, he taught me everything I knew. And so even though I was still worried about the video, I wanted to give it a shot. It would be hot, passionate love-making, just like we did all the time, although this time there would be a video camera. I didn't know if or how that might mess with our chemistry, but since we'd fucked in public before I doubted that the camera would be problematic.

"You wanna get the camera ready?" I asked him, staring my man in his green eyes. His whole face lit up in excitement, and I could tell that this was important to him. He really wanted this video. And I was ready to give it a try.

*   *

There was something special about Cole that night. He held his video camera tightly in one hand, as if letting it go would mean losing it forever. He had the most amazing look on his face: an excitement about the video we were about to film mixed with a pensive expression that clearly carried some worry about the way it would turn out. He wanted this to be perfect.

The lights were brighter in our bedroom. Since it was nighttime we needed to have good lighting inside the room, otherwise we'd risk making a video as dark as Cole's solo performance. I was laying on my

70

side, spread across the bed with my head rested in one palm as I stared at him. He was on the edge of the bed, nervously checking the settings on the camera. He was totally naked, and had asked me to wear a black jock strap.

I squeezed my nuts and slapped my cock against my abs as I waited for Cole's touch. I wasn't nervous anymore. Something about doing this for Cole got me so aroused that there wasn't any room for nervousness. As soon as I put that jock strap on and hopped into bed, and saw the excitement on his face, my nervousness faded. I didn't know what would happen when we'd be faced with actually putting the video online, or if the video would even be hot at all. But I had a feeling that it would.

My eyes lit up when Cole turned to face me.

"Smile," he said with a loving voice as he aimed the camera at me. He slowly moved the camera so that it scanned my entire body up and down. Somehow I couldn't imagine in the intimate setting we'd created that the camera in his hand was essentially the eye of the rest of the world.

I smiled for him, and for the camera, and he placed his free hand—large and masculine in its grip—on my thigh. He massaged the muscles in my leg, sliding his hand from my waist down to my knee. Both of his knees were on the bed and he sat facing me, his hard cock planted in the mattress. I shifted my body and slid towards him so that my head was in-between his legs, and I wrapped my fingers around the base of his large cock.

I knew that the camera was rolling but I didn't really feel it. It didn't feel like a performance. I didn't want to stare at the lens, and so I kept my eyes on Cole. I kept my hand on his quivering cock. And I took it deep into my mouth. My shoulders and head were in-between his knees. I didn't know where the camera was anymore, and I kept my eyes closed. I was in that erotic zone that only Cole could take me to. My lips were wrapped around him, and his huge cock pressed into the back of my throat.

I could tell he wanted more. He was craving it. He pushed his hips up towards me so that his cock slid deeper into my mouth, and just as he did I backed up. I licked all over, up and down his meat, working my tongue across every inch of his fat cock, starting with the head and slipping down to the base where his pubes leaped out around his balls.

With one hand still grasping the base of his cock, I licked up and down his balls so gently that just by exhaling I'd instantly dry them again, each time allowing them the fresh sensation of warm wetness on soft, dry skin.

And as soon as I brought my mouth up from his balls, I felt him grab a fist full of hair on the back of my head. His cock was rock hard, and he slapped me in the cheek with it. I stuck my tongue out to receive it, and he slapped me again, hitting me in-between the lips. I looked up at him while he playfully beat my face. He was craving me. Cole pushed down on my head, shoving my mouth onto his cock, methodically fucking my face. My mouth practically fell on top of it, absorbing its salty, masculine taste. I took my hand off his cock and squeezed his balls as I deep-throated him, again and again. And he responded in a series of deep groans.

As I kept working his cock, I felt him lean over me and slide his big hand behind me, feeling the slick coating of sweat that covered my hard, muscled lower back. When he reached the furry crack of my ass, I felt him work his wet fingers around my pink hole. The sensation was almost more than I could take. My ass arched to Cole's touch and I pressed my hole down on his fingers; I wanted him inside me.

Cole wanted to fuck me, but I was going to make him work for it. The second I pulled my mouth off his cock he grabbed my waist with one hand and tried to flip me over. I clasped my arms around him and planted my face on his belly. As he tried to pull me up towards his face, I stuck my tongue out, licking along his chest, following the trail of hair that led up to his pecs. Up to his neck. Until my lips were wrapped around his chin, and he was moaning with pleasure. His free hand held my ass, two fingers slipped just halfway into my moist and swollen hole.

I arched my back and stuck my ass out so that his big fingers slid deeper and deeper into me. I eased into it. And as he penetrated me with his fingers, I threw my hands up around his neck and put my lips on his. I've always loved the taste of his lips.

"I'm gonna fuck you," he said in-between wet kisses. I think he expected me to drop backwards and lift my legs up for him, but that's not how I wanted it that night. Instead I turned around and dropped down on my chest, lifting my ass off the mattress like a bridge over a stream. He rapidly hopped on top of my body, digging his knees into the mattress and rubbing his long cock against my wet hole, all the while kissing and sucking the back of my neck. He leaned forward to grab lube off of our nightstand, and soon after I felt the wet beads drip all over my ass.

"Man, I fucking love you," he told me as he rubbed his throbbing cock up against me. I think he was telling the whole world too. And that's when it really kicked in for me. I wanted the world to see this. And so I arched my back further and stuck my ass out for my man to have. I ached for him to be in me, and I knew at that moment that we were about to have the man-to-man beast sex I loved and craved so much. I've never experienced it with anyone but Cole. With him I didn't feel like I was bottoming for a guy; I felt like we were two gladiators fucking in lust and love. It was sex at its most primal form: sweaty, aggressive, and raw.

I felt him slide into me—that initial feeling of penetration that makes me feel like I could squirt without even touching my cock. I love the way his huge cock opens me up, and he did just that as he pushed all the way into my hole. All the while holding the camera on the two of us. I couldn't see him at all with my face planted in the pillow but I knew he was beaming. I could feel it the way he wrapped his fingers around my waist. It's the way you hold someone during sex when you know you're not gonna let go of them after cumming.

As Cole forced his whole body into mine—over and over—I could feel myself about to burst. I dug my shoulders into our sweat-soaked sheets and totally relaxed my ass. And as Cole's groans grew deeper and louder I could feel it coming. I could feel him entering that totally amazing space of full release. I stopped fighting the pressure inside me and just let myself go; let my mind and body totally surrender.

I exhaled deeply as cum pumped out of my rock hard cock, filling the inside of my jock strap. And within seconds I could hear Cole's loud groans of excitement as he shot his load into me. I could feel him shoot his seed deep inside me. Afterwards he fell on top of me, soaked in sweat, dropping the camera on the bed next to us and letting his wet lips slide across my sweaty neck.

"I love you, baby," he said in-between heavy breathing.

"I love you too."

And as we both looked into the camera for one final time, we broke out into laughter over what we'd just done. I couldn't wait to see this video.

*   *

When I woke up on Monday morning, Cole was already sitting at the computer desk, gazing intensely at the screen. He hadn't been able to sleep at all—for a second night in a row. After our amazing sex on Sunday night, Cole had laid awake, looking at the video and playing around with it online, and getting to know the editing software that was on his computer. He spent nearly the whole night in front of the computer, with a brief nap to satisfy his weariness. He was waiting for me to wake up, like a little kid staying awake for Santa Claus on Christmas morning.

I stayed in bed while he showed me the video. He played it twice—from start to finish. He pointed out each part that he'd edited. He pointed out his favorite sections. He told me how he wanted to handle the camera next time, and how much he thought people online would love it. Cole looked fucking hot in the video. Had I never met him and saw that video of him online, I would've totally been stalking him. Not in a *creepy* way, of course. But I'd at least e-mail him some dirty pictures.

"Can I upload it?" he asked me in excitement, and as soon as the words left his mouth I choked up. I couldn't respond. I thought about offering to go get him coffee, or finding some excuse to go downstairs and avoid giving an answer right away.

"Is everything okay?" came afterwards. He saw the way my eyes fell on the white sheets where we'd just fucked the night before. I wanted to respond to him. I truly wanted to give a confident *yes*, something I'd be proud to say. Something I'd be able to give him. He wanted this video so badly, and yet I couldn't even look him in the eyes to give the answer that he could obviously read through my averting gaze.

"Can you edit my face out?" I finally said. It's not what I wanted to say first, but somewhere in my mess of thoughts I found it to be the most diplomatic response.

"But you're gonna be the hottest guy on this website!" he protested. I knew he wouldn't be happy. "You're beautiful, Hunter. Why would I take your face out? Didn't you really want last night?"

"I did. I just don't think I can put my face online like that." I hated telling him no. Especially with the way he looked at me. I knew he wanted this so badly, and I just couldn't bring myself to say yes. I didn't want to have my face broadcast to the world in an online sex video.

"Do you want to see the video again?" he asked me, hoping for some small chance of a change of mind.

"I love the video, but—just for us. I'm not ready yet."

"I wanted us to do this as a couple."

"We can post it as a couple. As long as I'm not recognizable."

Cole turned his focus back on the computer screen where the video frames were loaded within his editing software.

"Are you mad at me?" I asked him.

"No—I think you'll do a video with me eventually. I want to show you off, Hunter. I fucking love you. Even if you're a pussy," he jokingly added.

"Fuck you, I'm not a pussy," I remarked. "I just don't know if I'm ready to do this. I'll do a video eventually, I think. Just don't be a dick about it," I added. "At least we still have the video with our faces. I'll think about it, and maybe we can post it later. In the meantime just post one without."

Had I known back then what I know now, I would've probably posted the video before Cole even got to it—faces and all. But I just wasn't ready for the possible consequences, and while I sat on the bed with a melancholy expression, all of the negative possibilities seemed to overwhelm the positive. I truly did need more time. Cole would just have to wait. The only thing I hoped was that my decision to pull out of our video wouldn't put a strain on the relationship. As I'd soon discover, not wanting to show my face in a sex tape would be insignificant compared with the other strains that were lurking around the corner.

CHAPTER SIX

narrated by Cole Maverick

"I've gotta go!" Hunter said for the seventh time, laughing uncontrollably as I tried to mount and tickle him. I was on top of him at that point, both of us on the bed, with his feet—clad in a pair of dress shoes for work—up in the air. He closed his arms around his face, trying to shield his neck and chin from my quick fingers. Each time he'd protect his face I'd go for his stomach, and then as soon as his guard was down I went right back for that chin. Hunter squeamishly rolled back and forth, trying to break free from my playful attack.

"I don't want you to leave," I moaned, with my best *sad face* to back up the words. I could see that Hunter was already feeling guilty about having to work, but it was Saturday and he needed to open the restaurant for lunch.

"I don't want to either—trust me."

"I'm really horny this morning," I said, and stuck a hand out towards his chin, but he shielded me with his thick arms.

"Can you save it until tonight?"

"What about now?"

"I wish I had time—. I literally need to be out the door—."

"I know, I know," I replied, and demonstrated my disappointment with a loud sigh as I stood up from the bed and allowed Hunter to do the same. "These Saturday shifts—."

"I know. Come by in-between lunch and dinner. I'll find an excuse to get out for a little while. We can cruise around in your car and—," Hunter didn't finish, but he winked at me and flashed his tongue in-between white teeth.

"Are you kidding? I'm there," I excitedly told him. As Hunter patted down his dress shirt and checked his tie in the mirror, I slowly wandered over to the glass computer table across from our bed, and planted my ass in the desk chair. "I'm so goddamn horny this morning."

"Look at some porn before you come see me."

"Yeah—maybe."

"What about that website you put your solo video on? I'm sure there are a million things to jack off to on there." he said, and came over to the computer desk to give me a kiss goodbye. He gave me a quick, wet peck on my lips, just as he felt up my erection with his left hand. "Damn, you're ready to explode."

"Yeah, that's what I've been trying to tell you."

Hunter looked me in the eyes, and I could tell exactly where his mind was floating off to.

"Okay, fuck it," he finally said, and revealed a brief grin. "You think you can cum fast?"

I nodded my head and leaned back as Hunter got down on his knees. My hard-on was fucking raging; standing at attention like a Marine in front of his officers. As Hunter pulled my boxers off, I couldn't pull my eyes off him. He looked so goddamn sexy, dressed up in jacket and tie. And when his fat cock emerged from those black dress pants, my eyes locked in. He was already dripping with pre-cum.

Hunter got right down to business. He held my cock in one hand, admiring it as he clenched with a firm, tight grip. And as I waited and craved for the sensation of his mouth, he slowly started to lick all the pre-cum dripping down the head. He worked his way from the head down the shaft, licking up every drop. I was shaking with anticipation.

I moaned loudly as Hunter's entire mouth wrapped around my cock. I could feel the head pressing against the back of his throat. I wrapped a hand around his head and pulled him into me, fucking his throat in deep, hard thrusts. After only five or six I was ready to shoot my hot, sticky load down his throat. He knew it was coming too, because as my moaning got louder and my thrusts harder, he yanked himself out and gazed up at me with that animalistic look.

"Wait, wait—shoot on my tongue. I wanna watch you jerk off on me."

How could I say no to that? He was still kneeling on the floor, his own red and swollen cock held tightly in one hand. I stood up off the chair, my sweaty balls hanging just over his moist lips. His mouth was wide open and his tongue was out, reaching up for my cock and begging for my load. I jerked my own cock with my left hand, and grabbed Hunter's hair to steady myself. He loved when I grabbed the back of his head, and he moaned in pleasure. The more I jerked myself the tighter my grip on his hair got. I tugged to pull his head back, preparing him for my load.

As Hunter's tongue reached out into the air, I stroked out one of the biggest loads I have ever shot. The hot spurts of cum shot all over his face and on his greedy tongue, pouring down into his throat. He moaned and quickly gulped down every hot squirt of cum. And just as he swallowed the last gulp, I saw his cock explode with cum, shooting a hot load all over my feet. As I crashed back onto the chair in exhaustion, Hunter fell onto my knees, panting for air, and savoring that bliss after an amazing orgasm. Finally he looked up and smiled at me with those big brown eyes, and I leaned down to kiss his cum-covered lips, and to taste that salty, sweet scent that still lingered on his mouth.

"I've gotta go. I'll shoot you a text when I can get free."

As Hunter hurried to zip up and get out the door for work, I thought about checking out XTube. Hunter's earlier suggestion hadn't left my mind, even after that cum we just had. Not to mention, it had been a few months since I'd even visited our page, and I was curious to see what was going on. After Hunter and I filmed that hot, passionate video together, and he decided he didn't want his face shown online, I edited the video down to a short clip and posted it. But hanging around the website looking at other people's videos only made me disappointed that my partner and I couldn't have our own videos up there. And so I forgot about it. Well, I didn't *forget*, but I also didn't visit the website. My last sign-on was just a few days after posting the edited and anonymous video that Hunter had filmed with me.

Hunter's suggestion did spark a certain curiosity in me. My solo video had been online for months, and so had my short clip with Hunter. And as I thought about all the warm responses I'd gotten to my solo video within just a couple days of posting it, I was filled with this extreme urge to see what people said about the second video. Of course, that was considering anyone had even seen it in the first place.

I heard the front door close just as I anxiously hurried onto the homepage to be greeted by columns of homemade porn videos. My heart was beating fast. There wasn't any logical reason to be so nervous about our video. It seemed like there were thousands upon thousands of videos on this website. Our two, short clips had a lot of competition. I guess all I was hoping for was some kind of consolation that we created something exciting, fun, and sexy.

Right after I punched in my username and password, the homepage re-loaded. And before I could even choose which of my two videos to check out first, another thing caught my eye. In the top, right-hand corner of the homepage, a little icon for their internal e-mail showed a startling number. *32.* I didn't think it was possible that within the past few months those short clips could've generated that many responses. If anything, I expected to see lots of spam mail and advertisements.

Out of curiosity, I clicked on the e-mail icon, and what I saw next was shocking. I scrolled down the webpage, my eyes wide open, my body hunched over the computer desk as if I needed to be inches away from the monitor in order to actually see the screen. I clicked on the first e-mail and read it, and then read it a second time. Then I moved onto the next. And the next. Suddenly I felt like I was back in the game. Thirty-two e-mails of support had renewed my spirits—my *need*—to try this online video thing again. One fan after another had written to us about the two videos asking to see more. They wanted to see my boyfriend's face. They wanted to see more positions. They wanted to know if we ever had three-ways. Some even asked if they could meet up with us just to fuck!

I had to check on the videos, and the one with Hunter was first and foremost. Even though I had edited out his face, I hoped that his hot body and ass would grab the attention of online viewers.

I impatiently tapped my bare foot on the hardwood floor as I waited for the page to load. But before our video had even loaded in the viewing box, I saw exactly what I was looking for. Even more jaw-dropping than the e-mails was the number of people who had seen our little piece of homemade and cinematic love-making. Over fifty-thousand views.

As I scrolled down the page to read all the supportive comments that viewers had posted about the video, I ran through the numbers in my head. I knew it wasn't fifty-thousand *people*, since there were probably some people who had seen it multiple times. But even if every viewer had seen it three times, we still had over fifteen-thousand unique hits!

There was no question. We needed to post some more movies. And Hunter needed to show his face. If we were getting this kind of a response after just a couple of choppy clips, then I could only imagine the response we'd get from long, hot, edited videos.

Cole

I leapt out of my computer chair with renewed energy. First I needed to tell the good news to Hunter, and second, we needed to make some more goddamn videos.

*   *

Hunter's restaurant sat proudly on Newbury Street in downtown Boston, occupying an entire street corner. The restaurant itself was designed in that style of old-world luxury, filled with mocha-colored woods and five service people to each table, and a high ceiling with gaudy chandeliers that elegantly lit the dining room. The menu was all high-end French, and their wine list was thick enough to be mistaken for the King James Bible.

I used to stop by Hunter's work all the time, usually late at night when he was in the process of closing up. I'd plant myself at the impressively enormous bar, and talk with the bartenders, servers, bus boys, and a whole host of regulars who would stop in for drinks and appetizers. I got to know the whole staff, and got along with everyone. This was one of those restaurants with a rule for everything, and so it took a while for many of Hunter's co-workers to break out of their strict disciplinary habits and just be themselves around me. But after the owner would leave each evening and the night would start to wind down, the place would no longer feel like a Marines base, and everyone would begin to loosen up.

When I reached the restaurant bar shortly before noon on Saturday, the wait staff was surprised to see me. I'd never come in that early to drink, and since lunch was just gearing up, it would be a long time before Hunter could go on break.

"Is it Mardi Gras weekend or something?" one of the bartenders asked me. Jenna was a sweet girl, about three years out of college, who had perfected the dirty martini years before she even left high school. She was no alcoholic, but she fucking loved alcohol. Watching her behind the bar was like watching a chemist at work. She was on her way to becoming a sommelier, and was having difficulty pulling herself away from the science of cocktails. I always thought of her as the Julia Child of drink-making. Tall with frizzy hair and a Jewish nose, she could've been a body double for Jennifer Grey pre-surgery. I always told her she'd make it on TV someday.

81

"Jenna!" I said, leaning over the bar to give her a kiss on the cheek. "I'm just looking for Hunter. Have some good news that was too big for a text."

"Be careful. Kelly's in. Showed up looking like hell."

That *was* reason to worry. Kelly was the owner of the restaurant, Hunter's direct boss. Kelly was a tall and elegant woman in her early forties, with long dark hair and an impeccable sense of style. She was of French descent, and spoke with a French accent that could be brutally difficult to comprehend, especially for employees getting yelled at by her.

Kelly wasn't a horrible person. She was just strict. The very *definition* of strict. Outside of the restaurant, she was one of the most charming people in the Boston social scene. But she was serious about her business, and refused to let anyone fuck up operations at her restaurant. And her methods worked. The strong would survive and flourish, and the weak would quickly return to browsing the job postings in the weekly paper.

"Any way someone can distract the boss for like two minutes so I can go talk with Hunter?" I asked Jenna, hoping she'd have a good idea, but she shook her head.

"That's like asking someone to go into the lion's den."

"He still shares an office with her, right?"

"Yeah, she and Hunter are in the same office in the back. Whatever your news is, it's not worth the risk," Jenna told me. "She likes you, but she sees you distracting Hunter from work and you're gonna find rat poison in your next order of soup."

"What if I just go in there and talk to them both?"

"Are you out of your goddamn mind?" Jenna asked, her eyes wide open in horror of what I was proposing to do.

"It's really important," I told her. Maybe my excitement for the videos made the news feel like it was more important than it probably was, but I knew Hunter and I were onto something life-changing. This felt big. And I needed to share with him the results of that video.

"At your own risk," Jenna said, and let out a big sigh. She pointed around the corner of the bar, back where the entrance to the kitchen was located. "Office is back there. Don't knock. It shows fear and submissiveness."

"Thanks!" I hurried around the side of the bar and walked in the direction of the kitchen. In all my visits—including my hot sex with

Hunter in the restaurant's basement—I'd never been in the kitchen or the offices. But after finding a little hallway near the kitchen that led to three doors, one of them with Kelly's name on it, I came to a stop and took a big breath. And taking Jenna's advice, I opened the door and peeked my head in.

"Cole?" Hunter asked. He was the first to see me, and looked shocked that I had shown up so early and had gone into the office. Hunter and Kelly worked off of a glass, L-shaped desk. Hunter's side had a flat-screen computer monitor, and hers simply had a laptop. As soon as Hunter spoke, Kelly glanced up to see me.

"Kelly, you look lovely today."

"Cut the shit. I look awful today."

Kelly essentially had two looks: colorful, and blindingly colorful. The worse her mood, the louder her outfit would become. This time it was fire-and-brimstone red, straight out of a Hellboy movie. I was quickly starting to fear for my safety.

"You are the fucking sexiest European girl I've ever seen," I joked with her, and she let out an all too brief smile.

"Hunter, you should bring Cole by more often," she said in her thick French accent.

"Is everything okay?" Hunter asked. He was still puzzled as to why I was there, and so I hopped in one of the two seats facing the desk, and rested my elbows on the glass surface.

"This'll be quick."

"And it better be work-related," Kelly added. This bitch was frightening.

"Uh—it is!" I said unconvincingly. "So um—Hunter. You know that new restaurant in the South End that we went to about uh—three or four months ago?"

"No."

"The one where I brought my camera and filmed a *video* while we were there?"

"What kind of video?" Kelly asked, diving into the conversation. "Which restaurant? Are they French?"

"Oh—they're definitely French. French-er than you, even."

"That's impossible."

"Right? I thought the same thing too," I said. "So I had forgotten about this restaurant for—oh, a few months—and when I looked it up online they had tons of e-mails saying how wonderful they are, and how everyone wants to eat there again—."

"What does their menu look like?" Kelly demanded to know. "Is it prix fixe?"

"Oh it's prix fixe, a la carte, whatever you want."

"Goddamnit."

"And get this—their website had over fifty thousand hits in just a few months of being up."

Hunter was following, and at first I couldn't tell if the serious expression on his face was because of my abrupt intrusion. His face was flushed and red with embarrassment. But as soon as I revealed the numbers his eyes lit up.

"Fifty thousand?" he asked, slowly enunciating each word.

"Over fifty thousand. And all of the comments said that if they see more *faces* around the restaurant, then it'll probably be—oh—I'd say the most popular place in Boston."

"What, you mean celebrity faces?" Kelly asked with a sour expression.

"Yeah!"

"But we have celebrities!"

"When's the last time you had a celebrity? Roman Polanski has been out of the country since '78."

"Well he used to come all the time," Kelly replied. "We've had Jacques Chirac."

"Who the hell is that?"

"Ignorant Americans," she said, rolling her eyes at me. "What is this new place you speak of? What is its name?"

"It's uh—called—um—Chateau du Ex Toobay."

"Chateau du Ex Toobay, huh?"Hunter asked me with a wry expression on his face.

"That's not French," Kelly exclaimed.

"I know! Some play on words, I think," I replied. I was starting to sweat.

"So they want to see faces?" Hunter asked, thankfully pulling the conversation away from the name of the restaurant. I knew I'd caught his attention, and I could tell he was considering doing another video. These were numbers that couldn't be ignored.

"What do you think? You think they'll get to see those faces?"

"Fuck Boston," Kelly said. "We have what—Mark Wahlberg? Is that it?"

"Please—you know you'd be in high heat if Marky Mark walked through that front door," I said, and Kelly frowned.

"I think there's an extremely good chance," Hunter said, and this bright smile burst onto his face. "Especially if it's the new thing, then it just makes sense for them to see faces, right? I mean—fifty thousand, wow."

"Hunter, I demand you find out everything you can about this restaurant," Kelly ordered, swiveling around in her chair to face him. "*French-er* than me. How dare they. Chateau du—whatever it's called. No one uses *chateau* in their name anymore."

"He'll investigate all right," I said, and nodded my head at Hunter as I stood up from my seat. "Gotta run, but just had to fill you guys in. Hunter—we'll start that investigation tonight!"

"Right after work," he replied, beaming in excitement.

"No!" Kelly exclaimed. She looked like she was about to burst through that red dress. "This issue needs to be addressed immediately. Hunter, after the lunch shift you will spend the rest of the night investigating this new restaurant. I want a full report tomorrow. Allow no nuance to pass you by."

"Really?" he asked in shock. "You don't need me to close tonight?"

"This is far more important. Cole—."

"Yes ma'am."

"Hunter is extremely bright. I assume you'll be joining him at this restaurant tonight," she said, that same sour expression still stiffly applied to her face.

"I will. I will be an incremental part of this research."

"Just don't fuck it up. I don't want my beloved Hunter to have any distractions."

"You're the boss," I said, winking once at Kelly.

"I know," she coldly replied. "That's all."

Just before I walked out of the office I glanced at Hunter with a big smile. I knew he couldn't give that same smile back, but at least I'd planted the seeds. He was worried that the wrong people might see his face in a video, but he was basing that on the assumption that we were essentially *nobodies* putting porn on a website alongside millions of other people. But if our videos were going to turn us into rock stars in a realm of millions of gay men, then it didn't matter as much what those "wrong people" might think. Popularity opens doors, and both Hunter and I were well aware of this. And so even though he couldn't return that big smile, I knew he was thinking deeply about doing another video.

*   *

As soon as I hit the light switch and our bedroom transformed from cave-like darkness to porn studio-like brightness, I expected to hear groaning from Hunter. Maybe a "turn the lights off!" or a mumbled "fuck you!" Instead: snoring.

"This boy can fucking sleep through anything," I said to myself, glaring in disappointment at Hunter's unconscious body comfortably sprawled out on our bed, his face shoved in a couple of white pillows.

When Hunter got home from work we wasted no time. The camera was out before our pants were even off, and we filled the late afternoon and early evening with some of the most intense sex of our lives. We pleasured each other for hours, until multiple cums later we dropped our sweaty bodies on the bed and passed out for a Saturday night nap. And I guess it was all the excitement of XTube and the sex and the videos, but within an hour I was wide awake and ready for more.

With the camera in one hand, I crept towards the bed where Hunter was sleeping like a baby in a pair of white briefs that he'd used to wipe the cum off his body just before slipping into them for a nap. As I hovered over the bed I got a great whiff of the sweaty briefs—their cum-stained, masculine musk letting off this tremendously thick scent. It was like he'd gone to the gym in them and they had just dried after soaking up all the sweat from his crotch.

I was in a gray t-shirt and a pair of briefs that I'd thrown on shortly after waking up. I thought about climbing onto the bed shoving my hard cock in his mouth. That would be a hot little video to film. Hunter was lying on his stomach, and so as I planted my knees on the mattress I used my free hand to try and turn him over. Instantly I heard the groans that I'd been waiting for.

"Ahh—," he complained, his eyes closed and his hair messy as he rolled onto his back. "What are you doing?"

"Waking you up! It's Saturday night."

86

"I have a headache."

He looked adorable, making little uncomfortable facial expressions as he rubbed his eyes.

"You were just getting fucked a couple hours ago!"

"That's probably why," he mumbled. "What time is it?"

"Time for you to get up. You're on camera."

"No——," he moaned. "Let's go back to sleep. My head hurts."

I knew that this was going to require special action. And so just as Hunter tried to roll back onto his stomach, I lifted one leg and sat directly on his upper chest so that his head was stuck in-between my crotch.

"What are you doing?" he said, groaning as he opened his eyes to the bright lights of the bedroom.

"Tell everyone on camera how much you love me."

"Maybe if you get me some Tylenol I will."

"Come on——," I joked with him, and held my camera-hand firm as I reached down with my other hand and tickled underneath Hunter's chin. He jumped and squirmed underneath me.

"Ah—I just want to feel normal again. I have a headache," he complained in the most adorable way as he wiggled underneath me. His arms were trapped by my thick legs, and my crotch was right in his face. As soon as Hunter realized that he was too tired and had too much of a headache to fight me off of him, he opened his mouth right beneath my sack and playfully bit down.

"Don't bite the nuts!" I shouted in fear for my manhood as Hunter chomped down within an inch of me. Suddenly I was the one squirming, shaking my body to get off of Hunter as he leaned his neck forward—a big smile on his face—playfully trying to bite at my balls through my thin briefs.

"Don't bite the nuts!" I said again, and anxiously dropped to my side to get away from him. I put the camera down on our nightstand, and Hunter rolled his body into me, hugging me with his thick arms.

"You're not gonna put that online, are you?" he asked in his tired voice. I had a feeling that he was done for the night. Though, I'd probably be able to convince him to relax and watch a movie with me downstairs.

"Of course I'm not gonna put that on XTube," I replied with a crafty grin on my face. Of *course* I was gonna post that video.

Maverick Men

CHAPTER SEVEN

narrated by Hunter

Of course Cole posted the video. Needless to say, he knew what he was doing, and within a month we'd uploaded a bunch of new, free clips. My fears of putting my face online had nearly disappeared. The first week was tough, and I kept waiting for that moment when a relative would call me up on the phone claiming to have seen me online getting a load of cum in my mouth, or when someone at work would make a joke about one of our videos. Thankfully, nothing like that ever happened. Cole and I were becoming an instant sensation online. We were so shocked by the tens of thousands of views our videos were getting, and yet our mini-celebrity seemed nonexistent in our daily lives.

Life was good. XTube, the video, and our online popularity had all given Cole this renewed spirit that was carrying success into his work life, and lots of happiness into our home life. Even if a work day sucked, I could come home and log online to see what our thousands of fans were saying about our love-making. I felt like an Internet rock star. And for some reason, all of the porn stuff didn't carry into our daily lives. Anytime I'd walk around Boston or show up for work, I didn't worry about being recognized. Nor did I worry that important people in my life—who didn't already know about the videos—would find out. It all felt disconnected. We'd created two lives, essentially. Our regular, day-to-day life, with normal jobs, and our wild online lives with hot, filmed sex, and tens of thousands of fans.

There was something about the celebrity that really excited me. The confusing thing—for me, at least—is that if our videos didn't get much attention, then I'd actually be more worried about backlashes. It was something about not knowing exactly *who* was watching us. But once we had an actual fan base of thousands of guys, I wanted to videotape our sex every chance I got. And I simply didn't care about negative opinions anymore.

I also have to admit that a big motive was wondering what all the popularity could turn into. If a couple hundred people were watching our videos, then that was one thing, but if thousands were continually watching them and interacting with us, then that was another. I couldn't help but wonder if we'd found our niche; something Cole and I were really good at, that we could grow into a business. With all the time we spent away from each other due to work obligations, I was aching for a sign that some other opportunity was waiting to deliver us freedom.

"So you sure this sale is going to come through?" I asked Cole as we walked into the locker room of Solaris gym in the Back Bay. Solaris was considered the hottest gym in greater Boston, and had a great mix of clientele. Mostly gay, but it also attracted a nice number of hot straight men who liked the attention. I was in love with at least a few guys who worked out at Solaris.

"The Marinelli deal is coming in. It's *for sure*," Cole said, as if the contract was going to be signed that evening. Cole was on the verge of selling a property that would land him his largest commission ever, and would set us up nicely for the coming months. On a whim, and in total confidence that the commission was guaranteed, Cole took me to Solaris on a Monday early evening and signed us both up for personal training. It was just over $7,000 of one year's worth of boxing and fighting training. Now that our bodies were totally exposed on the Internet, fitness was becoming a high priority.

"I trust you," I replied, even though I was slightly fearful. We weren't exactly in the financial condition to spend so much on personal training, but Cole was confident about this sale, and the commission would cover the price of the training package multiple times over. Not to mention, it was a great investment given our new online bodily exposure. We weren't trying to be muscle daddies, but we did want to stay in good shape. Health and fitness were very important to us.

The locker room at Solaris was massive. Not only was it massive, but it was a gay man's paradise. Beautiful bodies packed the spacious set of lockers, sofas, and the conjoining shower room, which had a sauna, steam room, and hot tub. Some guys would walk around naked, and some with a towel. The shower area could get especially cruise-y at night.

Cole and I had thrown our stuff in a locker in the very back of the locker room. It was tucked in the far corner near the toilets. Normally I liked to be right up front, where everyone in the locker room could see me taking my sweaty gym clothes off as I'd take that exceptionally slow walk to the steam room. It was fun to see the looks on some guys' faces. But the big draw that had sent Cole and I into the back corner of the locker room was a straight guy who worked out every Monday night at the same time.

This guy was beautiful. Clearly straight—unfortunately—although I'd made it blatantly obvious that if he ever wanted to swing my way, I'd be ready and waiting. He was about 6'2, solid body with thick pecs that would burst out of his tank tops, and short black hair overtop blue eyes. Since my work schedule only allowed me to see this guy once per week, I'd make each time count. Last week I'd followed him stalker-style from the showers to his locker—looking like an asshole when I realized I was stuck in the back corner of the locker room. I opened a random locker and exclaimed that my shit had been stolen. He asked if I wanted to borrow some dry clothes. I was deeply involved in a man crush.

"So you sure he's gonna be here?" Cole unenthusiastically asked me. He pretended to be jealous of this guy, although I didn't think he actually was. I mean the guy was straight. I think it must've just been an *alpha male* thing.

"Yeah. I want to steal a pair of his underwear. Is that fucked up?"

"A little bit. And that's why I love you, baby."

"Two weeks ago I saw him in a jock strap."

"You're shitting me," Cole said. Even in his feigned jealousy I could tell that he was into this guy too. Or at least appreciated how hot he was.

"His ass cheeks were out and solid," I said. I was getting hard just thinking about him.

When we reached our locker, Cole opened the lock and was the first to reach in. We were alone in the back of the locker room, and the gym crowd was slowly dying down as people went home for dinner. As I waited to change out of my gym clothes, Cole's hand re-emerged from our locker with his camera.

"What are you doing?" I asked, surprised that he even risked bringing it with him. That was his baby.

"I was gonna film you trying to steal this guy's jock strap."

"Please—I don't even know when he's coming back."

"Why don't you cruise the toilets and keep an eye out?" Cole sarcastically asked me as he turned the camera on.

"No thanks. Hey, how hot would it be if he just walked back here and started fucking around with us?"

91

"Not *my* definition of hot, but maybe you think so."

"I've seen you look at him too," I countered, staring Cole in his big green eyes.

"No way—when have I ever looked at him?"

"I've seen you take quick looks when you're spotting me; when you think I'm not paying attention."

"You're out of your mind," Cole said in protest.

"Okay. Whatever you say," I replied, shrugging my shoulders and grinning devilishly. "If you won't admit that you're always checking this guy out, then I'm not cooking you dinner tonight."

"Fine, I'll order in."

"Fine," I said. I pulled my wet t-shirt up over my head and tossed it on a wooden bench facing the lockers.

"Wait a second—are you really not gonna cook dinner? You were gonna do that, uh—that pasta thing I love."

"Not happening."

"What if I pay you, instead of admitting something that's *false*?" he added with extra emphasis.

"Nope, I need the admission," I bluntly replied. Cole frowned—I could tell he was thinking about whether or not the dinner was worth it.

"Well if I admit to it, then we need to be clear that I'm not telling the truth and only saying it so that you'll make dinner."

"I'm only interested in the *truth*, Cole."

"Okay! Okay! He's fucking hot. Are you happy? Is pasta night still on?"

"You know what I think?" I said to him, smiling in victory as I tucked my fingers into his gym shorts.

"What?"

"I think you're a whole lot fucking hotter than he is." I reached my hands down into his shorts and felt up his cock, packed behind tight briefs. As soon my hands were on his bare skin his cock began to grow, flexing against the cotton fabric with which it was contained.

"Yeah?" Cole said with a big grin as he glanced down at my hands on his hard cock.

"But seriously, if I was single and had never met you, and saw you working out at this gym, I'd stalk the fuck out of you in the locker room."

"We wouldn't even make it into the locker room," Cole said, breathing onto my neck as he wrapped one arm around my waist, and slid his fingers into the back of my gym shorts.

"You'd fuck me in the gym bathroom?" I asked him. I quickly looked to see if anyone had come to our distant part of the locker room, and then slowly dropped down to my knees so that my eyes were level with Cole's crotch. I pulled his shorts and briefs down so that his hard cock hung out in front of me.

"Yoga studio."

"How the fuck would we get in there?"

"Seven grand in training fees—they better fucking let us hang in there after hours."

Just before I wrapped my lips around Cole's thick cock I saw the light on the camera switch on. Something about being filmed in the locker room got me so horny and charged up that I grabbed Cole's ass and started pulling his crotch into my mouth.

"Yeah baby," he said, moaning as I sucked his sweaty dick. "Stand up—I wanna eat your ass."

I took my mouth off of Cole's cock and got up from my knees. My dick was already rock hard and hanging out of my gym shorts. I turned around and dropped my shorts to my ankles, exposing a jock strap that wrapped around two muscular, hairy cheeks.

"Look at that ass," Cole said, and grabbed at my cheeks with one hand. I loved feeling his big, masculine fingers squeezing my damp ass. I wanted to push him into the lockers and suck the cum out of his dick. Have him shoot all over my face, so that I could rub it in and then go chill in the steam room to enjoy that post-climax buzz.

And just before I turned around to drop on my knees and finish what I'd started with Cole, I heard a deep voice say "nice ass." And it wasn't coming from my lover.

I slowly turned around, my hard cock still popping out from my jock strap, and in total embarrassment watched as the guy who I'd been crushing on for months winked at me and then walked straight up to his locker. As I stood there—unsure what to do—the guy opened his locker with total collectiveness, as if the sex scene he'd walked in on wasn't the least bit strange. I turned around to face Cole, whose cock was also still out and who had a huge grin on his face.

"Hey, my boyfriend really wants one of your jockstraps," Cole said to the guy, who laughed as he went through his locker.

"Here you go," he said, nodding his head at me as he tossed a white jockstrap right onto my hard-on. As the cotton underwear hung there, and as I stood with my eyes wide open and my lips scrunched together, the guy closed his locker, and after one more nod, headed out of the little room.

"Oh shit," I said to Cole, without turning around.

"You're right. He's fuckin' hot. Time for pasta."

"Yeah—," I replied, reaching down to grab the jockstrap off my dick. "Time for pasta."

*   *

"Are you fucking crazy?" I asked Cole. Our XTube profile was loaded on the computer screen, and I was looking at one recent video in particular.

"Why are you awake?" he asked me from our bed. I could see him opening and closing his eyelids, glaring up at the high ceiling. The lights were still off in the bedroom, and even though it was a Monday I'd decided to wake up early and start my day. I've always felt more productive on days when I wake up early.

It had been a full week since our hook-up in the gym, and when I visited our online profile for the first time in a number of days I was surprised to see that Cole had posted a video from that night. It was a short, hot video of us messing around in the locker room at Solaris, right before the guy walked in on us.

"What if someone at our gym sees this and reports us?"

"Huh?"

"The gym video."

"Old news. I posted that like—four, five days ago," Cole said. He sat up from the sheets like a mummy rising from its sarcophagus, and in a zombie-like motion he turned to search for his coffee on the nightstand. "I can't believe you're just seeing it now."

"I don't check this every day," I replied. I leaned forward on the glass computer desk while the short video played. You couldn't tell what gym we were in, but if someone knew where the two of us worked out then the location would be obvious. "So you don't think there's anything wrong with having this video up?"

"It's hot!" Cole's typical argument rolled off his tongue in-between sips of his coffee. "It's hot. Sexiest video we've done, I think. I'd love to do a whole scene in there."

"Aren't there like—a million pornos that take place in a locker room?"

"Totally different," Cole was quick to reply. "That's *studio* porn," he added with such contempt in his voice that you'd think he was talking about the Taliban. "Yeah—they're in a locker room, but as they're faking a moan sequence there are two nasty-looking cameramen who you don't see, munching on meatball sandwiches and thinking about what elevator music to ruin the scene with. It's not real. That clip you're watching, in the locker room at Solaris—that's fucking real. As real as you can get."

Once the video ended I clicked on the e-mail icon for our online account.

"Have you been keeping up with e-mails?"

"Of course," Cole said. "Every day. Anything new?"

"A few."

I wasn't nearly as good about keeping up with our fan mail, mainly because my work demanded so much of my time and energy. Cole loved to interact with the people who sent us e-mails and supportive comments, so I usually just left it to him. I was actually surprised when I looked through our e-mail account at just how many people had written us to show their love and support.

"Is there a way to charge to see videos on XTube?" I asked shortly after I opened the most recent piece of fan mail in the account. It had been sent earlier that morning, and Cole hadn't seen this one yet.

"Yeah—I think you can upload videos and charge people to download them. Like uh—amateur downloads. I don't think the studios work off of XTube. Maybe they do."

"You've gotta come see this," I said as I scrolled through the message. "This is signed by the CEO of the company."

"What company?"

"XTube! The CEO of XTube," I replied. Cole began a slow walk around the computer desk to come see what was on the screen.

"So this is like the porn lord, huh?"

"Apparently. Read this," I said, waving my finger at the two short and supportive paragraphs. When Cole saw what I saw, a lightbulb went off in his head. His eyes seemed to burst open, as if a sudden eruption of energy woke him up from his tired state. The CEO of XTube had written to us that very morning, to tell us how much he loved our videos, and to add a line that was going to seriously affect us in the coming weeks: *I think you're crazy not to charge for your videos.*

It wasn't even something we'd seriously considered. Maybe because all the existing porn fit into that studio model that Cole so detested. Our amateur style with short clips just didn't seem like anything that should be charged for. It seemed natural, spontaneous, and just as much a public good as a local park or water fountain. The idea of charging for our videos seemed both unnatural and exciting, and I couldn't make up my mind whether I liked or hated the CEO's suggestion. At the bottom of his e-mail was his personal contact info, along with the phone number of his Site Administrator, who he said to contact if we ever had a problem with the website, or if we decided to start charging and needed help getting set up.

"We should talk about this later," Cole said. I could tell he was already thinking about it. He'd probably be thinking about it all day. "You know we're having dinner at Ron's tonight."

"Oh fuck, that's right. Oh God—really? His dinner parties are so fucking boring."

"We have to," Cole protested. "I invited Marinelli. I still haven't sold his house, and he's got his hand so far up my ass I could do a fisting video. Ron has a big, impressive place—you know that. And his— okay—so they're fucking boring. I agree. But there's good food and wine, and I uh—I like Ron. He's a good guy."

"So you sure Marinelli is showing up tonight?"

"Positive. And I'm showing the house to two clients today. So wish me luck."

"You know I always do. When do you want to talk about this e-mail?" I asked him. He shifted his lips to the right and breathed through his nose as he looked over the two paragraphs.

"Well—I mean this guy's gotta know what he's talking about, right? I'm gonna think about it today. You're off today—you have plans yet? You want to check out how the whole *charging for videos* thing works?"

"Yeah, I will. What time is dinner?"

"Eight."

Cole bent down and kissed me on my head full of wavy, black hair, and then turned to head downstairs for a shower. I had no idea what to do about the e-mail. There was something about charging for our videos that made me uneasy. In all the months we'd been putting out videos, we hadn't made a cent off of them. Our incomes were derived from full-time jobs that kicked our asses on a daily basis. By charging for videos, we could really supplement our income, but then we'd be entering this new world—this big industry of studios and porn stars and established norms, where everything has already been tried and done. I needed to consult some people about this one.

*   *

"I just don't see you as a porn star," Chris said, his chin resting on his two fists as he leaned forward on the café table. After Cole left for work, I called Chris and Jenna to see if they could meet up for coffee to talk about this big decision I was facing. Shortly after noon the three of us met up at a coffee shop on Tremont Street, and snatched a small table near the window.

"But he's already a porn star," Jenna countered.

"Yeah I know, and I just don't see it," Chris replied with a nonchalant shrug.

"That's because your idea of porn is all muscle and oil," I said.

"Right. And usually black. Or white if they have a mustache."

"I've never seen—in all the years I've known you—a boyfriend of yours with a mustache," I replied.

"Duh—I don't wanna *date* them. Just get fucked by them. Geez."

"You're a mess," Jenna took the words right out of my mouth. "Hunter, I think it's a good idea for you to charge."

"Really? I expected to hear that from Chris, not you."

"I think you should charge too," Chris added. "I just don't see you as a porn star."

"I think *porn star* is slightly different from what I'm going for. What makes our videos different is that they're real. Real love, intimacy, laughter—it's totally the opposite of studio porn. The type of guy who really loves studio porn probably won't *get* our stuff. But I think there are

97

a whole lot of guys who—well—I think they respect or yearn for the kind of relationship Cole and I have with each other, and just like to see it."

"And that's exactly why I think you should release videos," Jenna said, pointing a finger at me. "It's different. There's a market. It's something fresh. And just think about how many people are watching you for free. If only one percent of that entire group pays $5 to $10 for just one of your videos, and you release one video per month, then—. Well you know the numbers better than I do."

"I could quit my job," I joked. Well, it was a joke at first, but as I sat there with Chris and Jenna and ran through the actual numbers in my head, it didn't seem as funny anymore. It seemed real. Jenna had made a great point. And if our videos got better as far as the picture quality, the editing, and the video length, then we could start to pick up fans more accustomed to high-quality studio movies.

"Do you think your current fans will be upset if you start charging for material?" Jenna asked me.

"I hadn't thought about that yet. I don't think so. Do you think they would?"

"Look at it this way," Chris began, and spread his palms out on the table. "On one hand you have all the cheap assholes who download free shit because they're cheap. On the other you have respectable people like me who will actually pay for quality. Now the cheap ones—they're like vultures. They will *attack* and *devour* your free porn. What you're doing is not just charging for videos. You're literally moving from one market to another."

"Wow, Chris, do you have a background in economics that I don't know about?" Jenna jokingly asked him, but he ignored her and waved his palms in front of my face.

"One market to the next."

"I thought you download your porn illegally," I asked him, and I could see his cheeks getting red.

"No! That was like—a few times."

"So you don't think anyone would follow us over to the paid content? They'd just be resentful? You think our fans would actually be resentful?"

"I'm going to guess—," Jenna said, "that if you start charging you'll get some fans who get upset. But I think the number will be small.

What you need to do is make longer, better videos that are worth paying for. And then just continue to put out free stuff that's short, and like—a teaser for the paid stuff!"

"What if the videos explode in popularity and everyone in my life finds out?" I asked them the question that had been bothering me since the first video with my face was published online.

"The people who love you won't care," Jenna replied, "and the people who don't will let their close-mindedness show just how unimportant they really are in your life."

"What if it's family?"

"Before you get more involved with doing porn, whether you charge or not, you just need to be sure that this is what you really want to do. Unfortunately there *are* consequences. Not everyone is as open-minded as Chris and I. You might run into some nasty shit. You know how many dickheads there are out there, who thumb their noses at people who do porn? You'll need some thick skin. I know you already have thick skin, but this will be some *serious* practice in how to tolerate bullshit. Lost friends, hurtful comments posted on the Internet—there's a saying, you know. People who fly in the sun should be prepared to get burnt.

"But—it could also be really lucrative," she continued. "More importantly, it could create lots of opportunities for you and Cole. Imagine if you didn't have to work sixty hours at the restaurant every week and if he didn't need to run around Boston trying to sell houses, and you guys could just travel and be together all the time."

"It would be life-changing," I replied. What a reality that would be! If Cole and I could be totally mobile, and could just travel all over the world doing videos and having fun, and meeting new people. We wouldn't be tied down to one job, or one city, or awful working hours. We'd actually get weekends together.

"There's your answer," Jenna said, and just before she lifted her coffee mug to her mouth she smiled at me. And Chris, who had been looking at Jenna, turned to me and nodded. They both wanted this for me, and I think it was because I wanted this so much for myself.

*   *

99

About five minutes after 8:00 PM, Cole and I got out of a taxi in front of the townhouse of his friend Ron. Ron was more of a friend of Cole's ex-boyfriend. Cole wouldn't call him to chat on the phone about work or everyday life, and vice versa, but at least once per month Ron would host some kind of dinner party, and would always invite us. It was a nice gesture, and he never seemed like a bad guy. Sometimes he could take a joke a little too far, and didn't mind making someone uncomfortable at a party, but that was just his personality. It was a strange fusion of warm hospitality and cutthroat humor that marked his parties.

Ron lived in the South End in a beautiful, old brownstone. He was definitely into that old-world style, and this was apparent from the moment the front door opened. Lots of autumn colors, and old rugs that if not for their antique value would just appear dirty and decades past their prime. He was into landscape art, and fancy candle holders, and mahogany bookcases in just about every room.

"Is Marinelli already here?" I asked Cole, who had grown quiet from nervousness. This was his biggest client ever, both literally and figuratively.

"Not yet. He said he'd text me."

"You sure he'll be okay at a dinner full of gay people?"

"Yeah, he loves gay people," Cole unconvincingly replied. "He has a gay son. Haven't met him, but he likes to tell me all about him, and always reminds me that he's gay."

Within seconds of ringing the doorbell, Ron was at the door, wearing jeans and a beige cardigan. He was in his early forties and hadn't aged as well as Cole, but still kept in decent shape. He was one of those lifetime singles, but claimed he liked it better that way. He admitted to being very difficult to live with.

"Hey!" he greeted each of us with a hug, and waved us into his townhouse. "Is your friend still coming?"

"Yeah, on his way," Cole replied. "Good to see you."

"Thanks for inviting us, man," I said.

"The more the merrier. Let's go to the kitchen."

Ron had taken down some walls on the first floor to create an open floor plan, and from the entranceway one could see past the living room to the long dining table and spacious kitchen. There were already four people seated at the dining table, and another person in the kitchen preparing some food. All gay guys, closer to Cole's age than mine, and a couple in their fifties. I recognized all of them from past dinner parties at Ron's, and they'd all been very sweet towards me. I did have a small fear, however, that one or more of them had seen our videos. I don't know why I was so worried about that. Maybe they wouldn't care one way or another about the videos. But of course, my mind immediately drew up the worst-case scenario.

"Marinelli's here," Cole said, and I'd never seen him do a quicker one-eighty. As he hurried to get the door for the guy whose home sale could translate into a huge payout for Cole and I, Ron showed me to my seat at the dining room table. I had a feeling that this was going to be a long dinner.

*   *

This was my first time meeting Tony Marinelli, and after five minutes I could see why even Cole was a little intimidated by this guy. I think it was the way he'd look at you after asking a question; as if your entire fate hinged on the answer. It could be something as silly as "is the sky blue?", and he'd pause and stare into your eyes with the most serious expression, not saying a single world until about three seconds after the question was answered. And just when you thought you'd answered incorrectly, Marinelli would burst out into laughter and slap one of his huge hands on his knee.

He'd had a rough childhood. The son of Italian immigrants, and brother of five girls, he'd struggled throughout his teens and twenties working a number of odd jobs. He was always an entrepreneur. He told us that about fifteen times during dinner. Every job he ever got, he'd find some way to do it better than anyone else in his company. Before long, he started to develop his own little group of companies. And in his words, his dedication was always to the "blue collar men and women." This wasn't the kind of guy who would own a law firm or a consulting office. He owned "blue collar" companies. And the way he'd talk about them made it sound like everyone on his payroll was a hero to America. I wasn't about to argue, and neither was anyone else at the table.

Most of the conversation had revolved around Marinelli, and that was partly because no one else could get a word in. And it seemed that because Ron—who normally led the conversation at his dinner parties as if he was a composer at the Boston Symphony—was not the ringleader of table communication, he'd taken to drinking. And I mean *drinking*. Each time I'd turn to look at him he was refilling his glass of red wine.

"Oh my God, these are hot," said Ron's closest friend, Danny, as he hurried into the dining room carrying two trays with chicken and mashed potato balls. Danny quickly placed the trays down on the table in-between plates of vegetables and appetizers, and reclaimed his seat next to Ron. Danny was probably the sweetest guy at the table; a true queen, who never wanted to talk about himself—unless it involved gardening—and always seemed genuinely interested in the people around him. He was a regular face at these dinners, and usually helped Ron prepare the meals.

"Hunter—," Marinelli said in his boisterous voice. "Cole tells me you're a restaurant manager. Where in the city?"

"At Toast, on Newbury—."

"You know I own three restaurants in the city," he replied after the standard three second wait time. "Actually no—two in the city. One in Providence. All Italian, of course. Toast is eh—."

"French."

"I don't care much for French food," he said. "That's uh—Kelly *what's her name*. Real firecracker. Met her at a fundraiser. Ron, where's the pasta?" he asked, and patted the host on the back. Marinelli was already on a first name basis with everyone at the table, and poor Ron had gotten his back slapped about ten times already.

"Next time," Ron said, just before lifting a glass of red wine to his lips. "So is there anything else *new* in your life, Hunter?"

"Nah—just the usual. Busy all the time. I'm glad you were willing to do this on a Monday because otherwise I wouldn't be able to come."

"Nothing new and juicy?"

I couldn't tell where he was going with this, but there was a certain smirk on his face that was familiar of him. This was the face he'd use when trying to embarrass someone at one of his parties. When he'd turn the spotlight on an unsuspecting victim, all for a little dinnertime drama and gossip. And there was only one place my mind went with all this: the videos. Aside from being disgusted by the idea of Ron jerking off to us, I was instantly overcome with anxiety, thinking about what he might do in front of Marinelli.

"I wish," I replied, and turned to Cole. He was laughing, but I could tell in his eyes that he was thinking the same thing I was thinking.

I was growing more and more uncomfortable, and didn't even begin to know how I'd react if Ron blurted out our personal lives at the dinner table. This was what I'd worried about when I first told Cole I didn't want to have my face in our videos. I was proud of what my lover and I had created, but it was just natural to feel uncomfortable discussing it around strangers. These weren't close friends who Cole and I would regularly hang out with. I had no problem telling Chris or Jenna, but not a group of acquaintances that we'd only see once a month. And obviously not Cole's biggest client since he'd gotten back into real estate. If Marinelli found out and switched realtors, we'd be up shit's creek without a paddle. We'd just spent thousands of dollars on gym training and our rent was quickly approaching.

When I looked back over at Cole, he was calming his nervousness by eating. And just as I went to put chicken and potatoes on my plate, Ron said something that caused the blood in my face to rush out, revealing a pale, mortified expression.

"Don't bite the balls—I mean nuts!" he obnoxiously said, pointing his fork at Cole, who was sticking one of the fresh potato balls into his mouth. Cole's eyes lit up. Ron had seen our videos. He'd seen the playful video of Cole and I tickling and biting, where the "don't bite the nuts" line came from.

Marinelli burst out into laughter, and the other five guests awkwardly chuckled.

"Don't bite the nuts?" one of them asked.

"Don't bite the nuts," Ron loudly repeated. "I heard it online somewhere."

Asshole. He didn't even look at us. He just whisked his eyes around the table, looking at the other guests, absorbing our discomfort to feed his own little thirst for dinner table power. Cole looked ready to kick this guy's ass.

"So Tony—," Ron said, and turned to face Cole's client.

"Yeah?" Marinelli asked, his face still red from laughing.

"What are your thoughts on the porn industry?"

"Ron—you're gonna talk about that now? We're having a nice dinner," Cole countered, but Ron didn't pay him any attention.

"Let me tell you something, Ron," Marinelli said, and played with the napkin hanging from the top button on his dress shirt. "I was raised in a strict, Roman Catholic home. I had opportunities to move my money around into some questionable industries, but I knew my mother—God rest her soul—would kick my ass at the gates of Heaven. There was ah—strip joint in Boston I almost bought in the eighties. Closest I came to porn. What do I think of it? Sideshow freaks. All of 'em."

"You know—they're really changing the business landscape of porn," Ron said. And then, with a swift turn of his shoulders, he was facing Cole once again. "You know anything about that, Cole?"

"Dammit, I keep missing the porn section in the Wall Street Journal," he jokingly replied.

"There's a porn section in the Journal?" Marinelli asked, startled by Cole's comment. "Goddamn liberals. Cole, if Italians were running the Journal, things would be a lot different."

"No, there's no porn section in the Journal," Ron snarkly replied. "I'm not talking about pay-for-porn. I'm talking about the kind people give away for free."

"Now Ron," Danny started, and patted his friend on the shoulder. But there was no stopping Ron. He had a glass of red wine in his hand and waved it as if he was leading a marching band. I was actually hoping he might splash it on Danny or Marinelli, and that way the porn conversation would end rather quickly. Cole and I would have a much easier time apologizing for having an asshole friend than for having a collection of sex videos for free online download.

"I mean *free?*" Ron asked the table. "Who would go to the trouble of making porn and giving it away for free?"

"Do you mean the visitor sections of those websites?" one of the dinner guests asked.

"No! I mean there are websites where people upload free videos of themselves having sex," Ron explained.

"So do any of you think Mitt Romney has a chance at the Republican candidacy in 2012?" Danny asked, leaning his arms forward on the dining room table.

"We're talking about give-away porn, not Mitt Romney," Ron quickly intervened.

"Isn't he a Mormon?" Marinelli asked himself, and then returned his eyes to the food in front of him.

"I think that a table full of grown-ups can talk about something more intellectually stimulating than give-away porn," Cole said, staring Ron in the eyes. The latter looked back at him with a big smirk on his face.

"Would you ever do something like that, Cole?"

I nervously looked at my partner. All eyes at the table were on him. My hands were shaking on my lap, and I tried to conceal my heavy breathing.

"I was actually hoping to make an S&M video with you!" Cole replied, at which the whole table burst out into laughter. Especially Marinelli, who nearly choked on his chicken breast. "When you find time, I've got this great website where we can upload it."

"What's an S&M?" Marinelli asked after he finally swallowed his poultry.

"Certainly not a stock exchange," Danny timidly remarked as his eyes moved back and forth from Ron to Cole.

Ron held up his glass to salute Cole, and with a devilish grin on his face he nodded once. Even though the conversation ended there, and Cole seemed to have won this round, I could tell that he was boiling on the inside. And the scary thing was that neither of us knew just how far Ron was prepared to take this new slice of juicy gossip.

CHAPTER EIGHT

narrated by Cole Maverick

Two days after I almost leaped across the dining room table to strangle my *friend* Ron at his dinner party, another monumental thing happened for Hunter and I. Originally we were gonna do it the day after Ron's dinner party, but both of us were so stressed out that we spent hours re-thinking whether or not we should list our videos for sale. But the e-mail from the CEO of XTube, coupled with the thousands and thousands of fans who kept writing us every day to see more material, were so loud that we couldn't even hear Ron's obnoxious voice of antagonism in our heads.

And so on a Wednesday morning, Hunter and I both woke up right before sunrise and got to work. The goal was to edit some of our past material to make a longer video that we could put up for sale. Neither of us knew much about video editing, but I'd dabbled in it with our shorter videos. And hours later, after Hunter had gone off to work and I'd been staring at a computer screen so much that my eyes felt like they were gonna burst out of my head, I uploaded our very first video.

I didn't know how much to charge. Before I put a price on it, I looked at what the other popular amateur porn stars were charging. Some guys were doing jack off videos for $0.99, while others were doing full-fledged action for almost $5 a pop. I figured they wouldn't be crazy enough to charge that much if no one was paying for it.

And so I chose a modest amount, updated our XTube profile to point towards the Amateur page, and waited patiently. I don't know what I was waiting for—as if suddenly thousands of people would pour onto the new video within minutes of its creation. But it seemed like every three minutes I'd rush back to the page to see if Hunter and I were making any money.

This was one of the most exciting times of my life, and I wanted this video to do well. In fact, I'd even told Hunter that as soon as the Marinelli sale was completed, we could use that commission to relax for a while and focus on making videos. For some reason, even though we hadn't made a penny off of the videos, I saw them as our ticket to a better life. I wanted Hunter to quit his strenuous job and just enjoy life, without being held to some crazy work schedule that robbed him of his nights and weekends.

"Is it up?" were the first words out of Hunter's mouth as soon as I answered my cell phone.

"My dick's been up for hours looking at this video, *for sale*, on our new Amateur page."

"Has anybody bought it yet?" Hunter was excited, and every single word out of his mouth was soaked in this schoolboy thrill. His excitement fueled my own.

"Not yet, but it's only been up for about an hour. Let's give it some time. Hey—what time are you getting out of work tonight? The usual?"

"Yeah, it's a Wednesday," he replied.

My ex was visiting from Miami, and wanted to get together with us. Normally this would be a cool, relaxed visit, but I'd never told my ex about the porn videos. And since he was good friends with Ron, and *staying* at Ron's townhouse while visiting Boston, I had a good feeling that he'd gotten wind of our new online experiment.

"Okay—Barry is gonna be here around ten. I know that's a little early for you—."

"No problem, I'll be back. I might be a little late. I'll try to get Jenna to close up tonight."

"Awesome," I said. "I'm gonna go pick up a new computer. I hear the new Macs are great for video editing. I want these videos to be top-notch now that they're up for sale."

"Can we afford that?"

"The Marinelli sale is gonna happen soon. I can *feel* it. We have two interested buyers."

"I hope so, Cole," he said, although I could tell he was nervous about all this spending. "I just want us to be careful spending what we don't have."

"We'll have it soon. I wouldn't do it if I didn't believe it."

"Alright. I trust you," he said. "See you tonight."

"Take your time. Love you babe," I told him, and we both hung up. As soon as I was off the phone I rushed back to our Amateur page on XTube to look at downloads.

One download. It had begun. And I'd never been so fucking excited in my life.

*   *

When Barry showed up at the apartment, Hunter was still on his way home from work. I figured he'd be home any minute, but although I couldn't wait to see him, I was glad that I'd get to talk candidly with my former partner of ten years about what Hunter and I were involved in. I'd never done anything like our porn videos when I was with Barry. In fact, I was probably a lot more conservative in that relationship out of respect for him. Hunter and I were a totally different animal; sexually explorative, wild, and uninhibited. I don't wanna say that Barry and I were boring, because we weren't. It was just *different*.

As soon as I saw Barry at the front door of the apartment, I knew that he knew. There was something different in his face. And so not only did I prep to talk with him about my decisions, but I also silently cursed that asshole Ron, for ruining my first chance to share all this stuff with my ex-lover.

There wasn't much time or room for small talk, and it wasn't long before Barry and I were sitting on the chocolate brown sofa in the living room, one cushion apart, prepared to tackle the most controversial subject since our break-up talk.

"Ron must've told you," I said. Even though Ron never gave me the chance to tell Barry about the videos, I at least wanted to initiate *this* conversation.

At first Barry's expression grew grim. He lowered his eyes to the hardwood floor and scratched his blonde head of hair with one finger. I could see that familiar look of disappointment, and it instantly made me weak at the knees. I felt awful for not telling him sooner, or talking with him about this when it was just an idea between Hunter and I. But just as I went to open my mouth and break the ice, Barry's head sprung upwards and a thick smile was spread across his whole face. His lips were sealed, and he was trying hard not to burst out in laughter.

"It's fucking crazy!" he finally exclaimed. I wiped the sweat from my forehead, and sighed at the way he'd played me. "Cole? Porno? You? I'm—I'm blown away. Why would you be doing something like this? I mean, it's your life, but—porn? Are you at least making money on it?"

"Not yet," I said after taking a deep breath. "And by the way, don't scare me like that."

"You honestly think I would've been upset?"

"I don't know—I mean we never did anything like this when we were together," I told him. "I hoped you'd be cool with it."

"Well if anyone has the cock for shooting porno, it's you," he joked with me, still laughing from earlier. "But who else knows about this?"

"Very few people—."

"Are you gonna be okay when news gets out?" he asked me, his expression suddenly changing. He had that familiar, serious look in his eyes as he watched my body language for any sign of discomfort.

"Look, Barry, I'm a grown-ass man. I pay my own way in life. I don't really care who approves. It's hot and fun for both me and Hunter, and I think it could lead to a better life for us in the long run."

"So then I'm going to trust that you know what you're doing," he said. "And if I get any phone calls, I'll defend you. And if you think I'll pay to download this shit, you're sadly mistaken. I want free access—I'm pulling my ex-boyfriend privileges."

"Of course you can," I replied, and smiled for the first time since we both sat down. "Look—all Hunter and I are doing is making love—making fucking *hot* videos—and broadcasting them online. That's all. It's fun, hot, silly—the day I dread making another video or have some uninvolved cameraman filming us, you can tell me I've fucked up. But I think what we're doing now is awesome and exciting. It's beautiful."

"And you realize you'll have to defend your decisions to most people, right? Because most people aren't cool with this. Even if they look at porn all the time, a lot of people will look down on you."

"Come on, Barry. When have you ever known me to give a shit about what people think of me and my life? As long as I'm not doing anything illegal or bad. People can say or think what they like. I'm prepared for it all."

"Is Hunter?"

"Hell yes he is! We waited for months before he was comfortable putting up the first video. And now he loves it and wants to make more. It's great—sometimes I think he's more into these videos than I am."

"So you didn't pressure him into this?" he asked, his eyes narrowing upon me as he sat with his legs crossed on the sofa. It was

110

funny how even though Barry and I were no longer together, he could still rattle my cage when he narrowed those blue eyes and glared at me. It was his *Barry Face*. That familiar look of terror. He'd been a model and actor for most of his life, and knew how to use his skills to break my balls.

"It was his decision. I love Hunter. I wouldn't pressure him to do something that he didn't want to do. The videos would look so fake if I had pressured him into it."

"I haven't seen them," he replied. "I won't be your biggest fan on this, but you have my support. Even if I think it's a little nuts."

"Thank you," I told him with utmost sincerity. "It means—."

Before the words could leave my mouth, the front door opened and Hunter walked in with a big smile on his face. He was still in his work clothes, and instantly came over to the sofa to greet Barry.

"It's good to see you," he said, leaning down to give him a hug. They embraced and exchanged a quick kiss. "I need to go change real quick."

"No problem," Barry replied. "Actually, I should call Ron right now—let him know what time I'll be back."

As Barry pulled out his cell phone and dialed Ron, I relaxed for the first time since my former lover had walked into the loft. Coming out as a porn star was practically like coming out as a gay man all over again. With each instance of support shown by a close friend, I felt increasingly better about what Hunter and I were doing. I loved my friends, and wanted to be honest with all of them about who I was and what I was doing. And even though I knew that there was no way the whole world would be cool with our videos, at least our most important friends were being supportive. And situations like the one with Ron would just prove who was actually a friend, and who never really cared to begin with.

"I still haven't adjusted to the iPhone," Barry said as soon he was off the phone with Ron. He stuck the phone in his back pocket and sat down on the sofa in the same spot as earlier.

"Are you kidding? I love these things," I replied. "So how's that asshole doing?"

"Cole—."

"Come on, Barry. I'm actually surprised at you—that you're even staying with him after the way he treated me at that dinner. Did he tell you about that?"

"He's playful—you know that," Barry diplomatically replied.

"Playful? My fucking client of the century was sitting next to me—not to mention half the guys in there composed the gossip channel of Boston's South End—and Ron was spewing out quotes from our videos, and asking what I knew about the porn industry. It was just plain rude. I would never do that to him. That's my career—that's money that affects Hunter and my livelihood. Ron's a real dickhead. I wanted to punch him in the face."

Barry was laughing at this point. "Come on, Cole."

"Yeah, a real fucking dick. Just because he can't get any ass, and is therefore *miserable* all the time, I need to suffer? See if I go to one of his parties again. I'm so fucking pissed."

"Cole's right!" Hunter shouted from the second floor. "The whole dinner was one giant embarrassment. You know how much commission is at stake with the Marinelli deal?"

"I can imagine," Barry replied. "Look at you, Mr. million-dollar listing."

"All I'm saying is that I'm glad Ron didn't fuck that up, because I would've kicked his ass. He's like five years away from being the very definition of a curmudgeon. I don't know how his friends stand him. And I don't know how you can sleep at his house when you visit."

"He has a nice house—."

"Whatever. I know, I know. It's bigger than our place. But you know you're always welcome here. And if that asshole will talk shit on us, then he'll talk shit on you too."

Barry's laughing had ended, and with a plain expression on his face he nodded at me and shifted to pull his phone out of his pocket.

"And I'm sure he does," Barry calmly replied. "It sucks. I agree. Some *friends* just aren't good friends."

"I don't like that," I quickly told him. "You're either a friend, or you're not one. There's no such thing as a good friend or bad friend. If you're a friend, then you need to be good by default. The guy had me over for dinner and intentionally tried to make me squirm."

"Yeah—but you can't always expect so much of people. That's not the way the world works."

"It should."

As soon as Barry looked at his phone, his eyes widened, and an expression of horror covered his face, from his cheeks up to his forehead.

"Oh my God," he said as he stared at the small screen.

"What?"

"Oh my God," he said again, and covered his face with one hand as he held his phone across the sofa in my direction. Suddenly curious, I snatched the device from him.

I heard everything. Three simple words in a text message from Ron.

"What does this mean?" I asked.

"Oh my God—my phone must've hit re-dial when I sat down. Oh my fucking God—."

"You think he heard everything I was saying? Oh no, no, no—."

Just as Barry was freaking out on the couch and I was trying to figure out what had happened, I heard Hunter's footsteps on the ladder leading down from the second story.

"What's going on?" Hunter asked, sensing the sudden anxiety in the living room.

"I was talking shit on Ron, and Barry accidentally dialed his fucking number."

"Oh my God," Hunter said, and for a moment I thought he was going to fall off the ladder leading down from the loft. "You don't think he'd—," Hunter didn't ever finish. He just stared at me, holding onto the ladder with one hand as his feet touched the floor. I didn't know what Ron was capable of. Maybe nothing. Hopefully this guy wasn't too vindictive, and the only outcome of all this would be no more dinner party invites.

"Maybe I should sleep here tonight," Barry said, his face still pale from disbelief at what had just happened.

"You didn't talk any shit on him," I said. "It was all me."

"I need to go over there and pick up my stuff. I'll—I'll call you," he worriedly said, and then shook his head in disappointment. "I can't believe this," he said to himself.

As Barry hurried to leave the apartment and head down to Ron's, Hunter and I were left in the quiet loft, wondering what was going to come of all this. We just hoped it wouldn't be too severe.

*   *

"Cole? Cole?" Hunter's anxious voice was like a splash of cold water on Thursday morning. I'd had the most difficult time falling asleep the night before. Barry ended up staying at Ron's, yet I stayed awake for as long as possible, waiting for some kind of reassurance that was never going to arrive.

"What's the matter?" I mumbled as Hunter flicked the lights on in our bedroom. As I flexed my eyes open—which was very difficult considering I'd only slept for a few hours—I could see the pain written all over his face. "What happened?"

"I went to the gym this morning—I didn't want to wake you up because I know you didn't get any sleep last night. Cole—they wouldn't let me in."

"What do you mean they wouldn't let you in?"

"The girl at the counter kept saying that my membership card was rejected. She wouldn't give me any details. She wouldn't let me talk to the manager—I was going *crazy*. I just wanted to talk to someone, and this girl just kept saying *I'm sorry, I'm sorry*. She said we'd be getting a phone call from management."

"No fucking way! We just paid them like seven grand in training fees. You think it's a problem with the system?"

"No—I don't know." Hunter let out a deep sigh and sat on the bed. It was so difficult for me to see him like this. I knew what was going through his head, and it was the same thing that was going through mine.

I glanced at my phone on the nightstand. Two missed calls already, and one of them was from Solaris. As I sat up on the bed, I rested one hand on Hunter's back and dialed my voicemail with the other. As soon as the message started, I turned the loudspeaker on.

"This is Roger Mansfield, the General Manager at Solaris Gym. I'm calling with some very important information regarding your training membership at our gym. Please call me back at—."

Before the message ended I was dialing the caller ID.

"No fucking way. Ron must have ratted us out to the gym! He must have," Hunter said. All the joy and warmth in his voice had left, replaced by a sad realization that we'd been fucked over.

"Can I please speak with Mr. Mansfield? Cole Maverick. Thanks." I waited patiently. I could barely bring myself to look at Hunter. Had I caused all this? "Roger? I just got your message. What's going on?"

114

"I'm afraid we've terminated the training memberships purchased by you and your partner, due to a violation of our terms of property use." This guy didn't waste any time with pleasantries.

"What do you mean?" I asked the stiff voice that I was hearing over the phone; a far cry from the friendly staff members who'd made all of our past experiences at Solaris so wonderful.

"Management was pointed towards incriminating content, posted over the Internet, that shows the two of you violating our terms of property use."

Terms of property use, what a crock of shit. We'd been caught, and I didn't know whether to contest it over the phone or threaten to sue, or just swallow my pride and deal with this tremendous loss of money.

"Roger—I just spent seven thousand dollars on memberships— for a full year. We've hardly used any of it yet. This is outrageous."

"We're very serious about our rules," the manager coldly replied. "And you and your partner blatantly violated them. You're both banned from Solaris Gym and all of our U.S. locations."

"I could sue for this."

"I think there's enough evidence that a lawsuit wouldn't do you any good. I'm sorry for your loss," he said, and hung up the phone. He was done with us, and so was Solaris Gym. The seven grand was down the toilet. That was money that we didn't even have yet—money that was contingent upon a commission check for a property that still wasn't sold. I wanted to strangle Ron.

I turned to my partner, whose eyes had sunken into the saddest expression I'd even seen him wear. We loved Solaris—that gym had become an important part of our lives, and it had been taken away from us with a single phone call. Seven grand had been taken away from us with a single phone call.

"We'll be okay," I told him, but I don't think Hunter believed it.

"What's going on with the property? Does he want too much money? Is that it? Can you lower the price?"

"Hunter—don't worry about the money. We'll make it back."

"What else is going to be fucking taken away from us?" he asked. "Our apartment? My job? I have to go into work in a few hours. What if that fucker called Kelly? What the fuck am I walking into in a few hours?"

"You really think it was Ron?"

"Of course I do." Hunter wasted no time in his reply. "He heard you on the phone and wanted revenge. He saw all of our videos. He works out at Solaris. He knows we go there. Who else could it have been?"

I didn't want to face the idea that someone connected to us through my ex-lover Barry could've done something so cold and hurtful. I did say a bunch of nasty things about him, but he also tried to humiliate me in front of a client and a room full of acquaintances. Ron was playing a dangerous game, and I didn't know where it was going to end. And so all I could do was hold Hunter, and silently hope that he'd still have a job upon showing up for work.

*   *

You can't imagine my relief when I got that text from Hunter saying "everything's fine." I'd dropped him off to work after putting on a fresh suit in preparation for an important meeting with Tony Marinelli. The whole drive from Hunter's restaurant to Marinelli's downtown office was filled with anxiety. I was so tense and stiff that I had a difficult time even driving. And it wasn't until I was waiting for the elevator inside the high-rise where Marinelli's office was located that the comforting text came across from Hunter's phone.

That didn't mean my worries were over. Maybe Ron was holding that card to see what our next move would be. But somehow I didn't think he'd be that vicious. Fucking with a gym training membership—albeit a very expensive one—is one thing. Fucking with a man's job and livelihood is another. Although even as I tried to place all the blame on Ron, I couldn't help but listen to that small voice inside of me that asked if I'd fucked up my own livelihood by posting those videos. Fortunately, I wasn't going to let that voice get any louder.

For a guy who owned little Italian restaurants, gas stations, laundromats, car washes, and an assortment of small, single-location businesses, I was always surprised by Marinelli's office. He chose one of the nicest downtown high-rises to rent office space. Since most of his staff needed to be on-site, his office was actually very small compared to his Bostonian empire of working class enterprises. There was a pleasant secretary—an older woman who could've been Marinelli's sister or cousin, or friend of the family. She always had a big smile every time I walked into the office. I think it made her day to flirt with middle-aged, well-dressed Italian men.

"Lucille, how are you doing?" I asked as soon as I saw that white smile underneath her round glasses.

"Hi Cole," she pleasantly replied, blushing a little as she peeked up from her chair. "Let me get Tony."

Lucille hopped out from behind her desk and hurried down the short hallway that led to three offices. One of them belonged to Marinelli, another to his business partner, and the third to his son, who had the unenviable job of playing HR to all the small businesses.

It wasn't long before Lucille re-emerged and ushered me into Marinelli's office. It was a beautiful room with a conference table and a huge, mahogany desk, and an entire wall of glass that looked out upon Boston. He once told me that this office was a gift to himself, after cramming into a small room in the back of one of his restaurants for fifteen years. He said that even though he didn't really need office space, it had a certain aesthetic that kept him going, even in his old age.

"Take a seat," Marinelli told me as I walked into the office. Lucille closed the door behind us, and I sat down in one of the leather side chairs that faced his desk.

"How's your day going?" I asked as I placed a manila folder on his desk. "I think we're about to sell. We have two interested buyers and we're ready to start a bidding war."

But as I looked up to face the biggest client of my life, I noticed he wasn't smiling. At least, he wasn't smiling the way a guy should be after learning that he'd found buyers for his multi-million dollar home.

Marinelli didn't say a word. All he did was turn his massive, 27" flat screen computer monitor sideways, so that both he and I could see the source of his discontent. And there I sat, mortified, as one of the videos of Hunter and I streamed across his screen. The computer was muted, and so was the room. Marinelli didn't say a single word. He just looked at me in the eyes, as I went back and forth between him, the monitor, and the glass wall that looked out into my city.

"I'm okay with a lot of shit, Cole," Marinelli spat the words out. "I'm okay with gay guys. My youngest son is gay. You were always a good guy to me. A strong Italian. Aggressive. I wanted you to sell my house. But that was back when I thought you were clean."

"Clean? Tony—my personal life is a little creative. I don't know what to tell you. This video doesn't harm anybody."

"Let me tell you something about business," Marinelli said as he leaned across his executive desk. I could smell that awful, musty cologne leaking across the solid wood. "You think I got all this from playing fair? When someone you're in business with has a broken leg, you break the other. I don't have time to fuck around by playing fair, Cole. This video—this piece of shit—this is your broken leg. I thought you were clean, but now you've given people like me something to use against you."

"I don't know where you're going with this," I angrily replied. I wasn't even thinking about the money at this point. My whole body was stiff, and this prick—who had been a pain in my ass during this entire home sale—had gone too far.

"I have something to use against you, Cole," Marinelli replied, waving his chubby hands in the air as he smirked in delight. "This video is a gold mine of blackmail. You wanna keep your job? Keep your friends? Keep mama and papa smiling? Then as soon as my home sells, you're gonna take that fat, juicy commission check and shove it in my pocket."

"You can't possibly be that fucked up—."

"I can't be? You made yourself *vulnerable*, Cole. You're a wounded dog. And wounded dogs get put down," he spat out.

I sat there—I don't know how long I sat there for. Maybe ten seconds—maybe thirty. It felt like a lot longer. I thought about all the money on our credit cards. I thought about our struggling finances. Our rent. Our busy weekends and weeknights. All the vacations I wanted to take Hunter on.

"Fuck your home sale," I finally said, looking Marinelli straight in the eyes.

"Excuse me?" he said, seemingly astonished.

"You heard me. Fuck your home sale. Find someone else to blackmail. Or go get your realtor's license and take care of it yourself. You're selling a multi-million dollar home and you're trying to cheat an honest guy out of his commission? *Fuck* you."

Marinelli looked shocked. It was clear that he'd gone through life without anyone ever speaking to him like this. He was probably used to getting everything he wanted; having grown men constantly cower down to him.

I stood up out of the chair and looked at him one final time. He looked like an animal; not even quite human anymore. What a monster. As I turned to walk out of his office, I heard him call after me.

"Hey," he shouted from his desk, "Cole! I uh—I bought your video. Just wanted to see for myself that this was the real deal. Proved two things, Cole. One—I'm not a queer. God bless you and Hunter and my son. Second—you uh—I hate to admit this, but—you know what you're doing. I think if you put half as much love into selling my house as you did making that video, you'd have a commission check in your bank right now and you'd have won this round. If this is what you love—then do it. I'm happy to be your first customer."

I turned around and saw a brief smile appear on Marinelli's face. But there was no way I could smile. Hunter and I *needed* that commission. We needed to recover the money for the gym, paid for on a credit card. I needed to pay for the two-thousand dollar computer I'd bought for editing videos. I needed to pay our rent. There was nothing to smile about. And with that, I opened the door and walked out of his office; a broken soldier on his way home. The only thing on my mind was how I was gonna tell Hunter that the great life we'd been building for each other was falling apart. At least we still had each other. And I wasn't ready to give up yet.

CHAPTER NINE

narrated by Hunter

For the next two weeks we lived in fear. When I think back upon the saddest, scariest times in my life, I never slept as little as I did during the two weeks after Marinelli fired Cole. We'd lost not only our very expensive gym training memberships, but also a client whose commission was going to rapidly transform our financial situation. Someone was out to destroy us, and we didn't know what else they were capable of. Cole still didn't want to believe that Ron could do such a thing, but I didn't know anyone else who would have a motive to try and ruin our lives.

Even in our time of trouble, Cole and I still had each other. I was working harder and he was scrambling to catch up at work, but we tried to treasure the little amounts of time we'd get to spend with one another. And our one little beacon of hope, which neither of us really believed would come through, was that XTube Amateur page, where every day our video got more and more views.

Each day the dollar figures would keep growing, stretching into the thousands. But the money wasn't coming into our checking account, so how could we be certain that we'd even see it? This was a porn website, after all.

"It says we're finally gonna get a check," Cole told me on a Thursday morning, the week before our rent check was due at the management office. He was wide awake before I was, getting some work done from home before having to report to the office.

"I'll believe it when I see it," I replied, stretching out my body on our queen bed.

"Three to four business days. You know if this check actually comes—then we've paid rent and then some."

"I don't want to even think like that," I said, "because what if the check never comes and you and I slow down at work, thinking it'll be here next week? We need to just focus on work and see what happens."

"Do you really think it won't come?" I could hear the depression in Cole's voice. He really wanted this. For the past two weeks he'd felt personally responsible for the loss of the Marinelli account. I could hear in his voice that he wanted to make everything better for us.

"It has to, right? Something has to come," I told him, although I wasn't sure if I myself believed it. "If they didn't send money, then people wouldn't take the time to put all these videos up for sale. It's a business model."

"Yeah, you're right. They have to," he repeated. "And if it doesn't—Hunter, if anything happens and we lose the apartment—."

"Don't even talk like that," I comfortingly said, staring into his green eyes from my position on the bed. "This is *our* home. I know we're in for a struggle, but we'll get there. We can always sell some things in the apartment or borrow some money from our credit cards this month to cover rent if the check doesn't come."

"I don't want to have to sell anything," he complained. "And the gym memberships are already on the credit cards. What are we gonna do, put even more on there? I just want this check to come."

"Well *we* can't force it. We just have to wait, and continue to think positively."

And so we waited.

The original message to us, alerting us of the check, said we'd receive it in three to four business days. When Tuesday rolled around, there was no check. When Wednesday came, there was no check. Three to four business days had passed, and our rent was due Friday. Cole and I were still scrambling to make the payment. The management office in the building wasn't very forgiving. There were way too many people trying to rent at the Cigar Factory for the management office to excuse late or missing rent checks.

On Thursday, with a gut feeling that I couldn't describe, I left work in-between the lunch and dinner shifts and raced home. I didn't plan on going into the apartment, and I even told the taxi driver to wait for me at the edge of the property. As soon as my feet hit the pavement outside the factory lofts building, I jogged towards the entrance on my way to the mailroom. I wanted to sprint, but didn't want to look crazier than I already felt. It was true; I was rushing out of work on a hunch to come look for some check from an online porn website.

As I hurried towards the mailroom, I kept going over the logic in my head. They *had* to pay people, right? I'd always go on the website and see all these Amateur pages with lots and lots of videos. There's no way that people would continue making videos if they weren't getting checks. It just didn't make sense. I knew that this check had to be arriving soon.

I felt like my heart stopped the moment I put the small key in our mailbox.

"Please be in there," I said out loud as I reached into the box and pulled out some envelopes. Two bills and a credit card offer. I nearly sunk to the tiled floors. I was furious that the check hadn't come, that rent was due in 24 hours, that we'd been personally fucked just for posting a sex video on the Internet, and that I'd wasted money taking a taxi all the way home just because of a gut instinct. I was really struggling to stay positive about all this, but it was just so hard.

This was even worse than finding no mail at all in the mailbox, because then I could at least hope that postal delivery was running late. But it was Thursday, and the mailman had come and gone, leaving us with no check. Rent was due in one day, and we didn't have money in our account to cover it, and there was no way I was going to put my faith in XTube once again.

I shut the mailbox door and locked it, and immediately grabbed for my cell phone as I hurried back to the cab. The meter had been running ever since he'd dropped me off outside the building, and I was dreading the taxi fare.

"Cole? You busy?"

"Hi baby, I can talk. What's up? Are you at work?"

"I just checked the mail," I replied, trying to hide my anger, although it was difficult to keep from shouting into the phone. I didn't want to shout at Cole, or upset him, but I was furious at the whole situation. "Nothing. No check. They said three to four days, and it's now been five. I don't think it's coming."

"Goddamnit," he said, softly, as if he was trying to conceal his voice from other people in the office. "I'm gonna cancel the fucking account."

"Don't do that. Just—keep thinking positively," I told him, although I felt like the last person on Earth who should be giving that advice at that very moment.

"No. They're fucking us around, Hunter. I'm gonna cancel it as soon as I get home."

"We need them—even if it's just that small chance that a check will actually arrive," I replied, walking hastily out the entrance of the building. The cab was still waiting there, windows up and the engine on. "I don't know any other sites like this, and we don't know how to create our own site, so let's just—hope."

"Hope isn't gonna pay rent tomorrow."

"We'll just have to sell some things. That new computer you got. Can you return it?"

"I don't know—I don't know. I'll see. I can go by there in the morning," Cole replied. I knew he didn't want to sell that computer. He'd just gotten it, and had already fallen in love with the machine.

"I'll think about this today at work," I said. "Tonight we have to figure out how we can come up with this money. And not only that, but the money that we lost on the gym memberships. But rent is priority."

"Let me think about this one. Don't worry baby, we'll work this out," Cole replied, growing calmer as the shock wore off. But I could hear the distress in his voice. Not only was he pushing himself extra hard at work, but now he had this dilemma to deal with. I just hoped that whatever pit we'd fallen into wouldn't last much longer.

"I love you."

"Love you too."

*   *

Friday morning came too soon. Falling asleep on Thursday night had proved to be the most difficult in what seemed like forever. When my alarm went off on Friday morning I felt like I hadn't gotten any rest at all. And calling out on a Friday would be off limits with Kelly. I had to go to work, and I had to hand responsibility over to Cole for dealing with the management office. And for that I felt awful. He'd be sitting home, selling things on Craigslist or waiting around for the postman to show up, or maybe asking one of his friends for a quick loan. Cole's always had a lot of pride, and it made me feel awful to see him struggle like this. But in a way I also felt more connected to him. I wanted this man to know that I was going to be with him forever, no matter what kind of financial hardships we'd ever encounter.

As I achingly steered myself out of bed on Friday morning, it was Cole who had left a cup of coffee on the nightstand for me. He was wide awake, wearing only boxers, seated at the computer desk with a smile on his face.

"Everything okay?" I asked him in my groggy, morning voice. I was just surprised to see him smiling on such a miserable day.

"The check is gonna come today," he said, and pulled his eyes off the computer for a quick second to look at me.

"How do you know?"

"I just feel it."

"You've gone crazy," I said.

The night before, Cole had done a little book shopping. Whatever had led him to the self-help section of the local bookstore had produced a single, nighttime purchase. *The Secret*. That familiar book about positivity and the law of attraction. My first reaction was disappointment that he spent the money on the book, when I could've just stolen it from that douche bag in Provincetown, in that depressing guest bedroom. But Cole stayed up reading it all night, and by morning there was something *different* about him.

"The world likes us," Cole replied with a big smile on his face. "We don't need to sell anything, or do anything dramatic to try and make rent. The *law of attraction*, Hunter. We've been thinking positively about this for so long. When the postman shows up, I'm gonna march down to the mailroom and get our check, and then go pay rent. I've never doubted our relationship. Too many amazing things have happened to us. There's no way that check isn't coming today."

"And what if it doesn't?" I asked him. I was puzzled.

"It's coming. There's no way it won't come. It's coming."

"I hate to play devil's advocate, but if it *doesn't* come and we have no backup plan, what's stopping the management office from posting an eviction notice?"

"No worries. The check is on its way," he smoothly replied, as if he had no cares in the world.

"So you've got this under control?" I asked him. I didn't want to argue. There clearly was no way I'd win this argument.

"The postman has it under his control! And as soon as he arrives, I'll pay rent and put the rest in our account, and then we're gonna make a video number two. And it's gonna be fucking hotter than the first one."

Cole's confidence didn't rub off on me. I was still nervous as hell, and had no idea what was going to happen that day with the rent situation. I tried to block the check out of my mind. *There's no way that this will come*, I thought. I wanted to e-mail the company but knew I probably wouldn't even get a reply. What a lost cause.

My lunch shift was probably the longest shift I'd ever worked in my life. The restaurant operated flawlessly, with no problems to be found, but I couldn't stop thinking about our rent. And I hated it. I hated that money had caused me to be so obsessive. That's the thing that sucks about money. How easily problems can start when the money is gone. Even though it's just a game of numbers, Cole and I became so reliant on having money to do this or that. Money for our gym training, and for our perfect loft, and our vacation that we hadn't been able to take yet because work was overwhelming. And we couldn't quit our jobs, because then we wouldn't have any money. It was this awful, horrible cycle, and I think that's why the porn videos appealed to us so much. What a break from the cyclical nature of having regular jobs.

Now if we'd *only* get paid for it. That's what I kept thinking during my lunch shift. Life would be perfect if Cole and I could leave our jobs and just make videos, and live off of that income. I didn't know how much income it would be, but if downloads of the first video were any indication, then we could make a decent living each month.

But I didn't want to put all my faith in a check that might never come, or a website that might not be as legitimate as it let on. And so I just struggled to get through the lunch shift, sending my mind to all sorts of places, wondering what Cole would do to get the money for rent. It made me so sad to think about the look on his face, opening the mailbox to find it empty, or worse: to find a stack of bills and no check.

I was in the office with Kelly, shortly after the lunch shift ended, when my cell phone rang. I felt like my whole face was about to turn red. Cole was calling. Normally I wouldn't pick up my cell phone, but this was serious. And plus, Kelly—for whatever reason—liked Cole enough that her blood didn't start to boil whenever he'd call the restaurant, which was more than could be said about most of the employees' significant others.

"Hey, good news?"

"It didn't come."

I wanted to fall out of the chair and die. Even Kelly got a quick shock when she looked over at me to see all the color drain out of my face.

"Are you alright?" she asked. "If you're planning on throwing up, do it in the hallway."

"The mail came? Are you sure the mail came?" I asked, panicked.

"The mail came. No check."

"Oh my God. Where are you now? Home?"

"I'm at the bank cashing the check that never came," Cole replied, and burst out into laughter. "I told you it was coming today!"

My mouth hung open as I listened to Cole's laughter. I couldn't believe it.

"Heading back to pay rent," Cole said. "Nice fat check. I can't wait, baby. We need to do another one tonight. We've got something here."

"I love you so fucking much," I said.

"Love you too, babe. Get nice and sweaty for me. We're not even gonna make it to the bedroom when you come home tonight."

My phone clicked, letting me know that Cole had hung up. And with my mouth still open in shock, I placed the cell phone back on the desk and turned to face Kelly, who was staring at me with those little almond-shaped eyes, wondering what in the hell that call had been about.

"The uh—other French restaurant in the South End. They're going out of business."

"Out of business? Why?" she excitedly asked.

"Foie gras poisoning, or something like that. And I think it came out that the owners are actually Belgian."

"Bastards," she spat. A tiny smile crawled upon her face as she returned her attention to her laptop.

*   *

That night was pure magic. My spirits were lifted, and I carried the renewed energy and optimism through my work shift, until it was time to close the restaurant and head home. And as soon as I locked the doors to the restaurant, I jumped into a cab and rushed back to my apartment.

For a normal couple, their version of a romantic night would have been walking into a dimly lit apartment with candles all over the place and a nice bottle of wine on the dining room table. But let's not forget: we're porn stars.

127

I walked into an apartment so bright that it could've been sunlight coming through the windows. No candles—what a fire hazard that would be. Considering Cole and I were about to fuck all over the apartment, I didn't think either of us wanted to deal with accidentally burning anything down. And in place of that good bottle of wine was a nice, juicy bottle of lube, upright on the coffee table, ready for the both of us.

And Cole?

"Boo!" he shouted, nearly scaring me off my feet the moment I walked into the apartment. He'd been hiding behind the door, waiting patiently for my return. Already naked, his cock was rock hard, and he slammed the door shut before I could even regain my balance.

"Hey—," I started to say, but Cole pushed me into the thick door and shoved his tongue in my mouth. As he shoved his crotch into mine, he un-buttoned my dress shirt so quickly that it felt like he was seconds away from ripping it off my body.

I grabbed his cock with one hand, and put my other around his neck, pulling his tongue further into my mouth. His lips tasted salty, and the scent from his neck carried this hot, thick musk, that set my nose on fire. There was something about Cole's scent that always drove me so wild.

As I pulled my shirt off of my arms, Cole undid my belt and threw it on the floor. He wanted to get me out of my pants right away, but I had other intentions. With all of my strength I flipped Cole around, nearly taking him off his feet and pushing his back up against the front door. I bent down, grabbed his cock, and held the head right at my lips. Cole moaned as he felt his dry cock slip into my mouth, nice and slowly. My wet lips massaged the base, sucking his entire throbbing cock with this great mixture of brevity and intensity.

Cole had set up his camera in the living room on an old tripod that he rarely ever used, and the presence of the filming device gave me such an added rush. I sucked Cole's cock as if the whole world was watching us live. I made love to it. Squeezing his balls with one hand, and gripping the base with the other, I worked my mouth over his dick, sucking harder and faster with every one of his groans. As I pushed his fat cock deeper into my mouth I could feel the head hit the back of my throat. As Cole arched his back I could hear him moan with pleasure. His cock was dripping with pre-cum. It tasted delicious; perfectly sweet and salty. I was so badly craving his load.

When Cole pulled his cock out of my mouth I was panting for air, like a wolf who had just been yanked off of a raw piece of meat. Cole leaned down and kissed me again, tasting the fresh scent of his own dick on my lips. With his two big hands he grabbed me under the armpits and lifted me to my feet. Though he didn't stop there. He then bent down, put his arms around my thighs, and lifted me in the air. I wanted him to throw me up against the door, or throw me on the sofa and fuck me from behind. Instead he did something even hotter. With his masculine hands wrapped around my legs, he walked into the kitchen and put my body right on top of the stainless steel counter.

I was scrambling to take my jeans off, and with Cole's help we yanked them down to my knees. And with one swift move Cole came up in-between my legs, filling that opening in-between my crotch and the jeans still entrapping my feet, and pressed his hard cock against my ass. I leaned my back against the kitchen cabinets and slid down onto his dick, feeling the immediate intensity of his massive head entering my hole. Seeing I was having some trouble, Cole squirted some lotion onto his hands, from a tall bottle next to the kitchen sink. He rubbed the white, creamy lotion on his dick and the remainder on my hole.

Just before Cole entered me again, he looked me in the eyes. That's what really did it for me. That's what had always done it for me. That look in his beautiful, deep green eyes, telling me that he was there with me, in the moment, each time he'd stick his cock inside me. He wasn't just fucking for the sake of fucking. This was his non-verbal way of communicating his love to me; speaking with his eyes and his cock. And between then and whenever he'd cum, every other aspect of our lives would become unimportant. It would just be us, the way we fucked, and the way we looked at one another, in the most raw and natural form of sex ever to be had by two men, as if we were warriors on an ancient battlefield, celebrating life in the most erotic, masculine way possible.

As Cole's cock got halfway inside me, I breathed deeply and focused on relaxing the muscles in my ass. I wanted so badly for him to be fully inside me. As I relaxed into his huge cock, Cole leaned into me and kissed my neck, softly and passionately sucking on the space just under my ears. And once he was fully inside me, his cock filling up my ass and reaching me in those deepest, most pleasurable parts, he moved his lips from my neck to my cheeks. He kissed around my lips, gently sucking on my scruffy skin.

Cole rocked me back and forth, lifting his crotch up into me as my back and shoulders pushed up against the kitchen cabinets. I groaned each time I felt the full force of his cock go all the way inside me, stretching my hole and filling me with this amazing sensation. I squeezed my thighs into him, using my legs to propel him into me. And just as I did this, Cole's lips reached mine, and he stuck his tongue deep in my mouth. I sucked on it, tasted his sweat, and kissed him as he slid in and out of me. Perspiration dripped down my face.

I pulled my arms out from around Cole's neck and dug them into the countertop as Cole's fucking got more and more intense. My triceps bulged, and I saw Cole's eyes get stuck on my thick arms and pecs. Just as he grabbed my upper arms, squeezing them with his strong, rough hands, I felt him explode inside me. Those groans he made intensified as he fucked me with three final thrusts, pushing his cum deep inside me. The second it was over he let the weight of his upper body fall into me, resting his head on my shoulder and his wet lips on my sweaty neck.

"Don't get too tired," I whispered. Red marks on my arms were left where Cole's powerful hands had squeezed my triceps. I loved so much the way he manhandled me during sex.

"Huh?" he asked, panting for breath.

"I'll be ready for round two soon."

In-between deep breaths of air, Cole smiled and kissed my neck. Life was about to get a whole lot better.

Chapter 10

narrated by Cole Maverick

"To my good friends, who are changing the face of porn forever," Paul said, with his champagne glass high in the air. "And by *face*, Cole, I mean I've never seen an older son-of-a-bitch sell more videos than you, my friend."

"They must be watching for Hunter," I joked, and rubbed my partner's neck with my free hand. "I'd pay every day to watch him on video."

Hunter blushed as he took a sip from his champagne glass. Paul had been kind enough to invite us down the hallway for drinks on Saturday night. He wanted to celebrate our XTube success, and chew my ear off for not telling him about the financial problems Hunter and I had been having. I felt bad for not telling him about the Marinelli bullshit and the gym incident, but it was such a rough time for Hunter and I that I just wanted to focus on getting out of the dumps. I knew Paul would've been right there to help, but a big part of me wanted to do it on my own.

"You know, Ron is a real douche bag to give you guys a scare like that."

"Let's not point fingers," I replied, but Paul shook his head like he didn't want to hear it.

"Who else could it have been? Come on, let's be real. I know he's always had a crush on you, Cole. When you were with your ex, and now with Hunter, and he probably saw those videos, got super-jealous, and after wacking off to you thirty times—."

"Okay, okay, that's enough," I said, holding both palms in the air. "I don't wanna ruin my dinner."

"Fair enough. But if I see that asshole on the street I'm gonna set him straight," Paul aggressively replied.

"Please, you wouldn't hurt a fly."

"Those were the old days," Paul told me. "I'm a new man. Back on the prowl."

"Have you seen any guys lately?" Hunter asked him.

"Still working on that. I think you two need to send some my way! I can just imagine the fan mail you get."

"It's been pretty cool," Hunter said. "Great response to our videos."

"When are you going to start fucking fans on-camera?" Paul asked.

"What do you mean?"

"You can't just have two-ways. I don't know any porn couple out there who only have sex with each other. You need to introduce new, hot men into your sex life. People want to see threesomes. Keeps things fresh."

I looked at Hunter, who had an awkward look on his face. I knew he wasn't uncomfortable with the question, but like me he hadn't really thought about changing our videos to accommodate a third partner. So far it had just been us, and we'd been doing really well. But Paul did have a point. Every day fans would write to us, asking to hook up if we ever came their way.

"I don't know if I wanna get into all that," I replied. "Then you need to deal with forms and HIV testing and contracts and all this other crap. We'd probably have to pay them, like hiring porn actors or something. We're not paying each other to have sex on-camera, and I think that's what makes it hot. It's just—natural."

"This is the XTube generation," Paul replied. "Get some little bottoms who will do it for free, just because they like you guys. That'll seem more natural anyway. You don't want any big tops. Alpha male one and two are right here. I swear to God. Find some great bottoms who love you guys and want to hook up with you just for the sake of good sex."

"But if we're going to be putting it online and charging people, we can't just *not* pay them," I replied.

"These are inconsequential details, Cole," Paul replied. "There are a million options. Give them a check, a percentage, some material shit—take them on vacation. I don't care what you do with the money. Just *make* the money. At some point nobody is going to be downloading your videos anymore, and that's the sad truth of life. So in the meantime, ride this baby out, and have a good time!"

"You really think threesomes are the answer?" Hunter asked. I could sense the skepticism in his voice. I didn't know how I felt about it either. Hunter and I hadn't even explored a real threesome together yet, let alone doing one on-camera. We'd talked in the past about an open relationship, but our sexual attraction for each other was still so strong that neither of us really needed anything open.

"I think you two are foolish if you don't give it a try," Paul said. "Test it out. Guarantee the first video blows up the last one you put out."

"Why can't we just keep it between us?" I asked him.

"One-on-one videos? Viewers will get tired of it. You're both men, you know how it is. Sexual attraction is *raw* and fleeting. Keep it interesting. You guys are in a new relationship, and it's with the millions of gay guys who watch online porn. Don't let that marriage get stale. Keep it fresh, and they'll keep coming back."

Hunter and I turned to look at each other with the same hesitation in our eyes. I could tell what he was thinking. Paul had made a lot of good points, but the decision wasn't going to be that simple. Money was one thing, but my relationship with Hunter was sacred and special. I didn't want to do anything that would fuck it up. But, if this could be our ticket to a more relaxed life together, without all the pressures of a nine to five—or in Hunter's case, 10 AM to midnight—job, then it was worth a shot.

"We'll think about it," I carefully replied, and lifted the champagne glass to my lips.

*　　*

Paul's suggestion had sparked my curiosity. As soon as we got back to the apartment, Hunter went off to take a shower and prepare for bed, and I glued myself to the computer. I sought out any and every gay couple that released videos on XTube. I didn't find many, but there seemed to be a familiar theme. Threesomes were in. Paul had made a valuable point. I would've loved to just do videos with Hunter, but would there come a time when people would get sick of seeing just the two of us on camera?

The idea of filming threesomes worried me, and I guess because it was getting closer to the *studio feel*. I didn't know for sure, but I assumed finding third persons would mean a whole new process. We'd have to sign contracts, keep tabs on royalties, and probably deal with a bunch of other issues. What if we found someone perfect, signed the contract, and then as soon as the video came out they decided they wanted to shut it down? Would we keep the video up and profit from it,

133

or be the good guys and take it offline? I knew that if we were to do threesomes, we'd be going after younger guys. Maybe someone in their early twenties to add that third generation to our mix. My only issue was dealing with that age range. How many kids at twenty years old would confidently know that they want to be floating around the web forever?

"What do you think?" Hunter asked as he came up the ladder leading to the second floor. The lower half of his body was wrapped in a white towel, and his hair was wet and pulled back.

"I think it makes sense," I replied. "Just a lot to think about."

Hunter slowly walked over to the bed, and sat down so that he was facing the computer desk. He folded his arms on his knees, so that his thick, muscular pecs pressed outwards, hanging above his abs.

"I want to quit my job," he said, with such assurance that it seemed like he was ready to do anything to leave the restaurant. "I want to do this. If you think it'll be better for us to focus on threesomes, then let's do it. We just need rules. I mean—we haven't even had a regular threesome yet."

"What do you think about threesomes?" I asked him, and set the computer on its screensaver so that I could join my partner on the bed. As he rubbed his lips together and thought about the question, I walked over to the bed and took a seat right next to him, wrapping my arm around the soft skin of his back.

"I don't need them," he replied, quickly turning so that his eyes were staring into mine. "But I know that monogamy isn't always practical. And I don't ever want to get to a point where—well, when we're fighting or doing something behind each other's back. I just wanna be as open as possible, and share everything with you."

"I love you more than anything in the world," I said as I massaged his back. "You're so important to me. You drive me fucking crazy, you know that? I mean—look at me," I said, and pointed to my crotch, where my dick had already sprung out from underneath my shorts. "All I have to do is touch you and I get like this."

Hunter blushed, and he reached his hand down into my shorts, squeezing my erection with his fingers.

"I don't have any doubts," he said. "I just want you to know that I'll try threesomes. On video—and *off*, if you really want. We just need to have rules. Like, our *rules of engagement*."

Cole

"That's good," I jokingly replied. "How about no kissing." I relaxed my body as Hunter's fingers tickled along the head of my cock. "And neither of us bottom. We only do that for each other."

"So wait—basically that rule just means that I'm not allowed to bottom for anyone else?" Hunter asked me.

"Well—I only want you to bottom for me. I'm your partner. Your ass is mine, just like certain things of mine are yours. It's different," I said, trying to defend my request, although I could instantly tell by Hunter's face that I'd probably worded it the wrong way.

"How is that fair?"

"Hunter, why would I wanna sit here and watch you get pounded by some stranger?" I replied.

"You're such an Italian alpha male," he said, and playfully rolled his eyes. "What if it's just sitting here and watching me be pleasured?"

"Well do you *want* to bottom for other guys?"

"No," he said. "I don't know. But I'm afraid that if I'm not allowed to bottom, then the type of guys we'll be meeting won't be my type. Paul said the word *twink* like twenty times tonight, but I'm not really into twinks. I don't want to just be meeting twinks or guys who look like me, because then the threesomes are just to your benefit and not mine. We need to mix it up. Get some top vers guys that will bottom for us."

"I understand," I softly replied, giving him a moment to calm down. "How about we do this: if we're hooking up for a video, we pick guys who are fun, cute, will become friends of ours, and will make a great video. When we're hooking up outside of videos, we *both* have to approve them in order to meet them."

"So you only want to be open together?" Hunter asked. He turned to face me again, and I got the feeling that he thought this new openness meant I'd want to fool around on the side.

"Nobody does for me what you do. You're the most important man in my life. Anyone who wants to meet me better want to meet you too, otherwise it's not happening. If someday we want to be open outside of threesomes, we'll talk to each other, and bring it up then. Hunter, I want you to quit your job so we can be together all the time! The last thing I want is more time away, to fuck around with some trick."

Hunter lowered his head and smiled. His hand was still moving along my hard cock, massaging the soft skin under the head. I hoped he

135

knew how madly in love with him I was. I didn't think that we needed to make our relationship more open. Our sex life was going great, and I was more attracted to him than ever. I knew we'd find a way to experiment with these threesomes, and have a good time, and I just hoped that my relationship with Hunter would stay strong throughout.

"So no kissing or bottoming," Hunter said, repeating the two rules we'd created. "And unless it's for a video, I don't want to see someone more than once. Unless we really click, and they become a buddy, you know? Oh—and nobody sleeps in the bed with us."

"Yeah, I agree. No one in our bed," I replied, and knew exactly what was going through Hunter's head with that one. He was probably scared to death that some twink with a daddy/muscle top fetish would start hooking up with us and suddenly want to become a houseboy. We knew how to cook and do our own laundry, so we weren't exactly looking for that kind of a relationship. At least not yet.

"Anything else?" Hunter asked me, a pensive look on his face as he thought about any problems that might come up for opening our relationship to new sexual partners.

"Yeah, we're missing a big one," I said. "I like bareback."

"You *do* like bareback," he replied, and his eyes lit up. "Well can you use a condom when we have threesomes?"

"What am I—gonna fuck you without one and then put one on for them, and go back and forth? I don't want our threesomes to be a fucking carousel."

"You're crazy," Hunter told me. "I love bareback sex too, I'm not arguing with you. It sucks when you have a great, thick erection, and as soon as you put a condom on it your dick starts to deflate. Can we just get lots of testing kits? I mean—it depends who we're talking about, right? Because at least for me, if I was going over some guy's house, and he was like *hey, do you wanna take this testing kit before we fuck*, I'd probably lose my interest."

"Good point. So we'll do it before the day of the hookup. And for videos it'll be an absolute requirement. We all go together, and use it as a chance to get to know each other if we haven't met yet. That way everyone gets tested together, and everyone gets an answer together."

"I like that idea a lot," Hunter replied, nodding his head. "You think guys will be okay with doing bareback videos with us? It might narrow the field of people willing to film with us."

"Well, it's just about trust," I told him. "We'll all get tested together and get answers at the same time. And if they're cool, and they think we're cool guys, and we all have the piece of paper to prove we're totally safe and clean, then what is there to worry about? There's nothing more beautiful than bareback sex, and if we can manage to do it in a way that's safe and enjoyable, every hook-up is gonna feel great, and look great on-camera too."

"Just be prepared for some backlash," Hunter said.

"Don't worry about what people think. It's not like we're pulling guys off the street and fucking everyone and everything without getting tested. I'll get tested three times a week if it means we can have hot, uninhibited fun with our guys. And if the guys aren't into it, then we either use condoms or don't meet them. It's time that people stop being so fucking afraid of bareback sex. STDs don't get spread during bareback sex when both guys are clean. Infections happen when people don't know who they're fucking."

"Don't forget, with open relationships, sometimes boyfriends give it to each other," Hunter said, and took a deep breath. He had that worried expression on his face again. I knew it would take a long time for all this open relationship stuff to settle. It could be years before we were totally comfortable with an open relationship, but I was up for the challenge.

"You're right, they do. But sometimes long-time couples drift apart, and they no longer know who they're waking up next to every morning. I don't think that'll happen with us. We just need to be totally honest with each other. You think you're up for that?"

"Yeah, I can handle that."

"Then it's a deal. Our rules of engagement."

"You think we should try this first with someone for a video, or someone just for fun?" he asked. The same thought was running through my head. I wondered if our first threesome would seem any different if it was on-camera versus off. In fact, I wondered if off-camera might even be stranger. At least on-camera, all the emotions surrounding our first time with a third person might be repressed by the fact that we were all just doing something fun that would appear online.

"How about I'll search online, and we'll see what happens," I said. "If they wanna do a video, we'll do one. If not, then it'll just be a hookup. Sex isn't anything new to us, so this'll just be sex with someone else."

"Easily said. This open stuff can fuck with emotions though."

"Hey—," I gently squeezed Hunter's shoulder and pulled him a little so that he put his eyes back on mine. "Two things. First—we've got this. We can handle this, and we're gonna have fun doing it."

"I know." A small smile appeared on his face.

"And two—if you don't do something with this hard cock in your hand, then I'm gonna *attack* you right now."

"Oh yeah?" Hunter made this coy grin, and immediately released his hand from my dick.

"That's it!"

As I leaped at my partner, I tried to put the open relationship talk out of my mind. I was so happy with my relationship, and I was willing to do anything to make our lives better. And I have to admit, somewhere deep inside me I was going crazy thinking about how hot it would be for my boy Hunter to fuck the hell out of some twink. Him fucking the kid on one end, and me face-fucking him on the other. What a fantasy.

If on-camera threesomes were the answer, then I was ready and willing. Hell, I'd do ten-man orgies if it meant we could quit our jobs and just enjoy a new life together. Well—maybe not ten guys at once. But I did have a great feeling that venturing into threesomes would give us a chance to meet some cool new people, and maybe not feel so *alone* in the sea of XTube users. I wanted to develop our own little A-Team, although the only mission that *this* A-Team would be implementing was to fuck the hell out of each other on a daily basis.

We had just barely gotten our rent check in on time, but there were many more months of rent to pay for. Not to mention an expensive desktop and a costly—and extinct—gym membership, all sitting on credit cards that were just waiting to fuck us with high interest. We needed a lifestyle change. *Badly.* And even though I had no idea what was going to come out of this open relationship, I just hoped that it would make Hunter and I stronger. Looking back to that night when we agreed to start having threesomes, I wish I'd known just how much drama was going to follow our decision. We'd dived into our open relationship head first, praying that the worst of times were behind us. We couldn't have been more incorrect.

CHAPTER ELEVEN

narrated by Hunter

"Hey, I'm home!" I called as soon as I walked through the front door of our apartment. It had been a long Thursday at the restaurant, and I couldn't wait to take my clothes off, hop in the shower, and then relax for a while. Cole had been trying to arrange our first threesome, and I was kind of happy it wasn't happening that night. Cole said he was aiming for a Monday, which was my usual day off, although I didn't know if that would be better or worse. If I was into the guy, then it would be a hot way to spend my day off. If I wasn't, then it would basically be work on a non-work day.

"Cole?" I called again. Lately when I'd get home from work he'd be up at the computer desk, which was right at the edge of the second floor, overlooking the living room. All the lights were on in the apartment, so I knew he had to be home, unless he ran over to Paul's or the local convenience store.

"Did you know there's a frat house across the street from us?" he shouted from the second floor. I paused and thought about the local area. If there was a frat house across the street, I'd never noticed it for anything more than a building. I hurried over to the stairs, and climbed up to find Cole in the corner of our bedroom, staring out the massive window.

"How do you know it's a frat house?"

"It has to be. I've been seeing it more often now—usually after you leave for work is when they're all waking up. Walking around the yard like zombies."

"How do you know it's not just someone's place?"

"Well that university is a couple blocks away, so you know they're gonna have frat houses in the area. There are way too many guys for it to just be someone's apartment. It goes against the natural party law of guy-girl ratios. Let's say there are four to six guys living in that house, which there aren't, because there are far more. They're not gonna let many guys come to their parties, because they want a higher ratio of girls to guys. The more guys they let in, the more competition."

"What if it's a gay fraternity?" I asked, wandering over to the window to see what had grabbed his curiosity.

"Bullshit it's a gay fraternity. You and I are lucky guys, but we're not *that* lucky."

"So because there are a lot of guys around the house, you think it's a frat house?"

"It's sound logic," he replied, as if there was no sense in arguing.

I looked out the window, and suddenly realized what had Cole glued in the corner of our bedroom. Across the street from our apartment building was a house with flashing lights and a large concentration of young men, spread out across the outdoor patio and lawn with disposable cups in hand.

"This is a gold mine," Cole said. "I'm gonna buy a pair of binoculars."

"Oh my God—I'll never be able to get you out of the apartment."

"Come on. As if you won't be changing your jogging route tomorrow."

"Tomorrow?" I replied. "I'm thinking about going for a run right now. In the meantime—before those binoculars get here."

Cole turned from the window, and with that same piercing gaze from which he was staring at the frat house, he looked me up and down as if it was the first time he'd ever seen me. It got me so excited whenever he'd do that, and I couldn't imagine if a day ever came when that didn't happen anymore.

"I think I can wait for the binoculars," he coyly said, staring at my chest with a desire that made me want to rip my own clothes off and jump on top of him.

"Really?" I replied, matching his expression. "Well—sorry but I can't," I said, and as soon as I finished the sentence I darted for the ladder that led down to the first floor. I could hear Cole's laughter as he chased after me. I didn't know if I'd make it to the frat house before he caught me, but a little coyness is never a bad thing. Not to mention, we needed the exercise. How I missed our gym.

* *

It was only a couple days after we discovered the frat house across the street when two monumental, life-changing events happened.

Well, maybe *life-changing* isn't the best word choice. But on the same day that Cole purchased a beautiful, brand new pair of binoculars, he showed up at my work with important news about our search for an on-camera threesome.

"Have you tried these out yet?" Jenna asked from behind the bar as she admired the sleek, black binoculars. The restaurant was closed and the staff had dwindled down to a handful of people who were cleaning the tables, sweeping the floors, and getting the place in shape for the next day's shift. As I was sorting out the night's tips and financial numbers at the bar, Cole was seated with a manila folder and a dirty martini, ready to talk business.

"Just bought them. We're gonna try them out tonight," he replied.

"Very cool," Jenna said. "I might have to come over and uh— scope out the goods."

"We could use her to get us inside," Cole said to me, pointing enthusiastically at our bartender.

"So now I'm just bait?"

"Like you won't get laid too," he playfully replied as Jenna frowned and put the binoculars back on the bar. "I need to run someone by the commission."

"What's the commission?" I asked without lifting my eyes from the stack of receipts in front of me.

"Well technically you, but Jenna can be part of it since she's here tonight."

"What's this about?" she asked, and within a couple seconds her eyes widened and her face exploded with excitement. "Is this about the first three-way?"

"Candidate number one is in this folder."

"You actually made a folder for him?" I asked Cole, laughing quietly at his meticulous attention to details in all things porn.

"Of course I did."

"Did you pull a credit report too? Landlord references?"

"Very funny, wise ass," he remarked. "Jenna will take it seriously. Here you go, check him out."

Cole slid the folder across the bar, and Jenna stopped it with one palm. She quickly whipped it open and grabbed at the pages as if they hinted at the cure for cancer.

"Tye? Where are you poaching these kids? The local college track and field team?"

"He's twenty-three! Gimme that," Cole muttered as he snatched at the pages in Jenna's hands, but the bartender was quick to retreat with the sensitive information.

"Twenty-three? You're shitting me. What's his story?"

"He's an old hook-up I've kept in touch with off and on. Hot little fucker, total power bottom. Southern boy who moved up to Boston to try and find work and go to college, but hasn't had a great track record of either. He was living with his mom when I first met up, but now he's in an apartment with some friends."

"I love how *power bottom* precedes anything else in Cole's description," Jenna jokingly said to me.

"Yep, big power bottom who loves big dick," Cole repeated.

"Then what were you doing with him?" Jenna shot back at Cole. He rolled his eyes and shook his head.

"You love to bust my balls, huh?"

"I can't help it," Jenna said. "It's way too easy."

"Cole's been trying to recruit a twink for our first threesome video," I said, glancing up from the stack of receipts. "Since he and I are both that alpha male role, we thought it would make more sense to find some bottoms for our videos. At least, then the first video will seem less confusing. Two big tops, one small bottom—."

"Like that video Two Girls, One Cup?" she asked, holding the picture of Tye sideways to examine his lean physique.

"Yeah, except without the shit," Cole remarked, a frown wrapped across his face. "I can't believe you just said that, Jenna."

"Hey, that video blew up on the Internet. You guys might want to take some pointers."

"Nah, we'll leave that to your XTube debut," Cole replied. Jenna mouthed the word *ouch*. "Although we *are* pretty liberal—but the line's gotta be drawn somewhere." He shot me a funny look, and then returned his attention to Jenna. "So what do you think about Tye?"

"I think he's cute. I think lots of jock guys would love to see him get fucked by you two. How much does he want?"

"Of what?" Cole asked.

"Money. How much does he want for the video? Or are you guys doing profit-sharing?"

Cole and I both looked at each other with the same, anxious expression. We'd brought up this issue a few times together, but neither of us knew exactly what to do. We didn't know how to create a contract for doing a video, and Cole felt funny asking his lawyer to draft one up. At that point, all we wanted to do was have hot sex on-camera, that we could post online. We knew that it would be for sale, but we had no idea how much we'd make off of a threesome video, or what was appropriate to give our guests.

"He's doing it for free," Cole slowly replied, as if he expected the shock that soon came out of Jenna.

"For free? But this is like mass exposure. Does he know how popular you guys are?"

"I told him, but I don't know if he gets it," Cole said. "I don't even know if I get it yet. Who knows if people will even download this."

"But what about a contract? You guys need to protect yourselves. Say the video starts doing well, and this kid turns around and wants to cut it off. Your time is wasted, future income is lost, and worse—if you don't comply he can sue you."

"I don't think he'd do that," Cole confidently replied. "Look Jenna, I see it like this. If the guy is into us and wants to have sex, then it'll be fun and real. If he was just having sex with us in order to get a paycheck at the end of the day, I think the video would look like most of the shitty porn that's out there. We want the video to be the real thing; Tye is just coming over to the house for a hot threesome, and we're filming it. This isn't a big—*studio* setup."

"This is a whole new world for us," I told Jenna, since I could tell Cole was getting into one of his passionate rants. "We don't know anyone in the industry, and I guess by keeping it on XTube it's kind of detached from the studios. I know we'll be learning through our mistakes."

"Well I hope you don't make too many," she replied, and tossed the folder back on the bar. "I love you guys. Just be smart about this stuff. I want to see you both make a shitload of money, so you can take me on vacation somewhere! I don't want to see you have to spend it all on lawyers because of a stream of problems."

As I watched Cole stare at the closed folder, I knew he was feeling the same fears that were running through my head. We were diving into these threesomes head first, and even though Cole personally knew this kid Tye, doing a paid porn video with him would take the relationship to a whole new level, mixing laid-back pleasure with business. Neither of us knew what was going to come of it, but we both hoped that it wouldn't get too messy. And if anything was gonna get messy, hopefully it would just be the sex.

*   *

Keeping to the rules Cole and I had created together, we went with Tye to a local health clinic and the three of us all got tested, so that we could have as much uninhibited fun as we wanted. When everyone came back clean, we chose the upcoming Monday for filming. Even though I went to bed on Sunday with a tremendous amount of excitement for this new piece of material that we'd be unleashing online, I couldn't shake my nervousness about meeting this kid. I couldn't quite place where it was coming from.

Was it jealousy? This was about to be the first time that Cole and I messed around with a third person, and he was a lot more Cole's type than mine. The two of them had hooked up during the days when Cole was pursuing me, after he'd returned from living in Miami and I was still trying to figure out if I could open myself up to him again. I didn't expect him to be monogamous during that time. He'd get horny just like any guy, and since I wasn't ready to commit to anything serious, I couldn't blame him for seeing Tye. But I guess I had wished that when we did our first threesome, it would be with someone who was new for both of us.

When Tye showed up at our apartment I could tell he was a little nervous. The way he fumbled with his cell phone and wallet. The way his eyes would race around our apartment as he talked to us. His nervousness actually calmed me down, as I immediately empathized with the peculiar situation that he was in; about to bottom for two men— one of them a stranger—and have the whole session taped and published online.

Tye was much cuter than I expected, and looked a lot better than the few pictures Cole had shown me. I've never been into the twink thing, although Cole had been trying to recruit me to that cause for months. He thought it would create a hot scene: daddy, twink, and jock. I wasn't trying to recreate the Breakfast Club here, but it did seem like a good idea. And I had no doubt that I would get hard with this kid. Given how much I love a hot, bubbly ass, Tye's was perfect for me.

While Tye sat on the sofa and got caught up with Cole, who was doing his best to ease the kid's anxieties and create a comfortable and fun environment, I went to the kitchen to fix drinks. And it was somewhere in-between pulling a bottle of vodka from the freezer and pulling some glasses from the shelf that I looked over at Tye and my lover, sitting just a few inches from each other, when I started to tingle with this erotic sensation. It didn't make sense to me, at least not completely. Those small bouts of jealousy seemed to coexist with something that was driving me wild. My eyes followed Tye's bubbly ass and lean legs, wrapped tightly in blue jeans, up to his torso which was covered in a gray wife beater; and then his lean arms with their little bit of natural definition, and that soft, light brown skin. Those thick lips. They had me magnetized. And I followed them, back and forth, my gaze wandering from Cole's crotch to Tye's mouth.

I so badly wanted Cole to un-zip his pants, pull out his thick cock, and let me watch as Tye would slowly reach down and wrap his warm lips around it. I wanted to hear Cole's moans, and Tye's little grunts of pleasure as his head is pushed down into Cole's dick. I was craving seeing Tye wrap his lips around that thing, and suck with all the power of his mouth, soaking Cole's cock in saliva and eventually grabbing it with those small hands that looked tiny on the massive piece of meat. As Tye would suck on Cole, my lover's face would be ripe in ecstasy. His arms resting on the sofa cushions as he enjoyed the hot blowjob. And Tye would be sucking that cock as if he was in love with it; constantly bringing Cole to the point of eruption, and each time slowing down, keeping it hard, and massaging the base with those small hands of his. In fact he could wrap both around Cole's dick and still have room to suck on the head with those plump, juicy lips.

"Ride his dick," I imagined myself saying, since I would've been watching from the other sofa, or sitting there next to my man, his strong hand gripping my shoulder each time his cock went up into Tye's smooth throat. And as soon as I gave the command, Tye stood up and pulled that gray wife beater over his head to expose a lean torso with defined abs and a little bit of chest muscle. This kid was definitely a twink. Probably a 27-waist, and x-small everything. That was until he pulled his jeans down.

A long, thick, curved banana dick hung in front of Cole's face. Tye hadn't even bothered to wear briefs underneath his tight jeans. His big cock hung over the rough fabric of his pants, and thick, sweaty pubes emerged. I could tell he was totally into it, and I almost laughed out loud at the huge smile on his face as he turned to look at my crotch, and then back at Cole. He didn't even bother to pull his jeans fully down to his feet before he turned around and eased his ass down onto Cole's thick cock. I watched from my seat as Cole licked the sweat off of Tye's lean neck and back, just as Tye spit in one hand and then wrapped it around the dick he was about to sit on. I looked on intensely, reaching into my own pants to play with my own stiffening cock, as Cole's face warped into one of complete, uninhibited pleasure. Tye was dipping his tight little ass down onto Cole's dick, moaning as the thick cock dug deeper and deeper into his spit-soaked hole, rubbing his prostate and filling him with an ecstatic sense of pleasure.

Meanwhile my own cock was out, and I could tell that Tye wanted it. He kept looking at it, then up into my eyes, as he rode Cole's dick. He was begging for it; yearning to suck it with those perfect, wet lips. And so I came over to him, getting in front of Tye with my hard cock stretched out in front of his face. I watched his smooth ass bounce up and down on Cole's cock. My man's thick balls rested on the sofa, their sweaty residue leaving little stains on the fabric.

Tye leaned his head forward to suck my cock but I pulled back just in time. I wanted him to work for it; to beg for it. He looked up at me with huge, boyish eyes, as if to ask through his expression why I wasn't giving him what he wanted. Once again I leaned forward, holding the base of my pre-cumming dick with one hand as I stuck it in Tye's face. It touched his lips, and he immediately stuck his tongue out, licking the pre-cum off the head in long, sexy strides. And before he could wrap his lips around it I pulled back again.

Suddenly he reached out and grabbed my balls, which hung freely underneath my erect cock. I slightly winced as I felt his warm hand grab hold of them. As I looked down, I saw that Cole was fucking him harder; his hands cupped around the boy's ass as he repeatedly drove his huge cock into him. And before I had time to react, Tye gently pulled on my balls, forcing me forward so that my dick was once again in his face. He absorbed the whole thing into his mouth, practically

146

leaping for it; tasting the pre-cum that had spread along the head of my cock.

"Hunter!" Cole hollered from the living room. "You okay in there?"

"All good," I replied, shaking myself out of my daydream. I looked at the three glasses on the counter. Full. I didn't even remember making those drinks. It was like reading a book and daydreaming at the same time, and finding yourself ten pages in without any recollection of what you'd just read. I quickly sipped from one of the glasses in order to make sure that I hadn't botched the drinks. Good enough.

"Somebody's excited," Cole remarked as I walked back into the living room with glasses in hand. I followed his and Tye's eyes to my shorts, and when I glanced down I saw exactly what they meant. A huge bulge, shoving out of my red gym shorts. They weren't the best choice of clothing for hiding an erection. As I began to blush, Cole stood up and took the glasses out of my hands.

"Have any ideas about how we can get started?" he asked, and glanced down at Tye, who had made himself comfortable on the sofa.

"I have some ideas[2]," I replied with a wide grin.

*   *

"I have a great feeling about this video," Cole said to me, late on a Thursday night. It was just a few days after our on-camera sex with Tye, and my partner had spent nearly every waking moment creating two videos. One would be the full-length version that we'd sell online, and another would be a freebie to incite interest in the full-length. Neither Cole nor I had any background in video editing, but our one-on-one videos had given us enough of an education to become familiar with the software. We just hoped it would come out clean, and seem like a fun time. I'd never seen Cole more determined in all the time I'd known him. He really had high expectations for this video.

"The sex looks good?" I asked. I was by the window and he was at the computer desk. It'd been a long day of work, and since Cole was

---

2

http://olbmedia.site.metrixstream.com/site/MaverickMen/?page=videos&contentId=41

wrapped up in video editing and I was ripe in the middle of some nocturnal horniness, I'd taken the binoculars and set up in a position to spy on our fraternity neighbors. Thursday nights usually meant some kind of party. Hell, almost every night was a party. But for some reason, Thursdays were special. It might've been because it was so close to the weekend, and no one likes to edge more than a college boy.

"The sex looks mind-blowing. You were *on* three nights ago," Cole enthusiastically replied. "I was a little worried beforehand."

"Really?"

"Well yeah, he was an old hookup of mine. You'd never met the kid before, and he wasn't exactly your type."

"I still had fun."

"No shit," Cole said. "*Fun* is an understatement. Once this video hits the web I think we're gonna blow up. I've been thinking about that every day."

"Me too. I really hope so," I replied as I watched the frat house through the pair of binoculars. "I feel so creepy doing this."

"Doing what?"

"Spying on the frat house."

"Anything good over there?" Cole's head poked up from behind the computer.

"They're having some party. The crazy blonde one is out on the lawn, running around. Fucking non-stop energy. I would love to take just a quarter of his energy and bring it to work with me."

"Hopefully you won't have to worry about the restaurant much longer," Cole said. He smiled just before pulling his attention back to the video. He really wanted me to quit my job, and the whole plan hinged on the Tye video. If it worked, then we wanted to explore this new opportunity full-time. We both needed a break. *I* needed a break. I just wanted to have evenings again! Actual Friday and Saturday evenings, where Cole and I could go out to dinner like regular couples. When we wouldn't have to wait to make plans until midnight because that's when I'd be getting home from work.

"He just took his pants off."

"Who? The crazy one? Frat Boy?" Cole's head popped up again from the computer monitor. There was nothing like that frat house as a way to get his attention. "Can you see anything?"

148

"Boxer shorts, that's it. He is fucking cute! What a nice little man-boy body."

"It's a little cold out for that, isn't it? To be running around in boxers?"

"Tell him," I replied, focusing the binoculars to see if I could get a better view. "He's a cute guy. Too bad he's obviously fucking crazy."

"Fucking nuts. I love Frat Boy," Cole said, referring to the name we'd given the craziest of all the frat house regulars. "Let me take a look."

Cole leaped out from around the desk and hurried over to the window. I handed him off the binoculars and he quickly placed them up to his eyes. Outside the frat house some guys and girls had filtered onto the porch, with plastic cups in one hand and cigarettes in the other. In some cases, a plastic cup *and* a cigarette in one hand, and a cell phone in the other. And as new people showed up to the house in increments of about two or three every 15 minutes, a crazy, blonde frat boy in boxer shorts ran around the front yard like a puppy on the loose.

This guy was a regular, of course. A live-in, who complemented the fraternity the same way John Belushi did in Animal House. He was the unofficial mayor of his clan. It was all in the way he greeted people, the way each action and expression was so pronounced and jovial. Even the way he slammed down those beers on the front lawn. I had no idea what this kid was like sober, but as a drunk he brought the entire property to life. In fact, he made me want to be back in college.

"Oh—there he goes. Back in the house," Cole said with a hint of disappointment.

"He'll be back," I replied as I surveyed the front lawn of the frat house, and wondered how they got away with so much noise without police interference. I guess the police were used to it. And as long as they kept it contained and didn't piss any of the neighbors off, they were allowed to party. "Look! There you go."

"Where?"

"At the door."

Cole yanked the binoculars to the left and leaned forward against the window, peering down upon the porch where Frat Boy had re-emerged from the house.

"Oh my God."

"What?" I asked, and my eyes darted from my indistinct view of the frat house porch to my partner, whose eyes had widened behind the pair of binoculars.

"He's looking at us!"

"What do you mean? He could be looking at anything. We're one apartment in a building across the street from—."

"No—no, look!" Cole nearly shoved the binoculars into my face, and I had to step back so that I didn't topple over. I carefully lifted the device up to my eyes and then aimed it for the porch. Finally I saw what had startled Cole. Frat Boy was standing at the edge of the porch with a pair of his own binoculars, looking directly up at us.

"We've been discovered." We both hit the wooden floor of our bedroom like idiots, dropping to our knees with anxious looks on our faces. After waiting a few seconds and exchanging confused glances, we very slowly stood back up, poking our heads above the windowsill to see if he was still looking up at us. And there he was, his binoculars still aimed directly on our window.

"Why don't you flash your dick for him," Cole suggested amidst his own laughter.

"He's probably straight."

"Has that ever stopped you before?"

I turned to my lover and grinned. He had that look in his eyes that told me he wanted to get into some trouble.

"Do we have any large paper or poster board?" he asked me. "Or a dry-erase board or something?"

"A dry-erase board? When have you ever seen a dry-erase board in our apartment?"

"I don't know! Maybe you had one from college or something—," Cole replied, dismissively throwing his hands in the air.

"We might have some poster board. Let me check the closet," I replied, remembering some old art supplies from my previous apartment that I hadn't touched in years. They were probably dusty, and I don't even know why I'd brought them to the new loft, but I admit I have a tough time throwing some things away.

As I searched through the closet where we stored boxes, cleaning supplies, and our vacuum, Cole tried to keep the frat boy's attention by waving at him. He even made some lewd gestures. At one point when I stuck my head out of the closet—poster board in hand—Cole had his bare ass up against the window, shaking his thighs as if he was in a George Michael music video.

"You're gonna freak that kid out," I said as I rushed to the desk to grab a black marker, before joining Cole back at the window.

"He's having a good time. Look at him down there! Laughing his drunken ass off. You found some paper?"

"Right here."

Cole handed off the binoculars to me once again, and hastily bent down to start writing on one of the blank posters. I put the binoculars up to my eyes once again and looked down at the frat house, where our buddy was still looking up at us. I saw him laughing, and pointing us out to some of his friends, who were either too drunk to care or had no idea what he was obsessing over.

"Here, here," Cole excitedly said, getting up from the floor where he had been scribbling on the board. Just before he held the poster up to the window I read the brief message, written in a thick, bold font that seemed surprisingly neat given how quickly he wrote the letters and numbers. The poster contained Cole's phone number in huge font, and underneath were the words, *hey crazy, what's up?*"

I watched through the binoculars as Frat Boy seemingly read the message. After a few seconds, he pulled the binoculars away from his eyes, and his whole face beamed in excitement. I saw him reach down to his side and pat around until he remembered he'd taken his pants off somewhere in the yard. His eyes widened and shot around the porch and front yard. He looked like a guard dog who had just heard an explosion at close range.

Cole and I waited as the kid hurried around the property, searching for his pants, before finally discovering them laying along the path that led up to the front door. He reached in the pocket and pulled something out, and then placed the binoculars back in front of his eyes.

After a short wait, Cole's phone started to ring. He and I looked at each other with those same boyish looks of excitement. Those same wild eyes, curious to know how far this phone call would lead. Would we get invited over to the frat house? Would this be our ticket into becoming a couple of regulars at one of the hottest residences in Boston? Just the thought of it was putting a lump in my boxers.

"Hey," Cole warmly said after rushing to his desk to grab his cell phone. "Are you that crazy ass with all the energy? Yeah? No, we're a

151

little—what did you say? No, we're *older* than you guys. Only by a few years. Gray hair? I dye it gray. It's actually called *salt and pepper*, you asshole. If I don't dye it I look exactly like David Hasselhoff. Then I get bothered to sign autographs and all that shit—yeah, can't even leave my house without ending up in Tiger Beat. What's Tiger Beat? Ah, never mind," he said with a laugh.

"You want to meet us?" Cole shockingly replied, and then shot me a look of excitement. "We're great party crashers, you know—we can come meet your frat brothers, have some drinks—. Was I in a fraternity? No I wasn't. What an *asshole*, of course fraternities existed when I was in school. Dick head. Okay, okay, you want to come over and have a drink here? We can all spy on your own party from here. Great!"

Cole was beaming, and he waved his fist at me as if to say *victory*, before slowly pronouncing our apartment number and quick directions into the building.

"He's not even bothering to put his pants back on," I remarked, still watching from the window with the pair of binoculars. "What do you think that's all about?"

"Okay—see you soon. Call if you get lost in the hallway." Cole hung up the phone and set it back down on the glass computer desk. "I think we're in for a fun time."

Cole hurried to the ladder leading down to the first floor, and I was close behind, binoculars still in hand. The frat house was literally right across the street, so unless this kid couldn't navigate basic instructions, he was going to arrive any second.

"What do we do when he shows up?" I anxiously asked. "Too bad we can't tape this whole thing."

"Frat boys gone wild?"

"*Cole and Hunter Fuck a Frat House?*" I replied.

"I like it."

No sooner were we downstairs when three loud knocks signaled the frat boy's arrival. He must have sprinted to the apartment! This kid's energy was out of control, and I loved every second of it. As long as he didn't barf all over the apartment, I was totally ready for more of that frat boy energy.

Cole got to the door first. When he opened the front door, the kid nearly stumbled into our apartment. What a cute guy. He had that beefy, college boy build, with short blonde hair and blue eyes. His chest hair was almost as thick and full as mine. He wandered into our apartment as if he'd just discovered the Holy Grail. *So this was the mysterious place he'd seen with the binoculars.*

"You guys look just like you did through the binoculars," he remarked, although it wasn't clear which of us he was looking at. His eyes floated around the room, back and forth between Cole and I. The binoculars were still in his right hand, and his cell phone in the other.

"You look totally different," Cole replied, feigning disappointment. "I thought I was talking to a black girl with big titties. What a disappointment. You can leave now."

Frat Boy's face froze up for a few seconds as he waited for some sign from Cole, and then they both burst into laughter.

"You've been all over the place tonight," Cole said. "Why don't you chill out on the sofa or something. Come on in."

"You want to go back to the party?"

"In a little bit," I replied. Cole led the kid to the chocolate brown sofa. As soon as his body sunk into the sofa's soft fabrics, I could tell that exhaustion was finally catching up with him. I sat on one side and Cole sat on the other, and I waited for Cole to make a move.

"So what's your deal, Frat Boy?" Cole asked him once we were all comfortable on the sofa. "I'm Cole, and this is Hunter."

"This is a kick-ass place you guys live in," Frat Boy absently replied as his eyes wandered around the loft. "What do you guys pay in rent?"

Cole laughed and shook his head. This kid was clearly in a daze. "We're Cole and Hunter," he repeated himself. "What's your name?"

"Oh, sorry, my name's Bradley," he replied. "Nice to meet you," he added.

"So Bradley, here's the big question. Do you ever get with guys?" I almost died when the words left Cole's mouth. I couldn't believe that he came right out and said that.

"Whatever, it's all good," was Bradley's nuanced reply. "I do girls, but I prefer guys. No biggie." A huge smile spread across Cole's lips and he looked up at me with that familiar stare.

"Well that's great, glad you came over man," Cole said. And as I allowed myself to relax once again after Cole's blunt questioning, the two of them started to talk about the frat house and the neighborhood.

And for the next five minutes or so the conversation got really relaxed. Frat Boy got comfortable, and as I talked with him about what it was like to live in a frat house full of horny boys, Cole made his move.

And that move came in the form of a back rub. Cole carefully slipped one hand behind the exhausted frat boy's back and worked his magic, feeling the muscled body for any knots. When Cole hit the right spot, Frat Boy moaned in pleasure.

"That feels *so* good," he said.

"Why don't you get out the massage table?" I suggested to Cole. He gave a pretty intense massage, and actually had a table that he'd pull out from time to time when I was sore from work. Not that we'd ever stay on the table for very long, but such was our relationship.

"Perfect idea," he replied, and slowly leaned towards Frat Boy. Our lips met just behind the kid's head, though he didn't object to our affection.

Cole hurried off the couch to grab the massage table, and I leaned closer to the frat boy so that our bodies were touching. He turned to me and laughed nervously.

"So are you guys friends?"

"Hell yes, and we're lovers too."

"Oh—that's cool," he replied, and nodded his head in the affirmative. "Nice. You're both good-looking, and your place is kick ass," he said, repeating his earlier compliment.

"Thanks man, but I think we like your place better."

Cole didn't waste any time. He quickly returned with the massage table and set it up right in the living room, in-between the two sofas.

"Why don't you hop on here," he instructed our new friend. "Hunter, I'm going to get the *massage oil*."

Frat Boy was now in a state of exhaustion. He slowly got off of the sofa and eased his way onto the massage table, allowing his arms to fall at either side. I watched as a strange look fell upon his face, and suddenly he leaped up as if someone had poked him with a cattle prod.

"My frat brothers can't see into your place, right? Even from the top floors?" he asked in a paranoid sort of way.

"Nope," I comfortingly replied. "At least not into our living room. So just relax. Now how are we gonna massage you with boxers on?" I asked him. Without responding or even getting off of the massage table, he pulled them down around his knees. Since he could no longer reach them, I pulled the boxers completely off, revealing a thick, beefy ass with just the right amount of blonde peach fuzz. He had a perfect layer of hair covering his sweet, frat boy ass. My cock was rock hard at that point, and somehow I couldn't believe that we had our frat boy fantasy right there, butt naked on a massage table in our apartment. He laid still as I rubbed my fingers along his cheeks, massaging his ass muscles. Each stroke was hard and lasting, and it was great to hear his little groans of pleasure.

Cole was quick to return, and he brought more than just massage oil. He passed off a small bottle of lube and a couple condoms. Before I poured the lube into my hands I tossed Bradley's pair of boxers to Cole. He took a deep whiff of the musky smell of the boxer shorts and looked up at me with a great smile on his face. After tossing the boxers on the floor, Cole took over on the massaging end, digging his hands into Frat Boy's back and shoulders. I slowly began to rub the kid's sweet ass, slowly touching and rubbing his tight pink hole with my two fingers. It didn't take long for him to flip over, and that's when we got our first look at his cock. What a nice, thick piece of meat, fully erect. He was obviously ready for action, and I kept giving it to him, sliding my two fingers into his tight hole.

The way he responded with his groans and body language as my lubed fingers massaged along the inside of his hole was astounding, as if he'd never been touched that way before. His legs quivered and spread with feet dangling over the sides of the massage table. He was experiencing this awesome pleasure for the very first time. I decided to tease his penis, and so I slowly pulled my fingers away from his hole and slid them down along his crotch, massaging his erect cock. I rubbed just under the head and felt him get intensely hard. Cole was working the kid's neck and shoulders at a relaxing, stress-relieving pace.

Bradley was so excited that his dick reflexively bounced a little bit and relaxed on top of his balls, the head of his cock shiny with pre-cum. He looked up at me to see what I was going to do next. At this point I was already hard, with my pants pulled down and my dick out. As Frat Boy wrapped his hand around his own wet cock and started to play with it, Cole came around to the other end of the table. He took Frat Boy by the legs and dragged him to the edge of the table, and then pushed me between Frat Boy's legs. It was so hot and masculine to watch. I loved to

155

see Cole manhandle young guys. And once I was between Bradley's legs, Cole walked back to the other side of the table and smiled at me. I put my cock up against Frat Boy's hot little pink hole and waited.

At first I got this strange look from him, like he wasn't sure if he wanted me to enter him. I didn't know if he'd ever bottomed for anyone before. For all I knew, this could've been the first time another guy had ever touched him this erotically. But Cole went back to work, calming and soothing him with those big, masculine hands. He wrapped them around Frat Boy's scalp and dug his fingertips into all the right spots, allowing Bradley to relax and focus his eyes on the ceiling.

I decided I should go all out and take full advantage of this situation. Cole and I have always loved eating ass, and this kid had a real beauty. And so I pulled my cock away from his little hole and bent down so that I was eye level with his balls. As soon as I reached my tongue out and stuck it into his pink hole he moaned so loud that I almost burst into laughter. I guess he'd never been eaten out before, and so I went to town with it, working my tongue in and out of him as he writhed in pleasure.

Before I knew it, Cole was down at my side. He stuck his face into Frat Boy's crotch and began to share the kid's hole with me. We licked and sucked his furry little ass together, every few seconds turning our cheeks to kiss each other and share those amazing, masculine smells that were all over our mouths. I wanted Frat Boy's ass so badly, and I knew Cole could tell by the way I wouldn't let go of my own cock. As Cole stepped backwards, I stood up and climbed on top of Frat Boy, my knees resting on the massage table, hoisting up Bradley's thick legs. I heard the table creak and thought for a minute that it might collapse, but I didn't want to waste any time moving the fucking to somewhere else in the apartment. I wrapped one of the condoms around my hard cock and tossed the other packet on the floor. I wanted him right there and then.

Frat Boy moaned as soon as my cock started to enter him. I only got the head in, sliding into his tight, lubed hole as I held his knees up. With each little shove into him he grew louder and louder. At this point he was jerking his cock even harder, and holding onto Cole with his other hand. He was so tight that I could barely put my whole cock in, and so I started to fuck him in order to loosen him up. Frat Boy's entire body shook. Faster and faster his hand moved up and down his cock, and got louder with each of my thrusts. I let his legs wrap around my forearms.

They had a great weight to them—this masculine mixture of beef and muscle.

I could tell Frat Boy was close to cumming, and so I put all the power of my ass behind each thrust, fucking him as hard as I could. I looked up into Cole's eyes, who had forgotten about the scalp massage and was fixated on this hot scene in front of him.

"Yeah, Hunter, fuck that boy's ass," Cole told me, stroking his own thick cock as he watched us.

"Fuck me harder. Oh my God, dude," Frat Boy moaned. And just as Frat Boy's moans got loud enough to fill the entire apartment, this massive eruption of cum shot from his dick, flying overtop his chest and landing directly in his open mouth. Long ropes of hot cum kept jetting out over his chest and lips. His eyes were wide open in a shocked expression. I was amazed. I'd never seen anyone shoot like that far before. That was a direct cum shot from the cock to the mouth! It was an art form.

Just afterwards, Cole leaned down and gave Frat Boy a deep French kiss on his sticky, cum-soaked lips. Hadn't we agreed that there wasn't going to be any kissing? Even though it was hot to watch my lover kiss this beefy, sexy college boy, I didn't want to think that our rules were so fragile that they couldn't even survive our second threesome. Cole and I had some talking ahead of us.

"How was that?" Cole quietly asked Frat Boy as he lifted his lips just an inch above Bradley's. Frat Boy didn't skip a beat. He swallowed some of the cum that was in his mouth and flashed his eyes at us.

"I ain't complaining, am I?" he replied, and we all started laughing. And just as I looked back up at Cole, I realized that in my obsession and distraction with this hot, sweaty scene, I'd totally missed the small digital camera wrapped discreetly in Cole's free hand. I didn't know how much of this he'd caught, but clearly he'd gotten some of the sex on tape. He must've at least gotten that amazing cum shot.

"We've gotta do this again[3]," Cole told a sweaty Frat Boy, who was—after his long night of physical activity—finally panting in a relaxed state on the massage table. He nodded his head and slid his arm

---

[3]

http://olbmedia.site.metrixstream.com/site/MaverickMen/?page=videos&contentId=72

across his mouth, wiping the cum off of his lips and face. "And you've gotta teach us how to do that."

"No problem guys," Frat Boy said, and glanced up at Cole. I got a little nervous when he saw the digital camera, but to my surprise he didn't even flinch. Not everyone is into being filmed, but this kid didn't seem to mind. "You got my cum shot? Just keep that private. Don't show anyone, okay?"

"I promise," Cole assured him. Even more than my curiosity to go replay the footage was a burning desire to know if Frat Boy would want to do a video with us. This didn't seem like the best time to tell him that Cole and I were involved in online porn, but the night's events sure gave us a great segue into that conversation, and the request that he do a video with us. If we could do that same scene again and post it online, I knew for sure that our fans on XTube would go crazy. I had a great feeling about this kid.

*   *

Frat Boy quickly became a permanent part of our daily lives. No longer did we have to use binoculars to get a taste of the frat house across the street. Not only were we invited over—albeit the circumstances of our first time meeting Frat Boy were on the down low—but our new friend made frequent visits to hang out, hook up, and drink. He wasn't exactly closeted on-campus, but he didn't like everyone to know his business. He made it clear to us that no one even suspected his sexual inclinations, although it also seemed like he didn't give a shit if anyone were to find out. Still, the idea of filming a video with us worried him. Cole had asked him about fifty times already, and each time the kid gave the same answer. He was out of touch with gay culture, and was still terrified by the idea of doing porn. He was sweet enough though that he loved us, and didn't care that our cocks were all over the Internet. He didn't even mind when we'd pull the camera out while messing around with him. He knew we'd never post anything online unless he agreed to it.

It's funny how quickly our *rules of engagement* were amended. While we did go and get tested with Bradley right away so that we could have some uninhibited fun, our kissing rules became a lot more fluid. Even though we both felt that kissing is a very intimate thing that

158

shouldn't just be shared with anyone, we wanted to be able to kiss if the person and moment seemed right. And so we decided to pass judgment on a person-by-person basis. I didn't know how that was gonna work out. I didn't know how *any* of our rules were going to pan out in the long-term, but I had a solid feeling about our dedication to each other.

The morning after our amazing first night with Frat Boy, Cole uploaded our video with Tye. People were downloading it like crazy. All it took was that one video for me to see exactly what Cole's friend Paul had been talking about. Threesomes simply *worked*. Our fans loved the idea of us fucking a younger, smaller bottom. And not only that, but the video held to our ideals. It was fun, real, sexy, and seemed like three friends all having a good time and enjoying each other.

A little over two weeks after we posted the video, our next check was due to arrive. It was a combination of the first couple weeks of the Tye video, and some revenue from our one-on-one videos. Cole and I knew it was going to arrive, but after the last incident where the check came much later than expected, neither of us were ready to run to the building's mailroom.

That is, until a particular thing happened. It was a Friday afternoon, right in the middle of the lunch shift at my restaurant. Newbury Street was full of life, the sun was out, and Bostonians and tourists alike were enjoying the perfect Fall weather. Work was packed. Business people in suits, housewives gathering for some afternoon French cuisine, and plenty of out-of-towners who had just arrived for the weekend.

And as I walked towards the maître d', who was standing at an oak desk just in front of the entrance, a young couple opened the door to the restaurant. A cool breeze blew across my face. I could suddenly smell the city; hear the sounds of Newbury Street; taste the farmer's market just down the street in Copley Square. What a tease! Especially while I was stuck at work until eleven or midnight, only to get out when the crowds had left, the sun had long since gone down, and when that midday sense of leisure seemed once again unobtainable.

"Everything okay?" our maître d' asked me. She was a sweet girl—young—and only worked the lunch shift. In the evenings we had a French guy who had been working there since I was in diapers.

"I've gotta go," I replied. I don't know how the words came out. I was thinking it to myself, but for some reason I just blurted it out. And without looking back I passed by the couple who had just walked into the restaurant, and ran out onto Newbury Street. I grabbed the first cab I saw.

"The Cigar Factory," I said with such urgency that you'd think someone had been chasing me. The driver took off.

*　　*

I wanted to sprint from the taxi to the mailroom but I decided to just walk at a fast pace, only so that if I passed any neighbors they'd—at most—think I was just in a rush to get inside and use the bathroom or something. With all of our in-house video filming, loud sex, and stream of young hotties into the apartment, I couldn't afford to be raising any more local eyebrows.

But I quickly lost my focus on neighbors and gossip, as my mind went back to the mailroom and our box. In that box was potentially the key to my freedom; to enjoying those Fall days without being stuck in an office. This is what I'd been waiting for since I graduated college and wondered what the fuck I was going to do with the rest of my life. And I guess what changed over time is that I realized it didn't matter—at least for me—what path I went down. I knew that I was a hard worker, a good employee, responsible, and that I'd do well in whatever industry I got myself into. And so it didn't have as much to do with the industry. Maybe when I was in college I thought more about profession and titles, but as I evolved it became about love. It became about building a relationship; being in love, being happy.

My relationship with Cole was more fulfilling than any job or glossy title. I still enjoyed my job and earned my salary three-fold in hard work and motivation, but it was more a means to supporting the lifestyle that I wanted to have with my lover. And on our journey to finding jobs that would give us what we wanted most—time together, to enjoy in the beautiful, nascent years of our relationship rather than waiting until retirement age—we'd stumbled upon this fucking crazy idea. Online porn. Never in my life would I have ever done something like that. But it actually scared me to think of all the things I'd do for Cole; for more freedom to be with him.

Neither of us knew how long the porn thing would last, but in the meantime it seemed to be opening up all the right doors. The ability to travel without having to take leave time at a job, and wake up next to each other without the rush of throwing on work clothes and disappearing for ten-to-twelve hour shifts. Most people get what—two or three weeks vacation time per year? I was no longer ready or willing to tolerate that.

As soon as I passed through the opening to the mailroom I saw Cole standing by our mailbox, his entire face lit up. I loved when he looked like that. He just radiated this amazingly deep smile that immediately warmed my soul. I knew something great had happened the second I looked into his green eyes. I stood there in the doorway waiting for him to say something; my hands surrendered at my sides, and a chill running down my arms.

"Ready to tell Kelly she needs a new manager?" Cole said softly. He extended his hand, allowing a thin piece of paper clenched in-between his thumb and index finger to flop downwards.

"Oh my God," I said as I looked at the check.

"More than double the last one. We did it."

"We have evenings now—and Saturday afternoons—and—."

Before I could finish, Cole leaned in and kissed me with all the passion that had first drawn me to him. This wasn't the start of our lives together, but it was the start of a new, liberating chapter. I'd never been so happy in my entire life.

CHAPTER TWELVE

narrated by Cole Maverick

If there's anything Paul had drilled into my head since Hunter and I had started doing the videos—aside from an overzealous use of the word *twink*—was that we should keep in touch with the fans. And I made it my job to do that. Both of us loved interacting with anyone who appreciated our videos. In fact, it gave me the biggest buzz whenever someone would write to us in order to show their love for what we'd created. What a great feeling it was to have fans, especially when they were just horny guys like us who wanted to watch good porn.

But interacting with fans was only part of the huge amount of time I'd been spending online since we both quit our full-time jobs to focus on making videos. Finding new guys for threesomes was a huge undertaking in its own right. Sure, we had people writing to us left and right saying they wanted to be in a video, but for most of them that was just fantasy. Others, who had actually done porn, seemed totally money-motivated, and much more into the discussion of contracts and royalties and editing rights. They didn't seem to care whether the sex was fun or not. The guys Hunter and I sought were of a different breed: laid-back, cool guys who wanted to be our friends just as much as they wanted to have sex with us on-camera.

We hit the jackpot with one guy in particular. *Christo*. German dad, Persian mom, and raised in Berlin; Christo was a stunning mixture of exotic features, with a body to die for. He was an international dancer, who mainly worked out of Europe but did a lot of world tours, mostly for famous pop singers. Christo found our videos on XTube, but we connected on Myspace.com, where his profile was filled with beautiful pictures of himself. He had quite the fan following of men, and every day he seemed to get at least five to ten new compliments on just how goddamn pretty he was.

Christo wanted to do a video with us, but there was a considerable distance in-between Boston and Berlin. This guy was smoking hot enough that I would've flown to Germany just for a hot threesome, regardless of whether or not there was a video. But as it turned out, he was going to be dancing at a huge concert in Miami on

New Year's Eve. Hunter and I dived at the chance to meet him and do a video. In the meantime, we were glad to have a sexy European pen pal.

"Christo! What's up man?" I jovially said. In addition to browsing our fan mail and checking up on what other peoples' videos were currently popular, I spent a lot of time on Skype, which was a computer-to-computer chat software. It was a pretty brilliant system. Christo and I could talk for free using Skype, no matter where in the world each of us were.

"Just returned from the gym." His voice came out pretty clear over my computer's speakers. I was never a big fan of the German accent until I met Christo. I always used to associate it with villains in Indiana Jones movies. But Christo had this eloquent, soft-spoken accent that actually intensified his overall sexiness.

"Nice and sweaty?"

"Hot and sweaty, yes," he replied with a little laugh.

"Hey, when are you gonna get on cam for me?"

"On webcam? I need to purchase one!" Christo replied with a sense of urgency. "We dancers make only modest salary."

"You just wait. We'll set you up with the video you do with us. XTube won't know what hit 'em. What a perfect way to bring in the new year."

"Right? I'm so excited for New Year's Eve."

"How long are you gonna be there for, again?" I asked him. I knew we'd be flying down on New Year's Eve to see him in concert and then film the video later that night.

"Just three days. But it will be very special. You can follow my North American tour," he coyly added.

"Hunter and I would follow you to Afghanistan if it meant getting to touch that sweet ass," I said, and Christo replied with that little laugh of his. So adorable.

"So how are things on XTube?"

"Going great, although I noticed some backlash," I replied, followed by a long sigh. "I've gotten some hate mail—well, not really *hate* mail—but angry letters about charging for videos. I guess people think that because we did a video with that kid Tye, and are charging for everything now, that we're turning into a studio."

"How silly."

"That's what I said! What can you do though? A bunch of our fans just wanted the free stuff. I mean we still post those free teasers, and they're long enough to wack off to."

"This is your life now," Christo added. "Your income."

"Exactly! Hey, going to turn the volume up," I said, and put the volume on max just before getting out of my seat at the computer table.

"Bathroom break?"

"Nah—just being nosy," I replied, raising my voice so that Christo could still hear me as I walked across the bedroom to the huge window in the corner. The binoculars were perched on top of my favorite leather chair, and I picked them up and focused on my favorite piece of neighborhood real estate.

"Ah, the frat house?" Christo asked. His voice sounded choppy with the volume maxed out, but I still heard that sweet accent.

"Looks like just a regular—oh shit—."

"What?"

As I focused in on one of the second-story windows, I saw none other than our frat boy Bradley, buck naked, standing up against the glass. His beefy ass was pressed against the window. They looked like two big balls of gelatin.

"What's he doing?" I asked myself, sparking a curious remark from Christo. "Oh—*oh*."

As soon as Frat Boy turned away from the window I saw what was going down. When he moved to the side, pulling his cheeks away from the glass, I saw a sexy, younger-looking college boy with wavy brown hair bent down at our friend's crotch, his mouth working that cock in fast-paced motion.

"Hey Christo? I'll be right back."

"Are you okay?"

"Better than okay!" I replied, and tossed the binoculars on my leather chair.

*   *

An odd smell caught my nose as I passed from the sidewalk onto the stone path that led up to the frat house. It was a complicated mixture of colognes, beer, freshly-cut grass, and crotch. I guess when you have enough frat boys passing out in the lawn, that's what you get.

I passed over a condom just before stepping onto the wooden porch that ran the full width of the house, and turned the corner to form a massive L-shape. Sleeping on the hammock were two college kids, a boy and a girl. The guy looked big enough to be a linebacker, and the girl was tiny enough to fit in his pocket. I actually paused for a second, worrying about what would happen if this dude flipped over on top of her.

Just as I clenched my fist and was about to knock on the front door, it opened to reveal a skinny teenager wearing a football jersey about three sizes too large for him. This kid had big, curly brown hair, and bushy eyebrows. Totally adorable, and thin enough to pull off that whole twink thing in our videos. Unfortunately he also looked stoned out of his fucking mind.

"Uh—," he stared at me, and mumbled something with his little pink lips. This kid had the very definition of *crazy eyes*.

"Was gonna say hi to a friend of mine upstairs."

"Man, are you a professor or something?" he asked, his voice choppy.

"Do I look professorial to you?"

"You look old."

"Let me ask you a question," I said, speaking as clearly and eloquently as possible. "How old would you be if you didn't know your age?" The look of confusion on his stoned face was priceless. The kid stared at me for a good minute, until I think he forgot what he was looking for.

"Hey, I like that," he finally muttered. Then, after blinking those crazy eyes a few times, he left the door open and turned around to walk back into the living room. Seizing my chance, I hurried into the frat house, and gently closed the front door. The stairs were on my left, and I knew exactly which room belonged to Bradley.

I hurried up those stairs with a mission, and as soon as I got to the second floor I stepped over a girl who had passed out on the carpet, and I tip-toed down the hallway until I got to my friend's door. His bedroom door was the epitome of all college dormitory/frat house doors. A huge dry erase board took up most of the available space, and almost every inch was covered in little messages. Hunter and I had left one on there before, but it seemed to have gotten erased and replaced with some chick's number.

I didn't hear any noise inside the room, and so I knocked twice. Almost instantly the door opened to reveal that same guy I'd seen through my binoculars, although this time he wasn't on his knees with a dick in his mouth. This kid had a huge smile on his face, and I saw him wink at Frat Boy once before walking past me. The two of us made eye contact as he walked down the hallway, strutting that tight little college bubble ass, compressed in gray sweatpants.

"Unbelievable," I remarked as I strolled into the room. Frat Boy was laying on the thin, white bed, his arms folded behind his head. He'd thrown on a pair of boxers since his hook-up, but that was it. I wasn't exactly used to seeing this kid in clothing.

"Too bad you showed up late," he replied with a cocky expression on his face. "Already gave my goodies to that kid."

"Your goodies? What the fuck are your goodies?" I asked him, completely puzzled. I sat down on his bed and placed a hand over his bare chest, affectionately rubbing my fingers over his abs. He chuckled and looked down at his crotch, then motioned with his chin.

"You know, my knuckle children. My baby batter. My super spunk. The boys are all drained."

"*Baby batter*, you're ridiculous," I told him. "So how often do you hook up with guys around here, you lucky little fuck? I thought you were trying to keep a low profile on campus?"

"Did you see us in the window?" he asked me, playfully avoiding the questions.

"Did I see you in the window? Of course I saw you. Here I am on neighborhood watch, trying to make sure that our block is safe from criminals and bandits, and I see some beefy, blonde prick getting a blowjob in the window of a frat house."

"On neighborhood watch at—dude, it's like 11:00 AM."

"Of course there's neighborhood watch at 11:00 AM," I exclaimed, waving my arms for dramatic effect. "How do you think Boston stays safe in the daytime?"

"And you call *me* crazy," he replied. "I'm *kinda* closeted, but there are rumors, and to be honest with you, I don't give a fuck who knows now. I get approached by enough closeted guys that it works, and none of us get caught in the act. So fuck the haters. I'll do what I want."

"As they say, *haters gonna hate*," I joked with him, and a big smile appeared on Bradley's face. "I guess you won't get caught messing around like this. That is, until one of 'em moves into my apartment building and gets binoculars," I bluntly told him. "Hot kid though. Nineteen?"

"Just turned nineteen. Gave him a birthday present."

"So proud of you," I said as I tickled around his belly button. Frat Boy squirmed, and lifted his knees to shield himself from me. "When are you gonna do a video with us? Or at least let us post that insanely hot video from the night we met?"

"Are you nuts?"

"A little. What if you did a Zorro thing?"

"You want me to wear a fidora?" he asked, completely puzzled.

"No, you crazy ass, I want you to wear a mask. I mean it's not nearly as good as seeing that sexy face of yours, but it's something. We have fun sex already, so why not do this?"

"Can I wear a Michael Myers mask?"

"No dick head—I don't think our fans would get it," I said. "You wanna get fucked wearing a Michael Myers mask? You might fulfill some of my childhood fantasies, but I doubt anyone will download it. Come on, everyone would love to see us fucking a fraternity brother."

"I don't know—."

"Everyone who has walked by this house anytime past ten at night has seen your dick."

"Yeah but there's a difference between seeing my dick and seeing me get fucked by two guys," he replied. "What—are you and Hunter hurting for another video?"

"We have plenty of offers, but it's tough meeting the right kind of guys for these," I said, and relaxed my posture so that my lower back rested on his side. "There are like fifty studio actors asking to do a video, and some fans who've written in, but it's tough finding the right vibe. I want these guys to be buddies—not just actors. It looks a lot better in the video, when we're having fun and fucking around. You know—we need a guy who at the end of shooting won't throw his pants on and say *I gotta go, where's my money?*."

"You're right. I'd at least ask you for a drink first. Then my money."

"Wise ass," I said after some laughter. "We'd make an amazing video."

"You really care about quality, huh?"

"I do," I firmly replied. "And it's a *struggle* trying to keep the same quality. Sometimes I feel like I'm up to my eyeballs in an industry where most filmmakers don't give a damn what they're releasing. You know how hard it is to find human connection in porn? I think Hunter and I are onto something with this."

"Well buddy, I hope you get your next guy," he told me, and patted me on the back just as he leaned forward to sit up. "I've gotta get to class soon and I smell like cum and B.O."

"You're gonna ruin that great scent?" I asked him, but he shook his head as if there was no way I was winning this battle.

"I'll give you a call later. Any plans tonight?"

"Just enjoying vacation mode," I replied. No restaurant, no house showings; Hunter and I get to enjoy our evenings now. First time in— forever."

"Cool, maybe we can get together."

"Hey, go easy on that B.O., you smell good," I said as I stood up from the bed to leave the frat house. "And think about everything I've said. Hey, and don't be a selfish little fuck. The next time you get that hot boy over, *call us* so we can all get in on that."

*   *

It wasn't until I stepped off the front porch of the frat house that I checked my cell phone to see the seven missed calls and numerous text messages, all from the same person. Tye had been blowing up my cell phone, which I'd set on silent earlier in the day so as not to be disrupted while replying to fan mail. That was the worst: getting in a nice groove with e-mails and having it be interrupted by phone calls.

Even though I didn't know Tye *that* well, he'd never called me more than once at a time, and I couldn't tell if his message was going to be good or bad news. So within seconds of seeing all the missed calls, I dialed his phone number and let my curiosity go wild.

"Where have you been?" he impatiently greeted me. He sounded troubled, and it was clear that this wasn't going to be a happy phone call.

"Was with a friend. What's going on? Are you okay?"

"Someone I know saw the video and told my friends—spread it around."

"That's great news!" I replied. I too was excited at the rock star status we'd been receiving after releasing our video with Tye. He'd been transformed into somewhat of a gay porn sensation in what seemed like a week's time. We'd even received some e-mails from legitimate porn studios asking for his contact info.

"No, it's horrible news! I didn't think it would be this big," Tye angrily replied. His voice was ringing with frustration. "It's fucking up my reputation. I need you to fix this."

"How is it fucking up your reputation? So what, you had sex. Everyone has sex."

"Yeah, but you're selling that shit on a major porn website."

"And now you're famous for having sex," I jokingly replied, hoping it would ease his anxiety. But Tye wasn't in the mood to laugh.

"I don't wanna be. I'm the laughing stock of my friends now."

"Your *real* friends?"

"Not my real friends—like, people I see out," he answered, and I saw where this going.

"Don't sweat that," I told him in the warmest voice I could muster. "You're better than that. Me and Hunter had our own share of shit when people started to find out about us doing porn, but the people who love you are still gonna be there."

"Yeah? How am I gonna meet guys if I have this reputation in Boston. People are gonna think I'm some big slut—getting fucked by two guys online."

"Honestly, I think it's hot as fuck, and if I was single and had seen a video of you getting tag teamed by two alpha males, I'd be knocking on your door every single day."

He let out a long sigh, and I waited patiently for him to respond. It seemed like he just needed to be reassured that he was loved, and still desirable even after doing that video. But I still didn't envy what he was going through, and while I waited for him to speak my mind floated back to that awful dinner with Ron and Tony Marinelli. I knew just how he felt. Lower than life—as if one little decision to have sex on-camera had somehow made us less than human in the eyes of certain people.

"Really?" he asked after much hesitation.

"Really," I said, wasting no time in my response. "You're beautiful. And warm, and sweet—and any guy would be lucky to have you. Anyone who doesn't want to be your friend because you were in a porn movie doesn't deserve to be your friend."

"Yeah, but that's easy to say. The reality is different—when you call a friend and they aren't picking up, or see them out and they won't talk to you. Or worse—when they talk to you *differently*. It's hard to deal with that."

"I'm walking the same path as you," I reassured him. "I've had setbacks because of the videos. I know what it feels like. It sucks. Plain and simple. But it gets better."

"Does it really? I mean, we're in different places," Tye said, his voice still melancholy. "You guys are doing this full-time. I don't wanna be some porn star or anything. This might be the only video I ever do. So aside from some money, what do I get? I don't get this same thrill that you guys have. You go on to make more videos, and make this your life, while I go *back* to my life as some regular guy with a sex tape."

Tye's words hit me somewhere that I didn't expect. The studio routine would be to coax the kid into filming a video, and then tell him to get lost afterwards. And if he wanted to take it down, shove that signed contract in his face. But I was no monster. I was struggling with a side of me that hoped he wouldn't ask me to pull the plug on the video, since it was part of my household's primary source of income. I'd prepared him for the shoot and all, but we were still amateurs, and this was our first video. Hunter and I didn't know anything about contracts and disclaimers and all the things you're supposed to tell a guy who wants to have on-camera sex with you. The video was hot and exciting, but the post-production crap that followed was enough to make me re-think whether or not porn was a good career choice. I didn't know how long it would take for us to get this right, and I couldn't imagine becoming a hotline for 10-15 troubled young guys who suddenly regretted shooting porn. And that's the thing, I guess, is that there was no way I could tell them *no*. I was emotionally linked to these guys.

"If you think it's hurting you, and you want to take it down, we can talk about that," I hesitantly offered, but hoped he'd decline. "I know Hunter and I are in it for the long run, and you probably have no interest in doing these films anymore. I don't know what to tell you, other than that you've created something beautiful that thousands of people are enjoying. And if anything, all of the shit that's happening to your social life might be an indication that you're in a deeper, more open-minded place than the people you've chosen to surround yourself with. Maybe you just need to meet some new people who will really love you, and ditch some of the old ones who don't."

I held my breath, and waited again as Tye quieted down. I couldn't tell if he believed me or just thought I was full of shit, but it was the best advice I could give him.

"You're amazing," he finally told me, his little southern accent peaking out in-between soft-spoken words. "You have this great way of calming me down."

"I hope so. You still okay with the video? I'm here for you whenever you need me, Tye."

"I know. Yeah I'm cool with it. Let's see how things go."

"Alright babe, well I'm back at my apartment. Call me again soon and let me know what's happening," I said just as I got to the front door. I twisted the handle to see if it was open, and indeed it was. Hunter must've gotten back from his jog.

"Thank you," he said, and let the words hang out there for a couple seconds before I heard that familiar click of the cell phone. As I opened the door to the apartment a smile crossed my face. Something about helping these boys in need was really fulfilling, and I just hoped that he was over-analyzing his problems. If it was just gossip, it could very well be fleeting. Tye's call was also a signal that Hunter and I desperately needed to do another video. If Tye had asked to pull the video, then I conscientiously would have had to comply, which means my income would be suddenly and seriously hindered. If Hunter and I were truly going to make these videos our full-time job, then we urgently needed to find another hot third. It seemed like the money fears weren't quite over.

*   *

"What happened to your video?" That familiar German-accented voice greeted me with an unusually anxious tone only seconds after I'd logged onto Skype. Christo had dialed me immediately upon sign-in. I turned the volume down on the computer so as not to wake Hunter, who was fast asleep in our bed. The two of us had taken a post-dinner nap, but I'd awoken in a nervous mood after reflecting on the phone call with Tye, and our desperate need to film a new video.

172

"What do you mean?" I asked him, speaking into the computer. I was half-awake; my hair still messy from the pillows, and my eyes stuck in a droopy daze. I pulled up my regular Internet windows: XTube.com, e-mail, the news. They sprung to life in all the glory of high-speed Internet, although XTube was the first on my list.

"I just came home from the clubs and went on the computer, and I see your video missing. I haven't gone to bed yet. I was hoping you'd sign on."

"Which video?"

"The one with uh—Tye?"

It took that one sentence to knock me out of my sleepiness. Suddenly my game face was on, my eyes wide, and I was racing to our account page to see what Christo was talking about.

"Is everything okay?" I heard Christo's words, but couldn't respond. He was right. Our video with Tye had been taken down, and was flagged for complete removal from the website. It was no longer showing, and no longer making any money. In a panic I raced to our e-mail account, only to find a generic response from XTube stating that we'd violated some terms and that our video was going to be pulled.

I couldn't believe it. Had we really violated their rules? I'd seen a whole bunch of crazy shit on that website. In fact, our movie was PG compared to some of the stuff on there. So what had we violated?

"No, it's not," I finally said. I could hear Christo's nervous breathing. "Look, I don't mean to worry you. Go to bed, it's super-late."

"I am. No worries, I have no plans tomorrow. More worried about you."

"I need to call XTube," I said, and scrolled down my inbox for an older message that might point me in the right direction. "When their CEO wrote us, he included some guy's name in the e-mail. A Site Administrator or something—someone to call if we ever needed help. I gotta find that e-mail."

"You'll call this late at night?"

"Let's hope he's on the West Coast. Alright Christo, I've gotta make a phone call. Go get some sleep. I'm on top of this."

"Okay. I hope so. Tell Hunter I said hi."

No sooner did Christo exit out of the Skype call than I was on my cell phone, dialing the digits listed under the name of the XTube Site Administrator. Luckily I'd saved the e-mail, and found it quickly amongst our other mail. It was close to midnight, but I figured that if this guy worked for the biggest online porn website, he probably was keeping late hours. I just hoped the phone call wouldn't piss him off enough to delete our account. XTube had become our income.

"Please be in LA, please be in LA," I said to myself as the phone rang. It was beginning to seem like an absolutely crazy idea, calling this guy so late at night. I could've waited until the next morning, but my livelihood was at stake, and I've been known to act on impulse.

"Hello?" a guy's voice answered. He sounded young—probably still in his twenties, or early thirties at the very latest. He also sounded prompt and awake, which was at least somewhat of a relief for me.

"Hey," I quickly said. "Listen—this is Cole Maverick from the XTube Amateurs—."

"I know who you are," he interrupted. "Why are you calling me at midnight?"

"So you're not in California, huh?"

Frank, the System Administrator, surprised me by bursting into a quick fit of laughter.

"No, I'm not in Cali. What's up?"

"Look, I'm sorry to bother you so late at night, but my partner and I have been putting our hearts into these videos, and the most recent one just got taken down. I got some e-mail that it was flagged for deletion, and—."

"A computer does all that," he nonchalantly replied. "Let me take a look. That was hot, by the way."

"You've seen it?"

"Of course I've seen it. You guys are the hottest thing in Amateurs right now," he said with the first bit of excitement since he'd picked up the phone. "Sometimes these things can get flagged for deletion if an XTube user contacts administration and makes a serious case against it. Like if someone in the video looks underage, or if there's excessive violence—you get the idea."

"Why would someone do that to us?"

"Finding out right now," he replied. I could hear him typing away at his computer. "I'm actually glad you called. Was kind of bored."

"Are you up working?"

"Yeah, are you kidding? Midnight is like lunchtime for me. I like the night shift. Not so much of a morning person." There was a short pause, and then I heard Frank let out a long sigh. "Did you guys sign a contract with the kid in your video?"

"No—we didn't. He's a friend of ours, though. I didn't think we needed a contract."

"Ouch. I'm sending something to your e-mail. Check it now. Are you online?"

"I am," I said, and quickly switched back to my e-mail account. I clicked on the new message from Frank, which contained a single website link. Nervously I pressed down on the mouse. Obviously this had to be something serious, otherwise he would've just shrugged off the flagging and put the video back online.

As soon as the new page loaded I froze in my seat. Frank had sent me an XTube profile of the guy who flagged our video. I looked at the pictures, the description, the likes and dislikes. He listed everything from his favorite movie to what he looks for in a sexual partner. Tye had flagged our video.

"Why would he do this?" I asked in shock.

"What drama. Well, the flagging citation basically reads that he never signed a contract with you guys, and wants the video pulled. He cites that you have no legal right to use his image. This is serious, Cole. We can't put this back up until we get written permission from him, otherwise we're liable to get sued."

I just sat there for a moment, staring at the screen; at the sweet pictures of Tye with that big smile on his face. I didn't even know he had an XTube account. My mind was racing. Why would he have called me earlier and not said anything? Had he changed his mind and didn't want to tell me? There was no telling when or if we'd get that video back online. Our income was suddenly cut short, and my friendship with Tye was seriously jeopardized.

"You there?" Frank asked in a worried tone.

"Yeah—yeah I'm here. Thank you for telling me all this. I don't know what got into him. I just talked to him earlier today and everything seemed okay."

"Sometimes these young guys don't know what they're doing," Frank replied. "They think making a sex tape will be fun and all. If Paris did it, then why not them, right? But when reality hits, and thousands of people are watching the video every day—," Frank grew silent for a few seconds, long enough that I wondered if the call had been dropped.

"Hey—give me a call if this kid is willing to send written permission, and I'll get the video back up in seconds. I just need the paperwork. You understand."

"I do. Thanks man. Thanks so much," I said, and we both hung up. I put the cell phone down on the desk, and immediately stood up from the chair. I didn't want to look at Tye's profile anymore; at that smile that deceived me all along. I didn't even want to call him to ask *why*. I could wait for that. I'd do it in the morning, after calming down.

I walked to the far corner of the bedroom, where my favorite brown leather chair sat against the huge window overlooking the neighborhood. My binoculars were rested on the leather cushion, and I put them in my lap as I eased into the seat. Hunter was still knocked out, and I wondered if he'd wake up before morning. He was still enjoying his post-restaurant life. Being able to take a nine o'clock nap was new in his world. I really didn't want him to suffer as a result of my pursuit of this new career. I just wanted someone to throw us a bone. I needed some kind of sign that everything would be okay. Something to ease what I knew would be nights upon nights of money worries, as Hunter and I would struggle to put together another video.

I turned around in my leather chair and glanced out the window. What a perfect Fall night. The frat house was once again alive with partiers. I never bothered to check my phone to see if Frat Boy had texted during my nap, and instantly felt bad about that.

I didn't see him on the front lawn, but as my eyes wandered up to the porch I noticed that familiar outline. Well, it was more the fact that I saw someone without any clothes on. He was jumping up and down, although I couldn't quite see what all the fuss was about. And so I lifted the binoculars to my eyes and focused in on the porch.

As soon as Frat Boy fell into view, I saw his same baggy boxers, his hairy chest, and that short blonde hair. And to my surprise, it seemed like he was jumping up and down to get my attention. He was looking straight at me! Leaping into the air and waving at the window with both hands. And as soon as he realized he'd gotten my attention, I watched him lean down and pick up a huge piece of poster board from the porch. He held it above his head and smiled with those perfectly white teeth.

I'll do it!, the sign read.

As I pulled the binoculars away from my eyes I didn't know if I should run down to the frat house or wake up Hunter with this amazing news. Although I was still shocked and upset about the issue with Tye's video, I'd found my sign. And I was ready to make a new video that would top anything Hunter and I had done prior.

CHAPTER THIRTEEN

narrated by Hunter

As soon as the weekend hit we were pumped and ready for filming. One of Cole's good friends lived in a beautiful mansion out in Rockport, and he invited us to one of his famously huge pool parties. He said we could bring along Frat Boy, and do some filming at the mansion. Cole hesitated for about half a second before taking him up on his offer. This friend, Adam, was a big mover and shaker in the business world, and had made a fortune in computer technology. He and Cole had known each other for years. Adam had a reputation for having the hottest boyfriends and lovers, and he threw some of the best parties in Boston. I was psyched to go see the place and spend a perfect Sunday partying; something that would have been impossible during my restaurant days.

And in addition to a great weekend, we were expecting an ever better video to come out of the trip. We had a beautiful Fall day and an incredible home on tons of private land. And since Frat Boy was more a friend to both of us, and totally my physical type, I felt a lot more comfortable than I did going into our last video.

Speaking of Tye, he'd been MIA ever since Cole learned about the video flagging. He avoided phone calls, text messages, e-mails, and just about any attempt to get in contact. And even though Cole was doing a good job of covering it up, I could see all the pain that my lover was carrying. Not only did he feel betrayed, but he felt like he screwed up for us. As if Tye's actions were his own fault, and he wasn't doing a good enough job of ridding all my worries. And that's why I loved my man so much. He fully and whole-heartedly wanted me to have no worries in life. And even though the removal of Tye's video was a big hit against us, I did my best to convince Cole that I was okay.

Rockport was a perfect city to spend a relaxing Fall day of making a video and hanging out. The three of us had no real agenda for the video. We figured we'd just do whatever seemed fun, and keep the video camera around for any moments that seemed worth filming.

As soon as we pulled up to the mansion I was awed. Cole had obviously been there before, but for me it was a first. Rockport, MA, is a beautiful little city along the Boston North Shores. It borders the ocean, and is known for its palatial homes on the oceanfront. What a beautiful place to live! Even though I enjoyed city life, I could easily see myself living in a town like Rockport someday.

"Uh, did you guys bring bathing suits?" Cole asked as we pulled into the massive driveway of his friend's mansion. To the right of the estate was the ocean and shore line, and off to the left was a massive state of the art poolhouse with a large indoor, in-ground pool. The pool area boasted a double-sided fireplace and a ten-man jacuzzi, built around an impeccably landscaped collection of stones and boulders that kept the pool area completely secluded from neighbors and passersby.

"No—you didn't say anything about a pool," Frat Boy replied from the back seat.

"I specifically asked you if there would be a pool and you told me no," I said, and couldn't decide whether I wanted to laugh or be frustrated.

"Oh well, guess that means we're going skinny-dipping," Cole replied with a sly grin.

*   *

Cole's friend Adam, the owner of the mansion, greeted us on the front lawn. He was a tall, beefy masculine guy with a handsome complexion, who kept his salt and pepper hair short and well-groomed. As soon as Cole and Adam saw each other they instantly embraced in a big bear hug. While Bradley and I unloaded the car, the two old friends shared some laughs, and then quickly got into a discussion about how hot they both though Frat Boy was. Once we'd all been introduced and exchanged some words, Adam left to head inside to prepare for the evening's party, and the rest of us decided to check out the pool.

Frat Boy was the first to dive into the lukewarm water. While Cole went into the shed to look for pool toys, I quickly stripped out of my shorts, boxer briefs, and tank top, and leaped into the pool. The temperature was perfect for a cool Fall day. Any colder and I don't think we would've lasted very long.

I swam over to Frat Boy, just as he lifted his head up above the water. The pool was surprisingly deep, and even while standing the water came up to my nipples. As soon as I reached Frat Boy I reached my arms around his shoulders, holding his thick body. Under the water I felt his hairy ass back up into my crotch, and stretched his lower back so that he could push himself up against me. My cock was quickly getting hard as Frat Boy backed into me. He held his ass cheeks apart so that my dick was nestled in-between them.

"Whoa!" I heard Cole shout out from the side of the pool. "At least let me get the camera rolling."

"I don't know if I can wait," Frat Boy shouted back, just as Cole began to throw a pile of pool toys at us. A volleyball, a floating mattress, and some pool noodles all landed around our heads.

With my arms wrapped tightly around Frat Boy, I lifted him upwards, and dropped him across the floating mattress. There was a quick splash, and then silence as the kid clung to the plastic bed. His hairy bubble ass was now just out of the water. He spread his legs apart, beckoning me with that amazing view of his backside.

As Cole started up the camera and focused in on us, I rested my hands on Frat Boy's thighs, gently digging my thumbs into his leg muscles. And as he laid there with his butt up in the air, I stuck my face in-between his cheeks and extended my tongue. Instantly I heard him moan in pleasure. I licked around the outside of his hot little hole. Each time it would get a little too wet, I'd pull back just an inch and blow gently on his ass, allowing those cool Fall breezes to pass down and tickle him from behind.

My man was on his way over, holding the camera with one hand and his cock with the other as he walked slowly through the deep pool water.

"You want it?" I asked the kid as he squirmed on the mattress, and he shook his head yes. He was biting the plastic bed, waiting for that pleasure to hit. And so I stuck my face back in-between his cheeks and fully extended my tongue, thrusting it into his hole. I felt his whole body wiggle as he dealt with the sensation. His fingers were gripping the mattress so tightly that I thought the whole thing might burst.

I wasn't ready to let up. I kept my tongue in there, twirling it around and gently sucking on his little hole with my lips. I loved the way that I was making him squirm. His whole body was responding to my tongue. His legs kept bending at the knees, the soles of his feet pointed upwards toward the sky. He started to push his ass into my face, back and forth, as if he was getting fucked by it. I couldn't wait to fuck this boy; I could tell he seriously wanted it. That would come soon enough.

"You like that?" Cole asked him, but Frat Boy couldn't respond, as his teeth were still biting down on the plastic mattress. But he nodded his head in approval and kept giving me his ass. Cole came around to my side of the bed and lifted his hand under the water, clenching Frat Boy's thick cock. As I worked this kid's ass with my tongue, Cole squeezed and stroked his throbbing cock underneath the water.

I buried my tongue deep inside him, fucking him with my face so hard and fast that I was beginning to sweat. He tasted amazing; this mixture of salty perspiration and natural musk. His groans were getting louder and louder, until he let go of the plastic with his mouth and let out an amazingly long noise.

"I want you inside me," he ordered as he squeezed on the mattress with his strong hands.

"How many loads you got for us, sexy boy?" Cole asked, his hand still wrapped around Frat Boy's cock.

"As many as you want, sexy man. All of 'em."

Cole looked at me with a big smile and a seriously excited expression on his face, and then back at Frat Boy's hairy ass. I had just pulled out for air, and was breathing deeply while Frat Boy recovered from all the rimming.

"Let's not waste one underwater," Cole finally said with a smirk on his face as he let go of Frat Boy's erect dick. "I'm in the mood for a drink. How about you guys?"

*   *

We didn't even bother to put our clothes on. We ran stark naked from the pool into the mansion, assuming we'd raid the bathroom for towels. The estate felt like a giant playground, and we were like a trio of horny kids who had been unleashed upon it. Running naked through someone's lawn wasn't something I'd do regularly, you know. Maybe for Bradley it was just a normal day in the neighborhood, but Cole and I were grown-ups. We were mature guys. Or at least, I liked to tell myself that.

Cole was the first to stop dead in his tracks as soon as we hurried through the front doors of the mansion with our cocks hanging out. I couldn't tell why he'd ground to a halt, other than maybe he had no idea where he was going within the monstrous house, but as I looked around, I too stopped cold.

"Whoops," Bradley said, looking back and forth between us, and then at the two people we'd interrupted.

None of us had expected to run into Adam, since the mansion was enormous and we were going to be staying in our own private wing, but as fate would have it when the front doors opened and we barged into the grand foyer, Adam and his date were standing there amidst boxes of decorations. Adam had a mixed look of both humor and shock as he watched us quickly fold our hands in front of our junk. The image was priceless. There we were, dangling cocks and all, standing around awkwardly in front of Adam's hot Brazilian boy toy who we hadn't yet met.

"Umm, these are my friends, Cole, Hunter, and Bradley," Adam said, leaning in towards his date, but keeping his eyes on the three of us. "They're uh—nudists—don't mind them. You know—Bostonians."

Adam's stunning Brazilian boy quickly looked us up and down, and then let out a brief laugh.

"It's nice to meet you," he finally said, speaking in a heavy accent. "Hope to see more of you tonight."

"Cole, you know where your bedroom—."

"On our way," Cole quickly replied. And with that, Adam nodded and escorted his date out of the foyer.

It had all happened so fast that the three of us stood around for a minute even after Adam was gone. Finally we burst out into laughter.

"Who was that kid?" Bradley asked as Cole led us towards the guest wing of the mansion. "Damn, I'd tap that—."

"That's his date," Cole quickly replied. "I don't know the kid's name—Adam is like a fucking Hugh Hefner; every time I see him it's one beautiful guy after another. He was probably too shocked to even remember to introduce the kid."

"I'm sure we left a good impression," I said.

"The party's tonight, so we don't have that much time to film before people start arriving," Cole said. "Let's grab towels and uh—see what happens," he added with a thick grin.

*   *

We grabbed towels in our suite's guest bathroom and headed back downstairs to the massive kitchen. Adam dropped by real quick to say he and his date would *disappear* during filming. That was great for us, since the last thing we wanted to do was shock this unsuspecting Brazilian.

As soon as we hit the kitchen, Frat Boy began to raid the refrigerator. Meanwhile, Cole and I mixed up some cocktails. It was fun to go through Adam's kitchen and see all the high-end flatware and silverware, and intricate china. This was a real fucking kitchen.

As I was pouring out some drinks in a few martini glasses, I glanced up to see Frat Boy, butt naked, sitting on the granite kitchen counter with his legs dangling in the air. He was devouring a turkey sandwich as if he hadn't eaten in days. I patted Cole on the shoulder, and motioned towards Frat Boy, and as soon as he saw the same crazy scene he burst into laughter.

"What?" Frat Boy asked with his mouth full as he glanced up to look at us.

"Nothing, Bradley," Cole replied. "Just get that cute ass over here."

With the sandwich in hand, Bradley leaped off the granite countertop and walked up to us. His dick was semi-hard, and every few seconds his free hand would go back to playing with it. What a horn ball.

Just as I was about to give Frat Boy one of the cocktails I'd made, I brought it up to my lips for a quick taste. Not that Frat Boy would care if it was too strong. I just wanted to make sure I'd made a decent rum and coke. As I sipped the drink, I watched Bradley's free hand go back to his thick cock, rubbing it up and down alongside those huge balls that hung freely in mid-air.

"I have an idea," I suddenly said. "Cole, grab the camera. Hey Bradley, jump back on that countertop and stand up."

"What? I thought you were gonna make me a drink?"

"That can wait. And—get rid of that fucking sandwich. Come on."

"I'm almost finished," he said, hurrying to devour the remaining bite as he climbed back up onto the slab of granite.

At this point Cole had turned on the camera and was focusing it on me.

"I think this drink's missing something," I said as I walked towards Frat Boy, and ran my hand up along his hairy, muscular legs, all the way up to his cock and balls. Cole was already following along.

"What did you say about these drinks?"

"I said it was missing something," I repeated. Frat Boy stood up straight, anxious for what was about to happen. The scene was great; like a strip joint in someone's kitchen. All we needed was a pole.

"Yes, it is. Hmm, well it's a cocktail, so let's try some cock," Cole said, the camera in one hand and his rum and coke in the other. We each raised our glasses up to his low-hanging balls, and allowed them to dip right into our cocktails.

"Yup, much better," I said as soon as I took a sip from the glass. Cole was laughing, and Frat Boy was quivering excitedly from the cold liquid on his sensitive balls.

Cole turned his camera off and Frat Boy hopped down from the counter, but at that point he was so hard from our hot little scene that he asked if we could film some more stuff. Even though a part of me wanted to film a scene in the kitchen, there wasn't enough time to clean up before partiers began showing up, and so we decided to take Frat Boy back to our suite's bedroom.

Cole and I brought our towels back, and Frat Boy led the way. As soon as we walked through the bedroom door he jumped onto the bed face down. His ass was up, and he was ready for some serious man-on-man action. As I watched him arch his muscular lower back, his beautiful little ass popping straight up in the air, I couldn't believe that this was how we were going to be making a living.

This time I'd be doing the filming. Cole handed off the camera to me, and I walked around the side of the bed as Cole climbed on top of Frat Boy. I watched him as he slid his hands up the back of Frat Boy's hairy, muscled legs, up to his little peach fuzz ass. Frat Boy's face was wedged in-between two pillows held in place by his thick arms. Cole was moving in. I watched as he dragged his five o'clock shadow over Frat Boy's butt cheeks. Bradley arched his ass higher, totally surrendering his body. Cole leaned down further and started by licking Frat Boy's cock and balls, slowly working his wet tongue along those big, low-hanging genitals. Frat Boy was moaning into his pillows, and by the time Cole's tongue reached Frat Boy's ass, the pillows couldn't even withhold the sounds of pleasure.

"Come on, fuck him already," I joked, given how loud Frat Boy was getting. Cole pulled his face away from Bradley's ass and chuckled. He then climbed on top of Frat Boy, covering his hard body. Frat Boy was shaking. Cole started by gently licking along Frat Boy's neck and ears, and while he did that, I wet my hand with my own spit and began to massage Bradley's tight hole. It was already nice and wet from Cole's mouth.

"Reach back with your hands and spread those ass cheeks," Cole ordered, and Frat Boy immediately flattened his chest across the bed, and did as told. He reached around and grabbed those beefy cheeks, and spread them open for Cole's fat cock. I watched as Cole rubbed his dick against Frat Boy's moist hole. Buckets of pre-cum were already pouring onto Frat Boy. This was going to make penetration much easier.

Frat Boy started to squirm as the thick, chubby cock slid into him, and so Cole grabbed the back of Frat Boy's head in order to keep him from moving.

"I like that," he moaned, and so Cole grabbed even more of his hair. Cole pulled back on it just as he thrust the rest of his throbbing cock deep into Frat Boy's ass.

"Yeah, fuck that boy," I said as I lined up the camera. Cole loved when I talked dirty to him, and I could tell it got him excited. He was really giving it to Frat Boy, putting all of his weight into pounding that tight little hole. The two of them were sweat-soaked beasts.

I pulled the pillows away from Frat Boy and got up on the bed, my cock solid and bulging, and Bradley immediately went for it. He consumed the whole thing in his mouth, just as Cole's pounding was getting harder and harder.

Cole was about to cum. His face was red, and beads of perspiration dripped from his forehead. He pounded deeper and deeper until finally he pulled out of Frat Boy and leaned back, and cum spit from his cock like a jet stream, covering that bubbly ass. It was so hot that as soon as I saw the explosion of cum, I released right into Frat Boy's mouth. I could hear his little gags as cum burst from my dick, shooting down his throat and splashing all over his lips.

The next thing I knew, Frat Boy had rolled over onto his back. His mouth was still full of cum, and he pulled down on my legs so that my ass came right down into his face. Frat Boy was jerking rapidly; he was ready to cum. Cole bent down to help him out by licking his balls.

And as I felt Frat Boy's tongue climb deeper and deeper into my hole, cum burst from his dick, shooting all over his stomach. Within seconds after the explosion, the three of us collapsed on the bed in a tangle of sweaty, cum-covered bodies[4].

*   *

"Oh my God," I said as I watched Frat Boy run naked through the front lawn of the Rockport mansion. Cole and I were sitting on the trunk of our car, which was parked on the circular driveway in front of the estate. We each had a beer in hand, and casually took sips as we watched our friend run laps around the water fountain. "I feel like we bought a puppy. Is this what parents go through? I couldn't imagine dealing with this for ten years."

"Me either," Cole remarked, shaking his head at the mere thought.

When Frat Boy rounded the fountain for the twentieth time he jogged back to us, with his tongue hanging out of his mouth like a dog gasping for air. He'd spilled most of his drink, which he still clenched tightly with one hand. We didn't allow him to take a glass outside, but there were still plenty of plastic cups from the evening's party. Neither of us were sure if the cup was even Bradley's, or if he'd just found it on the ground. It wouldn't surprise us if he did.

"I'm getting another drink."

"No, I think you're done," Cole said exactly what was on my mind.

"Dude, who do you think you are?" he replied. I didn't like his tone of voice. We hadn't seen Frat Boy this argumentative before, and I was taken back by the immediate rush of anger.

"This is my friend's place, and I'm responsible for whatever happens here. You're drunk, and I'm flagging you before you fuck up his house," Cole said. "You can either come sit here with us and enjoy this beautiful night, or go lay down."

"Try to stop me," Frat Boy replied, waving his disposable cup in the air as if it was a weapon.

4

http://olbmedia.site.metrixstream.com/site/MaverickMen/?page=videos&contentId=138

I'd never seen Cole move so fast. In the time it took me to blink, Cole had leapt off the back of the car, and was standing face-to-face with Frat Boy. Cole towered over him, and his deep green eyes—which usually were the most calming part of him—stared straight into Frat Boy. The latter looked terrified. He dropped his plastic cup and grabbed for his cell phone.

"I'm going home," he angrily replied, taking a couple steps backwards.

"We can drive back in the morning," Cole said. "It's too late, and we've all been drinking."

"Chill out," I told Frat Boy, although he was too busy dialing numbers.

"Hello? Hello?" I heard him shout into the phone. He was so loud that I was beginning to worry one of the neighbors would overhear. Even though the mansions in the neighborhood were far apart, it wouldn't take much for neighbors to hear some college boy shouting in the late, quiet hours of the night. Adam had already gotten some local heat for his parties, and he tried to enforce a 1 AM closing time on all of his events. This wasn't the big city, after all. Rockport didn't have a reputation for being noisy at three o'clock in the morning. And the last thing we needed was a police car rolling into the driveway.

"Who are you calling?" Cole asked.

"I need a taxi," Frat Boy ignored him, speaking into the phone. "Where am I? I'm on the water. In Rockport in a big house on the water. What the fuck? It's a big fucking mansion right on the water in Rockport, there can't be that many. I—dammit!"

"Let's go inside," Cole said, but Frat Boy looked up from his cell phone with a sneer.

"Whatever we gave him—we have to remember to keep that bottle capped next time," I told Cole, who nodded his head in the affirmative.

"Hello? I need a taxi," Frat Boy shouted into his cell phone. "I'm on the water—in Rockport on the water. I don't know what the fucking address is, it's—hello? Hello?"

"Give me a hug," Cole said, trying another route of persuasion. He didn't wait for Frat Boy to come to him; instead he walked up and wrapped his arms around our friend. Frat Boy dropped his cell phone, and within a few seconds he had tears in his eyes. He dug his head into Cole's chest and began to cry in short, quiet sobs.

"I'm tired," he moaned. "I'm tired."

"Let's go to bed," Cole told him, and turned his head to look back at me. I winked, and hopped off the trunk of our car. "Come on— let's go play nice inside."

We led Frat Boy into the mansion, and decided to put him in our bed. Even though we had a strict rule about fuck buddies sleeping in bed with us, he was so drunk that we were worried he might wake up at some point and cause trouble. The last thing we needed was for Frat Boy to break something valuable in Adam's house. And so we made adjustments to yet another one of our relationship rules, this time so that we could take care of a drunken Bradley.

As soon as his head hit the pillow, he passed out. We put him in the middle of the wide four poster king bed, and crawled in on either side of him. It was kind of funny sleeping with this kid in the middle of us. A part of me wondered if this would be our story someday. The aging gay couple with a young, pretty third, who would sleep with us and live with us and do our laundry. It was an interesting fantasy.

"You're gonna see him tomorrow?" I quietly asked Cole as he pulled his clothes off. I did the same, pulling my jeans down to my feet, and then my t-shirt over my head.

"Yeah. We're supposed to have coffee in the morning."

"You think he'll let us put the video back online?"

"I don't know," Cole replied, with some sadness in his voice. Tye had texted him during the party asking to have coffee in the morning. After days of ignoring phone calls, Tye was suddenly ready to talk, and I was extremely curious to hear his side of the story. We both hoped that he'd agree to put the video back online, but neither of us were counting on it. "I feel bad about this, Hunter. I feel like we dived in without really knowing him."

"If that's true, then we did the same with Frat Boy," I replied.

"Yeah, but who knows at twenty-something years old that they really want to have a sex tape of themselves floating around forever. I don't even know at my age. You know, this stuff never disappears. And we've only seen two guys so far. If this is gonna be our income, we need to be doing this with at least one or two people every month."

"I know," I softly replied. "I feel like we might need an HR department at this rate."

"I think I have a better understanding of the studios now," Cole said. "That's why they sign contracts—why they don't pick up their phones when a guy like Tye calls to say he wants his video pulled out of circulation."

"But that's not us."

"I know it's not. But I think it's an unfortunate reality that we may have to deal with at some point. I just hope it doesn't make us jaded, or regret doing all this," Cole added, and then leaned over Frat Boy's soft, sleeping body to give me a kiss on the lips.

"I think we'll find a balance," I replied as our lips parted. "Let's get some sleep. You can't miss this meet-up with Tye tomorrow morning."

"It's gonna be hard to sleep with it on my mind," he told me. I turned off the lamp and laid down on the scattering of pillows. Cole reached his hand out and took hold of mine, and we rested them on top of Frat Boy. How our uncomplicated lives had changed.

CHAPTER FOURTEEN

narrated by Cole Maverick

I can't even describe the knot in my stomach when I pulled into the parking lot of a diner in South Boston. Some of it was lack of sleep, and probably also hunger, from waking up so goddamn early to drive from Rockport all the way back for this meeting. Tye hadn't given me any clues about his intentions, and as far as I knew I could be walking into some kind of lawsuit. If this kid really thought that his reputation was tarnished, then what was to stop him from suing us? My household's income and livelihood were at stake, and their return to stability was about to be decided by one of the least stable people I knew.

"Hey, just pulled in," I said as soon as I heard Tye pick up his phone. I'd found a parking spot on the side of the diner. As I reached to open the door, I saw Tye's twinky frame hurry towards my car from around the front of the building. He was wearing a tight-fitting t-shirt and a baggy pair of jeans, and was shivering as he jogged to the passenger's side door. I gave him a surprised look as he opened my car door and hopped inside.

"Aren't we going inside?" I asked as he shut the door behind him. He looked up at me with those innocent brown eyes and shook his head *no*.

"Can we do it in here?" he asked me with that boyish Southern drawl. It really did have an effect on me. As nervous and aggravated as I was upon pulling into the parking lot, as soon as Tye stepped into the car my stress level sank.

"Yeah, this is fine. Was hoping to get some food—."

"Five minutes. I just wanna talk about this stuff in private," he said. He adjusted himself on the seat, and stretched his long, slim legs. "It's really personal."

"I get that," I said as warmly as I could. "And I know you freaked out about the video, but I hope we can reach some kind of agreement. You know—this stuff is what Hunter and I are living on these days."

"I didn't call you about the video," Tye replied, giving me this awkward look as his eyebrows narrowed and his lips tightened.

"Tye, I've been calling you for days about the video. Ever since you flagged it and took it offline."

"It's offline?" he asked, seemingly in shock. "I haven't even been online to look at it. I haven't returned your phone calls because I've been fucking scared to death all week."

"Scared of what?" I asked him. Suddenly I was just as confused as he was.

"I've been partying every night, and—something happened."

"Like going out to clubs?"

"No, I mean *partying*, Cole. I have a problem. I didn't realize it, but then I was out at the clubs this week, high off my ass, and met some guy who had seen the video on XTube. He was flirting with me all night. Finally he offered me more drugs, and so I went back to his place and—I don't know what happened. Everything's blank from there. I don't know if we fucked. If we did, I don't know if it was safe. I woke up in a fucking alley."

"Are you physically okay? Do you have any bruises or—."

"Nah, I'm not hurt. I always thought I could control that shit, but now—I don't know what the fuck to do."

"Don't freak out," I told him, and placed an arm around his lean shoulders. "Why were you scared to tell me about this before? I have friends that work at the Health and Addictions Center here in Boston, and I can take you over there right now—."

"No, I don't need that. It's all this fucking stress from the video—God," he angrily exclaimed.

"But it sounds like these problems started long before we ever did the video," I calmly replied. "You could have told me about this."

"Can you just give me some money? Look, this won't happen again. I was broke and couldn't buy my own shit, and so I took some from this *asshole* at the club. It's all good. I just need money for my own shit."

I couldn't believe what I was hearing. Somehow the soft-spoken, shy Southern guy who had evolved into a hot, erotic friend to Hunter and I, had become a total wreck. I'd never seen any signs of this before. And Hunter and I weren't the kind of guys who were at the Boston nightclubs all the time, so if Tye was out getting fucked up every night, neither of us would've known about it. I felt so awful that he couldn't share his problems with me sooner, but then again, I wondered if he'd confided in *anyone* in his life. Was I the first?

"Money's not going to solve your problems," I told him. "I can take you to a help center right now."

"What about work? I need to work."

"We'll help you find another job if you go get yourself help. I'll drive you over there now. You can tell me how all this got started—how long you've been on this shit for—. Lots of people get addicted to meth, at all ages. It'll be okay. Hunter and I have been around for a while, and we know the deal. What, with all the drugs we've had around us in our lifetime it's no wonder we haven't fallen into that hole. But Tye, I want you to be totally honest with me. If you were in some drug-induced state and flagged your own video on XTube, just let me know."

"Why would I do that to you guys?" he replied with the most convincing, wet eyes. As I sighed and shook my head, unsure what to believe, Tye leaned his head on my shoulder, stretching across the car to rest against me. I felt one of his hands crawl across my jeans, and something about his fragility at that moment, and his sexy, lean body wrapped in my arms, stirred this incredible energy down below. I could feel my hard-on pressing against my jeans, forming a bulge through the rough fabric.

"So you'll take me to the help center and stay with me?" he softly asked me. I guess he realized I wasn't going to give him any money to fuel a drug habit. I cared a lot about this young guy.

"Yeah, I will. These guys will take care of everything, and Hunter and I will be there as friends throughout all of this. And once all this shit is over, we'll sit down and figure out how to get this video back online."

"You know—you don't need to make a video just to get with me," he replied after a short pause, and before I even had time to think of a response his hand was wrapped around my erection. There was no hiding it. I was as hard as ever, and a huge part of me just wanted him to whip it out and suck it right there in the parking lot.

"I can't without Hunter," I said, but it was as if I hadn't said anything at all. As Tye massaged my cock through my blue jeans, he used his other hand to slowly undo my zipper.

"Lemme just suck you off real quick," he whispered, and lowered his head towards my crotch as he squeezed my dick with one hand.

"Stop—," I replied, hating myself for not really wanting him to stop. "Stop," I said more loudly, and lifted him off me. I didn't push him, but I gave him enough of a shove that he'd get the point. It wasn't easy to do. He was so cute and vulnerable, looking up at me with his big sexy, sad eyes, filled with a mixture of tears and lust. I wanted his beautiful full lips and hot mouth wrapped around my cock. I wanted to fuck my load into his pretty little face and down his throat. Hell, I would've thrown him in the back seat and pounded out his hot ass right there, but I needed to be realistic and not think with my cock.

"You can't without Hunter?" he asked in a patronizing tone. "You guys do online porn and you wanna pull the monogamy card on me? Are you fucking serious, Cole?"

"Come on Tye, don't be like that. You know we have rules. We have a relationship and we have rules for a reason," I replied. I wished I could've just said that I didn't want Tye. I wish I felt that. Instead I felt like an idiot—making my relationship with my true love sound more like a contract and an obligation.

"You think any of the rules are going to still be around after a few more videos? How soon until one of these guys is someone you or he can't resist?"

"I love Hunter. I'd fight for him—kill for him. Listen Tye—I think you're sexy, and yeah—you get me hard—but no hookup is worth a strain on my relationship. Relationships are about trust and respect. And if Hunter doesn't trust and respect me, then what am I?"

"Someone who wants to have fun," he angrily replied, and then quickly opened the passenger's door.

"Come on, Tye! Let me drive you to the center," I hollered as Tye rushed out of the car.

"Don't bother." He slammed the car door and hurried off into the cold. I watched him wrap his arms together to shield himself from the chilly morning winds. I was left with this sick, helpless feeling in the pit of my stomach. I wanted to help him, but I knew he wasn't ready to listen to me. And I feared his problems could be much worse than he was letting on.

* *

I didn't know whether or not to call after him. Twice on my way back home I went to dial his number, and then stopped. The second time I even threw my phone into the back of the car, just so that I wouldn't be tempted. I couldn't help but feel personally responsible for all the nonsense with Tye, and I didn't know how to fix the situation. He wasn't ready to come with me to get help. Maybe a couple of warm voicemails to let him know that I cared, and that Hunter and I would be there when he was ready? I wanted to get close to him, without getting *too* close.

By the time I pulled into the parking garage of the apartment building, I was overwhelmed with a fear of confronting Hunter. I'd met with Tye on behalf of the both of us. That video was part of our livelihood, and I just couldn't bring myself to walk through my front door and explain to my lover that I'd failed. I couldn't bear to see the look on his face. To see his lips bunch together, and his eyes fall towards the floor. I absolutely hated to see Hunter stressed out.

And so I stalled for time. With my car parked in the garage, I sat in the driver's seat and—having retrieved my cell phone from the back seat—scrolled through new e-mails. There were a couple new fan messages, plus an e-mail from Christo giving us his flights and travel info for Miami during New Year's. I wished that I could have fast-forwarded time and went right to New Year's Eve so that Christo, Hunter, and I could tape the best love making in the history of porn. Then we wouldn't need to worry so much about Tye's video. Poor kid. It would've been nice to know even just one of his friends, who I could call and talk to about all this. Then again, I didn't know what he had told his friends about Hunter and I.

As I scrolled to the end of my new e-mails, I caught one that mentioned Boston in the subject line, and so I clicked on it. The message was short and sweet. A young guy in the Boston area had written to express how much he loved our videos, and how much he wanted to be in one of them. He left his name and a phone number, which I didn't recognize as a Boston area code. Maybe he was just going to school in the city. After all, Boston was a big college town, with a constant stream of beautiful young guys every August.

The thing that really struck me was at the end of the e-mail. I scrolled through three little pictures, each taking up most of my cell phone screen, revealing one of the cutest little guys I'd ever seen. He had this late-teen cuteness, with rosy white cheeks and big, dreamy eyes.

And his body was perfect for what Hunter and I were looking for: tall and slim, twinky, boyish; a third person who looked distinctly different from either of us.

There was something angelic in this kid's face. And without any thought, I dialed the phone number in the e-mail.

"Hey, this is Cole Maverick—I just got your e-mail," I said into the phone after a deep, boyish voice answered.

"No way," he replied.

"No, it really is! I just saw that nice e-mail you sent. Hunter's inside, and I actually have a crazy question for you. You want to get together tonight, hang out, and see if we click for doing a video?"

"Are you serious?" he asked, laughing at my spontaneous phone call. "Um—yeah, I have nothing else going on. But are you cool with picking me up?" he asked. He sounded normal, like a regular kid in his late teens, bored and hanging out at home.

"Of course! Where do you live? Which neighborhood?"

"Uh—I'm not exactly in the city," he slowly replied. "But I still want to hang out tonight! Honestly I'm kind of out in the middle of nowhere, and there's nothing to do, and it would be so cool to come meet you and Hunter—."

"So wait. Middle of nowhere as in—an hour away?"

"Try three hours," he replied, and let out a huge sigh. I could tell at that moment that he gave up hope.

"And you don't have a car, huh?"

"Nope."

I glanced out the window into the parking garage, my eyes falling on the entrance to the building. Hunter was inside, maybe taking a nap. Maybe waiting for me. Maybe nervously awaiting an answer from my meeting with Tye.

"I'm coming," I said.

"Really?" he excitedly responded.

"Yeah—just text me your address. I'll leave now."

"Wow—that's awesome. I'll see you soon! Or—in three hours!"

As I turned off my cell phone, a smile popped onto my face. Maybe he'd be our answer. And I wasn't going to return home to Hunter empty-handed.

* *

For about two hours and forty five minutes I didn't have a single nervous feeling in my body. I drove smoothly with the windows open and the Fall breeze sweeping in and out of my car. I listened to music. I called some friends, and had a nice chat with my neighbor and close friend Paul about the whole Tye situation. I even got an international call from Christo, who had called using Skype, and was at an Internet café in Berlin having a late cup of coffee. We talked about our excitement for New Year's Eve in Miami, and I filled him in on my morning's encounter with Tye, and on the kid I was driving to pick up.

But in the last fifteen minutes of the long drive, there was no scenery, music, or phone call that could distract me from the increasing nervousness in my gut. I wondered if he'd flake out and not show—if this drive was going to be for nothing. I worried about whether or not he actually looked like his pictures. I'd had that experience meeting guys off the Internet a couple times in the past. I made plans with some hot twenty-something, and the guy that showed up looked about ten years older and thirty pounds heavier than in his pictures.

When I'd left Boston to drive three hours to pick up this young guy, I didn't think it was a crazy idea. But as I got closer, the reality started to kick in. I was just sick of seeing Hunter get depressed over our struggle with the Tye video, and all I wanted to do was make him smile. I would've driven down to DC to pick up a guy if it meant putting a smile on my lover's face.

I was only a few minutes away from the house, which was buried in the boondocks of New Hampshire. He should've just put "Canada" in the subject line of his e-mail to us. His neighborhood was mostly woods and long, empty roads, and so I was thankful to be doing this drive in the daytime. At night I would've been completely lost.

I grabbed for my phone as soon as my GPS told me to make my final turn on the trip. As I dialed his number, I took a deep breath and held it. I was fifty feet away, on a thin road surrounded by trees. Long driveways on either side of the street led to ranchers, each with a decent amount of space in-between. Enough for some reasonable privacy.

As soon as the call went to voicemail, I panicked. There was his sweet voice again, asking to leave a message after the beep. The GPS notified me that the address was only twenty feet away, on my right. As I slowed my car down, gliding at a slow speed towards my final destination, I re-dialed the phone number.

By the time my car pulled up in front of his house, his voice greeted me again with that same voicemail message. Why wasn't he picking up? I'd called him from the highway, and he picked up then, telling me he was going to shower and get ready. All sorts of horrible things were rushing through my head. Maybe this young guy just wasn't who he said he was, and I'd driven three hours to figure that out. As I re-dialed the number for a third time I was preparing myself for that sad, lonely car ride back to Boston, and that awful moment when I'd need to stand face-to-face with my lover and tell him that I'd screwed up twice in one day.

Voicemail. I didn't see any lights on in the house, or any cars in the driveway. It was a modest rancher surrounded by forest, with a spiraling driveway covered in yellow and brown leaves. I thought about knocking on the door, but how would I explain my visit to one of his parents? They'd never met me, and I had no excuse to be at their house. Not to mention, I was a little bit older than the guys he was probably used to hanging out with.

As my cell phone screen went dark I could see my reflection in the glass. I could see the deep frown on my face, and the worry behind my eyes. I didn't want to sit parked outside the house like some stalker. I thought about taking the car for a drive around the block, although back in these woods there weren't exactly *blocks*. I turned my phone on for one final time to see if I could get a hold of him when my passenger door opened. My head shot upwards, my eyes fixed on the car door, when suddenly a slim, young guy in blue jeans and a hoodie hopped into the passenger's seat and tossed a backpack on the car floor.

He had those same rosy cheeks; the same big eyes that made him look years younger than his age. He looked totally innocent. I don't know why, but the first thing I did upon laying eyes on him was picture him getting fucked in a porn video. Not necessarily by us, but just any porn, where some older muscle daddy was fucking his hot little body. I could see that adorable face, staring up at the camera, an innocent expression in his eyes, like it was his first time taking cock. He could've done it one-hundred times and it would still look like his first time.

"Sorry—just wanted to check you out to make sure you seemed normal," he said with a little smirk on his face. "I'm Billy."

"Cole," I replied, and shook his hand. "For a second there I was worried you wouldn't show up."

"Of course I showed up," he replied, as if there was no reason to doubt him. "So—long drive. You ready to go?"

He shut the door, and adjusted his backpack so that it sat in-between his feet. I hadn't even thought about the fact that he'd be staying over, or that the next day I'd have to drive him three hours up, and make that three hour drive home. The more I thought about it, I hoped that bringing Billy back to the apartment wouldn't upset Hunter more than if I'd come home alone. But I had a good feeling about this.

"Let's hit the road," I said, and smiled at him as I switched on the ignition. He stretched out his legs and adjusted his seat backwards. I loved the way he just made himself at home in my car. It was as if we'd been buddies for years. There was no longer any nervousness—especially not from him. He was relaxed and unpretentious.

"So where's Hunter?" he asked as we drove away from his house. It struck me that I'd never told him I'd be coming alone.

"He's at home. You'll meet him in a few hours," I replied, and grinned. It was going to be a *long* drive back to Boston. "I uh—actually haven't told him that I'm picking you up yet. I'll call on the way home. We um—there's been a little drama with the first guy we did a video with—."

"Yeah, what happened with that?"

"It's down. I met with the kid this morning, and it didn't go too well, so I didn't want to come home to Hunter with bad news. And then I read your e-mail—."

I glanced over at him, pulling my eyes from the road, to see if I could get any expression. However, his face didn't change at all. He merely sat there, relaxed, with his hands folded behind his head.

"I'm surprised you came this far," he finally replied. "I'm really glad you did though. You look much better in the flesh."

"Thanks," I told him, flattered. "I'm glad I came too. I think we'll have a lot of fun. Have you been to Boston before?"

"Never."

"Really? You've been stuck up here?"

"Yeah—I haven't been anywhere," he said. "Haven't even been with a guy before."

I'm surprised I didn't swerve off the side of the road. Had he said what I thought he said?

"You mean you've never had a boyfriend?" I asked, hoping he only meant that he's never had anything committed. Maybe some hook-ups and random sex with straight boys, but never a solid boyfriend. But when I looked over at him, he was shaking his head *no*.

"No boyfriends, no sex. I mean—that doesn't mean I've never done *anything*. I've fooled around with some straight guys. But I've never gone all the way."

"You're a virgin?" I asked with wide eyes. "And you want your first time to be on-camera with us two guys? Total strangers?"

"Why not?" he replied as if I'd asked a stupid question. "You guys seem like you have a lot of fun in your videos, and you're both hot, so—?"

"You know, a lot of guys have problems the first time they bottom," I said.

"Did Hunter with you?"

"No—but we were so into each other—."

"Well I'm really into you guys," he shot back, cutting me off before I could even finish my response. "It'll be fine."

So he said, but I couldn't wait to see his face when he saw our thick, erect cocks, lubed and ready to enter his hot little ass. I almost laughed out loud at that mental image. Suddenly I was worried that this video wasn't going to happen. If he did indeed have trouble bottoming, then it could take forever just to get quality footage. After all, I was assuming he didn't even know how to get his ass cleaned and ready to be fucked. We'd probably have to keep him around for a week or so, to give him the opportunity to practice.

"We'll make it work," I said, deciding to end that conversation. If he was up for bottoming for Hunter and I, then I'd give him the benefit of the doubt. Plus, who wasn't into fucking a cute, virgin twink? That was like every alpha top's fantasy. I already knew that Hunter was going to love fucking this kid.

"Do you care if I take a nap?" he asked me. I turned to see those dreamy eyes drifting off to sleep in the comfort of the passenger's seat.

"Go ahead beautiful. I'll wake you once we're back to civilization."

He smiled at me in the most charming, adorable way, and then lazily started to unlace his sneakers.

"You mind if I take my sneaks off?" he politely asked me.

"Sure, go ahead," I replied. He slipped his sneakers off and then lifted his legs up, intentionally placing his socked little feet in my lap. He was light enough that it didn't cause me any problems in the driver's seat. In fact, I loved having his feet on my lap. I briefly turned to look at those dreamy, innocent eyes, and then returned my focus to the road. I had an instant hard-on, but I didn't know if he could tell. Either way, I had a good feeling about this new relationship, and just hoped Hunter would feel the same way.

CHAPTER FIFTEEN

narrated by Hunter

"He's moved in," were the first words to leave my mouth as soon as Cole and Billy left the apartment on trek to the grocery store. I was upstairs on the computer, with a Skype connection to Christo, who was in Barcelona preparing for a show.

"This is good or bad?" he asked me.

"It's been what—a week since Cole brought him home? And he hasn't left! Now he's talking about looking for an apartment in the city, but he doesn't have a job, and we've messed around, but there's been no actual fucking. I mean we all had to get tested first, so that's understandable, but we all came back clean and there's *still* no fucking, and he hasn't said we could post videos of him yet, so—wait—I'm sorry. I'm rambling."

"It's okay!" he reassured me in that calm, German accent. "You're—what's the word? Frustrated?"

"Very! I mean—I like Billy. I do like him. He's super fucking cute, and really nice. I just didn't think this would turn into a roommate situation."

"Have you gotten to know him?"

"Not really," I said. "He's bonded a lot more with Cole."

"And how does that make you feel?"

"I don't know, I think it's a daddy thing or something," I replied. I didn't know if I was in the mood for this type of questioning. Or rather, I didn't know if I was in the mood to figure out the answers. "I'm fine with it. He's cute and young, and Cole is intrigued by him, and wants to help him. It's not a big deal. You know? Billy's from the middle of nowhere and isn't in college and isn't working, and Cole is just trying to set him up with a good life. Cole's always had this paternal thing about him. I think he knows we probably won't have kids so he gets something out of helping young guys get their life started."

"Do you suspect anything more?"

"No. No, I don't. It's not like that."

"Well if you'd like to talk more about it, I am here," he reassured me. I knew he didn't believe a word I said. But I didn't want to doubt my lover. I didn't even want to voice any suspicions, for fear that they might come true. "I love the video with Frat Boy. Adorable! Wish his face was shown."

"Yeah, me too. And you saw that the Tye video is back up?"

"Yes, yes. So strange. He changed his mind?"

"I guess so," I replied. "Cole was surprised too. All of the sudden we got an e-mail from the XTube guys this week—a few days after Cole and Tye met up—and it said the video was back up. They got the signed paperwork they needed. No word from Tye yet, but Cole has left that alone."

"At least it's back," he cheerfully replied. "Now you have two up! And soon a third."

"If we get some decent footage with Billy, then yeah. I wish New Year's would hurry up and get here already. I've jerked off to you like three times this week."

"Which picture?" he asked amidst some boyish laughing.

"All of them. I don't know how anything we do before meeting you is gonna compare! Or anything after. We'll just have to convince you to move to Boston."

"Maybe," he coyly told me. "But please—I like you and Cole. Make sure things are okay at home. I want New Year's—for us to meet. If anything worries you—."

"I'll let you know," I said. "I appreciate it, Christo. It's hard to talk about this stuff with my regular friends, you know? It's so foreign to them. A year ago this would've all been so foreign to me."

"I'm happy to fill this void," he cheerfully replied. "I must go. Big show tonight."

"Break a leg."

"Oh God no, I hope not!"

"Do well!" I corrected myself. "Bye Christo."

"Cheers."

Once the Skype call ended, I leaned forward on the computer desk and rested my chin on my two fists. Was I making a big deal out of nothing? I liked Billy—I mean he wasn't totally my physical type. A bit too *twink* for me, but we still had fun in the bedroom. He had a sweet little ass, and whenever the three of us were together there'd be lots of laughing and pranking. The situation just bothered me. Cole and I had never had a fuck buddy *live* with us. And I guess that's what was so different about this one: he wasn't just a fuck buddy. Billy was becoming a friend to the both of us, but I felt like it was happening more quickly with Cole than with me. And not only that, but Cole and I no longer had the privacy to have all those important conversations that had kept our relationship going strong.

I guess if we had been doing the whole open relationship thing for a bit longer, I would've felt a lot more secure. But the fact is, we were still brand new to including new sexual partners in our relationship. And our rules weren't even totally stable yet. Look how quickly the kissing rule was broken, and then amended. I guess I couldn't count Frat Boy sharing a bed with us the one night in Rockport as another broken rule, since he was just drunk, and we were taking care of him. But would something like that ease Cole's feelings about having a guy sleep in bed with us? Would I soon be fighting for pillow space with Billy?

And so in an effort to be optimistic I decided that all we really needed—or all I *hoped* we needed—was some bonding time. I didn't know if this would take the form of a simple night out or a weekend getaway, but something had to be done. I at least wanted to challenge all the things that were bothering me about Billy's new residency in our home, and figure out if I was just being crazy, or actually had some legitimate fears. And so without further delay, I grabbed my cell phone and quickly typed a message to Cole, asking that we all do something to bond that upcoming weekend. Once the message was sent I took a long, deep breath. I just hoped he'd come up with something good.

*   *

It was sometime after eight when Cole and Billy finally got home. I'd gone to the gym—a new gym, that wasn't quite as nice as Solaris but got the job done—met up with Jenna and Chris for lunch, took a power nap, and had many hours of productive activity. Okay, so my productivity was mainly looking at porn, and browsing other videos to get ideas for our upcoming releases. I'd even met a cute Southern guy online, who lived in Tallahassee but was interested in driving down to Miami to meet up with us around New Year's. Between he and Christo, we'd be hitting the jackpot on that trip.

I could tell that Cole and Billy were on their way back when they were still in the hallway of our monstrous apartment building. Cole's voice was louder than usual, and it was coupled with grunts and groans, which led me to believe they were dragging groceries. But when the front door swung open and a loud clunk sounded on the hardwood floor, I could tell that this was more than a gallon of milk and some Cap'n Crunch.

When I got out of my seat to peer over the railing on the second-floor loft, I saw Billy and Cole nearly collapsed on the ground, surrounded by shopping bags and three huge green duffels. I was impressed that they were even able to carry all of that into the house!

"Why didn't you call me to come help you?" I shouted down to the first floor.

"It was—a—surprise—," Cole was panting in-between words. He smiled up at me with those loving green eyes. Billy seemed even more out-of-breath than my lover did.

"What's all this stuff?"

"We're going camping," Cole replied, and rested his back on top of one of the duffel bags. "I got your text earlier and the idea came to me almost immediately. Spent all afternoon driving around to camping supplies stores looking for stuff."

"Camping?" I repeated.

"Aren't you from Utah?" Billy asked. "You should be a pro at this stuff."

"You know how long it's been since I camped?" I replied. "And anyway—those were family trips. Stuffed in a 2-person tent with three cousins. Bears and feral animals all over the place. It's been forever, but yes, camping was pretty cool. Uh—probably much better without the extended family."

"Come help us un-pack and I'll tell you what I'm planning."

"I was thinking more of a weekend in New York or Montreal. You really want to go *camping*?"

"Just imagine—," Cole's voice grew softer as he began his sales pitch, "shooting a hot video in the deep trenches of the wilderness. Fucking in cabins. Getting pounded in tents. It's gonna be a blast."

"Trying to give someone a blow job, then tripping, and falling in poison ivy," I interrupted. At least Billy laughed.

"This trip is going to be *epic*," Cole promised me, his sales expertise as a former realtor leaking out into his delivery.

"Because no one's ever fucked in a tent before?"

"No! Because no one has ever done a camping video before. Or at least not on XTube. Or at least not a gay one. I think—."

"You don't seem too sure of this," I replied. "Can't we just do Montreal? Billy—wouldn't you rather do a big city?"

"I'll do whatever," he replied, uninterested in getting in the middle of the heated discussion.

"And listen to this—," Cole called up to the second-story loft. "It's a *gay* campground."

"Oh hell no," I instantly replied. "Are you serious?"

"No I swear, it's like Provincetown in the forest. The only kind of bears we're gonna encounter will look like Bruce Vilanch. Probably some skunks though—. We'll have to bring tomato juice."

"Forget it," I said. "I'd much rather go somewhere without skunks—without any wild animals, for that matter."

"There'll be sexy mountain men," Cole said, a thick smile on his face. "The kind you won't find at any gay bar here in Boston."

I tried to keep from grinning.

"Mountain men?"

*   *

"You know I've been here before?" Cole said from the driver's seat, his green eyes on the highway.

"When? You never told me that," I replied.

"Years ago. I was probably around his age; eighteen or nineteen," he said, glancing in the rear-view mirror at Billy, who was playing around on his iPod.

"I'm sure," he remarked without taking his eyes off the device. "Did you bring your pet dinosaur when you were here as a kid?"

"Don't make me come back there and kick your little pre-pubescent ass," I jokingly told him. "Yeah, I had an older friend back then who took me. Nice guy—a lawyer, I think—who I'd drink with sometimes. Kinda sexy in a nerdy way. If I knew then what I know now, something might've happened with him. But he was very cool with me; never pushy about getting with me or any of my friends. I think he just liked to be around young, cute guys. Who knows. Maybe he was *boinking* all my friends."

"*Boinking*?" Billy replied.

"Actually, come to think of it, he was probably trying to get with me on that camping trip. But he was always very respectful. Plus, back then I couldn't pick up on a signal from a guy if it was flashing in my eyes. But luckily we had a great time and this guy never tried to slip his hand into my sleeping bag. But I always remember it as being *so* much fun—the gay camping jamboree. You have no idea how happy I am that we can actually do these trips now."

"Yeah, when I worked for the restaurant it was impossible," I remarked, and then put a hand on Cole's right leg. "Life is much better."

"Hey, why don't you get the camera," Cole suggested. "We need to start filming the trip! We could have a Cannes submission by the end of this weekend."

"Tell me again why we waited for the weekend, when none of us have jobs?" Billy asked from the back seat, which led Cole to raise an eyebrow.

"Hunter and I have very important, busy jobs. We keep strict *fucking* hours Monday through Friday. Come on, guys, the weekend is when everyone will be there. When normal people have off work."

"There better be mountain men," I said as I pulled the camera out of its box and switched it on.

"I'm the only mountain man you should be focused on right now," Cole quickly replied. "Hey Billy, why don't you come stick that cute little face up here in the front seat and let us show you the wonderful world of road head."

As Cole un-zipped his pants I got this little rush—the same I experienced the first night Tye came over. Just the fantasy of this young twink servicing my man was so exciting for me. I got hard the second I saw Cole's fat cock popping out of his blue jeans. And it wasn't even because I wanted to suck it or jump on it! I just wanted to watch Billy take it in his mouth—hear those faint moans as he absorbed the whole thing into his throat.

Without a moment's hesitation, Billy put down his iPod and leaned forward between the two front seats. Cars whizzed by us, although none of us seemed to care. In fact I was kind of excited by the idea of onlookers.

I held the camera steady as Billy leaned forward and took Cole's thick cock in his mouth. It was so hot to watch this sexy little twink wrap his lips around Cole's meaty dick. Cole fully relaxed in his seat, resting his shoulders and keeping one hand on the wheel as the other gripped the back of Billy's head. Meanwhile I tried to keep the camera steady as I un-zipped my jeans with my free hand and brought out my own dick, already hard from watching those two.

After a couple minutes, Cole directed Billy over to my side. He quickly obeyed, moving his wet mouth over to the passenger's side of the car, where he bent down and took my cock between his lips. I felt that first warm sensation, then the hint of coldness as he took his mouth off of it. I placed both hands over his head of short brown hair and pushed him down on top of my cock. He gagged a little, but then sucked harder. I have to admit, he learned very fast how to give great head. He really wanted my cum, although a big part of me wanted instead to jack off while watching him suck Cole.

"Start of a good trip," my partner said as Billy's mouth moved up and down on my erect dick.

"Definitely."

*   *

As soon as we checked into the campground and learned that there were cabins for rent, our tents became old news. No longer would we have to sleep in a pyramidal piece of a plastic. We'd be in a classic log cabin with three rooms. Unfortunately all of the log cabins were shared space, and there weren't any cabins that were completely empty. This was campground strategy for forcing fellow campers to meet and socialize, but wasn't the best policy for campers looking to shoot porn scenes.

And since we couldn't get our own cabin, we settled with one bedroom in a 2-bedroom cabin. At least there was a living room separating us from the other campers, although the cabin's wooden walls weren't going to be thick enough to block out all the noise we'd be making.

The campground itself was slightly different than what I expected. Actually, I don't know what I expected. Probably some early 1980s San Francisco scene with tons of long-haired hippies and a bunch of plaid-wearing mustached men all parading around tents and bonfires, as wild sex parties took place right out in the bushes and passing streams. Instead the campground was no different than a regular campground, aside from the fact that the tents and cabins were filled with gay guys. I knew that in a gay campground there had to be some sort of sexual playground, hidden somewhere within the premises, and I just hoped I'd find it before the end of the weekend.

"You think they do gay camps here in the Summer?" I asked Cole, who gave me the strangest look just as we entered our cabin. The front door was always left unlocked, but each of the bedrooms were key-entry. We walked into a modest living room with some sofas facing one another, and a coffee table with magazines and board games. There was a small kitchen tucked away in a corner, and a breakfast table in the other. The most exciting part of the living room was a fireplace positioned directly across from the entrance. On either side were thin doors that led to the bedrooms. Ours was on the left, and our cabin mates weren't anywhere in sight.

"That would be hot," Billy finally replied with a pensive look on his face. "You guys could be camp counselors."

"And our next video would be from the state prison, right?" Cole replied. "Camp counselor—meh."

"It'll be an eighteen-plus camp," I said. "College boys. I think it sounds fucking hot."

"Well if we're ever rich someday maybe you can start one up, money bags," Cole jokingly replied. "Don't expect me to be a counselor."

"You can be the fitness instructor."

Cole muttered something under his breath as Billy and I laughed. The door to our bedroom was unlocked, and so while Cole inspected the living room I wandered into our new home for these next couple of nights. The room was pretty bare, with only two bunk beds and some chairs. The cabin was definitely designed to get people out of their bedrooms.

"We should've asked if they had a jacuzzi cabin," Cole called from the living room.

"A jacuzzi cabin? You're out of your mind. Why would there be a jacuzzi cabin? What is this, the fucking Westin Boondocks?"

"Like a honeymoon cabin! They've gotta have a honeymoon cabin."

"If I'm gonna catch crabs, let it at least be with a guy. Not a heart-shaped bed in Vermont."

"Luckily they make creams for that," Billy remarked. "So how's the bedro—oh," he cut himself short as soon as he peeked into our closet of a bedroom. "Should we go back and get the tent?"

"Oh come on, it's not that bad," I replied.

"Yeah!" Cole said from the living room. "You know that people in the—uh—third world—sleep on uh—dirt and wood? Dirt and wood, Billy. So be thankful you're in a cabin with a mattress. *Are* there mattresses?"

"If you call a piece of foam a mattress, then sure," Billy replied, followed by a long sigh. "I don't see any plugs for my iPod."

"Keep looking. Two days without your iPod won't kill you," Cole said.

"Yes it will."

"Hey, let's drop our bags and go check out the campground," I suggested, noting that there wasn't much to do in the cabin. I wanted to explore, to find out where everyone was cruising and having sex, and to meet some of the other campers.

"Sounds good," Cole quickly replied. "You gonna behave?" he asked Billy, who frowned and glanced at his iPod.

"I'll try."

*   *

The campground was much bigger than expected. We walked two full nature trails, one of which brought us along a beautiful stream that peacefully flowed through the forest, and yet in all of our hiking we barely found any other campers. On one of the trails we passed two seniors, both men, who smiled and kept on their way without making any conversation. And along the stream we ran into a scruffy middle-aged guy sleeping against a tree. But aside from that, it was just us.

It became clear by the end of the second trail—and the fact that it was almost dark out—that we needed to figure out what to do in the campground. Clearly there was something going on that was eluding us, and it sure as hell wasn't nature trails. And so we sought out the cabin of the campground manager, which turned out to be a white version of our cabin. His living room was more of an office, and one of the two bedrooms had been converted into a little living room.

Trailer Dan. A former Teamster, this Jerry Garcia look-alike spent an hour telling us about how he used to be an unintentional drug mule for the Vegas mob, until he found out exactly *what* the guys at the factory were putting into his truck. It prompted an identity change and a cross-country game of hiding, until he finally settled in San Francisco, where he claimed to have taken part in just about every gay protest for just about everything. He apparently protested so much, that after showing up on national TV in jean shorts and a rainbow bandana, some old mob guys recognized him. Trailer Dan narrowly escaped, moving East, where he found work in this gay campground.

For all we knew he could've just been a retired dentist from Chicago. But he liked to tell his story, and he looked crazy enough that most people probably believed him.

"So what do we do for fun around here?" Cole asked, and I shook my head immediately afterwards. What an awful question for a guy who made his life out of this place.

"There are a million things to do around here," he exclaimed, his eyes growing eerily wide. Cole, Billy, and I were sitting on a plaid sofa in his living room, and he was just across from us in a lounge chair, with his bare, dirty feet rested on a leather ottoman.

"Let me rephrase," I said. "We haven't run into anyone, yet when we checked in, we were told that most cabins were full and there weren't any full cabins for rent. We've gone on trails, and walked all around the campsite, and we can't seem to find *anyone.*"

"Of course not!" he replied. "You think you're gonna see these people on a fuckin' trail? They're all getting stoned over on Devil's Peak."

"Devil's Peak?" Cole suddenly exclaimed with the same excitement with which Trailer Dan had replied. We were all on the edge of our seats.

"Well—they only call it that because a couple people have gotten too stoned out of their wits and fell right off. Great scenic views though. I'd give you a map, but I actually just got back from there and am too high to move. Go check my desk."

Cole, Billy, and I turned and faced each other with the most intrigue we'd felt since setting off for the campground.

"I think that's the end of trail walks this weekend," I said, to which Cole and Billy nodded their heads.

*   *

"Oh my God! Someone painted the walls!" Cole shouted as soon as he switched on the lights to our cabin. As we wobbled in, stoned, exhausted, and feeling philosophical, our eyes wandered around the square living room.

"They're post-its," Billy said in disgust as he pulled a small piece of paper off of the wall. "It says: *do not remove my phone charger to charge your iPod. If there's no space, too bad.*"

"What kind of dickhead would write that?" I asked, as I pulled one off the coffee table and read it. *Please keep your shoes in your bedroom, rather than leaving them in our shared living quarters.* "Guys, we're clearly rooming with some fuckin' assholes."

"Can someone read this for me?" Cole asked, glaring at a post-it attached to the refrigerator.

"I know, the print is really small," I replied. "Be right over."

"No, I'm just too stoned to read right now."

"Alright, let me see. *Please keep your food items on the left, and don't leave half-empty bottles of iced tea on their sides. Sit them upright.*"

"What the fuck?" Cole said, staring at the fridge with a look of shock on his face.

"I say we go give them a little face-to-face message," I said, clenching my fists as I glared at their bedroom door, but Cole quickly grabbed a hold of my arm.

"I say instead we go have the loudest, hottest sex possible. And make sure to bang on their wall so loud that they think there are B-2 bombers in the air raining shells down on the campground."

"You ready to bottom, Billy?" I asked, turning my attention to him. He blushed in that usual, shy way of his, and then flashed his white teeth.

"I think that's a yes," Cole said.

*   *

"Fuck! Yeah!" Billy shouted, thrusting his arms forward and punching the bedroom wall that separated us from the assholes who left us about fifty post-it notes on bad roommate behavior.

213

"Yeah—give it to me," Cole said loudly and deeply, shoving Billy forward, his big hands wrapped around the latter's thin waist.

"Oh my God! I'm getting close!" Billy hit the wall harder, this time with both his palms, pushing all of his slim frame into it.

"Okay—," I finally said in my regular tone, as I kneeled beside them on one of the beds. "Can we actually fuck you now?"

Suddenly Billy's theatrics came to a quick halt, and he glanced over at me with that boyish face.

"We can try," he replied, and nodded nervously. He then sat up and marched his naked body over to the bed opposite mine, and laid down with his hands folded behind his head.

"Who should go first?" Cole asked the both of us as he grabbed his camera with one hand and stroked his erection with the other.

"I think you should," I suggested. "You know—you were the one who went and picked Billy up, and first got to know him, so—I think you should." I looked to Billy for approval, and he seemed to be fine with it.

"You open him up," Cole replied, and smiled at me. "Then I'll do the rest of the work."

Cole's casual reply didn't fool me for a second. Nor did his silliness or claims of being "stoned out of his mind." This was calculated. Billy was still a virgin. Neither of us had ever entered him before. No one had entered him before. We'd messed around since Cole brought him down to stay in our apartment, but we gave him lots of space to get comfortable with us.

Cole knew that I needed a little more than *bonding time* on this particular camping trip. For me, Billy wasn't just some cute twink who was imposing on my privacy at home. He was an example of the lifestyle that Cole and I had chosen for ourselves. There would easily be more guys like Billy, whether they lived with us or just became frequent friends-with-benefits. And I badly needed to get in that same zone of comfort that my lover was in. I needed to chill out on my imaginations and fears of Cole leaving me for someone like Billy. Realistically, I knew it would never happen, but insecurities have their way of popping up. Clearly, if Cole was craving this kid so badly then he'd never give up that ego-tripping chance to be Billy's first. He was handing it over to me. We were going to fuck Billy as a couple.

I wasn't quite clear whether this was romantic or not. I think in our world, it was about as romantic a gesture as any. I would've gotten weak in the knees and maybe shed a few tears, but I had a cherry to pop.

I pulled my t-shirt off and dropped my boxers, and climbed into bed with Billy. He was already preparing himself, squeezing some lube onto his hand from a bottle sitting next to the bed. His dick got hard as he watched me lean over him. He quickly rubbed the lubricant all over his asshole, and then took my cock in that wet, slippery hand, and lubed it up. Slowly he tickled his lubricated fingers up and down my erect cock, teasing my head and then working his way down to my balls. I was getting really excited for this; to penetrate that cherry hole.

It was suddenly almost surreal looking down at him with his face propped up on his elbows, totally naked, his sweet lean body and erect cock aching for me to mount him. As I knelt down between his legs he lifted them so that his ass was elevated and his cute, sweaty little feet were practically in my face. He reached down between his legs to caress my cock some more. And as he rubbed up and down with those small hands of his, I began to gently suck the toes on his left foot. His response was a surprising mixture of giggling and moaning. And after a little while he placed both his feet on my face and gripped them like a monkey would. Cole and I immediately started laughing.

There was something so sensual about him too—he was nothing like Tye. Not that Tye wasn't good in bed—he was pretty amazing. Billy was just different. He was connecting to me, through those big, boyish eyes. This wasn't just a fuck for him. He really wanted us. He wanted me inside his cherry hole.

As I stuck my hard cock up against his lubed hole I watched his whole face change. He looked at first helpless, and then curious. I slowly slid into him, the head going in just enough to make Billy open his mouth and close his eyes as he got into that mental space where he could relax his ass muscles and just enjoy my cock. I could tell he was feeling that first pain, those first sensations that are both uncomfortable and wildly exciting.

"Can I keep going?" I quietly asked him, and he nodded without opening his eyes.

I pushed harder, inching myself into him. My cock was throbbing, and I could feel the tight ring muscle of his hole pull and squeeze my cock as it inched its way in. He finally opened his eyes, just as our faces were practically touching at the nose. And yet we didn't feel like we needed to kiss each other. He just looked deep into me, and held my upper arm muscles with his little hands, gently squeezing my triceps as if letting go would cause him to fall off the bed.

"You like my ass?" he asked me.

"Love it," I whispered into his ear.

"Oh my God." He closed his eyes again, and took a deep breath. Then he put his lips up against my neck and pushed the lower half of his body up against my crotch. I could feel his fingernails dig into my arms as I got deeper. With each inch his little moans grew louder.

"Stick your tongue into his mouth," Cole told me. "Kiss that boy. Kiss him hard." And so I grabbed for Billy's chin and slipped my wet tongue into his mouth. He sucked on my tongue as I penetrated his hole.

"Stay with me," I whispered to him as I moved away from his lips and started to kiss his face and around his eyes. His eyes were still closed and his face was full of discomfort, but he still nodded. He moaned and squirmed under my weight, brushing my cheek with his light brown hair. I was loving the feel of Billy's sweet ass, and I had to fully go for it. With one final thrust, I pushed my cock deep into him. I could feel him open up; his cherry was popped. He moved his hands up my arms, resting them on my shoulders and sinking his back into the bed. I couldn't believe that this was the first time anyone had entered him. I'd never been into the virgin thing, but there was something really amazing about this. Aside from the fact that he was this beautiful, hot, young, slim guy, it just felt special being the first person to penetrate him. I wondered if he'd always remember this moment.

"Guys, I'm about to blow over here," Cole remarked. Billy and I both burst into laughter as we turned our heads to see my lover sitting there on one of the little chairs in the bedroom, stroking his dick with one hand and holding the camera with the other.

"We're having a moment here," I said, still smiling. "How are you doing?" I directed towards Billy, whose eyes were open again. I was relaxed inside him, my cock still hard and fully penetrating his tight little ass.

Billy turned back to face me, his lips just an inch apart from mine, and he widened his eyes in this beautiful, boyish, curious way.

"Fuck me Hunter, fuck me," he whispered, just before resting his lips upon mine.

It seemed like an hour of fucking Billy's sweet ass before I came, but when I did it was pretty fucking amazing. I had him doggie-style, face down and ass up, and I was soaked with sweat, pumping my hardest. I remember looking over to Cole to tell him I was close. Cole kissed me while I was pounding Billy, and just before I came I pulled my cock out and blasted a huge load on the small of Billy's back. I gushed so much cum that Cole was actually in shock.

"That was a great shot," he exclaimed as I relaxed on top of Billy, who was shaking a little from that intense fuck session. "I got every second of it on camera. You guys are fucking porn stars."

Billy didn't comment, rather he moaned and then collapsed onto his stomach. He finally looked up with a grin on his face; those boyish eyes full of excitement.

"How you doing, sexy boy?" Cole asked him. "Ready for round two, or do you need a break?"

"Bring it, daddy," he replied, both to my surprise and to Cole's. My partner arched an eyebrow, and I got off the bed to take the camera and let those two go at it.

As soon as Cole got onto the bed I could tell that he was ready for some fucking. His cock was dripping with pre-cum. It was obvious that he had been dying to pound Billy.

I focused the camera on the two of them and watched their movements. Cole was looking Billy up and down, not unlike a hungry bear staring at a bowl of honey that was about to be devoured. Cole reached down and grabbed Billy by the hair, and then said, "you wanna get fucked, sexy boy?"

"Yes please," was his soft response. Cole instantly leaned down and sucked on Billy's mouth for a minute, kissing his deeply before pushing his face down into the pillows. Billy responded by arching his back, and sticking that perfect little bubbly ass up in the air. Cole's cock was already slathered in lube; he'd been playing with himself while watching Billy and I fuck.

I was so excited by all the build-up that even I was getting hard again after my explosive cum. When Cole saw my erection, he motioned for me to come towards him. And as he pressed his thick cock up against Billy's tight little hole, he grabbed my sweaty body and pulled me into him. Cole kissed me passionately as he stuck his fat dick into Billy's wet hole. Billy moaned so loudly that I thought it was over, that maybe he'd

217

already had enough. Two big cocks in one night was a lot to ask of a twinky virgin.

Cole let me go, and I got back to filming as my lover took control of Billy's ass. Billy was clenching the foam mattress as tightly as possible, pushing his flat, lean back up against Cole's crotch. He was humping that big cock in long, deep strides. And once Cole was all the way in, he fully took control, fucking Billy harder and harder. I could only imagine what the guys next door were hearing as Cole talked dirty to his little virgin.

"You like that dick in your ass, boy?"

"Yeah, fuck me daddy," Billy said loudly. He was practically shouting in-between those long moans.

I felt ready to cum again. I'd been stroking with one hand while filming with the other, and as I focused the camera on Cole's fast-paced fucking, I came around the side of the bed and stuck my cock in Billy's mouth. Billy was sucking me and getting plowed at the same time.

I could tell Cole was getting close, because he had this strange—almost angry—look on his face, that was typical whenever his fucking got really intense. His nostrils flared and his eyes focused on that sweet virgin ass. As I watched my man get close to shooting, I blasted my load into Billy's mouth. He wasn't expecting it, and so I heard those first moans of surprise as cum shot all over his tongue.

"I'm gonna fucking shoot," Cole shouted, and he pulled out of Billy's tight hole. Within seconds, ropes of hot, salty cum shot as far as Billy's head, covering his cheeks and neck. Billy's cum-covered tongue flung out in an attempt to catch some of Cole's hot juice.

When Cole fell backwards in exhaustion, Billy was quick to respond. He practically jumped onto Cole's dick, mounting his sweaty body. As he bounced up and down on that fat cock, he jerked himself harder and faster, doing all the work as Cole laid back on the bed. Finally Billy let out a loud moan, and within seconds hot cum squirted from his dick, shooting all over Cole's hairy chest. And with the meaty, cum-covered cock still inside him, he collapsed forward into Cole's arms.

*　　*

There weren't any post-its to greet us in the morning. Unfortunately, our classy and courteous cabin mates had packed and left that same night. Apparently not all gay people are comfortable with sex. And so the cabin was ours for the rest of the weekend. From that special night onwards, Billy somehow relaxed into the space needed for bottoming. He wasn't quite the bottom that Tye was. That kid could suck a golf ball through a 40 ft. hose, and get fucked for thirty minutes after cumming. But Billy was on his way to becoming a full-fledged power bottom, with our eager help. And after we opened him up in our cabin, all he wanted to do for the rest of the trip was get fucked in every position and every place possible. We fucked him up against a deserted cabin, along trails, against trees—and he was loving every second of it[5].

On Sunday night, with a camera full of video material, we said goodbye to our cabin, to Trailer Dan, and to the gay campground, and hit the road for Boston. We had no plans for the week other than to get this new video up online, and Cole seemed like he wasn't going to sleep or eat until the video editing was done with.

"You still okay to drive?" I asked, although I already knew the answer. I was asking more out of courtesy. Billy was fast asleep in the backseat, with headphones on and his iPod rested awkwardly in one hand.

"Wide awake. I don't even know if I'll sleep when we get home. Might start putting this weekend together."

"Don't go too crazy. We have all the time in the world. It's not like when we had full-time jobs. But I guess it's cool that you're so excited about this. You were never this excited about real estate."

Cole turned and smiled at me, and then put his attention back on the road.

"Our new lives," he remarked.

"And I have no reason to worry about our new lives?" I asked, throwing the question out there.

"What do you mean?"

"Well, since Billy's been staying with us I haven't had any alone time with you. Frat Boy is one thing. At least he has a house—or sort of a house—across the street. But I guess I just don't know what our life is going to turn into."

5

http://olbmedia.site.metrixstream.com/site/MaverickMen/?page=videos&contentId=16

"Like if we'll become an orphanage for horny nineteen-year olds?"He asked, and I laughed at the way he phrased it.

"Yes, like an orphanage for horny nineteen-year olds."

"I know—we need to start investing in other properties."

"Seriously?"

Cole instantly shook his head *no*.

"I love having Billy over, but I miss just waking up next to you, and sharing the whole day with you and you alone. We'll put Billy in an apartment. Don't worry. Look at all this beautiful freedom we have."

"True—but the videos come with their own burdens," I replied. "Look at the whole mess with Tye. Even Frat Boy the night of the video. Could you imagine if we had to deal with that every time we did a video with him?"

"He gets like that even without shooting a video," Cole remarked. "That crazy ass. Too bad we couldn't bring him along this weekend."

"It was important that it was just the three of us."

"Yeah, I agree."

I reached for my cell phone and clicked on our joint e-mail account, deciding to go through the weekend's mail since service up in the campground wasn't particularly reliable.

"I love you so much," Cole said as I scrolled through a few days' worth of messages. "I mean it. This is all for you."

"But it's fun for you too," I replied. "I don't mean to sound unappreciative, because I really am. I think we've created something beautiful. But it has its downs. And the ups are obvious. I mean now I feel like some sort of a—sexual *rock star*. How often are nineteen-year-old virgins knocking at the door of guys nearly twice—or in your case *actually* twice—their age—."

"Hey," Cole snapped back in a funny tone.

"But it's true, right? How often does this happen?"

"Not often enough," he said, and then laughed to himself. "But I just want you to know the difference. I'm madly in love with you. These guys we're meeting are friends—great fucks—probably some won't be so great. I think you just don't know your own power. If tomorrow you said that we're not doing porn anymore and are going back to our old careers, I'd delete the XTube account."

"Really?"

"Oh yeah, in a heartbeat. I love the freedom and fun that this life gives us, though. I want to be able to give this to you forever."

He knew how to make me smile. I rested a hand on Cole's knee and he immediately took one hand off the wheel and placed it overtop mine.

"Oh my God."

"What?" he asked. "I'm not going too fast. I'm not! Look, the speed limit is—."

"You won't believe this e-mail," I said. I was stunned, and I could barely get the words out. "He's suing us."

"Who is suing us?"

"Tye. He has a lawyer," I anxiously replied. I scrolled up and down the e-mail from a law firm in Boston, intensely scanning each sentence. Every single word.

"But for what?"

"He wants a higher cut of the video. Look at that—*no contract*. We're fucked. We're fucked."

"Are you sure this is legitimate?" Cole asked me, but I could barely hear him in the loudness of my mind. What a little shit. "I'll call him as soon as we get back. There must be some mistake. Maybe he tried to call all weekend and we didn't have service, and this was a last resort—."

"We need to deal with this before it gets ugly. Cole, if this blows up—I mean, we have family—."

"I know, I know," he replied, placing a hand on my shoulder. "It'll be okay."

"I hope so," I said, defeated. The idea of a lawsuit scared the hell out of me. We'd quit our jobs to focus on making videos, and I didn't want to think that one angry guy could bring us down. We still had family members out there who didn't know about the videos, and we also still had bills to pay for. I was beginning to obsess over every which way we could get fucked by Tye. "I'm starting to understand why studios become *studios*."

"Yeah," Cole calmly replied, keeping those green eyes on the road. "Me too."

CHAPTER SIXTEEN

narrated by Cole Maverick

"We keep getting these studio offers," I mentioned from the computer desk in our bedroom. Hunter and Billy were sprawled out on the bed, watching a movie. From time to time I'd glance up to see Billy cuddle up to Hunter like a cute, little puppy, and some of the expressions on Hunter's face were priceless. "I don't know what to do with them."

"I thought you're anti-studio," Billy replied.

"Well—I am, but I'm open to *talking* to a studio if they can give us more resources to keep doing what we're doing. I'd need to have a lot of freedom, you know, to film the way I want. Try getting an erection while two cameramen in another world of ugly are kneeling beside your bed, as some curmudgeon studio exec is taking a loud shit in your bathroom."

"Is that really your impression of studios?" Hunter asked me, poking his head up to laugh in my direction. "No wonder you hate them."

"Cialis works wonders," Billy said, although I doubt that horny kid had ever needed one.

"Maybe we can meet with one—I don't know. There's one in Boston that wrote us. I've seen their site—they do the whole twink thing pretty well."

"Any more word on this nonsense about the lawsuit?" Hunter asked, out of the blue.

"Tye sent me a text saying he'd call this morning," I replied. I'd been trying to stay off the topic. I'd been miserable since getting home from the camping trip, and couldn't mask my anxiety over this lawsuit. My fears weren't even strictly financial at this point. I just didn't want to get distracted from our work, and bogged down with adolescent drama. We were trying too hard to create a new, more relaxed life for ourselves, and we both worried about any drama that might steer us off course.

And in addition to the worries about drama and wasted time spent on a silly lawsuit, there was also that fear of having more situations like the one with Ron. If news of the lawsuit got out, lots of people in our lives could find out about the videos. We planned on eventually telling our friends and family in our own time, and on our own terms.

Obviously there were still many people in both of our lives who didn't know about the videos, and we wanted to keep it that way. Not everyone is sexually mature and comfortable enough to appreciate and understand pornography, or differentiate between the good kind and the bad kind. And sure, I could name a bunch of relatives who I knew wouldn't be cool with the videos, and that didn't mean I loved them any less. It just meant that they never had enough positive exposure to the porn industry. They just didn't understand it.

"That kid sounds like *big time* drama," Billy remarked from the bed, which prompted Hunter to raise an eyebrow.

"At least he didn't move in after the first time we messed around," Hunter replied. "Had I known there was a U-Haul attached to your ass——."

"Who does your laundry?" Billy shot back. "That's right, *bitch*. I have the power to ruin all your clothing in a fifteen-minute timeframe."

"Yeah? See what I do to your hot little ass."

"Keep it up, I may just slip with the bleach," Billy replied with some laughter, and laid his head back down upon Hunter's lap.

Just as I pulled up a recent e-mail from a Boston porn studio, the doorbell rang twice, creating a loud buzzing throughout the apartment.

"That's probably Bradley," Hunter said. "He said he was coming over today. Can you get it?"

"Yeah, I can see you're *so* busy," I replied.

"You need the exercise more than I do."

"Son of a——," I muttered as I stood up from the computer desk and stretched my arms. This anxiety needed to go. Even the idea of Frat Boy, Hunter, and Billy, all in bed with me, didn't lift my spirits. As I climbed down the ladder to the first floor of the apartment the doorbell rang again.

"Coming!" I shouted, although the upstairs TV was loud enough that I didn't know if Frat Boy could hear me behind the front door.

My expression transformed as soon as I opened the door. Tye was standing there in my doorway, looking cute as usual in black jeans, an open, puffy gray jacket, and a tight t-shirt underneath. He looked sad, distraught—in fact, just looking at that face made me forget all about my anger surrounding this lawsuit.

"Can we go for a walk?" he asked in a calm, melancholic way.

"I don't know, Tye—you've been putting me through it," I told him, but he just kept looking at me with that sad expression. "Okay—let me grab my sneakers."

I grabbed a pair of shoes beside the door and hurried out into the hallway. I didn't want to invite him in, mainly because I didn't want to make a scene. I also knew he felt he could trust me more than he could Hunter.

"You been staying away from the clubs?" I asked him as I put my sneakers on. I glanced up to look him in the eyes, maybe for some sign of honesty. Or some reassurance that he wasn't fucked up on some drug.

"Been trying to."

"Well that's good news. And staying away from crystal?"

Tye slowly nodded his head, but kept his mouth shut. As soon as my feet slid into the shoes, I started to walk at a slow pace down the hallway. Tye followed next to me.

"So you want to explain this lawsuit to me?" I asked him. "Hunter and I have been good to you, and I can't figure out why you're trying to hurt us?"

"I don't know what you're talking about," he quickly replied.

"Of course. Just like the video flagging."

"I don't! I just—I need some money," he bluntly said. "I know the video's doing well, and I want a bigger cut. I was gonna threaten you with a lawsuit if you didn't give me money, but I don't want my parents finding out about the video and all."

"That's nice," I sarcastically replied. "Well it seems you've taken more steps than just *thinking* about a lawsuit."

"What are you talking about?" he asked me, appearing dumbfounded. He seemed legitimately confused about the lawsuit, but for all I knew, he could've realized how awful the legal action was, and therefore felt embarrassed by it. Embarrassed enough to deny getting a lawyer involved. "You know I'd never hurt you."

"I don't know that," I shot back. I kept my voice low as we neared the exit to the apartment building. "Where are you parked?"

"On the street."

"I'll walk you to your car."

"Can't we go back to my place and talk about this?" he asked.

"I don't think that's a good idea."

"Cole, I would never hurt you," he said again, although his words didn't have the same effect on me as they used to. "I just need some more money. I want to move away from Boston. I was thinking LA. Or Atlanta."

"You try to destroy the video, then you threaten us with a lawsuit—why the hell would I want to give you more money? Not long ago you were pouring your heart out about a crystal addiction—."

"It's not an addiction," he interrupted.

"Well it sure sounded like one. Going home with some stranger and waking up in an alley? That's a sure fucking sign that you need to get some help. The offer is still on the table from me. But why would I want to help someone who is threatening my family with a lawsuit?"

"Stop talking like that," he said. I could tell from his face that he was getting upset. I didn't know how to deal with this kid anymore. "I'm not threatening your family."

"Hunter is my family. You threaten him, and you're threatening my family."

"He's your boyfriend," he angrily replied, as if he didn't want to accept that Hunter was anything more than that. As if our threesome had somehow diminished my relationship with Hunter in the eyes of Tye.

"So if I give you more money, is this a buy-out? We won't ever have to deal with your shit again? Or see you, for that matter?"

"Why are you saying that? Why wouldn't you want to see me?"

"Tye—do you realize what you've done to us?" I replied, growing increasingly frustrated. We walked through the front doors of the building and started a slow walk across the lawn to his car, which was parked along the street outside the complex. "The lawsuit thing is serious! You don't just go around suing people you care about. You've caused us lots of stress and anxiety. And you've lied out your ass."

"Why don't you move down south with me?" he asked, and it took me completely by surprise. "We can do videos together. You don't need Hunter."

"You don't know what the fuck you're talking about," I said, and sped up my pace.

"I know you still think about me like that," Tye replied, hurrying to keep up with me.

"How much money do you want? I'll go to the bank today and I don't want to see you again after that. And if you want me to take down the video—consider it gone. In fact, I'd rather just get rid of it."

"I just want another shot with you!" he said, loudly enough that it was embarrassing. I glanced around to see if anyone had overheard him.

"There was never any *shot*," I softly replied, lowering my voice as we approached his car. "Do you understand that? Hunter and I are lovers. We invited you in to have hot, exciting, fun sex, but that's all it was. Sex with a cool friend."

"No—we were connected while you were fucking me."

"Tye—tell me what I did to lead you on? I didn't do anything. I can't think of *anything* that I've done. I've wanted badly for this to work out as a friendship," I honestly told him, and I could feel my eyes getting wet as I talked to him.

"Just give me another shot, and you don't have to give me any more money," he said. "We can leave today if you want. I'll do anything you want. I'll sexually please you whenever you want. You can have boys over all the time. You can fuck me whenever—have other guys fuck me for videos."

"Tye, come on, you're talking crazy. I'm in love with Hunter," I replied. "It's not about the videos, or money, or submission. I'm just in love with him. We're doing videos for freedom and fun. I'm sorry if you got confused, but I laid everything down from the start, and you know it."

I opened Tye's front door for him, but he stood there staring at me with those sad, boyish eyes. He looked vulnerable and anxious. I don't know if he was on something at that moment; I wouldn't have been surprised if he was, the way he was acting. As I waited for him to get into the car I could feel my cock getting hard. Something about that vulnerable, sad look on his face, or the way he held his body against the cold winds.

"I'm gonna go inside and take the video down, and if you want money—."

"I just want you," he interrupted me. "I can't beat my addiction without you."

"Just a minute ago you were saying that you *don't* have an addiction!" I replied, raising my voice in frustration. "What is it, Tye? What happened to the sweet boy I knew?"

"You need to help bring him out again," Tye said, staring at me with those boyish eyes. He looked uncomfortable in the cold, but I didn't want to get in his car, and we weren't having a conversation that could've taken place inside my apartment or building.

"It means a lot to me that you feel this way about me. It really does. I think you're sexy and sweet, and you were such an amazing, cool guy. I don't know what's been going on with you lately. But my heart's been with Hunter for years, and it's not going anywhere."

Tye bit his lower lip and then lowered his eyes from me to the pavement. I didn't know what else to say, and so I just stood there, waiting for him to do something. And after about a minute of silence, he did. He stepped forward in a calm and intimate way, leaned his chin upwards, and gently kissed me on the lips. It was short and close-mouthed, and as soon as he withdrew he averted his eyes, looking instead into his open car. As he stepped into the driver's seat and started the ignition I just stood there, wondering what had happened with this kid. Wondering if I'd somehow fucked this up along the way. Wondering if there would be more like him. What if this would be Billy in another couple of months?

Tye drove away without saying a word. I stood there on the pavement, so uncomfortable with my emotions that I wasn't even bothered by the chilly winds that swept down into the city on that particular day. And for some reason the neighborhood suddenly seemed empty. No life over at the frat house across the street. No one outside on the front lawn of my apartment building. No cars driving down the long street that surrounded the complex. I let my eyes wander around me until they fell on the window of my apartment, tucked away on the second-floor in the corner of the building. Hunter was standing there. I was far away but I could still see his outline, watching me from above. I wondered how long he'd been standing there, and how much of everything he'd seen. And for some reason—although I'm not quite sure why—the morning's victory didn't seem like much of a victory at all. There wouldn't be any lawsuit, or any more threats from this kid, but the ones that had passed had already left their scars.

I did my best to smile, although I knew Hunter couldn't make out the expressions on my face from that distance. It was time to go back inside.

"We're going on a road trip tonight," I announced as soon as I climbed up the ladder to the second floor of our apartment. Hunter was back in bed with Billy, and he placed the movie on pause as soon as my feet hit the wooden floor of our loft bedroom.

"We just got back from one," Billy remarked.

"I have a friend down in Providence, and we're gonna go spend the night."

"Providence is hardly a road trip," he replied.

"Well, it's something," I said, and immediately went to the bedroom closet to grab a duffel bag that I typically used for the gym.

"Is everything okay?" Hunter asked. His tone was warm and worried, but I did my best to give him a reassuring smile.

"No more lawsuit. But we're gonna take down his video tonight. And that's fine, because once this camping video with Billy goes up, we'll be playing in a whole new ballpark."

"Is there even anything to do in Providence?" Billy asked.

"Yes, there's a lot to do. Grab your bags," I said, and Billy reluctantly rolled off of the bed to collect some of his things.

"I don't feel like bringing a bag. Can I just throw my shit in yours?" he asked.

"Yeah, of course."

"What about Frat Boy?" Hunter mentioned, and I realized I'd totally forgotten that he was supposed to come over.

"You snooze, you lose. That kid gives a six-hour timeframe for hanging out. For all we know he might not show up until ten tonight."

"Does your friend even know we're coming?" Hunter asked me.

"He will as soon as we're on our way."

*   *

"So this is it?" Billy casually asked from the backseat as we drove through the East Side of Providence, Rhode Island. I looked in the rearview mirror to see him glaring out the window with an expressionless face, his headphones still on and his iPod laying next to him on the seat.

229

"Yeah—welcome to Providence," I said. "If we're lucky, all the hot Brown and RISD boys will be out."

"The only seniors I'm seeing are the ones collecting social security checks," Billy remarked.

"You know what, turn your iPod volume up and just wait to comment until after the trip."

"It's a very beautiful neighborhood," Hunter diplomatically said. "You're not gonna find big nightclubs, but the houses are really classic. Do we have time to walk around before dinner?" he asked me.

"Yeah, yeah, we'll explore. Then we're having dinner with my friend Miguel, and he's taking us out to a strip club here in Providence. He said it's the only reliable place on a Monday night."

"I bet there are a few bingo nights around here," Billy said. "You know, retirement communities love those."

"Are you gonna keep this up all night?" I asked, reaching my arm in the back and playfully grabbing his leg. I shook it, and watched his body shake back and forth in the rearview mirror.

"Maybe," he coyly said, and giggled. Billy had never been to a gay club, let alone a strip club. This was mostly due to his age. At nineteen years old, there weren't many gay clubs that actually catered to a non-drinking crowd. I don't know whether this strip club had an age limit or not, but my friend Miguel said it was seedy enough that they wouldn't really care. As long as we were buying drinks and tipping the strippers, we'd have nothing to worry about.

"So have you guys been to this strip club?" Billy asked. "Lots of straight muscle guys, right? Maybe some sailor hats?"

"We're actually gonna drop you off and put you in their employ," Hunter said, turning around to face the backseat. "Let them deal with your sarcastic little ass."

"They'll give me back in a few days."

"Hey Hunter, what's the address? Odds are on the right. Keep your eyes open."

"It's right there," Hunter said, pointing out an enormous house at the end of the block. The house was pale yellow in color, and looked big enough to be split into many different apartments. I didn't know how many suites they rented out, but I told the guy on the phone to book us the largest available.

"No street parking? Is there a garage?"

"Around back there's parking," Hunter said. "Around the side of the house."

"It looks creepy," Billy remarked as he took his headphones off, observing the old house with a sudden spark of curiosity.

"It's supposedly haunted," I said. "Awful story too."

"What?" Billy asked, his eyes darting back to me as we pulled into a parking spot behind the house, in a little driveway surrounded by overgrown grass.

"He's full of shit," Hunter remarked.

"No! I'm serious. I checked this place out online. Hunter—how much do I love scary shit?"

"You live for it."

"Exactly my point. So wouldn't I *naturally* pick the most haunted place to stay? Couldn't I have just booked a cheap hotel room somewhere in the city?"

"Yes," Hunter reluctantly conceded.

"Okay, my point exactly."

"Well what's the story?" Billy pressed on. I could tell that he was suddenly a little nervous. His eyes were shifting from the house to me, switching every five seconds.

"Okay—if I tell you, will you be able to sleep tonight?" I asked him as I turned off the ignition, and turned around to face him. Billy nodded his head. I couldn't help but think how much he looked like a little owl, all wide-eyed and curious, sitting with a perky posture in back. "This place has been a bed and breakfast for about twenty-five years. They'll claim that the house used to be single family. But, they're *lying*. You see, the current owners bought this magnificent piece of real estate that no one else would touch, and they did so on the verge of it being torn down. They got a steal, basically paying for the land, and less than the land was even worth. No one was going to even develop on this lot after what happened in the late 60s and early 70s."

"What happened?" Billy asked, this time more nervously. His eyes were wide, and completely drawn into mine. Even Hunter looked a little bothered by what I was saying, although he was trying to play it off like he didn't believe me.

"Before this place became a bed and breakfast, it was closed down for nearly ten years. No one would dare go near it. The place was rotting. I'm amazed the current owners were even able to renovate. I mean the windows were all barred up—pipes rotting—this place was a disaster zone. But one thing was still intact. One very important feature. Hotel suites."

"It was a hotel?" Billy quickly asked me.

"Well—you could say that. More or less. You see, this house was only owned by one family ever since it was built early last century. The place is over one hundred years old, you know. And one family owned it up until 1985. Or—1976, when it was seized by the State. That's the year a neighbor tipped off the police to a strange sighting outside the property.

"This neighbor was an old man—raised in one of the old red homes built in the last quarter of the 19th century here in Providence. He was a lifer. Eventually bought a place across the street from this one with his wife. One night he was walking his dog around the block and decided to take it down the street. Right down this one next to us, that passes this house. As he walked his dog down the street he heard a tapping sound coming from the house. Brief, painful taps, something that couldn't possibly come from birds or the weather, or even a tree brushing up against the window.

"But he just kept going. Kept walking. It wasn't until the return, walking back up that street with his dog, that he heard the noise again and decided to look up. And up in one of the second story windows he saw what would go into the very first police report. A man—foaming at the mouth—trails of blood starting where his eyes used to be—tapping at the window like a madman.

"You see, this bed and breakfast that we're about to stay in was inherited by a psychologist whose parents tragically died young. The dad was killed in World War II, and the mom raised her son while dealing with severe depression, that led to a suicide right here in this very house. But that's not the scary story. It's what happened after this young man's parents passed away.

"He inherited the house while he was in med school. Upon returning and setting up practice, he realized he could make a few bucks on the side by renting out bedrooms in this palatial estate. Not a bad idea, right? And so he used some of his inheritance to fix up the floor plans and turned the place into an inn. Hired staff and all.

"What quickly became apparent to our young psychologist's staff and hotel guests was that his troubled past had resulted in some severe personality disorders. As word of mouth spread about his outbursts, his odd behaviors, and the creepy way he'd stalk the hallways and social rooms at nighttime brought down the hotel. All the staff quit or were fired, and no one was showing up to stay overnight. Instead of accepting that hotel management may not have been his specialty, he grew angry. And his anger was unleashed in the worst possible way, on one of the most vulnerable groups of people in society.

"You see, the psychologist always resented the fact that his father was killed during a war. It made him obsessed with war. He was both terrified and fascinated with it. He wanted to know everything about it. To *see* it, without actually being there. And he resented those who fought in wars, maybe because that's the way his father died. Maybe because he was too much of a coward to serve his country. But given this dark fascination and fetish, he re-launched his hotel as a cheap place for men returning from the Vietnam War.

"A night's stay was often dirt cheap, if not free. He didn't hire any staff. He went after people who had lost everything in the war. Guys who either lost their minds, or had sold all their possessions before departing for Southeast Asia, and had nothing to return to. He accepted these men into his home. Very few at a time. And from Johnson to Nixon, our young psychologist would lure these vulnerable people into trusting him—into sleeping in his house with their doors unlocked. And one by one he'd do his experiments. He did unspeakable things to these men— all in an attempt to extract from them something about war. Something about why they went. Or so he could hear the same way they cried out in pain when on the battlefield. Or see the same *hell* in their eyes that they saw out in the jungles of Vietnam. He wanted to kill soldiers. And he did, for a decade.

"At least, it's assumed that it was for a decade. Obviously no one knows the exact dates. When the cops broke down the door and searched the house they found the psychologist dead. That guy in the window— the one the neighbor saw—had stabbed him to death, forty times. Apparently he broke free, but since he had no eyes and was too injured to walk, he couldn't make it out of the house. The police found so many corpses in the basement that just opening the door to the cellar from the kitchen unleashed a smell so nauseating that it could make you throw up everything in your stomach.

"And that's the history. The place was cleaned out and left for dead. The bloodiest property in all of Providence. That is, until a quirky, older couple bought it in 1985, totally renovated the house, and re-launched it as a bed and breakfast with themed suites."

"There's no fucking way I'm staying here," Billy said. This kid's face was ghost white at this point. Even Hunter was breathing heavily.

"It's pre-paid. Too late," I replied.

"But I—ah!" Billy screamed so loudly that I leaped a couple inches off of the driver's seat. A tapping on his car window had sent him howling in fear. When my eyes shot to the window I saw Billy hunched over in fetal position, and an older man waving at us with a confused look on his face.

"We're getting a hotel," Hunter exclaimed.

"Too late," I replied, and instantly opened the car door. "Hey! I'm Cole—talked with you on the phone earlier today about the suite."

"Is he okay?" the older man asked, pointing towards Billy, who was just starting to peer up in curiosity.

"He's totally fine," I replied, shrugging it off as if Billy's reaction was nothing. "You must be—."

"Howard," he said, his tone becoming more friendly. He stepped around the car and shook my hand. I recognized him instantly from the picture of he and his wife on the inn's website. He was in decent shape for a guy his age, which I guessed was around late seventies. He dressed plainly; flannel shirt and old Levi's. "Welcome to our bed and breakfast. How was your drive?"

"Nice and easy."

"Terrific. Come inside and I'll get you all set up," Howard replied with a congenial smile.

As he walked back towards the house, I leaned down and glanced into the car, where Billy and Hunter were both staring at the house with terror in their eyes.

"You guys aren't *scared* of this place, right?" I asked them.

"No," they each unconvincingly replied.

"Good. Let's grab our stuff and check out the most haunted place in Providence!" As I turned from the car and headed into the guest house, not even a crowbar could've pried the smile off my face.

*   *

"I'm afraid the Edgar Allan Poe suite only has one bed, but there's a sofa with a pull-out couch," Howard's wife, Melinda, remarked as she led us upstairs to the second floor. She looked even younger and more vibrant than her husband, and it was clear as soon as we got inside that Melinda ran the show. She seemed to take great pride in the bed and breakfast.

"One bed and a pull-out sounds great," I told her.

"When did you guys buy this place?" Billy asked her. His eyes were still darting all around the house in total discomfort.

"In 1985," she replied without hesitation. "Needed a lot of work, though. Howard and I were able to fix it up nicely. It's been an on-going project. Oh—and watch your step in the second floor hallway at night. It gets very dark up here when the sun goes down."

"Something to remember when we get home from the club," I whispered to Billy, who responded with a dirty look.

"Here we are," she said, stopping outside a door made out of a dark wood. "Welcome to tonight's home away from home." She opened the door and led us into a suite with two rooms and a small bathroom that featured one of those old, huge white tubs, completely enclosed by a wrap-around shower curtain. This was the Edgar Allan Poe suite, and every detail of decoration was just as creepy as the writer. The walls were painted in a blend of violet and mauve, which in a suite with very little natural sunlight created an eerie daytime color. All of the furniture was as dark as wood can get, and the walls were covered with paintings of headless men and women. The grand centerpieces were wood-carved ravens that sat above the queen bed, and in dim lighting looked so creepy and authentic that even I was wondering if I should opt for the pull-out couch.

"Oh my God—," Billy said, and I looked over to see him at the window. "It's facing the sidewalk. It's facing the sidewalk on the side of the building."

"About that," Melinda said, and cleared her throat. "Something about the glass—I don't know—but many guests have reported hearing a tapping sound on that window, late at night. I don't know if there's a bird's nest up there, or maybe just the wind—oh, either way, just so you know."

"Tapping?" Billy asked. The poor kid looked terrified.

235

"Yes, tapping. Oh—and—well, the house was in awful condition when we purchased it. And so much of it was gutted and renovated. The walls were, how should I say, very *thin* when we bought the house. We've since sound-proofed them. So you'll have plenty of privacy."

"Which means no one can hear you scream," I quietly said in Billy's direction. He turned around and gave me the dirtiest look imaginable.

"Melinda, we're going to meet some friends tonight, and will be home very late," Hunter said. "Will the house be locked after a certain time?"

"Yes—but I'll give you a key. The kitchen will be open if you'd like a late night snack. Just make sure you don't go down into the basement. It's the old white door in the kitchen with the lock on it. Unfortunately Howard misplaced the key last week and we had to break the lock, since the water tank is in the basement. We haven't gotten a new lock yet, and I just don't want to encourage anyone to—go into the non-*common areas*."

"Do you want us to buy a lock for the basement? We can do that today," Hunter quickly replied.

"Are you shivering?" I asked him.

"No. Why would I be shivering?"

"Howard has some errands to run tomorrow, so he'll do it then," Melinda replied. "But thank you for the offer. Well I'm headed downstairs, but stop by the office on your way out so that I can get you a house key. Enjoy your stay."

"Thanks Melinda," I said with the biggest smile I could produce. When I turned back to face Hunter and Billy, they were each looking nervously around the room, inspecting every closet, corner, and window curtain. "Are you guys ready to go see Providence?"

They hastily nodded their heads.

*   *

We met up with my friend Miguel at around 8:00 PM, and after a casual dinner the four of us headed to the strip club. The day—albeit on the chilly side—was perfect for exploring Providence, and I was happy that we got to introduce Billy to a new city. Hunter and Billy quickly became comfortable with Miguel, who was a friend from the old days.

He was about Hunter's age, but could pass off as a freshman in college. Something about that dark, smooth Puerto Rican skin, coupled with his warm eyes and affectionate behavior.

"Just some warnings before we go in," Miguel said as we parked in a poorly-lit, shady lot outside the strip joint. "First off, about three-quarters of these guys are hustlers. About three-quarters are also straight. That doesn't mean all the straight guys are hustlers, but I'm just giving you the statistics. Some of them will try to sell you a blowjob, then take you in the back alleyway. There's a good chance that they've got some thug back there waiting patiently to take your shit. Obviously he's got a deal with the stripper."

"Is there a safe place for blowjobs?" Hunter asked. I couldn't tell if he was serious or not.

"If you pay for a lap dance, and they like you, then you'll probably get one. Oh, and the rate is always a third of whatever they tell you. They start high for any newbies."

"What the fuck is a newbie?" I asked him, and Miguel replied with a surprised look.

"You don't know what a fucking newbie is? It's someone who is *new* to something."

"Oh, so like—new to the strip club?"

"Precisely. Rule three: don't order anything with tequila in it. And whatever you do, *don't* order the bar food."

"Even the peanuts?"

"For God's sake, definitely don't order the peanuts."

"But aren't they usually complimentary?" I asked.

"Go ahead and see what happens," he taunted me, and I worriedly glanced around the car. "So that's it for the rules. Don't do anything stupid, and we'll have a lot of fun tonight. Don't need to be bailing anyone out of jail. It's a Monday."

Miguel was the first to open the car door, and the rest of us swiftly followed suit. He led us into the entrance, where a grumpy-looking old man stamped our wrists and waved us into the club without saying a word.

"Oh my God, Miguel, this is the trashiest, slimiest, sleaziest joint I've ever been to. A hive of pure scum."

"And don't you love it?" Miguel turned to me with a big smile, and all I could do was nod a slacked jaw in approval as I watched the trashy scene.

"Yes, I fucking love it."

"Let's start up a pool game," Hunter remarked after giving a once-over to our soon-to-be favorite dump in Providence. This place was your standard, trashy strip joint. There were two bars, one on either end of the club, and a catwalk down the middle for dancers to perform. On the left side was a pool table surrounded by some red, ratty-looking sofas, that looked like a burgundy in the dim lighting of the club.

"Fuck, the sofas are nasty," I remarked as we neared the pool table. "And they look wet."

"Yeah, I don't think they really worry about steam cleaning the sofas around here," Miguel replied. Hunter went off to get change for the pool table, and so Billy and I took a quick walk around the club. The opposite side had a little dance floor that was completely empty, and a second stage for dancers. The crowd was pretty scarce, but then again it was a Monday night. Most of the patrons looked like they were either truck drivers or retirees. There were only about five or six strippers floating around, socializing with customers as they took turns getting up on the pole.

"You wanna get a lap dance?" I asked Billy, who suddenly looked up at me as if I'd asked him to do a shot of heroin.

"Seriously? I wouldn't even know where to begin."

"To begin with what? You just pick out some guy you think is hot, and they grind up on you."

"I don't know, I don't know," he dismissively replied. "I don't know if I want some skank humping me."

"We're getting you a lap dance," I said. "And that's final. Skanks, huh? You know you've been eyeball-licking every stripper in here since we walked through that lube-covered front door."

Billy frowned and folded his arms.

"Hey, what are you guys drinking?" Miguel called out as we walked back to the pool table. "First round's on me."

"Gin and tonic," Billy replied.

"Oh—*excuse me*," I said with my raised eyebrows. "When did *we* start drinking? You have an ID to back up that order?"

"No, but that's why I have you here."

"So hold on—do you even know what a gin and tonic tastes like?"I asked him. He looked kind of puzzled.

"Yeah—it's just gin and tonic water. Duh."

"I think we'll just stick with the tonic water for tonight."

"But that's not fair! Everyone else is drinking."

"*Fair* is a fluid concept," I reminded him.

"I'll remember that next time you want to release some of your *own* fluids," he shot back, and walked off towards the bar to get his water.

For the next couple of hours we played pool, laughed, were entertained by some strippers, and even chatted with a couple of the dirty bar patrons. But between the hours of 10:00 and 12:00, it seemed like each time we looked up from the pool table there were more and more people. It was amazing, but the strip club—on a Monday night—went from being completely dead to nearly a full house. Suddenly the number of strippers had tripled. The dance floor was active. There was even a cheap light show up on the main catwalk, probably something to take everyone's attention off the fact that none of the straight strippers could actually dance.

And at midnight on the dot, somewhere into our ninth or tenth game of pool, a hideous drag queen emerged on the main stage dressed as Marie Antoinette. Or, Marie Antoinette's much older, much less attractive sister.

She announced that there would be a wet thong contest among the night's strippers, and immediately afterwards broke out into an awful rendition of a classic Elton John song, opening with the tragic lines: *don't let your son go down on me; he's much too young to get a venereal disease.*

"This drag monster is out of control," Hunter said, midway through her performance. Miguel was playing pool with Billy, and Hunter and I were sitting on one of the red sofas, drinking dirty vodka martinis and observing the crowd.

"*Drag monster* isn't nice," I scoldingly told Hunter. "They prefer *gender illusionists.*" He gave me a perplexed look, until he realized I was joking. "This place is a fucking trip," I added. "I'm glad we came though. I'm having fun. And it gives Billy some exposure."

"Yeah—I guess he needs it."

"How are you two holding up?" I asked him. Hunter sighed, and then took another sip of his drink.

"I think it's been pretty solid since the camping trip. But I'm just worried that he's not going to move out. I think that we should sit him down as soon as the video is out—."

"It'll be out this week, I promise."

"Well—as soon as it's out," he repeated himself. "That way he'll have some money, and we can start pushing him to get an apartment. I mean the kid is nineteen and he's not in school, not working. It's not healthy for him."

"I think he really needs us," I said.

"And I agree. And even if he gets an apartment down the street, that's cool. We just have to start being a little tough with him. I know it's hard, because we've come into this laid-back lifestyle. But had he met us before we started with the videos—I mean we worked our asses off."

"I'll talk to him," I reassured Hunter. "But I know that Billy is definitely a good guy, and I think he'll do real well as soon as we get him into his own place, into school. I want him to be in school by the spring. Let's just motivate him. He feels like a little brother to me."

"I hear you," Hunter calmly replied, nodding his head. "I feel the same way. I just want our home life back the way it is."

Back up on the stage the drag queen was butchering the vocals to "Happy Birthday," singing to some heavy guy in a button-down who looked like he was probably a sleazy state legislator in Western Massachusetts. As the drag queen obnoxiously sang and waved the microphone in front of the guy's face, a beefy stripper hovered inches above his lap.

"You should go tell them that it's Billy's birthday," Hunter jokingly said, and then chuckled as he thought more about it. "Could you imagine the look on his face?"

"Actually—that's brilliant," I replied, as the lightbulb in my head went off.

About fifteen minutes later, after a few strippers had painfully danced while getting their white thongs sprayed down by staff members, the massive drag queen re-emerged from the shadows with her microphone.

"Providence!" she screamed, and a little squeal came from the audience. "I was just informed that we have another birthday in the house. But first, I want to bring up the guys who are going to help me sing 'Happy Birthday.' That's right boys, we have some grade-A sexy celebrities here. I want you to give a big applause to the sexiest couple on XTube.com: the Maverick Men!"

"Oh God, I didn't realize she was gonna call us up too," Hunter said, shooting me a quick look as we slowly stood up from the sofa. "Did you tell her who we are?"

"No! I guess she recognized us."

The two of us hesitantly walked through the crowd and hopped up onto the stage. I admit; there was a great rush of excitement being recognized for our videos by a live audience. It was one thing to get lots of fan mail and Internet feedback, but to be clapped for by a bar full of gay guys was really astounding. It totally reinforced my pride in the videos, and in the hard work that Hunter and I had put into this new career.

"You two are lookin' *good* tonight," the drag queen said. "Aren't they, boys?"

Once again there was a little squeal from the audience, accompanied by some clapping.

"When are you gonna put me in a video with you two?" she asked us, and shoved the microphone in front of my mouth.

"You're telling me that a lovely lady like you would want to be in gay porn?"

"Maybe I can fuck the both of y'all?" she replied, and slapped me on the shoulder.

"As hot as that sounds, I think we might have to pass," I jokingly replied. At least she was laughing.

"So before you boys go home and jack your little dicks off to the Maverick Men, I'm gonna let these guys call up the birthday boy."

She stepped aside and handed Hunter the microphone, just as one of the staff members brought a folding chair up onto the stage.

"Cole and I would like to invite onto the stage a very special person in our lives. He's a loving, sweet, adorable young guy, who just did his first video with us. He's an amazing fuck, and just turned twenty-one. Billy, will you please come up here?"

Billy looked horrified throughout Hunter's entire introduction, but before he could even register what was going on, Miguel grabbed a hold of his arm and started to lead him towards the stage. As soon as the crowd got a good look at him, the whole place was roaring in applause. When Billy got to the stage he struggled to break free from Miguel, but at this point there were too many people pushing him onto the platform. Reluctantly, he rolled on and stood up, looking out into the crowd in shock.

"Take a seat," Hunter directed him, and Billy did as told, planting his little butt in the folding chair. Almost as soon as he sat down, the light show started up, and the drag queen seized her microphone. And as soon as she hit the first note of "Happy Birthday," some 6'4, ripped stripper with arms about as big as Billy's head, leaped onto the stage and began to give the kid his first lap dance.

We all belted out the song for him, and it was great to see the mixture of joy and confusion in Billy's face. He didn't really know what to do with the stripper—or the attention. But I could tell that whatever he was feeling, he was enjoying it. And I felt thrilled that Hunter and I could be the ones to help him explore the world. I had a good feeling that this kid was going to be a friend for life.

*   *

It was nearly 3:00 AM by the time we pulled into the parking lot of the bed and breakfast. We'd danced and drank until 2:00, got a quick bite with Miguel, and then dropped him off at home. The whole College Hill area was deathly quiet upon our return, and it became evident that as soon as we got back into the neighborhood, the fear in Hunter and Billy began to materialize. The night's excitement had made them almost entirely forget where they were spending the night.

"Maybe we should just stay out and come back in the morning," Hunter suggested as soon as I turned off the engine. "I'm sure there are diners around here. We can go walk around the waterfront."

"A diner for what—an hour?" I replied. "And we'll be too tired to walk. It's fine, let's just go in."

I was the first to get out of the car, and the other two methodically followed. As creepy as the house looked during the daytime, it looked even worse at night. Maybe it was because there wasn't a single bright color in the inn. Howard and Melinda's taste for decorating was all based on dark colors, big furniture, clutter, and a variety of spooky shit that made the interior look much more Addams Family than your standard Providence bed and breakfast.

"You guys hungry?" I asked them as soon we stepped foot inside the house. Hunter and Billy hustled in, and I locked the door behind them. "I feel like that burger wasn't enough."

"I told you to get two," Hunter said.

"I should have. Let's check out what's in the kitchen."

"Hey, I'm gonna head up to the room and take a shower," Hunter replied. "But if you see anything light and healthy in the kitchen, bring it up. Nothing heavy!"

"Ok babe," I said, and gave him a quick kiss on the mouth. "Keep nice and steamy for me!"

"I will," Hunter replied as he walked off towards the stairwell.

"Looks like it's just me and you," I told Billy, who still had a frightened look on his face. I led him into the kitchen, which was easily one of the biggest kitchens I'd ever seen in a single home. It looked like they'd expanded it during the conversion of the house into their own style of bed and breakfast. It made a terrific space for accommodating lots of guests.

"So that's the white door, huh?" I asked, pointing towards an old, paint-chipped door in the corner of the kitchen. As Billy stared at it, I opened the cabinets to search for some late-night snacks. "I'm really in the mood for pancakes."

"Are we allowed to cook?"

"Probably not," I disappointedly replied. "Hey—Melinda said the lock to the basement was broken, right?"

"You're fucking crazy," Billy said, already sensing where I was headed with this.

"No, I'm just curious! That's where he buried all the bodies. Even some of the experiments took place down there. I'm just so curious to see what it feels like to be in a place with that much fucked up, scary energy."

"I'd rather pass—."

"Come on," I said, and took a hold of Billy's hand. "If Howard goes downstairs to check the water tank, then it can't be *that* bad."

I led him over to the white door, and we stood in front of it for a full minute. Billy's heart was racing fast, and I could see it all over his face. I could tell in the way his whole body shook. Even his hand, wrapped tightly in mine, was shaking with fear.

"I don't think it's a good idea, Cole. We could get in trouble. What did they say about the basement?" he quietly asked me.

"Nobody knows. The owners never let anyone down here. There've been a bunch of requests by psychics and ghost hunters to come check this place out, and they've never allowed anyone. We could be the first to tell that whole community."

Before Billy could voice his dissent, I put my hand on the door handle, and slowly opened it. The door pulled out towards me with a long creak, revealing wooden steps that descended down into darkness. I flipped the light switch on the basement wall, but nothing happened.

"Billy, check the kitchen drawers for flashlights," I ordered.

"Oh hell no."

"Billy—."

He looked up at me with those big, innocent eyes, and then hurried over to the drawers on the oversized kitchen island. After opening the first two, he found a third drawer that had some small flashlights. They didn't have much of a beam, but it would have to do.

He handed one to me and clutched the other as if it was his only source of protection. I aimed mine down the basement stairs and flicked it on, revealing a long path of deteriorating steps. I could just barely see the floor of the basement, which was entirely dirt. This was clearly the one place that Howard and Melinda had never decided to renovate.

"I bet these are the same stairs the psychologist dragged his victims down."

"Oh my God."

I took the first step down onto the flimsy wooden stairwell. The whole thing creaked underneath my weight, and I felt like it could break at any second. Billy nervously followed behind. There was no railing to hold onto, so I did my best to maintain my balance, and hoped that Billy wouldn't trip and fall into me.

As we neared the bottom of the stairwell I stopped about three steps from the dirt floor, and aimed my flashlight at my surroundings. The basement was pretty long—the length and width of the entire house, and mostly consisted of beams, dirt, and various crates that looked like they hadn't been opened in decades.

"What's that in the back there?" I asked as my flashlight came upon what looked to be a makeshift room. It was an area of the basement enclosed by pieces of wood that fell about one foot short of the ceiling. Most of the wood was either rotting, or at least showing some nasty signs of water damage. "I bet that's where he kept the bodies. Come on."

"You're out of your mind—."

"Come on," I said, and tugged Billy down the stairs with me. He reluctantly followed, keeping his flashlight aimed at his feet.

There was definitely an eeriness to the basement. A cold chill that descended upon the air from above. And the smell—there was this peculiar smell, something that I'd never tasted in the air before. And it wasn't just that smell that old books get after sitting in a basement for twenty years. I don't know how to describe it, other than that it was uncomfortable enough that I had to constantly cup my free hand over my mouth.

"It's dug up," I said in excitement as soon as the beam of my flashlight crossed into the little opening in the wooden room. Two large holes had been dug in the dirt ground, with the brown excess tossed alongside the wall. "It's not clear what's—Billy, do you see anything?"

Billy was literally an inch from my body at this point, practically holding onto my back in fear. He poked his head under my armpit and directed his flashlight on the holes that had been dug into the dirt floor.

"I think we should leave," He whimpered.

"Are you kidding? How many people have gotten a chance like this? Hey, I left my camera upstairs in the room. Can you go get it? I wanna take some flash pictures."

"I'm not walking through the house alone."

"Just go do it," I said in a more authoritative tone.

"Are you crazy? You want me to leave you down here alone?"

"Please—what do I need to be afraid of? Ghosts?"

And just as Billy was about to respond, from somewhere in the darkness the word, "yes" leapt out at us. The change in Billy's face was instant.

"Did you say that?" he whispered to me, his eyes wide with fear and his entire body stiff.

"No—," I nervously replied.

We didn't waste any time. In a coordination of sprinting and screaming, the two of us darted through the basement towards the stairs.

We couldn't hear anything over our own shouting, and neither of us bothered to look back. We knew what we heard.

"We have to get Hunter!" I shouted to him as we neared the top of the stairs. Billy was practically flying up the stairs, maybe afraid that someone would grab him from behind—or worse—shut and lock the kitchen door.

"We need to get the fuck out now!" he called back.

"The bedroom!" I said. "The bedroom!"

Billy was the first to cross into the kitchen, and I followed quickly behind. I was in pretty good shape, but this kid's legs had some real speed behind them. As I panted on my way up to the second floor, Billy sprinted up the stairwell screaming out Hunter's name.

"The bedrooms are soundproof!" I shouted after him. "He can't hear you!"

I didn't catch up to Billy until he was through the suite's bedroom door. I hastily shut and locked the door behind me.

"Hunter!" I called out.

"He's—." Billy didn't finish his sentence. I hurried into the suite's living room, where Billy was standing alone in the darkness, facing the bathroom, where the only light in the suite illuminated half of his body.

"What's the matter?" I asked.

At this point he had tears in his eyes. I walked slowly, fearful of what he might be looking at. Fearful of whether I wanted to see it. And when I got to the bathroom I peeked over Billy's shoulder to see a trail of blood on the white tiled floor, leading up into the grand bath tub, which was completely enwrapped by a shower curtain. We each could see the dark outline of a body up against the curtain.

"Oh my God," I said.

Billy turned up to me with little tears soaking his rosy cheeks, and looked into my eyes for guidance. And what he saw was that I couldn't open that shower curtain, for fear of what I might find.

Without saying a word Billy stepped very slowly into the bathroom. He stepped over the puddles of blood, methodically approaching the bath tub. And when he reached the shower curtain he took a deep breath, and looked back at me. I mouthed the words *thank you*. Billy put one hand on the shower curtain and closed his eyes.

But before Billy could open the curtain, something reached up and grabbed him from within the bath tub. He leaped into the air, and toppled forward into the bath tub, where Hunter—covered in fake blood—began to tickle his belly amidst my laughter and Billy's own screams, which quickly transformed into curses.

"You assholes!" he shouted as Hunter lifted him out of the bath tub and carried him into the living room. "I was really worried!"

"You were *scared shitless*," I said. "Own it."

Hunter tossed Billy onto the sofa bed and immediately stripped out of his stained boxers.

"Come on, this stuff doesn't even look real," he said to Billy.

"How would I know what it looks like?" he shot back.

"Make some room," I said as I hopped onto the bed next to Billy. Hunter joined us on the other side, and the three of us laid on our backs, facing the ceiling.

"I will admit—that was pretty good," Billy said. "But how did you guys pull off the tapping?"

"What tapping?" I asked.

Billy held his index finger up to his lips, and the three of us quieted down. I hadn't even realized it with the screaming and shouting and anxiousness of the sprint back to the suite, but as soon as silence embraced the room, we could hear the unmistakable sound of tapping on glass. Hunter and I sat up immediately, staring at the window in the living room that faced the street.   And in perfect synchronization, we each turned to face each other with that same look of bewilderment.

*   *

"So was there really a mass-murdering psychologist that lived here?" Billy asked Melinda, who broke into laughter.

"Oh, silly boy—," she replied, but didn't offer a response. "I hope you all enjoyed your stay?"

"Loved it," I said. "But I think we can only handle the one night's stay."

"Oh, that's too bad," she remarked as she swiped my credit card downstairs in her little office.

"You guys wanna go get the car ready?" I asked Billy and Hunter, who each nodded and took off for the parking lot. Once they'd left and the door had shut, I turned back to Melinda. "You put the *incidentals* on the card, right?"

"Of course," she said, and handed me a little receipt and a pen for my signature.

"Tell Howard thanks for the basement scene. But I just have one question—."

"Yes?"

"How did you guys pull off the tapping on the window? I've been thinking about it all morning, and I can't figure out how you did that! Do you have speakers hidden in the room or something? It actually looked like the window was being tapped."

As I handed Melinda the signed receipt, I noticed her entire expression change. She scrunched her little forehead and shrugged her shoulders, looking at me as if I was crazy.

"You heard tapping? Probably the wind," she dismissively replied. "But you know—a hidden speaker would be a great idea for a tapping effect. I'll have to take that up with Howard."

"It definitely wasn't the wind that I heard—."

"Then maybe it was your imagination," she said, and pursed her lips to form a very brief smile. "It was a pleasure having you at our bed and breakfast. Enjoy your ride home."

I left the bed and breakfast in a puzzled state. Billy and Hunter had already loaded our few bags into the car, and were waiting inside with the heat on.

"Back to Boston," Hunter remarked as I stepped into the car, and he affectionately placed a hand on my right knee.

"Back home," I echoed.

As we pulled out of the parking lot and made a left onto the street that ran alongside the old house, I looked up once again at that window.

"Scared?" Billy asked me from the backseat, noticing my pensive expression.

"No," I hastily countered. "But I'm sure as hell not staying there again."

CHAPTER SEVENTEEN

narrated by Hunter

"You sure a suit would've been too much?" Cole asked me, probably for the fifth time since we'd left the house.

"Yes, a suit would've been way too much. We're meeting a porn studio head. He wants to see us in our natural form. I mean look—if you were interviewing two twinks to be in a series of videos, then wouldn't you want to see them looking sexy?"

"I mean if it was a nice suit, I'd be pretty impressed."

I shot Cole a raised eyebrow, and then returned my attention to the directions I'd printed out.

"So it's on this block," I said while observing the print-out. "Looks pretty barren to me, though."

"Of course it is. It's a porn studio," Cole remarked as if he was the leading expert on porn studio real estate. "Discreet—probably cheap rent. I bet it's that warehouse at the end of the block. Big piece of shit in the middle of the ghetto, but I guarantee you walk in there and it'll be like the lobby of the Bellagio."

"So that's where Steve Wynn got his inspiration, huh?" I sarcastically replied. "Actually I think you're right—it looks like that warehouse is—yep. That's it. Big metal door right there near the corner."

"Where do we park? Do they have a garage? They must have a garage because you know the studio head isn't gonna be driving around in anything that can be parked out here."

"The e-mail didn't say anything about a parking garage," I replied.

"Then give him a call!"

"Why should we call him? There's parking right across the street. Look—right there."

"If someone breaks into the car—."

"No one is going to break into our car," I quickly said as Cole frowned and set up the vehicle to parallel park. "I wonder if we'll get to see any filming."

"Maybe even join in some filming," Cole replied, his frown quickly transforming into a smile.

"Let's see what happens," I casually replied. I was worried about going in with too many expectations, although I'll admit the idea of a fat paycheck and all the perks of studio work made me a little giddy. Cole and I wouldn't have to screen guys on our own anymore. The studio would take care of finding people for our videos, and dealing with the contracts, age checks, and STD testing. And they'd even fly us around the world to film! What a life. Of course, on the flipside, I wondered if a situation like Tye's would still happen even with a studio and a contract. There's no way Cole and I could just ignore a kid like that, especially one who had become a friend of ours. Maybe it was just a messy business to begin with. I was still way too early into the game to make any vast assumptions about the whole industry.

Cole and I stepped out of the parked car and looked down the street as we crossed towards the front entrance. There was one big metal door and a buzzer to the right of it. Just an address, but no names or labels. Not even a slot for mail. Police sirens sounded like they were just a couple blocks away, and the neighboring intersection had a grimy feel to it. We clearly weren't in the best part of Boston.

"You sure we're not dressed too casually—."

"No, I promise," I assured, and pressed the buzzer next to the metal door. It was barely five seconds before the door opened out towards us, prompting Cole and I to step back onto the sidewalk. Out popped a tall, good-looking guy who was probably around my age. He was dressed entirely in black, and had a clipboard in one hand. I assumed he was part of the production crew.

"You guys look just like you do in the videos," he cheerily said after quickly looking us up and down.

"The cameras aren't *that* good," Cole remarked.

"I'm sure," the guy then said with a brief laugh, and I didn't know whether to feel complimented or insulted. "Come in, come in."

Cole affectionately placed a hand on my lower back as I led the way into the studio. My expectations weren't very high to begin with after seeing the neighborhood, but I never expected the scene that greeted us. The small sets looked straight out of a low-rent Detroit casino. And the office was another tragedy entirely. It was more like a few large boxes thrown up against the wall of the warehouse, each with glass windows that hadn't been cleaned in months and cheap plastic blinds descended about a quarter of the way from the ceiling. And what dumbfounded me most was that this very studio had a successful track record for their videos. These guys weren't broke. It just seemed like they had no concept of the important difference between being tactfully frugal and embarrassingly cheap.

"So I'm Steve, and I run production here at the studio," our greeter warmly announced. "As you see, we're not filming this morning. But we have some scenes that are being filmed tonight if you all would like to stop by again. Depending on how your meeting goes," he added, and smiled at us.

"That might be interesting," Cole said. Who knew if he was paying attention. He couldn't take his eyes off the camera equipment, the lighting, and all the other set pieces. I wondered if this was the kind of stuff he dreamed of buying for our home, or our *own* studio if we were someday able to rent a little space to film our videos in.

The walk to the offices was short and sweet, and as we passed by the window of the third office, I took a good look at the guy behind the desk. This office was the same size as the rest, and wasn't any easier on the eyes. The desk looked like cheap particle board, probably purchased for fifty bucks at a local office supplies store. And even the two chairs set out facing his desk were falling apart. One of them had a couple cigarette burns in it, and the backrest of the other was hanging on its last screw, ready to fall off at any moment.

"Mr. Bucci has helped grow and mature many porn careers," Steve said once his hand touched the metal door handle that led directly to the boss' office. "I hope you guys make the right decision."

Neither Cole nor I said anything. I nodded, and Cole mouthed *thanks*, and then I took a deep breath as the production guy opened the office door. I don't know why I was so nervous, but I guess it was because this studio boss had the power to really improve our lives. And so naturally I had my hopes up. Even Cole had relaxed his tough stance on studios after all the drama with Tye. Maybe this was what we needed.

We had no intention of signing anything on the spot. Even if they made a great offer, we didn't know if we'd take it. The whole point of visiting the studio and meeting with Mr. Bucci was largely informative. Cole had always had this strong dislike of the *studio method*, and amidst all of our problems trying to manage a little homegrown studio, we just wanted to see what made the big studios work. We wanted to know what it would be like to work for one.

The smell of Mark Bucci's office was instantly off-putting. The small room reeked of smoke. There were two dirty ashtrays on his desk that he hadn't bothered to clean out, and an opened pack of cigarettes lying on top of some paperwork. I couldn't imagine how this guy could run such a low-rent operation given how much money he was probably making off of his videos. If anything, that made me nervous about whatever he was planning on offering us.

"Take a seat," Mr. Bucci said. He didn't bother to stand up, but instead maintained his relaxed posture in his swivel chair. The boss was nothing to look at. Short and stocky, and about as dirty as his office, he wore a wrinkled button-down with hair popping out around the front of the collar. And for some reason I thought about what some of the young, aspiring porn actors had to do for this guy to get a role, or to keep their jobs. My mind was reeling with images of young, aspiring porn actors, having to please this guy in a series of awkward and uncomfortable moments just for career advancement.

"Lemme see your cocks," he said as soon as Cole and I were in the two disaster-prone chairs facing his desk.

"Uhh—," was the only response that came to mind. I don't know whether Mr. Bucci was serious or not, but as soon as he saw the looks on our faces he burst into laughter.

"I'm kidding, I'm kidding. But seriously, be prepared to un-zip later. Gotta inspect the investment."

"Our videos are a pretty reliable representation of our bodies," Cole said. I was glad that he too found Mr. Bucci's request to be appalling.

"Chill the fuck out," Bucci replied. "We're gonna be working side-by-side here. Fuck—if I want to pull out a lawn chair and jack off while you guys are fuckin' some twink on my cameras I'll do it. That's normal in my studio."

"So what exactly would our partnership entail?" I asked, although I was already uncomfortable, and ready to dart out of there. I at least wanted to hear the specifics.

"I have a studio," he exclaimed, waving his arms in the air as if this fact was something we weren't previously aware of. "Equipment. Boys. Distribution. Connections. You guys ain't got shit right now. Amateur is *shit*. You don't meet nobody in the industry."

"So basically, you'd provide guys, shoot the videos, and distribute DVDs," I replied, summing up his proposal. "How often would we be doing videos? What would be the in-take per scene?"

"I'm gonna re-launch you two as the baddest ass twink fuckers in the world. I wanna create a *series*. Colt Stallion and Falcon Fuck Face— you two will be fucking every twink up and down the East Coast."

"Whoa, whoa," Cole intervened. "It's *Cole Maverick* and Hunter."

"I have Colt Stallion here. Who told me that? Steve!" he shouted at the top of his lungs. "Steve!" he screamed again, before breaking into a sickening gag. The product of years of smoking.

The production guy popped his head into the office and waited until Mr. Bucci was finished choking.

"Yes?" he asked.

"Who the fuck are these guys?"

"The Maverick Men."

"Then who the fuck is Falcon Fuck Face?" Bucci demanded to know.

"Isn't that the younger one?" Steve asked, sticking his index finger in my face.

"Did you just say *who the fuck are these guys*?" Cole asked, looking back and forth between Bucci and Steve in shock. "Are you fucking kidding? Please tell me this is a joke?"

"Cole, this was a bad idea from the get-go," I remarked, shaking my head in disappointment.

"Falcon Fuck Face is a good name," Steve replied with a shocked expression on his face as Cole and I stood up to leave the office. We'd had enough. "There are a thousand Hunters out there."

"The only *fuck face* here is you," Cole shot back. "Don't bother following us. I'll just follow the slime tracks out of here."

"Fuck 'em," Bucci remarked. "I need a smoke."

Neither of us had ever walked out of a building so quickly. As the metal door closed behind us, Cole hurried to keep up, and as soon as we were out the door and crossing the street I looked back to see that look of shock and disappointment on his face.

"I'm sorry," I said as I crossed over to the passenger's side of our car. "I couldn't take it. Those guys were freaks. I don't know *how* people can work for a place like that."

"It's fucked up, but it just confirms what I've always thought about places like this," Cole replied. "I don't know. Maybe there'll be another one that's not like that. They can't *all* be like that."

"No, you're right," I replied. We opened the car doors and sat inside. I took one final look at the door of the porn studio, and then turned back to face my partner.

"Can you believe he said *lemme see your cocks*?" Cole said to me, and then burst out in laughter. "I wish I had a camera. The look on your face was priceless. Especially when he called you Falcon Fuck Face."

"What the fuck was that about?" I asked. I couldn't help but laugh as I rewound the whole incident in my head.

"I thought you were gonna kick his ass."

"Wouldn't have been worth it," I said. "You know, if we have to go this alone, I know we can do it."

"Me too," Cole replied after some hesitation. "Me too."

*   *

"Awful," I said loudly and clearly into our computer's microphone. I could hear Christo sigh in disappointment. It was really touching that this guy we'd never met had developed so much love for us, that he'd be equally hurt by our trials and tribulations in figuring out this world of porn.

"I'm so sorry, Hunter," he said in that soft-spoken German accent. "How does Cole feel?"

"He's disgusted and disappointed. You know, he was so anti-studio for the longest time, and this just cements his opinions."

"You must have checked your e-mail?"

"Just logging on now. Why? Did you send us some more pictures?"

"Even better," he said. I didn't know what it could be, aside from maybe a jack-off video. Christo was smoking hot, and knew that Cole and I were in love with him. A jack-off video from him would be like pure gold on the scale of hottest things in the universe. The only thing better would be our planned video on New Year's Eve. The fuck of the year.

"I don't see anything from you," I said to him as I scrolled through our e-mail.

"Oh no, this is not from me. You know of Manhunt.net?" he asked, referring to the popular website dedicated to gay male hook-ups and connections.

"Of course I know of Manhunt. What gay guy doesn't?"

"That's who it's from," he replied with a little chuckle, and I suddenly got very curious. I hurried through the day's new e-mails until I came upon the one he was talking about. I hastily opened it and scrolled down to the body of the letter.

The message itself was short and sweet. The Webmaster of Manhunt had been tipped off to our material by Christo, who had hounded the office with letters and e-mails in order to promote the Maverick Men videos. In fact, he was so excited by our style that he was inviting us to audition to headline a new website that would basically be Manhunt.net's take on user-submitted porn.

"Oh my God—Christo—you're amazing," I said, practically speechless over this opportunity. A hole-in-the-wall porn studio in Boston was one thing, but Manhunt was an online empire. And, as fate would have it, they too were based in Boston.

"You and Cole deserve it. I simply—umm—how you say, *pointed* him in your direction."

"I think we're just going to kidnap you on New Year's and bring you back to Boston with us."

"Oh—no—then you'll grow sick of me so quick," he replied amidst some laughter. "I know how you are with Billy."

"Well—that's another story," I replied. "If you move in with us I'll just have to convince Cole to get a bigger apartment. That or Cole will finally need to move all his storage stuff out of the second bedroom."

"You should give him the good news."

"I will. He's downstairs cooking something up. This is great, Christo. You're the best."

"What can I say. I'd do anything for the people I love."

*   *

Cole was thrilled with the news, and we wasted no time in calling Manhunt. The Webmaster was extremely friendly over the phone, and asked if we could meet with he and the CEO at the end of the week. And so Cole and I celebrated this new opportunity with a bottle of champagne, some good food, and our favorite pastime outside of sex itself: looking at guys online.

"Isn't he fucking sexy?" I asked as Cole scrolled through the online profile of a Southern boy from Tallahassee who had emailed us asking about doing a video. "He's going to drive down to Miami over our New Year's trip. Almost gives Christo a run for his money."

"No one comes close to Christo," Cole said, looking up at me with a serious expression, as if my comparison was sacrilegious. "But you're right. This guy is sexy as hell."

"We have to get Frat Boy to show his face," I said.

"You know he's hanging out with Billy tonight?"

"Oh really?" I asked in surprise. Billy had been out for a few hours, and I guess it didn't click for me to ask where he'd go. He hadn't really made friends yet in Boston, and Cole and I didn't know anyone of the same age except for Bradley. "There we go—we can get him enrolled at the university and he can go live across the street from us."

"Could you imagine Billy living in a frat house?" Cole asked me. "Between he and Frat Boy I think they'd turn just about every straight guy that stepped foot in—."

Cole's sentence was interrupted by a louder-than-usual opening and closing of the front door. I peeked over the balcony that overlooked the first floor and saw Billy hopping into the apartment, marching towards the ladder that led up to the bedroom.

"What's gotten into you?" I called down as he practically danced his way up the ladder.

"I found an apartment!" he shouted. I'd never seen Cole's head turn more quickly.

"You found what?" Cole asked.

"I found an apartment!" he said, peeking his head out into the bedroom. He gave one final push and lifted himself onto the second-story loft. "We passed one that's a few blocks away from here. I already called the realtor and left a voicemail."

"So all the sudden you want to get your own place?" Cole asked him. Billy sat down on our bed, facing Cole and I, who were behind the computer desk.

"Yeah—I mean my video is out now, and I feel like I have a good thing going. I was even thinking of applying to Bradley's college.

Obviously I can't start now because the semester is almost over, but I could do it in the Spring."

"I think that's a great idea," I said. I was shocked that this was coming out so suddenly. Cole had been taking a very long time to push Billy towards his own place, school, and a job, and all it took was a few hours of hanging out with Frat Boy to reach some epiphany. "What made you change your mind?"

"Well—I think I just need my privacy if I'm going to be living in Boston for now on."

"I think you do too," I replied, and Cole playfully wacked my knee underneath the computer desk.

"Privacy can be very important," Cole said after giving me a quick look. "Especially when you meet that special someone. It's nice to have your own space with them."

"I'm still going to come over every day—don't think you won that battle."

"I think we need to start looking at apartments too," I whispered to Cole, who tried to contain his laughter.

"How about we start looking this week," Cole said. "We'll start with the apartment you saw, and we'll look at some others in the neighborhood. And you know you're welcome here as often as you want. We both love you."

"We do," I honestly told him. "You're very special to us. But I'm glad you're going to find a place for yourself, so you can start developing your own life here."

Billy's news couldn't have made me happier. I was expecting Spring to come around before this kid found his own apartment, meanwhile worrying if the next boy in our series of videos would also try to live with us. I really loved this kid, but it would be nice for Cole and I to finally have our space back. Little did I know that apartment-hunting wasn't quite as easy for porn stars as it was for those in everyday life.

CHAPTER EIGHTEEN

narrated by Cole Maverick

"So what do you think?" Hunter asked me as soon as the cold air hit our faces. I waited as the taxi driver fumbled in his pocket for change.

"Keep it," I muttered, and offered a quick smile when the cabbie's face lit up. I was in a good mood. I shut the car door and began to walk with Hunter towards the entrance to our apartment complex.

Earlier that day we'd had our first meeting with the Manhunt guys. We met with two of their top brass: the CEO and the Webmaster, both of whom were fans of our videos. The meeting was mostly informative. Both guys kept a poker face as they explained that they wanted to launch a website that involved user-submitted porn. They'd witnessed the whole XTube sensation, and they liked the concept of real-life, *captured-on-film* porn. And most of all, they liked the way we did it.

They wanted to set us up with a website. As a result, we'd put our material on there, and we'd recruit guys to upload their own videos. It all sounded interesting. I mean, XTube was easy for us, since we could upload videos whenever we wanted. A deal with Manhunt would mean a ton of new responsibility. We'd essentially be building a brand, and recruiting guys who did the same kind of work as us to come support it.

The problem was, neither of us really knew if we wanted that kind of responsibility. Hunter and I had tons of questions, and unfortunately since it was just our first meeting, the Manhunt executives couldn't give us fine-tuned details. The longer the meeting went on, the more overwhelmed I felt. Like I mentioned, the XTube stuff was easy to manage, and gave us a ton of freedom at home. Suddenly we were talking about quotas, and brand building, and doing a certain number of blogs per week. I'd never blogged once in my entire life.

I respected that these guys knew what they were doing, but I couldn't shake the anxiety that somehow Hunter and I were heading in the reverse direction with this contract; that maybe we'd be back to being way too busy again. Too busy for casual weekend trips and late mornings in bed.

At the end of the meeting, the CEO and Webmaster surprised us with a visit to the home of one of Manhunt's two owners. It was a nice touch at the end of a long, technical meeting. The co-owner, Larry, was an awesome, relaxed guy, and we spent the afternoon drinking champagne with he and his partner in their palatial, artsy apartment.

"I think it went well," I told Hunter as we crossed the lawn towards our building. "So the Christmas party is next?" The Christmas party would be our big *test*. Even though the CEO and Webmaster were each pulling for us, the big decision maker was the other co-owner, the one we hadn't yet met. And he was hosting a Manhunt Christmas party in his Boston home, where he wanted to meet us and see if we were worth the investment. Money wasn't a topic of conversation in our first meeting with Manhunt, mainly because that big issue would entirely revolve around our success at the Christmas party. If this other co-owner liked us, then we could be looking at a really lucrative deal. If not, we could probably kiss the whole website goodbye.

"We'll nail it," he confidently said. "Talk about the polar opposite of that other studio."

"Yeah—they really had their shit together. But then again, this is Manhunt. You know, I think this could be a big thing for us," I told Hunter, who slowly nodded in response. "We just have to keep thinking about it. This could really change our lives. We just have to be totally upfront with them about our style and what we want. We have a certain style with our videos—a brand. Yeah, people who love studio porn probably won't like us, but for all those guys who want to see real-life, fun sex, we're reliable. We need to keep it that way. That means creative control. I don't know if they're gonna want to give that up."

"Well the Webmaster said he's a big fan of our stuff," Hunter said. "So he'll understand, don't you think?"

"Hell yes, I think he'll definitely be on our side when we negotiate this contract."

"Well let's just make sure that it's the right decision. We have a little homegrown studio right now, if you want to call it that. If we start playing in the big leagues, well—I mean—you heard him. We'd be contracted to do a certain number of videos per month. We'd have to attend events all over the place. We decided to start charging for our videos because we thought it would create a comfortable life for us. Is this going to make us less comfortable?"

"I think it's a challenge," I said. "I think you have some good points, but I also see it this way: we're clearly creating something beautiful and real, that people enjoy and want to pay money for. They're not gonna be paying forever. At some point we'll be yesterday's news, and I think if we get this opportunity with Manhunt, and take it, we can only get bigger. We'll learn more about the industry. We'll meet people. And we'll set something up so that someday when people aren't downloading the videos anymore, we'll be behind the scenes, still making a good living for ourselves."

"Or just living off our royalties," Hunter joked, and revealed that sexy smile that always had a way of making me feel like a giddy school boy.

"So what do you say we go meet up with Billy and see the next apartment?"

"Oh my God, this kid is going to look at fifty before he makes up his mind. You'd think we're in Manhattan."

"I'm keeping my fingers crossed that this is the one."

*   *

Hunter and I waited in a tense posture, holding each other's hands as we breathed deeply and prayed that Billy would finally settle on the apartment. He was looking at a small one-bedroom in a building about three blocks from ours. It was the same building that he'd initially wanted to rent in, having passed by it while on a walk with Bradley. It was mostly occupied by college students who had rejected the dorm lifestyle, and was a perfect choice of location if Billy were to indeed register for Spring classes.

"I don't know about the kitchen," he said as he stopped and observed the cabinets. They were a bit outdated, but still in good shape. The whole kitchen was white, which I'm sure raised some concerns with him. He'd have a much more difficult time keeping it clean.

"Billy, the kitchen is fine," I said. "You don't even know how to fry an egg—why the hell are you worried about the kitchen? You know you're gonna eat pizza every day."

"All the kids are trying to have a white kitchen," his obnoxious realtor added. "It's like Miami Vice all over again. White is the new black. Or stainless steel. Yeah—white is the new stainless steel."

"That makes no sense at all," Hunter whispered to me, and I casually nodded my head. I don't know where Billy had found this realtor, but he was a piece of work. He was a handsome guy with great arm muscle and a nice chest that popped out of his polo shirt, but every time he opened his mouth he only hurt his chances of selling.

"I don't know why he didn't just let me set him up with one of the guys I used to work with. For God's sake, I *was* a realtor," I whispered back.

"He wants to be independent. What can you do?"

And so it had come down to the kitchen. Hunter and I were a nervous wreck. The realtor was breathing heavily. And Billy—well, he was just standing there, looking over the kitchen, and those white cabinets that seemed to be the one thing holding him back from an immediate *yes*.

Billy opened his mouth, and the three of us—all hanging on his decision—inhaled.

"I like it. I'll take it."

"Hallelujah," Hunter said as we all exhaled.

"Perfecto!" the realtor exclaimed. "Let's go back to my office and sign the paperwork. Then you'll have your keys tomorrow, bro."

I'd never seen Billy so happy. This was such a big step for him, and I felt proud that I could be part of it. It gave me hope that positive stories would come out of the guys we met. That maybe Tye was just the exception to the rule.

We went straight from the apartment to the realtor's office, which sat on a busy Boston street in-between a Greek restaurant and a boutique store that sold greeting cards. Billy's realtor led the way into the office, marching in as if he'd just won a war. I couldn't imagine how his co-workers dealt with him on a daily basis.

"Phil, can you prepare this gentleman's paperwork for unit 718 at the big S?" he directed towards a middle-aged effeminate assistant who was seated at the front desk. The realtor gave him a little punch in the shoulder, and the assistant responded by glaring at him in disgust.

"The Strauss—."

"Duh, bro, the big S. Set it up. Set it up."

Phil, the assistant, stood up to greet us, and then paused awkwardly. It was strange enough that I immediately looked down at my jacket to see if I'd spilled something on myself, or if a bird had crapped on me during the trek over to the realtor's. The assistant's mouth hung open for just a few seconds, before he quickly smiled and then sat back down at his desk without shaking our hands.

"Welcome to the office. Can I get you three anything to drink?"

"Just some water would be great," I said. Hunter shook his head, and I could tell by his face that he picked up on the exact same vibe that I got. Meanwhile Billy had his hands full between his cell phone and iPod, and didn't even hear Phil's offer to get him a drink.

"So one water," Phil slowly replied. "Okay, I'll be right back. Um—for this property the owner requires just one month's security deposit, and first month's rent. If you can prepare the checks, I'll get the paperwork printed right away and then we can go over all the details on the lease."

As soon as he hurried to the back of the office to get my water, I turned to Hunter and narrowed my eyes.

"That was weird."

"Did he know you from somewhere? Were you a bully in high school?" he jokingly asked me.

"No—of course not. Well maybe a little. But I don't recognize this guy at all. I thought he was looking at all of us. You think he saw the videos?"

"I don't know," Hunter replied with a quick shrug, and sat down in one of the gray waiting area chairs. "You can't just assume that every gay guy we meet has seen the videos."

My curiosity got the best of me. I wandered over to Phil's desk and looked at the name on his little stack of business cards. It still didn't ring a bell. And so I casually drifted around the other side of the desk so that I could get a view into the back of the office. Phil was at the water cooler talking to Billy's realtor, who had his eyes wide open. Whatever Phil was saying, it sure was interesting enough to elicit a big reaction.

Just before Phil came back with the water I hurried back over to the waiting chairs, where I took a seat next to Hunter.

"Let's get you your apartment," he said with a perfectly friendly smile on his face.

*   *

"I think this is gonna be the easiest move that I've ever been a part of," I said. Hunter and I were sitting around the apartment, dressed and ready to hear from Billy that he'd received the keys. He was already up at the realtor's office. The car was packed with his few belongings, and the plan was to drop everything off at the apartment, and then go furniture shopping for the rest of the day.

"Yeah—hopefully he stays there for more than a year!" Hunter remarked. He was laying on the bed with his arms folded behind his head, and I was at the computer checking up on our XTube activity and responding to some e-mails.

"Yeah, and you know what? We're gonna have every piece of furniture delivered. I'm not carrying shit."

"It's too bad it doesn't come furnished already."

"Yeah, that would—ah, hold up, he's calling," I said as soon as my cell phone went off. "What's up, Billy? Say again? We'll be right there."

"Everything okay?" Hunter asked with a worried expression. He must've seen my face change.

"I don't know. He's crying, and asked if we'd come to the realtor's office right away," I said. I had never heard Billy so upset. This kid had thick skin, and even when we'd all playfully bust on each other, he'd never got hurt or offended, so I had no idea what could've happened to make him lose it. I wondered if maybe his lease got denied, but then why would he cry about that? He could always just get a new lease on a different apartment. I had a bad feeling about this.

"Oh no—I wonder what could've happened."

"No clue," I replied as I rushed to the ladder that led down to the first floor. "How hard can it be to rent an apartment?"

We were quickly about to find out. Hunter and I hurried out to the car and raced to the realtor's office. Billy sent me some texts but he was so upset that his spelling and grammar were totally incoherent. And with each text and every minute closer to the realtor's, I could feel myself growing increasingly nervous.

We found parking on the same block as the realtor's office, and rushed inside. As soon as we walked in we got a nasty look from the queen sitting behind the front desk. The realtor was nowhere in sight, and Billy was sitting on one of the gray waiting chairs, completely in tears.

"What's going on?" I asked, marching up to the front desk as Hunter hurried to comfort Billy.

264

"The landlord has terminated the lease," the assistant, Phil, said in a cocky little voice. "Your *friend* over there has violated the terms of agreement."

"Okay, so the landlord is an asshole and we didn't get the lease," I replied. "Give us back the checks so we can go find another realtor."

"They won't give them back," Billy said, glancing up with big wet eyes.

"That doesn't make any sense," I replied.

"The landlord *signed* the lease, and so it went into full effect," Phil told us. "And then when he learned of Billy's *occupation*, which is in direct violation of a clause in the terms of agreement, he terminated the lease. And since Billy violated the contract, the landlord is keeping the security deposit and first month's rent."

"Whoa, whoa," I replied, shocked at what I was hearing. "Are you an office of con artists? You sign contracts and blow them the next day, putting decent people out of thousands of dollars?"

"How dare you call *us* indecent," Phil snapped back. "At least I have a normal job."

"Ah—so that's what this is all about. I knew from that look on your face yesterday. You've seen our videos."

"And I think it's repulsive."

"Yeah? So repulsive that you'd spend enough time to go in search of them, and then watch them in their entirety? I guess not *that* repulsive that you wack off to our porn often enough to be able to recognize us."

"You can leave," Phil coldly replied. At this point a little scene was gathering in the back of the office, although I still didn't see Billy's realtor.

"Get me your manager."

"There's nothing you can do about this."

"The owner is here," Billy said, once again lifting his head from Hunter's shoulder. "He came in to cancel the lease."

"The unit owner?" I asked, and Billy nodded his head. "Where is this asshole?" I directed to Phil.

"I'm about a minute away from calling the cops."

"You'll have beaten me to it! Because I was just about to call some of my good friends over at the station, who are *well aware* of our videos, and let them know we're being extorted by a self-loathing queen, and a poor excuse for a realty office. I *was* a realtor. I know how this shit works. And if you think we're gonna leave here today without our two checks, then you're out of your fucking mind."

Suddenly the obnoxious smile was wiped off Phil's face, and he sat up and turned around to face the little group of employees watching the scene. Finally one of them stepped forward; a guy about ten years my senior with thin gray hair, a button-down with the sleeves rolled up, and khaki pants. I noticed a manila folder in his left hand.

"I'm Gregory," he said as he neared Phil's desk. "I'm the unit owner."

"I don't want an explanation or argument or apology," I replied as I rounded the desk to get up in his face. "I just want the two checks back."

"I'm not a homophobe, but I find your *work* to be reprehensible," he spat out as he reached into his folder and pulled out the two checks we'd written for the apartment. I quickly snatched them out of his hand. "And I don't want my property to be a goddamn porn studio."

"I don't give a fuck what you think is reprehensible. That's your opinion. And you know what they say—opinions are like ass holes, and everyone's got one."

"The only reprehensible thing about this situation was your bullshit ploy to try and rip this kid off," Hunter chimed in, keeping a comforting arm around Billy. "*That* was reprehensible. You're lucky I'm in a good mood right now or else both of you dick heads would be looking up at us from the ground."

There was nothing left to say. As Gregory turned away from us, I stuffed the checks in my pocket. And with that, Hunter, Billy, and I left the office.

*   *

"I'm never going to find an apartment," Billy exclaimed as he fell backwards onto our bed. He'd stopped crying, and had settled more into a quiet melancholy. He was happy that we got the checks back, but his buzz about getting his own place was completely crushed.

"Trust me, Billy. I think what just happened is pretty rare," Hunter said. He sat down next to him on the bed and gently massaged his chest. "We'll find you a place."

"But what if this happens again?"

"Let me set you up with one of my realtor buddies," I offered. "And—don't worry. You can live with us for as long as it takes."

As soon as I said that I could see the change in Hunter's face. Even though he was tending to Billy and taking care of him, I knew how much he was looking forward to our alone time. Suddenly we were back at square one.

"Thanks guys," he said from his spot on the bed. "I hope you know I don't take you for granted."

"We know you don't," Hunter softly replied, with a little bit of sadness in his voice.

CHAPTER NINETEEN

narrated by Hunter

"It's the gay Hugh Hefner," Cole remarked as we parked in front of the massive estate, located in a suburban mansion just minutes outside of Boston. As we stepped out of our car, we could hear the noises of music and chatter pouring out from the back yard. It was Christmas Eve, and the Manhunt Christmas party was underway, located in the home of one of the company's two owners. This was the co-owner we hadn't yet met, and the one who we needed to impress.

"Nervous?" I asked Cole, but he shook his head.

"Well, maybe a little," he finally admitted as we walked up the long driveway towards the open fence that led around back.

"Let's just go in, grab some drinks, and relax," I told him. "I'm sure it'll be fine."

Neither of us knew exactly what to expect. We both understood that Manhunt was a website for online cruising and hook-ups, and so we didn't expect to walk into a super-formal party. This wasn't going to be cocktail hour at the library. Our nervousness stemmed out of a combination of the pending contract, the responsibilities attached to it, and the professional atmosphere of the Manhunt office, which was nothing like the seedy porn studio we visited in Boston. As soon as that image came back into my head, I let out a little laugh, which prompted Cole to look at me as if I was crazy.

"What's so funny?"

"Falcon Fuck Face," I remarked, and shook my head.

"Oh God. What if that guy is the other Manhunt co-owner? Could you imagine if we walk in here and see him again, and he's like *hey, Colt and Fuck Face! What happened to ya?*"

"I'd die."

"You mean you wouldn't accept the contract?" Cole jokingly asked me.

"Hell no. Well, at least I already have a porn name in case we ever work for a big studio."

Cole shook his head at me. We were at the open gate which led into the back yard of the mansion. When we peered into the back yard, we saw a beautiful, oval-shaped pool surrounded by a walkway that led to a large canopy on one side, and a small poolhouse on the other that contained an indoor pool. No one was swimming, obviously, since it was freezing out, but we saw lots of guys standing outside with drinks.

We followed the walkway around the pool until we got to the back entrance of the mansion, where a handsome middle-aged guy was standing in the doorway wearing a tuxedo.

"Hey, Cole and Hunter, we're here for the Christmas party," Cole said, pointing to each of us respectively.

"Welcome!" the tuxedo-clad guy at the door said, and smiled as he led us into the house.

The interior was beautiful and classy, and you could tell that a gay guy lived there. I mean, the first thing we saw was a life-size stone statue of a naked man, modeled after an ancient sculpture. A santa hat sat atop its head of stone curls. In the other rooms, statues and pictures of men meshed alongside antique furniture and expensive chessboards.

There was a great mixture of people at the party. We saw every type of guy there, from older businessmen to muscled porn stars to cute twinks. We saw old love, young love; handsome professionals with their young lovers. Even though there was a certain maturity to the party, there was no mistaking that an exciting level of sex and desire were circulating throughout the party. This was a good-looking crowd, and everyone was having fun, smiling, socializing, and admiring one another.

"What a great place," I said to Cole as we walked through the crowd, looking at both the home and the people in it.

"You think there's a grotto?" he asked me, and we both chuckled. "Come on, he's gotta have the *sex cave* underneath this place."

"I'm wondering what he'll look like. You think a velvet robe, and three blonde twinks on his arms?"

"I have no clue," Cole remarked, still laughing. We'd never met this co-owner, and had no idea what he looked like, or what he was all about. I was definitely getting a Hugh Hefner impression. The secluded, private mansion, with its multiple pools, and all the sculptures and pictures of men. This place was designed for a gentleman who took interest in being surrounded by beautiful men.

"Your hands were empty," the handsome guy in the tuxedo said to us, reemerging with two beers. "Jonathan is in the kitchen."

"Thank you," we each graciously said, and took the beers from him. "Should we just—go in?"

"Yeah, it's a party," he replied, and shrugged his shoulders. He offered us one last smile before returning to the back entrance of mansion.

"Here we go," Cole said to me, and raised his eyebrows. He tapped my beer bottle with his own.

We passed through the crowds until we got to the massive kitchen. It truly was enormous, and fitting for the size of the mansion. The first thing I thought about when I saw it was actually Billy. I don't know why he came up, but something about a huge kitchen and house, and that if we lived like this, I don't think I'd mind having him there. I could just see waking up every day to Billy making coffee and preparing breakfast for the three of us in that white kitchen. It was slightly far-fetched. I mean, that would require Billy learning how to cook, and waking up *before* us. But it was a nice thought.

"Cole! Hunter!" we heard the familiar voice of Manhunt's Webmaster calling to us just seconds after entering the kitchen. When we both looked over, he was standing by the window, having a glass of wine with a casually-dressed older guy.

Gary, the Webmaster at Manhunt, waved us over to the corner.

"Guys, this is Jonathan," he told us. So *this* was the co-owner. "Did you just get here?"

"We did," I said. "It's really nice to meet you."

As Jonathan shook our hands, he looked each of us up and down. I think Cole was just as surprised as I that this was the co-owner. He seemed like a normal, relaxed, down-to-earth guy. Someone you'd want to have a drink with. He definitely didn't have the Hugh Hefner ego, or any kind of pretentious attitude that might come with running such a successful company. I knew instantly that this was the beginning of a great relationship.

"So, the boys tell me we'll be doing some business together soon," he said to us.

"We hope so," Cole replied. "Still a lot to talk about, but yeah, we both hope this works out."

"Well, if it does, we're thinking about having an office raffle to decide the name of the website," Jonathan said.

"With all due respect, there's no need for a raffle," Cole told him. "MaverickMen.com," he added, and the words rolled off his tongue. Jonathan turned to Gary and raised his eyebrows, and then nodded in approval.

"Not bad," he replied. "Not bad."

*   *

"Merry Christmas!" I said into the computer microphone. We'd just returned from the Manhunt Christmas party when in my slightly drunken state I signed online and messaged Christo. It was early in the morning on Christmas Day over in Berlin, but Christo was packing for his trip to the United States, where he'd be dancing on tour for an entire month.

"Is it Christmas for you, yet?"

"Yeah man, it's nearly one," I replied. "Did you pull an all-nighter?"

"I did," he replied in exhaustion. "No wonder I'm so delirious."

"You leave when? Today?"

"Correct. Will see family in the south of Germany, then off to Miami! Rehearsals, rehearsals, rehearsals, and then the tour starts on New Year's Eve."

"I can't believe I'm going to be sliding into you in one week," I said in excitement. "I wish I could orgasm a bunch of times in a row. I have a feeling that I'm not going to last long when we first get together."

"Aww, well we have more than one day," he replied, laughing at my sexual impatience.

"I know, I know. Hey, we also met this kid who lives up in Tallahassee, who wants to do a video with us that weekend, after you leave."

"How nice! What is Tallahassee?"

"City in Florida. But way up there," I said. "It's a long drive from Miami."

"I see. Oh I'm so excited to see America, finally. How are Cole and Billy? Has he moved out yet?"

"No, he's still here," I replied. Cole had set him up with a new realtor, but Billy hadn't found an apartment that he liked quite as much as that last one. "He's seen a bunch of new places. I don't know if he's purposely not trying to rent one, or what. But this kid's been living with us for so long now—. I like him and all, but come on, I'd like some privacy with my partner, you know?"

"I know."

"They're sleeping now. Billy didn't come with us to the party— he was exhausted earlier. I'm just over it, Christo. It would be one thing if he came over a bunch. I don't care if it's five—six times a week. But I'm feeling smothered here."

"Have you given him a—ah—deadline?"

"No, we haven't. And that's the problem. Cole is way too easy on him."

"Speak with Cole," Christo softly replied. "Maybe you can give him a deadline, say—by when you return from Miami?"

"Well there aren't many people around to rent between Christmas and New Year's, but we'll see. And he's not coming to Miami. Do you think I'm being a dick? I don't know—maybe it's just a mood. But it comes and goes all the time. I think I have a right to privacy with my guy."

"You do. Just talk to Cole. Maybe I will say something too, although I'm just an online friend—."

"No, Christo, the both of us honestly feel like we've known you for years. Even though we haven't met in person yet, you've become a major part of our lives," I said. "And I can't wait till next week."

"Me either," he replied, and I could tell that he was just as happy as I was. "I might try to sleep now. Speak with you soon."

"Talk to you then," I warmly told him, just before a loud beep notified me that he'd signed off of Skype. I didn't know when I'd talk to Cole about Billy, but I knew I had to do it soon. It was Christmas, and not exactly the best time to discuss kicking someone out of your apartment. And my biggest problem was that Cole didn't seem to mind if Billy decided to live with us permanently.

"Heading out!" I heard Billy call from downstairs, and instantly my stomach churned. Had he heard my entire conversation with Christo? I could've sworn that he was fast-asleep. At least, he was asleep on the sofa when we got in from the Manhunt party. Suddenly I felt awful. Even though I believed everything I'd said, I didn't want the kid to feel unwelcome. And as I reflected on my own embarrassment, I realized that Cole had probably been soft on the *move out* topic for the same reason.

"See you in a little bit!" I called back. I didn't know where he was going at this hour. Maybe to a local 24/7 convenience store, or some late night party in the city. I just hoped he hadn't heard me; that maybe he was in the bathroom getting ready, or listening to his iPod, or anything. Fuck.

*   *

"Shouldn't you be at your family's or something?" Cole asked from one of the downstairs sofas as Frat Boy walked into the apartment, accompanied by Billy. I was cooking Christmas breakfast while Cole laid around in boxers and a white t-shirt.

"I'm going over there in an hour," he replied, and hurried over to the couch to give Cole a hug and kiss. "This is for you?"

"What the hell is this?" Cole asked. I glanced out of the kitchen to see Cole holding some sort of candy cane.

"I have one for you too," Frat Boy said, and walked into the kitchen to greet me.

"Merry Christmas," I told him as we embraced and kissed. And that's when I saw his gift. From a little plastic bag, he pulled out a candy cane in the shape of a huge cock and balls.

"For the two biggest dicks in the neighborhood."

"That's hilarious Bradley," I replied, and laughed out loud. "Where did you even find this?"

"I made them!" he proudly responded. "By the way, I love your Christmas tree."

"Yeah, it was sort of a last-minute thing. We bought it a few days ago, and Billy helped us set it up."

"Is it real?" he asked.

"Of course it's real!" Cole loudly replied. "You think I'd get a fake tree when we have a houseboy to clean up all that shit that falls off it?"

"I'm not vacuuming any pine needles, if that's what you're implying," Billy replied.

"Hey Cole," I called out from the kitchen as Frat Boy wandered off to look at the tree.

"Yeah?"

"I need to get more milk. You know any stores nearby that would be open on Christmas morning?"

"There are like—a *million* Indian-run convenience stores. You can't go a block without seeing one."

"Actually, that's not true," I replied. "There's only one that you always *claim* is nearby, yet for some reason I can never find it when I'm out."

"It's right on Mass Ave. Go up the street and make a right."

I threw on my sneakers, and grabbed my coat, when I noticed Billy putting his sweatshirt back on.

"Can I come with you?" he asked me. It was a little unusual for him to tag along with me on errands, so I naturally wondered if he'd overheard my conversation with Christo about him.

"Sure, of course," I replied, and waited for him to squeeze into his hoodie. As soon as he was ready I opened the door and we headed out of the apartment.

It was a while before either of us said anything. We walked all the way down the hallway, down the stairwell to the ground floor, and out onto the pavement without even a whisper. Our hands were in our pockets and our necks were clenched as we fought the cold, late December winds.

"It's too bad there's no snow on the ground this year," he finally said as we approached Massachusetts Avenue.

"There's a little bit. I'm sure we'll get it in a month or two."

"Yeah, but up north I'm used to more snow around this time."

"You overheard me last night, didn't you?" I bluntly asked him, bypassing the conversation about the weather.

"Yeah."

"How do you feel?" was the only thing I could ask him. I didn't know what else to say. I was kind of struggling with this; whether or not I should apologize, or maybe hold to my guns and tell him that even though I really like him, I miss my alone time with Cole, in the household we've worked hard to create for ourselves.

"Look, I know I'm probably a big intrusion sometimes," he said as we waited for the light to turn green so that we could cross the street. "But I'm really new to this stuff. I never bottomed before I met you guys. I never lived in a big city. I never went to any gay clubs. And I really need you to help me figure this stuff out. I don't know what life on my own will be like, but I know it won't be as much fun. Since I've met you and Cole, I've learned and done so much. Just a few months ago I was a teenager living in the boondocks, hours from civilization, with no job, and no college program."

"But we'll still be a huge part of your life even after you get your own place," I reassured him. "The last place you looked at was like three blocks away."

"Yeah, but then I move away, and how do I know that you guys will keep in touch? Or that some other kid won't move in?" he asked me, and for the first time, his fears were completely aligned with mine. *What if some other kid moved in?* "I'll start seeing you less and less—. You guys have to keep meeting people for your videos, right?"

"You're right. We have to keep meeting guys in order to produce videos," I said. "But trust me—we're not looking for the next guy who will move in and replace you. I think you're pretty irreplaceable. I mean, Bradley is fun and hot, but a little crazy, so who knows where that is gonna lead. And you're definitely more stable than Tye."

"Southern boys."

"Yeah, really. You don't need to worry. I promise you that we'll be honest and open about whatever comes up, no matter what," I said, and turned to look him in the eyes. His cheeks were red from the cold winds, and there was this great honesty in his eyes. "I love you like a family member. Or—like a family member that I actually love," I corrected myself. "Obviously you can't pick them, and some aren't so great. Bad analogy."

"It's okay. You can try again," Billy joked with me.

"My family is out West, but Cole's is right here in Boston. And we wanted to wake up and have Christmas day with you before you head up to see your mom. Trust me, there are a whole bunch of Italians at Cole's who can cook much better than I can, so I'm giving up two awesome meals to cook your ass some french toast and eggs."

"That's better," he replied, that mature smile still on his face.

"I have an idea," I said as we neared the convenience store on Mass Ave. "How about for Christmas, I give you a key."

"To a new car?"

"No—hell no—you think I'm made of money?"

"I don't know. Cole won't give me the money info on that Manhunt deal."

"We haven't even gotten to the money part," I replied. "You're such a little hustler. We're still waiting to hear back from them. No, I meant a key to the apartment."

"I have one!"

"No, but I mean you can actually keep it after you move out."

"You were gonna take it away?" he asked me in surprise.

"Just—just hold on to it," I replied, and laughed at his reaction. "Remember—there are *rules* that come with that key."

"Like if I show up and you're having sex, then I just join in, right?" he asked me.

"Forget it. Just—don't abuse the privilege," I said just before we walked into the convenience store. Billy split off to look at food and candy while I went straight for the milk. My entire family lived in Utah, so they were two hours behind us, and I decided it was probably early enough to give them a quick Merry Christmas call. But when I pulled my phone out of my pocket I was surprised to see five missed calls from Cole. I'd set the phone on silent that morning so that we could relax a bit before all the Christmas phone calls, and had totally missed my partner's attempts to reach me. Assuming he just needed something else at the convenience store, I dialed his number.

"There you are!" he boisterously said.

"What's up?" I asked him.

"I just got off the phone with the CEO of Manhunt. He had *two* things to say. The first was Merry Christmas. The second was that he wants to make us an offer!" he practically shouted the last sentence into the phone.

"You're shitting me. So Jonathan liked us?"

"Hell yeah, and they want to meet with us before we go to Miami, because they want to finalize everything the week after New Year's Day, when everyone's back in the office. They're gonna go over everything: terms, money, obligations. They're gonna make us an offer, and then we can decide if we want to take it or make some demands. We definitely need to talk to them about editing control."

"Yeah, I agree. Wow—can't believe this is happening. Tell him tomorrow!"

"I already did!" Cole excitedly replied. "See you back at the apartment. And Merry Christmas."

"Merry Christmas babe. Love you," I said with a huge smile.

*　　*

Like any busy holiday filled with friends and family, our Christmas flew by. Frat Boy and Billy spent the morning with us, and then each left to see their families. Since we lent Billy the car for his long road trip back home, one of Cole's brothers picked us up for Christmas dinner. Unfortunately, that brother wasn't around to drop us off at the Manhunt meeting on the 26th, and so around 11:30 AM we hopped in a taxi and headed for an interview that could change our lives forever.

"What do we do when they bring up money?" Cole nervously asked me.

"Aren't you the guy who has negotiated all these big real estate deals?" I asked him.

"Yeah, but I always get nervous talking about money."

"Well let's just listen to whatever he has to propose. We don't have to give him an answer today. We can ask for a couple days to think this over. I mean—he didn't say we have to make a decision today, right?"

"Yeah, no decisions today," Cole replied. "Today's the big meeting. They're gonna put forth an offer, and then we'll lay out our demands. Editing control is the big one—we need to be in charge of editing our videos. And we need to still be able to put videos on XTube. They've been too good to us this whole time, and there's no way we're gonna abandon them just because of this contract."

"I'm so nervous," I replied. "I've been nervous all morning. It's way more than the money—I mean who knows what they're gonna offer. This would be a huge commitment, Cole. Can we handle getting deeper and deeper into the porn industry?" The two of us sat in silence for a couple minutes after that, each watching the buildings and people go by as the taxi rode through the streets of Boston. It was difficult to be chatty when we both were so nervous, and it seemed like Cole would rather think about the questions I'd asked than voice any kind of opinion.

The Manhunt deal would transform our lives. There was absolutely no question about that. It would be a totally different ballpark. We were used to doing these infrequent amateur videos that we'd upload to XTube, but something about them *did* work. Because we weren't forced to hook up with lots of porn stars, we could keep our videos to a small group of people who we'd personally befriended, and who weren't in it for the money. I guess my biggest fear was that our whole style would have to change with a Manhunt deal. Would we be required to do a lot more videos? Would the guys be gay-for-pay, instead of real, cool gay guys who were into us? Would we be so busy that the money wouldn't be worth it? Our decision to do XTube videos was prompted by the fact that we were always too busy to enjoy our relationship. Neither of us wanted to get back to that awful pre-XTube period.

"What's the matter?" I asked Cole as soon as I turned to face him and noticed a big smirk on his face. He slipped one hand into his jacket and produced a single, white envelope. Then, without saying a word, he placed it on the seat in-between us.

"I couldn't hold out any longer."

I slowly picked up the envelope and reached my hand inside. My eyes were still focused on Cole, who looked as illuminated as ever. It was as if the nervousness of our upcoming meeting had completely dissipated within him. He was waiting anxiously to see my expression change.

Inside the envelope was a thick piece of paper, and when I pulled it out I narrowed my eyes.

"What airport code is AMS?"

"Duh, it's Amsterdam!" he exclaimed loudly enough that the driver jumped in his seat. "Merry Christmas."

"The week after Christmas?" I said in excitement as I read the receipt for the airline tickets.

"It'll be cold as hell, but I wanted to give us some time away together. *Real* alone time. I mean, Miami doesn't count. That's all about Christo. Amsterdam is gonna be just us. And—whatever guys we might meet who are willing to shoot a video."

"This is fucking awesome! I love you so much," I exclaimed, as I leaned forward to kiss him. Cole embraced me with his big hands and stuck his tongue in my mouth, and we kissed passionately in the backseat until the cab driver—for the third time—obnoxiously cleared his throat. I could see that Cole was getting ready to call him out on his homophobia, but just as Cole was about to open his mouth, the cabbie finally spoke.

"Are you two *the* Maverick Men?" he asked us in a thick Indian accent. Cole and I turned our heads so quickly that we almost got whiplash. It wasn't just that we were recognized as porn stars in the back of a Boston cab, but because of who was recognizing us. Our Indian cab driver was in his late 50s, complete with turban and a huge mustache. Of all the people on the planet Earth to recognize us, he seemed like the last one I'd ever expect.

"Uh—are you a fan?" Cole asked. I'm sure he didn't know what else to say. I sure didn't.

"I'm not gay, but I have seen it. Listen—you ever need a third guy for your videos, you call me."

Our cab driver tossed a business card into the backseat, and I casually tucked it into the white envelope.

"Uhh—thanks for the offer," I replied.

"But remember. I'm not gay," he reminded us.

"Yeah—okay buddy, your secret's safe with us. Hey, the building's right there!" Cole said, pointing to the building where Manhunt's offices were located. We were both thankful that the ride was over. It was pretty shocking, but it both made us smile in a big way.

"Hey, my new friends Maverick Men, hit me up," the driver said in a nasally pitch as I pulled out my wallet to pay. "I come over—cook for you. Clean your place. We have hot sex. Make that money." He offered a toothy grin.

"Make that money, yep. Sounds good, sexy man," Cole said. He held the door open for me as I jumped out of the cab. "You take care, boss."

"Well that was fucking hilarious," I remarked as our Indian friend sped off.

"Tell me about it—."

"You ready for this?" I asked, glancing up at the office building. We were fifteen minutes early, but I knew that Adam, the CEO, was up there waiting. Cole proudly nodded his head, and then looked at me with those piercing green eyes of his. And in one swift move, he grabbed me once more, harder than he did in the taxi, and kissed me right there on the sidewalk in front of the building. My mind drifted back to that first time he kissed me, so many years ago, overlooking the city of Boston at that party where we met. And as we prepared for the next big chapter in our lives, with all of our transformations and changes along the way, he was kissing me again, in public; a statement of our love and on-going trials.

"Now I'm ready," he said just after pulling his lips an inch away from mine.

*　　*

"So I have only one final concern," the CEO said to us as he looked over a legal pad scattered with notes. The three of us were occupying a maple wood conference table in Manhunt's executive boardroom. The rest of the office was completely empty, which gave us a nice level of privacy for such an important meeting.

We'd talked numbers. We'd talked details. We requested to still be able to put material on XTube if the deal went through, and to have total control of editing our videos. And during all of this the whole *studio* feeling didn't sink in until we got around to the requirements of how many videos we'd be obligated to produce each month. It was something Cole and I would need to discuss after the meeting. We both loved sex, but neither of us wanted to be sexed out. We also worried that too many videos would hurt our style of befriending and building rapport with our fuck buddies. We didn't want to ever get to the point where we'd be cranking out redundant porn just to keep a deadline.

The contract with Manhunt would essentially act as a steroid—without all the negative health effects, of course—in helping our careers. We'd be heading a major new site developed by their people, and would be catapulted into a much bigger world of professionally-produced videos, celebrity events, and distribution in outlets that we had no access to. The partnership would also help to prevent situations like the one with Tye. We'd be safe from threats, lawsuits, and from having a video pulled on us because one of the participants got angry and decided to flag it on a website. Essentially Manhunt would be our business partner and big brother.

"I have to admit that everyone we considered in the past was an individual performer," Adam, the CEO, continued. "I have seen all of your work, and I absolutely love it. I can see why you guys have millions of fans. There's a real *natural* quality—a hotness to your videos, that's totally different from most of what's currently out there. Our only concern is that you're a couple. And part of my hesitation revolves around the—what's the best way to put it—*turbulence* of relationships. You see—we can form an agreement with you both, create a website,

281

and get underway, and if the two of you break up then the whole thing has collapsed. So I guess I need to know where the two of you are in your relationship?"

"Actually, I think the single individuals are at a disadvantage," I said, and quickly shot a smile to Cole. "Everyone wants to be with somebody. What's to stop one of them from meeting a guy who wants them to tone down their porn? Or worse, stop it altogether? Cole and I had good jobs before we started putting up videos on XTube. We worked *hard*—sacrificed long weekday nights and weekends that could've been spent together for the sake of our careers. And all this while we just wanted to spend more time together in the same lifestyle that we'd become accustomed to.

"Cole introduced me to the idea of doing porn, and I *slowly* gravitated into it. When I saw how much free time it gave us to be together, there was no going back. We're best friends, and it's cool to be able to wake up next to my best friend every day and just do whatever we want, without worrying about reporting to some office."

"So if you're doing well now, then why pursue a contract that could potentially make you very busy once again?" Adam asked, leaning forward on the desk and looking into my eyes with piercing curiosity.

"That's an easy question," Cole stepped in. "You're talking about two totally different worlds. In our past careers, we were extremely busy and barely saw each other. Now you're offering us a lot of money to spend as much time with each other as humanly possible. Not to mention, you're asking us to partner with you, and do exactly what we already want to do: have sex with each other and film our hot, fun moments! Which is probably the most amazing thing that any loving couple could dream up."

"And we want to become a lot better at this," I added. "We've chosen this industry for ourselves, and we want to dig our hands in. We want to leave our imprint. So we have no problem with working hard."

"However, difficulties may come up," the CEO remarked. "Say the sex starts to get boring because you're doing too many videos. Or maybe you find you're spending *too* much time with each other. Or maybe the videotaping will take something away from your intimate space, and it'll become burdensome thinking that every time one of you wants to cum, you have to pull out the camera."

"Let me tell you something about Hunter," Cole said after a couple seconds of silence. "Have you ever been in love?"

"Yes," Adam replied without hesitation.

"Then you may get what I'm about to say. I think there are a few different ways we find our lover. And I mean *lover*—someone who you're really in love with. Someone who deserves your love. The first is beauty. Every so often someone will pass into your life who you'll fall in love with the very second you look at them. This is someone who just *does it* for you. Sometimes you can't even look at them without tearing up—on the inside or the outside—because seeing a smile on their face is the only thing that makes you want to wake up and face each day.

"Second is intelligence. Some people are stubborn, and close themselves off from finding a lover who is smarter than they are. But have you ever felt that raw beauty that radiates from a person whose conversation leaves you wanting more and more? It's something that no porn in the world could ever capture. We all know beauty is fleeting, but a solid mind is the fuel that guides love into its old ages.

"And the third and final is most important. And that is compatibility. Sometimes we find lovers who are beautiful and deeply intelligent, but just aren't compatible. As time goes on, the differences just become more and more blatant, as we begin to replace the lack of compatibility with physical and emotional affairs.

"But sometimes, even less often than finding someone who is really beautiful, or intriguingly smart, you'll meet someone who is so compatible that you can't imagine life without them. Someone who can lift you from the darkest place in your life with the kind of conviction that can only come from a soulmate.

"I found all three when I met Hunter. My whole world would fall apart if he left me, and I know he feels the same way about me. And that's why you don't have to worry about our relationship. The top priority on my mind every day is to make him happy. Everything else falls after."

"Well," Adam said, and then paused as he went to collect his items on the boardroom desk. He was doing his best to keep a poker face, but I could tell that he was touched by everything Cole said. If not by the words, then by the way I looked at my partner as he reminded me why I'd fallen so passionately in love with him back in my college years.

"I can see that you make a good team," Adam finally said once his papers and notebook were aligned in a thin pile. "Have fun in Miami. We talked about a lot today. I have to talk with the owners and the executive team, and if everyone agrees to the requests that you outlined today, we'll have ourselves a deal."

CHAPTER TWENTY

narrated by Cole Maverick

"I actually miss Billy," Hunter turned to me and said with a little frown on his face.

"Please, he's having a better time than us right now. All alone in our apartment—who knows how many guys that kid will have over."

"I think we should fly him down. At least for the weekend. Christo leaves Saturday morning."

"Well I'll check out flights when we get to the hotel room," I remarked. "Billy *and* Frat Boy would be a lot of fun down here. But that's considering we have anything left after Christo and this Tallahassee kid. Actually once Christo gets here, I don't even know if I'll want to leave the hotel."

"Yeah, same here. We need to convince him to move to Boston," Hunter said. "I'm so excited to finally see him in person though."

"Me too! Our little best friend from abroad."

As our plane touched down on the runway at MIA, I noticed Hunter turn around in his seat and look in the back of the plane. This was at least the twentieth time he'd done that during the flight, and I was beginning to get irritated, mainly out of my own curiosity.

"What? What do you keep looking at?" I asked as I stretched my neck to follow his attention.

"Nothing," he casually replied. "Just wondering if you wanna start the trip with someone other than Christo."

"Huh?"

"Aisle seat, seven rows back."

I stretched my neck a little further and counted the rows until my eyes fell upon a beautiful, young Brazilian guy with lean muscle and dark features. He looked straight off the gay beach at Ipanema, sitting there in a cute tank top and board shorts, listening to his iPod, with his gaze held firmly upon Hunter. What a little hottie, with his short hair and boyish brown eyes. When he noticed that I was also looking at him, he turned his head and grinned in my direction.

"We haven't done an airport bathroom video yet," I told Hunter as the two of us turned around.

"Well—whether this is a video or not, I think we should go for it."

"I'm kind of hungry—."

"You just ate before we left!"

"It's a three-hour flight," I remarked, rubbing my stomach in feigned pain.

"You're gonna pass up a threesome with a guy like that because you want to snack? Save it for dinner. Earn those calories."

I once again tilted my head to get a look at the Brazilian sitting behind us.

"Yeah, you're right. I guess I could survive on some sweet Brazilian boy ass until later."

And so we played the eye contact game. And as soon as the cabin door opened and everyone started to get off the airplane, we maintained that eye contact, turning around every so often to give the Brazilian a little smile. Every time we'd look, he'd smile at us.

"He's gonna follow us," I confidently told Hunter as we walked off the plane and casually made our way out into the terminal at MIA.

"Should we wait?" he asked me.

"Nah, he'll follow," I said. And as predicted, when the Brazilian emerged from the tunnel that connected the terminal to the plane, he immediately started to follow after us. We walked for a short while, continuing that trend of eye contact, until we reached the first public restroom in sight. This time when I looked back, I nodded my head as if to suggest that he follow us in.

"What are you doing? Are you seriously considering tricking out with this kid in an airport bathroom? What do I look like, a U.S. Senator?" he sarcastically asked me.

"Chill out Hunter, I just want to see if he will go for it."

It worked like magic. Hunter and I took turns walking into the same handicap-accessible stall. It was the only spot big enough to contain the three of us.

"What if someone with a wheelchair has to—."

"I'm sure there's more than one handicap-accessible stall in MIA," I quickly countered in a light whisper.

"Well for the record, I think this is fucking crazy," he whispered back. "We could get arrested." And after about ten seconds of waiting up against the bathroom wall, inside the handicap stall that was relatively— and surprisingly—clean, the Brazilian hustled in and locked the door.

Without saying a word he pushed his bags up against ours, and went first for Hunter. *Attacked* is probably a better word. Before Hunter even had time to get comfortable the Brazilian pushed him up against the wall and stuck his hands down the front of Hunter's pants.

Meanwhile, I tried to step over the luggage and toilet in order to get in on the action. Unfortunately what resulted was that I ended up with a leg on each side, hovering above the toilet, when the Brazilian decided to attack me. He wrapped his muscular arms around me and leaned in close, nose to nose. He was looking into my eyes, as if waiting for me to say that it was okay for him to kiss me. His breath was hot and fresh, and this guy's face was fucking sexy. He kissed voraciously. My entire tongue was submerged in his mouth, and he was sucking it as if it was a lollipop. I could taste his sweet, sweaty aroma, unaffected by any colognes or deodorants. And as we made out in my awkward position, I felt the Brazilian's hand grab hold of my rock hard cock. Hunter got behind him and pulled the guy's shorts down. Within seconds Hunter was inspecting his hot ass. I saw Hunter's face dive in, and he quickly started to eat the Brazilian's clean, muscular ass, his hands wrapped around those magnificent tan lines.

I decided that my squatting position was either going to result in a collapse upon the toilet or upon them, so I sat down on the lid in order to check out this kid's meat. What a big, fat uncut cock, with lots of foreskin, and just enough head poking out. I had a huge smile on my face. I loved uncut cock, so this was a great surprise. I buried my face in his hairy balls and was rewarded with the best, sweaty man smell ever. His scent alone was enough to make my entire cock throb. I couldn't wait to put his thick cock in my mouth and choke it down.

I stuffed the Brazilian's uncut cock deep in my mouth. Instantly I was hit with that amazing, sexy smell of sweat, as his hard cock pounded the back of my throat. His cock was out of this world. An uncut piece of thick perfection, nice and moist. I could taste his pre-cum oozing out; it was salty and sweet, and more and more leaked out as he stuck it deeper into my mouth. I could tell he was trying hard not to moan. The three of us were being as quiet as possible.

"Ugh," we heard from outside our stall, and we all ground to a halt. I heard the stall next to us slam shut, followed by more groans as someone assumed position on the toilet next to ours.

"Shh!" Hunter motioned towards me, looking around the Brazilian's ass to wave his index finger in front of his lips. None of us wanted to get busted. I raised my eyebrows and my palms. I had a huge uncut cock in my mouth, which meant my only breathing was by means of my nostrils. And our neighbor wasn't making nose-breathing too enticing for me.

As I tried to stop myself from gagging, I attempted to focus on the Brazilian and forget about the potential of getting caught. As hot as that feeling of almost getting caught is, I finally couldn't take it any longer. The bathroom was starting to get too busy, and people were randomly tugging on the stall handle to see if it was in use. I attempted to pull my mouth off the Brazilian's cock, but as Hunter saw what I was doing he pushed the poor guy forward, shoving his thick, uncut dick deeper into my throat. As I tried to push the Brazilian off of me, Hunter pushed him up against me, which probably made for a pretty hot blowjob. Unfortunately I wasn't getting any pleasure from it, given my precarious position.

There was only one more solution, and I didn't want to have to do it. But as they say, desperate times call for desperate measures. And so I bit slightly down upon some foreskin.

"Ow!" hollered the Brazilian, and suddenly our neighbor's bathroom moans stopped. The Brazilian pulled out of my mouth, and Hunter—on his knees—just sat there with his cock in hand, and a worried, surprised expression on his face.

"Wait for it—wait for it—," I whispered. And no sooner had I finished my sentence than a little head poked down underneath our stall. It was a chubby businessman, probably my age, but he hadn't been to a gym since it was forcibly required in high school. He glanced around. First looked at Hunter, sitting on his knees with his cock out. Then at the Brazilian, and the big piece of uncut meat. Then at me, sitting on the toilet, waving at him with a wry smile on my face.

His look of shock was hilarious. I had to bite my tongue just to keep from laughing. He stared for what seemed like an eternity, and then pulled his head back like a turtle. He flushed and scrambled out of the stall so fast that I wasn't sure if he even had time to wipe his ass.

"Can we get the fuck out of here now?" I asked Hunter, who groaned, and then looked up at the Brazilian.

He didn't follow us to our hotel, but we did share a taxi down to Miami Beach. As it turned out the Brazilian was no stranger to our videos. He'd recognized us on the flight, and was actually interested in doing a video someday[6]. If we weren't meeting Christo that night we probably would've asked to film one right then and there, but we each needed to save our energy. The fuck of the year was just hours away.

*   *

"Wow, I can't believe I'm talking to you on an actual phone!" I remarked as soon as Christo picked up his cell. He had bought a pay-as-you-go phone upon arrival in the United States, since he'd be in the country on tour for long enough to require a cell phone.

"Right?" he replied in that pleasantly soft German accent.

"So listen, Hunter and I are getting dressed right now—we're in the hotel room. I'm psyched to see you perform, and of course to meet up afterwards."

"So am I, so am I. It's been *so* long," he replied.

"Tell Christo I said hi!" Hunter called from the sitting area of the hotel room, where he was cracking open some beers for us.

"Hunter says hi," I told him over the phone. "By the way, what's this area code? You should've gotten a 305, since you bought it here in Miami."

"What's a 305? Tell Hunter I say hello."

"It's the Miami area code. Hey, where's the VIP entrance located for this concert? I know you said there's a separate entrance entirely."

"Not sure," he replied. "I know there's a separate VIP check-in."

"I feel so important!" I joked.

"You are to me."

"Aww, I can't wait to see you tonight. This is gonna be great," I said. I was thrilled that we'd be finally meeting, and the setting made it even better. Where else but South Beach for the hottest sex of the year? "We'll go out for drinks right after the concert, watch the ball drop, and then come back to the hotel room to start the new year off right."

6

http://olbmedia.site.metrixstream.com/site/MaverickMen/?page=videos&contentId=111

"I can't wait. Gotta rehearse. See you tonight!"

"See you babe."

Talking with Christo left a huge smile on my face, and I leapt onto our king-sized bed in a fit of excitement. Hunter looked over at me with narrowed eyebrows, probably wondering why the hell a grown man was jumping around his hotel room, but I was so thrilled for this New Year's Eve. Not only were Hunter and I meeting one of the hottest, sweetest guys we'd ever known, but we were about to spend two wonderful days with him.

"Want a beer?"

"Yes," I quickly replied as I rolled over to my laptop.

"Here you go, crazy man," Hunter remarked. "Hey, watch him be even better looking than in his pictures."

"I bet you're right. What's his XTube account again?"

"Just go to Myspace if you want to see his pics. He has like two hundred on there."

I took Hunter's advice and logged onto our Myspace account. We didn't use it too much, but every so often our fans would leave some love on that profile. I wasn't nearly as good about checking the Myspace e-mails as I was about checking the XTube fan mail. And as a result, when I logged onto Myspace and noticed six unread messages, a little wave of panic hit me. I don't know why I panicked, but I guess I've always liked to be on top of responding to our fans. I never took for granted a person who would take time out of their day to write us an e-mail. Of course, some e-mails were crazy, but most of them contained a sweet, loving message.

The first message in the pile was the newest, and it was oddly titled "Christo." It wasn't from his account, and so I assumed it might be a friend who he told about us.

"This is odd," I said out loud as I scrolled through the short, one-paragraph e-mail.

"What's that?" Hunter asked as he sipped his beer.

"Some guy claiming that he's been dating Christo online for the past six months. They were supposed to meet last night in New York City and Christo never showed up. He said that Christo mentioned us all the time as his friends in the U.S., and he's asking us to confirm that Christo is real."

"The guy is delusional," Hunter hastily replied. "Christo was in Miami last night. He's never even been to New York."

"I'm just telling you what's in this e-mail."

"Who is it from?"

"Just some kid who lives in New York—pretty hot, actually. I'd do him."

I honestly didn't know what to think about the alarming e-mail. As I looked through the Myspace profile of this kid in New York, I didn't see anything that would suggest he was strange or crazy. He actually seemed like a pretty normal guy. The e-mail wasn't harsh or threatening; it just asked for reassurance that Christo was a real person.

"I'll wait until after the concert and ask Christo about this, before I write him back. Did Christo ever mention this guy?" I asked, and looked up at Hunter, who was shaking his head.

"Nope. Never mentioned anyone in the U.S."

"Hm—I don't know."

"Me either," Hunter replied, "but what I *do* know is that you need to take a shower because we're out of here in twenty minutes."

"Okay, okay, I'm coming," I replied, trying to snap myself out of lazy mode. I couldn't get over how strange that e-mail was, but I tried to push it to the back of my mind. We had a concert to attend, and I didn't want to be late for our VIP seats.

*   *

Our taxi dropped us off at the American Airlines Arena, a beautiful piece of modern architecture in downtown Miami, tucked in-between the expansive Biscayne Bay and the massive high-rises along the adjoining boulevard. We had about thirty minutes until the opening act, and had no idea who was going on first, but since Hunter and I were confirmed for VIP we wanted to arrive early and check out the scene. As hundreds of people poured into the main entrance in a chaotic, unorganized rush, we did our best to cut through the crowds and make our way around the side of the building.

It didn't take us very long to find the VIP entrance, since everything was marked and there were signs directing us to a little entrance off the beaten path. A few people were outside smoking within a roped-off area, and two suited thugs stood by the door. One of them had a clipboard, which I assumed was the entry list, and so as Hunter and I approached we decided to talk to him first.

"Your names, please?" he pleasantly asked us before we could say anything. I was actually a little surprised by the congeniality in his voice, since this guy looked like he could have played for the Philadelphia Flyers in the early 1970s.

"Cole and Hunter. One of the dancers—Christo—got us the tickets."

"There are a lot of people associated with the production," he replied as he browsed through the list, as if it didn't matter who got us the passes. "I don't see you on here. Did you bring the print-out of your receipt or ticket summary?"

"No—we didn't buy tickets. We're friends with one of the dancers in the show, and he said he used his passes to get us into the VIP section," I replied. I knew there had to be some kind of mistake. "Is there a separate list for employee passes?"

"A dancer in the production wouldn't have the ability to get you VIP seats, unless he or she paid for them," the bouncer told us, still maintaining that same cordial tone. "I'm sorry, buddy, but you're not on here."

"No one by the name of Cole or Hunter?"

"See for yourself," he casually replied, and held out the list for us to see. It was a single page, with names filling two columns down either side of the paper. Hunter and I both scanned the list for our names, and just as the bouncer had informed us, they were nowhere to be found. "I'd give your friend a call. Maybe he can get you into general admission."

"We will, thank you," Hunter said, and the two of us walked away from the VIP entrance. As we walked away from the building and towards the bay, which was empty save for a single yacht with its lights on, I pulled out my cell phone and dialed Christo's number.

"Anything?" Hunter asked me, although I could tell that he didn't expect anyone to answer. His mind was going exactly the same place as mind: that strange Myspace message that I saw before we left for the concert. "Maybe he freaked out about meeting us."

"You think he got scared at the last minute? I just got voicemail for the second time in a row."

"He can't just be fucking around with us," Hunter said as he sat down on the side of the bay, dangling his feet above the water. "I mean—this kid has been talking with us for so many months. He got Manhunt to notice us! Why would he make plans and then just blow us off?"

"I don't know," I honestly told him. "I have no freaking clue. I've never experienced anything like this before. I don't know what to do."

"Try him again."

"Already on it. Third missed call. He's not gonna pick up."

"Maybe his phone is in a locker or something," Hunter said. I could tell that he wanted so badly for this to be some simple misunderstanding.

"I think we should leave," I said as I turned back to the VIP entrance, where a young couple was being ushered inside.

"Maybe he'll see the phone call before the concert. Or after."

"I hope so."

*　　*

But the concert passed, and so did New Year's Eve. We tried to cheer ourselves up by going to a party with Barry, my ex, who lived down in Miami with his boyfriend. The party was great, hosted in a beautiful penthouse overlooking Biscayne Bay and the Miami downtown scene. Barry tried to comfort us, but even with his kind words and all the flowing champagne, I still couldn't shake the disappointment. We were supposed to be having the hottest sex of our lives with one of the coolest people we'd ever virtually met. I couldn't understand why Christo would ditch us like that.

Shortly after midnight we headed back to the hotel. There was still no word from Christo, and the whole trip down to Miami was starting to look more and more like some fucked up game. I'd imagined a hundred times over what our New Year's Eve would be like. I saw ourselves at the concert, partying in the VIP section. I saw the three of us celebrating midnight at some luxurious club, or rooftop party, talking about this past year as if Christo had been there with us in Boston for every second of it. And I even saw all the different ways that we'd come back to the hotel room and make that video: the hottest sex tape that we'd probably ever make. Something so beautiful that it couldn't ever be topped. Raw love-making.

I must've called Christo's phone twenty times in-between when we left the American Airlines Arena and when we got back to the hotel after the penthouse party. And about five minutes before 1:00 AM, Hunter and I were still sitting around the hotel room; he was watching TV and I was browsing e-mails, or looking at Christo's Myspace profile, or re-reading that strange, single-paragraph e-mail from the guy in New York City who wanted to know if he was *real*. But how couldn't he be real? Hunter and I had spent countless hours talking with him on the computer. We'd confided in him. He'd told us intimate details of his life that couldn't possibly be fabricated.

When I returned to our e-mail account, I was surprised to see that a new message had showed up in our inbox shortly after midnight, although when I realized who sent it my surprise faded. Frank, the XTube employee who I'd spoken with on the phone regarding the whole Tye flagging, had sent an e-mail asking to call him when I was free. He also told me to enjoy my New Year's. That gave me my first laugh of the evening.

And so about thirty minutes into January 1st, I picked up my cell phone and dialed his number.

"You're not at some hot porn star party?" he asked me in bewilderment.

"You're not at some hot XTube fan party?" I replied. "Hey, you emailed me first."

"I didn't expect you to call me now. I expected to hear from you in like—three days," he said. "Shit, everything okay?"

"Unfortunately not. We were duped big-time. Made plans with someone—flew down to Miami to get together with them, and were completely blown off."

"Oh man, that sucks. Someone for a video? You know, these guys can be flaky."

"You're telling me," I replied. It actually felt nice to be able to tell this to someone. I'd thought about calling my friend Paul, but even hours after the concert I was still worried about getting on the phone with someone for fear that Christo might call, and I wouldn't see it.

"Hey man, I have to apologize to you. I sort of fucked up."

"What do you mean?"

"Well—," he began, and then took a deep breath. "I didn't *fuck up* per se, but I probably led you to get angry at someone who didn't

Cole

deserve it. I actually stumbled upon this by accident. You know how I
told you that Tye had flagged his own video?"

"Yeah."

"Well I was tracking an IP address of an XTube user who has
been harassing some other users in recent months, and it turns out he has
about eighteen profiles. You'd never be able to tell that any single one of
them is a fake. They're seamlessly created. All very different. I mean—
one of the personalities is some Colombian personal trainer, and his
profile and e-mails are in Spanish."

"So what do you mean? He was impersonating Tye?" I asked.
Not that I needed him to repeat what he was saying, but it all sounded so
devious and crazy that I didn't really want to believe it.

"Sort of. He created an entire profile for Tye. Pulled real pictures
and information from elsewhere on the Internet. Then flagged the video.
Probably knowing you'd find out and get pissed off at the real Tye. Do
you guys have any enemies? Any fans who would be out to get you? We
found a fake profile for that kid in your camping video too. He was
probably getting ready to do something with that."

"You're kidding me," I replied. "No—no, we've always been
very good to our fans."

"Maybe you'll know the guy who did it. I'm emailing you his
profile now. I'm gonna pull all of them in the next hour. The IP address
traces back to a two-year old profile, used by some kid who lives in
Kansas City."

I felt so much discomfort in my chest as I clicked on the new e-
mail Frank had sent me that I could barely breathe. I felt like I was
drowning in air—as if the oxygen levels had been sucked right out of our
little hotel room in South Beach. And as the profile loaded on my
computer screen, my whole body froze. There was something incredibly
disturbing about it—about that main picture. An overweight white guy
with long, greasy brown hair, lots of facial stubble, and piercing brown
eyes. He was wearing a dirty white t-shirt in the picture. There was
something about him that just touched me the wrong way.

"Can you do me a favor?" I slowly asked Frank as I rushed back
to my e-mail.

"Anything, man."

"I'm sending you a picture right now. A kid named Christo, a pen pal we met shortly after joining XTube. He's who we flew down to Miami to meet. Tell me if this picture matches one of the profiles?"

"Christo, the German dancer?" Frank asked before I had even sent the picture. My heart sank. I turned to Hunter, who had muted the TV and was now watching my face and listening to the conversation. "Yeah, he's one of the profiles."

"He—I mean the guy had a German accent."

"And apparently he reads and writes Spanish, and probably has an accent for that too," Frank casually replied. "I'm sorry that you guys wasted your time. He's clearly a sociopath with an addictive personality. I don't know what the guy does all day long."

"He knew what time zone it was in Berlin when we'd call—."

"Cole, the guy's a fake. That profile I sent you—that greasy-haired kid who looks like he's never missed a Dungeons & Dragons convention. That's Christo. But hey—I don't know what you resolved with Tye, but give the kid my regards. I wouldn't be surprised if this psycho is responsible for a lot of the shit you might've incurred. And I can just imagine what he was planning to do with that cute kid in your camping video. Fuck—I wish I could do more than just delete his accounts. He's bound to pop up again."

"Yeah—," I replied. I didn't know what else to say. I didn't even have it in me to compose a full sentence. All I felt was the pain of betrayal. "Thanks—Frank."

"No problem. Hey—hope you have a good holiday in light of this. It sucks, but you still have thousands of *real* fans who love you."

"Thanks," I said again, and then hung up the call. When I turned around to face Hunter, his whole face was filled with shock. "You heard all that?"

He nodded his head slowly, and then reached out his arms for me. And we finished the rest of our New Year's Eve in each other's arms, without saying a word. We each needed to sit with this, and figure out where to go next. And we needed to heal after a year of deceit. At least we had each other. I couldn't imagine being alone in a hotel room after getting off that phone call with Frank. Even though we got screwed over, I was fortunate to have Hunter there with me.

*   *

We woke up late on January 1st, mainly because it took so long to fall asleep. But one thing was for sure: when Hunter woke up, he did so with a vengeance. Like me, he didn't want to think that the whole trip was a waste, and so before he even brushed his teeth or got out of the bed, he was emailing the kid in Tallahassee who had expressed interest in doing a video with us. *Jack.* A cute boy from Georgia who was living in Tallahassee for school, meanwhile trying to make it as a musician. I didn't know if I was ready to shoot a video after learning the awful truth about Christo, but Hunter was determined.

"He said he can chat on Skype in about fifteen minutes," Hunter said, right before hopping out of bed.

"Doesn't he have a cell phone?"

"He doesn't own a cell phone."

"Who doesn't own a cell phone?" I asked in surprise. "That's a long drive, Tallahassee to Miami. He's going to come down today?"

"That's what he's saying," Hunter replied from the bathroom. "I asked him if we could talk on Skype before he starts to head down."

"Why?"

"After last night, you have to ask? We are not going to be tricked like that ever again."

"Good point," I replied as I slowly pushed myself out of the bed, and drearily wandered over to the coffee maker. "That sucks. It's like—I don't even know a good analogy for it. Maybe like finding out your boyfriend has been cheating on you for the past year with your best friend. I bet that would feel like this."

"I don't want to lose any more sleep over this," Hunter replied.

"Well you can't get over it *that* quickly. I mean, give it time to heal on its own. Otherwise he wins, and we'll just become jaded and pessimistic about everyone we meet. We can't let this change who we are."

"How can I *not* be pessimistic?" Hunter asked. "How do you think this makes me feel? I confided in him. Told him secrets and personal stuff that I hardly share with anyone. It just frustrates me. I mean our income depends on meeting people for videos, and I think it's cool that we're trying to become friends with all these guys, but so far our batting average isn't so great."

"Yeah—but we've met Billy and Bradley. I'm fine with writing off ten bad experiences for the blessing that they've been to us. How often do you meet sweet, sexy, great guys like that? And you know—as we get better at this, we'll get better at meeting the right people, and knowing what to say and look for."

"I should've known all along," Hunter said in frustration. "How could he not afford a webcam? Everyone has a webcam."

"You're right. We're not meeting anyone without a webcam from now on. We're adding that to the rules. They have to go on video for us before we meet them."

"Hey, can you check Skype to see if Jack is on?" Hunter asked me.

As the coffee maker worked its magic, I hopped back onto the bed and logged onto Skype on our laptop. As the buddy list loaded, I'll admit that I got a quick sting upon seeing Christo's name. He wasn't online, and I didn't know if he'd ever be online again.

Within a few seconds of the buddy list loading, a little notification popped up on the computer screen that alerted us to a call from Jack.

"Hey! Jack!" I cheerily said as soon the call was activated.

"Hey guys," replied a young guy with a charming Southern accent. His voice wasn't as deep as Tye's, and you could tell that he was from the deep South. "How are ya'll doin'?"

"Not so good, Jack. Unfortunately we were duped into coming to Miami by some hideous psychopath from Kansas City who created false identities because he clearly has no life of his own. It's really quite sad."

"Oh—that's not cool," Jack replied. There was something funny about his response; sort of an uncertainty about how to react.

"Yeah, and XTube sent me his real profile. Hideous, greasy guy. No wonder he invents these online personalities of beautiful, sweet boys. What a monster. Hopefully you never have to deal with someone like that."

"Maybe he just doesn't have many friends where he's from."

"No, I think he's an evil sociopath. This guy is pure scum. Probably a virgin who obsesses over creating these identities because otherwise guys would never bother with him."

The sad part about the whole mess—which struck me as I ranted about *Christo*—was that it didn't matter what this kid looked like in real life. If he had been sweet and honest from the start, we wouldn't have given a shit about his looks. Sure, he wasn't our type for doing a video, but that didn't mean anything. In fact, I wondered if our friendship with him would have been just as strong had he been honest with us.

"Well—uh—."

"Hey Jack, do me a favor and turn your webcam on," I asked. I glanced at the opening to the bathroom, and Hunter was leaning his head out into the doorway, part of his face covered in shaving cream, and a worried look in his eyes. He clearly hadn't expected me to go so rough on this kid, but he understood why I was doing it.

"I don't have one," he replied with that sweet Southern accent.

"Oh, that's too bad. So hey—you're driving down today, right?"

"Well uh—can I do it tomorrow? My sister's here right now visiting from Georgia but she's leaving tomorrow."

"Do me a favor and put her on the phone."

"I think she's on the toilet right about now—."

"I can wait," I hastily replied. "You see, after we got duped by this kid Christo, I just want to make sure that you're real, since I obviously can't see you through a webcam. It would be great if you could put your sister on the phone to verify this. If that's not a trouble."

"Uh—yeah, sure," he slowly replied. I waited patiently for a full minute of silence before I heard an effeminate, soft-spoken Southern voice pop onto the laptop's speakers.

"Hey! This is Angela, Jack's sister. I've heard so much about you guys."

"Hi Angela," I replied in a friendly tone. I glanced again at Hunter, and I know he saw the look on my face as the dreaded realization started to creep into my head. "It's so nice of you to get on the phone. Do me a favor. Can you both say *I've heard so much about you guys* at the same time? That would be wonderfully reassuring."

And as expected, within seconds of my request the Skype connection was cut.

"Fuckin sick," I shouted, as I shut the laptop and hopped off the bed to return to my cup of coffee.

"Oh my God—you've gotta be fucking kidding me," Hunter loudly exclaimed as he stood in the doorway, shaving cream still covering part of his face. "So our buddy in Kansas was not only Christo, but also Jack. So nice of him to drag us all the way down to Miami. This is so fucking twisted, I really cannot believe this shit. We have—what—four full days left here? I don't know, Cole. I just want to go back to Boston."

"Yeah, I hear you," I replied. I was doing a good job of hiding it from Hunter, but that call with Jack had infuriated me. I wanted to call the number back and scream at him; demand why he wasted our time for so long. But I knew he wasn't going to answer. Besides, I didn't want to feed into his games any more than we already had.

"I'm gonna check out return flights for today. It's January 1st. I'm sure no one is flying," Hunter said as he disappointedly walked over to the bed to seize the laptop. "I'd rather be back with our friends."

I didn't contradict him. I too was ready to go home. Miami had turned out to be a total flop. And it pissed me off even more that this kid had created the Jack personality, just to prolong his sick little game with us. And I couldn't help but wonder if he would pop up again as some other fan, or some other hot guy who wanted to do a video with us. At least we knew how to avoid the mistakes that had led us to Miami, but I felt like all of this was too harsh. Why did this bullshit have to happen to us in the first place? We never hurt anyone in the course of doing our videos. We were always appreciative of our fans, and kind to anyone who'd write us an e-mail. I felt like our kindness had been taken advantage of.

The hotel room phone began to ring just as I was fixing my coffee, and so I glanced up at Hunter to see if he'd pick it up. He caught my eyes, and quickly answered the phone.

"Hello?" I heard him say. "Oh—um—sure. Yeah, send them up. Okay, thanks—thanks. Take care."

"What's that?"

"Did you invite your ex over?" Hunter asked me. "That was the front desk, and they said that a *Barry* is downstairs with one guest, and asked to come up. I obviously said yes."

"Yeah, I guess he's trying to cheer us up after last night," I said. I felt bad that we weren't able to stay and enjoy the New Year's Eve party with Barry and his partner, but there was too much going on.

"Watch it be Christo and Jack," Hunter joked, and the both of us burst into laughter for the first time all morning. "Get that videocamera ready!"

"Yeah, right. It's fine. We'll go have breakfast or something with them. Any excuse to get out of the hotel room."

I took another sip of my coffee and then pulled a white bathrobe out of the closet, sliding my arms into it so that I'd at least be somewhat presentable upon opening the door. I will admit that a small part of me hoped that Christo was real, and that it was him coming. I wanted to open the door and see him standing there—maybe with another one of his dancer friends. I wanted to get some excuse that his cell phone broke, and there was a problem with the VIP list, and he was so sorry for everything. A wild fantasy, I know, but it was fun to replay it in my head a couple times before I heard the light knock at the door.

"Got it," I told Hunter as I briskly walked to the door and grabbed hold of the handle. I let that fantasy about Christo replay one more time in my head before I opened the door, and as soon as I opened it I forgot about Christo entirely.

"What the *fuck* are you two doing here?" I asked the two last people I expected to see in our hotel doorway on the morning of January 1st.

"Dickhead," Billy said with a smile on his face. "Bradley and I found out about Amsterdam. Had I known you were going there too I would've never let you leave me in Boston."

"Yeah, really," Frat Boy said in a more serious tone. "You can't go on *two* trips without us. Where's Christo?"

Before I could even reply, Hunter was already at the doorway, pushing past me to give Billy and Frat Boy a bear hug.

"It doesn't matter," I casually replied, waving a hand in dismissal.

"Yeah, well we almost didn't make it," Frat Boy said as he peeked over Hunter's shoulder, who seemed to be hugging him for an unusually long period of time. "Billy was such a pussy about getting on the airplane."

"No I wasn't."

"Oh that's right—your first flight," I said as we waved them into the hotel room. "Are you staying through the whole weekend?"

"We only booked one-ways," Billy replied. "We figured we'd just focus on getting *down* here, and then you could pay for the return."

"Oh my God," I replied, and although I did my best to frown, it was pretty clear that these two had saved the trip for Hunter and I. And suddenly the whole mess with Christo and his army of alter egos didn't seem so damaging. Because when all was said and done, we were with the people who truly mattered, the ones who we should've planned to spend our New Year's with all along. And all it took was a little detour to Miami Beach to figure that out.

CHAPTER TWENTY-ONE

narrated by Cole Maverick

The four of us got back to Boston on a chilly Sunday night, and early the next morning I got in my car and drove to a part of the city I'd never previously seen. It was a place that didn't have any meaning to me other than that it contained an address, scribbled on a piece of paper a long time ago. And at some point in time I'd put that address—scribbled on a little piece of paper—into my computer for safe keeping.

The neighborhood wasn't one of Boston's finest. Depressed rowhomes littered each block, and so did old cars that hadn't seen a good year since the 90s. This was a place where shirtless teenagers played basketball on deteriorating public courts, and where some people might be afraid to come out onto their porches for fear of who might drive down their block. Hunter would've never let me go to this neighborhood, and that's why I didn't tell him where I was going. But I had an apology to give, and forgiveness to ask for.

The problem is, after learning about all the manipulation coming from Christo, I didn't know what to believe. I knew that Tye had a drug problem and was definitely a little bit of a mess, but I assumed that the legal notice and the flagging were probably constructs of Christo's mind games. This guy had been trying to fuck with us, and even though Tye had definitely caused his own drama, Christo's interference just intensified things. I couldn't help but wonder what would've happened with Tye if Christo was never in the picture.

The address on one of the rowhomes matched the one I'd written down, and I parked close enough that I could keep an eye on my car from the house's porch. I walked across the weed-infested sidewalk and hurried up the steps to the rowhome until I got to a white screen door. I could see into the dark living room, and I heard a TV on in the background, but didn't see anyone. And so I rang the doorbell and patiently waited.

I didn't have to wait very long. After a few seconds an older woman appeared in the doorway, peering at me through the screen as if to ask why I was intruding on her property.

"Can I help you?" she asked without opening the door. Her Southern accent was a lot thicker than Tye's, but I could see where he got it.

"Are you Tye's mom?"

"How do you know my baby?"

"I'm a friend of his, ma'am. My name's Cole. I don't know if he ever mentioned—."

"He didn't," she replied. She wasn't smiling, and she wasn't opening that screen door. "What's someone your age doin' hangin' around my boy?"

I wasn't about to get *that* personal with her.

"Well ma'am," I hesitantly spoke up, "that's a long story. I just need to apologize to Tye for a misunderstanding. I know he doesn't live here—he had a roommate somewhere else, but I'd like to know if you can give me—."

"Tye's gone."

I could feel my knees getting weak. I wasn't sure if I wanted her to say anything further.

"What do you mean, *gone*?"

"He moved down south to live with his daddy," she replied. "Said he'll move back if he can't find a job. Economy's bad enough here—can't imagine it's gonna be better down there."

"I tried calling him, but—."

"Doesn't have a cell phone, sweetheart," she interrupted. "Was broke, and I wasn't gonna give him money for another one. I have his father's number."

"It's—it's alright," I said, holding my hand up. I recalled him telling me once that his dad wasn't cool with his sexuality, and the last thing I wanted to do was call his father's number and risk causing a fight between those two. E-mail would be a much better option. "Thank you. I'll just send him an e-mail. Hopefully he still has that."

"Maybe. Don't know."

"Well, thanks for your help," I told her, and she nodded her head and left the doorway. I slowly walked from the porch to my car, the whole time wondering if I'd ever see or hear from him again. Tye was certainly no angel, but it hurt knowing that Christo—or whoever he was—had come in-between the two of us.

Cole

I knew that Tye would've still wanted more than I was able to give him, but without Christo's interference the whole situation could've been handled a lot better. Maybe we'd still be friends, and maybe he wouldn't have left Boston so suddenly. Maybe he would've sought help with his drug problems. I planned on writing him an e-mail, and I hoped he'd read it. Whether or not I'd ever hear from him again, I wasn't too sure. In some ways I was happy that this chapter with Tye was closed. But I guess in some odd way, shooting a porn with anyone other than your lover can be the same as having virgin sex. You'll always remember your first. And if you're lucky, you'll always have a soft spot for them.

CHAPTER TWENTY-ONE continued...

narrated by Hunter

"There you are," I greeted Cole as soon as he walked through the door. "You were gone a long time."

"Hit up the grocery store," he said with a smile on his face as he put a couple bags of groceries down on the kitchen floor. "Made another stop too. I'll tell you about it later."

"Is everything okay?"

Instead of responding to my question, Cole walked up to me, looked me in the eyes, and leaned forward to place his lips on mine.

"I guess so," I said as soon as he pulled away. "We'll talk later. But listen, I'm glad you're back, because Billy and Frat Boy are here and I have a huge announcement to make."

"Did you hear from Manhunt?" Cole asked, his eyes widening in excitement.

"No, no, don't get your panties all tangled. Something else. It's only the 5th, chill out! January 2nd was a Friday. They're probably just starting the conversation today."

"I don't know—they really seem to have their shit together," Cole replied as he turned back to the groceries to start putting them away.

"You're telling me."

"Cole—put those away later!" Billy shouted from the sofa. He and Frat Boy were waiting patiently for my announcement. It was actually the first time I'd seen the two of them sit still with such obedience.

"Okay, okay, I'm coming. I don't want anything to spoil."

"Nothing's going to spoil," I assured him. "This will take two minutes. Maybe not even."

"Okay, fine, I'm coming," he repeated himself, and allowed me to drag him into the living room, where he sat down on the chocolate sofa opposite the one containing Billy and Frat Boy.

I anxiously took a seat next to Cole and leaned forward so that my elbows rested on my knees.

"So—I have an announcement to make."

"You're pregnant," Frat Boy said.

"No—I'm—listen, just keep quiet. So, I've had a big change of heart since the Miami trip. I think the biggest lesson we learned in Miami was that it was foolish of us to go spend that holiday with complete strangers when the people who mattered most to us were right here in Boston. When you two showed up, you quickly turned a horrible trip into one of the happiest vacations of my life."

"Even when I puked in the pool at the Gansevoort?" Billy asked with some embarrassment.

"Well—that was your fault. And I actually found it pretty entertaining."

"I didn't—," he replied with a frown.

"But look, didn't we all have an amazing time?" I asked, and everyone nodded in agreement. "So—wow, this is exciting. Billy and Bradley, because you both are so wonderful and important to us, and—don't make me regret this—we're letting you stay at our place while we're in Amsterdam for three weeks. You each get keys, and the loft is yours."

The two of them nearly leapt from the sofa in excitement. Neither had expected to be able to hang out in our place during the long trip to Amsterdam. In fact, Cole had already made arrangements to have Billy stay with his friend Paul during our vacation.

"We're gonna stock it with food and call a cleaning service to come twice a week while we're gone, so you guys don't have to worry about anything," I said.

"Are you sure you want these clowns turning our home into a bachelor pad?" Cole asked me as he laughed at their reaction.

"I'm positive," I replied. "I think they've earned it. But if you try that Miami shit where you flew over to meet us without a return ticket—well—I hope you like Holland, because you'll be staying there for a while."

"Don't worry," Bradley replied. "Your place is *exactly* what we need."

"I'm sure," I said with a cocked eyebrow. "Just go easy on it."

*   *

Thursday came quick, and before we knew it we were boarding our plane for Amsterdam. Luckily the plane to Amsterdam was a wide-body, so Cole and I had our own two seats next to each other, with no one seated next to us.

"So were you serious when you said that no one speaks English in Amsterdam?" I asked Cole. I had a feeling he'd been pulling my leg with all his remarks on the city.

"Yeah, Hunter, no one speaks English over there. Only Dutch and French," he confidently answered.

"You're full of shit."

"No I'm not," he quickly replied, looking at me with a wide-eyed expression, as if I'd accused him of a crime. "Wait until you get there. You're lucky I speak fluent Dutch."

"Yeah?" I asked him. "Say something in Dutch."

As Cole proceeded to go into a fit of coughing, throat clearing, and grunting, a smile spread across my face.

"I just asked how the weather was," he wryly told me. "Hey, phone call," he added, and pulled his cell phone out of his pocket. "Hello?"

"They're going to make you turn that off real soon," I said, but instead of replying to me I saw his expression completely change. Suddenly the smile left his face and the chuckling stopped, and he looked frozen in space as he sat there with his cell phone against his ear.

"We're actually on a plane that's about to depart for Amsterdam," Cole said into the phone, "but yeah, can we do the call on Skype as soon as we land? That would be perfect. Yeah—that's perfect."

"Excuse me sir," a voice startled me from the aisle. I turned to see a handsome flight attendant who looked about five years my junior. He was motioning for Cole, and pointing to the cell phone. "Could you please turn that off? We're going to depart in five minutes."

"Yeah—yeah—it's a really important phone call."

"But sir, we can't leave until you're off the phone. The Captain needs all electronic—."

"Okay, okay, one second—alright," Cole said into the phone. "Talk with you when we land. And thank you."

He quickly shut the phone off, then glanced up at the flight attendant with those big green eyes of his.

"If you weren't so hot, I would tell you where to stick this," he joked with him. I nudged Cole, but to my surprise the flight attendant laughed.

"Well be careful, because if you guys told me that, I might just do it," he replied with an adorable little smile. "You know, I feel like I've seen your face somewhere."

"Probably in a few places," I jokingly replied.

"I was a realtor," Cole slowly replied, although I could tell he was expecting this guy to know us from our videos.

"Oh my God! You were my dad's realtor," the flight attendant giddily said.

"Wow, I didn't expect you to have recognized me from *that* occupation, but sure," he said, and chuckled. "Who's your dad?"

"Tony Marinelli," he said, and both mine and Cole's jaw dropped simultaneously. "I'm the gay son," he added, and waved his hand.

"You know he fired me from that deal!" Cole said after the stun of the flight attendant's revelation wore off. "You're Tony Jr., right?"

"That's me," he said, and pointed at the word *Anthony* on his name tag. "Yeah, my dad is a dickhead. That's why I didn't pursue the family businesses. But I'm sorry to hear that he fired you."

"Well I do have to say—," Cole began, and narrowed an eyebrow, "if I had to choose which Marinelli I'd want to get in bed with, I'd easily give up that nice commission for you."

Tony Jr. smiled, looked up and down the aisle real quick, and then leaned in close to the two of us.

"Well in that case— Are you guys busy, say, four hours into the flight?"

"Does this mean that we're gonna join the Mile High Club in a threesome?" I asked him, and he turned towards me and grinned.

"You might as well just skip college and go straight to grad school." And with that, he walked off down the aisle. I watched his tight bubble butt as he headed back towards the galley, and got excited just thinking about putting my face up in there.

"So how do you think Marinelli's gonna feel about us fucking his son?" I asked Cole, who was laughing and staring at his cell phone.

"That was Manhunt," he said, totally ignoring my question. "On the phone. We got it."

"We *got* it?"

"They accepted all the terms we set out. We got the contract!"

A smile spread across Cole's entire face, giving him this amazing glow just as the Captain announced over the loudspeaker that we were preparing for take-off. What an ironic statement.

It didn't seem all that long ago that I was sitting in the guest bedroom of that Provincetown apartment, with a wise older man and *The Secret* to keep my sadness company. I can still remember his words—his reflection on love. And I can still feel the way I felt when I saw Cole in the crowd. When I turned and ran, and when he came running after me. I'll admit that a bunch of times after that night I wondered what would have happened if he hadn't chased me. But in reality, the chasing didn't only happen once. He chased me for months after that night. He chased after me even while we were living together in our loft apartment. This entire time, my lover had been part of a marathon, and the sole purpose was to create a comfortable and happy life for the two of us.

And I'll admit that I haven't always understood his reasoning. It took me a long time to warm up to the XTube videos, and an even longer time to gather enough faith in this new venture to quit my day job. I never would have imagined this life for myself, but now being a part of it, I can't really imagine anything else. I get paid to make love to my amazing partner, and to meet the kind of life-changing people—like Billy and Frat Boy—who bring countless smiles to each new day.

I think back to that meeting with Manhunt's CEO, and the beautiful speech that Cole gave about the ways a person knows that they've met their best friend and true love. And as eloquent and precise as his observation was, I think he missed an important fourth quality. Aside from finding someone who is stunningly beautiful, or intriguingly smart, or perfectly compatible, there's one more tenet that Cole didn't identify at that meeting. And that's dedication. Because even better than meeting someone who is beautiful, intelligent, and compatible, the most precious part of any relationship is the dedication that two people have for one another. If anything, my story is a testament to dedication. If it had ever escaped from our relationship, even just for an instant, then I wouldn't have ever made it to that Manhunt deal, or that airplane to Amsterdam. We completely rearranged our lives for each other, with no guarantee that we'd make it out of the changes in one piece.

I can honestly say that I don't know what lies ahead. I don't know what the Manhunt contract will bring. I don't know if MaverickMen.com will catch on. I don't know if we'll meet more guys like Billy and Frat Boy, or if we'll meet more guys like Christo out in the vast pool of people who we come into contact with every day. But one thing I do know is that we'll tackle it all together. And regardless of what path our lives take, I know we'll have a damn good time along the way.

THE END

About the Authors

The Maverick Men are the most popular couple on XTube.com, with over 86 million video views. You can follow their weekly blog at MaverickMen.com, or their tweets at Twitter.com/TheMaverickMen.

ACKNOWLEDGMENTS

This book would not be possible if the publisher, Anthony DiFiore, wasn't a huge fan of our work. His quiet, soft spoken voice and professional manner coupled with the fact that he is STUNNINGLY hot helped us decide to write this book, so thank you very much Anthony for coming up with this idea, we love you. Also it is without saying that if it were not for the help and support of our amazing friends at XTube, specifically Kurtis and Adam (poor Adam had to endure countless frantic phone calls and unsolicited advice, all while having a big smile on his face). Thank you XTube for helping to create a fan base of over 86 million followers, you boys rock. Our fans are where we got started and we love them and will continue to stay true to them with the very best video content. Hunter and I have enjoyed sharing our lives with you all here in the pages of this book and online. Firstly and most importantly to our fans! XOXO. We fucking love you guys so much. Your support has helped Hunter and I to create a fun, special life together. Without you boys there would be no MaverickMen.

To our Boyz: Thank YOU to our amazing, loving boyz, especially the guys that were mentioned in this book. Billy, the boy love of our life, our crazy-hot-sexy-fun Frat Boy Bradley. Much love to Lil'T the hyper sex machine. One boy that was not mentioned in the book is our boy Johnny Rio, he was with us from the inception of our videos, we love him and hope someday he will share his hotness with us on-camera for you guys. Special thanks to Gary Blumenthal, our kick-ass Webmaster for MaverickMEN.com. Without his help we would be lost. He is the brains behind the site. All of the guys at ManHunt and On Line Buddies, especially Adam Segal for realizing how important it was for us to maintain control of our creativity and not trying to change what we do or how we do it. He had the foresight to see or potential. And to Hector, or as I like to call him, Macho Camacho, made us feel very welcome with his big bear hug within the first few minutes we met him. So many people have been so great to us and knew our potential before we ever did.

Larry Basil and Jonathan Crutchley, the owners of ManHunt and On Line Buddies, have been amazingly helpful in understanding the business side of what we do. They are a font of wisdom, born of hard work, hard knocks, and great ideas. They are two of the most amazing businessmen and fun guys we have ever met. Through their many inspirational stories and sound advice, we were able to focus on our own vision. Hunter and I are both very proud to be able to call them good friends.

To my Hunter, I love you with all my heart and soul, you are the reason I wake up in the morning. Without you I would not be.

Cole Maverick & Hunter

Check out these other books by inGroup Press

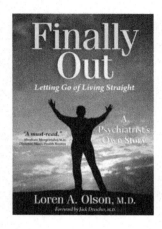

Finally Out: Letting Go of Living Straight, A Psychiatrist's Own Story by Loren A. Olson, M.D.

Dr. Loren A. Olson has frequently been asked two questions: How could you not know that you were gay until the age of forty? Wasn't your marriage just a sham to protect yourself at your wife's expense? In Finally Out, Dr. Olson vigorously answers both questions by telling the inspiring story of his evolving sexuality, into which he intelligently weaves psychological concepts and gay history. This book is a powerful exploration of human sexuality, particularly the sexuality of mature men who, like Dr. Olson, lived a large part of their lives as straight men - sometimes long after becoming aware of their same-sex attractions. FinallyOutBook.com.

A Pale Existence by Gillian Paige

Four troubled young women embark on a suicidal road trip in the most haunting new title in LGBT fiction. This is the gripping and thrilling story created by emerging author Gillian Paige, who has created a modern gothic that will both frighten and intrigue its readers. Long roads, a lonely city, and a terrifying forest all act as backdrops in a tale that shakes the foundations of reality. As the four women move deeper into societal isolation, the whole world changes around them, and the only hope is a small beacon of reason that may be too far out of reach for any of them to see.

CPSIA information can be obtained
at www.ICGtesting.com
Printed in the USA
LVOW13s1110270617
539532LV00005B/1203/P